Marshal Huntington Bright

True stories of American history for our young people

Marshal Huntington Bright

True stories of American history for our young people

ISBN/EAN: 9783337124946

Printed in Europe, USA, Canada, Australia, Japan

Cover: Foto ©Andreas Hilbeck / pixelio.de

More available books at **www.hansebooks.com**

THE CAPTURE OF MAJOR ANDRE

Mu... ...gath was ... in Ame... ...A... ...t the ...tle ...The ...t... ...was it ... was neve... ...tione... H...
...c... t ...n... Pau... Van Wa...t an... W...ams ...were b...oted with auto...ts at ...w... as a sea...t ...ch...

THE SURRENDER AT YORKTOWN

TRUE STORIES

...OF...

AMERICAN HISTORY

...FOR...

OUR YOUNG PEOPLE

A BOOK FOR HOME AND FIRESIDE

CONTAINING

oroughly Truthful Narratives of the Greatest, Most Interesting, and Romantic Incidents
from the Earliest Days to the Present Time

TOLD IN EASY, FAMILIAR LANGUAGE

BY

COL. MARSHAL H. BRIGHT

AND OTHERS

EMBELLISHED WITH ABOUT

ONE HUNDRED AND FIFTY FINE ENGRAVINGS

BY THE BEST AMERICAN ARTISTS

Illustrating that which is Best, Noblest, Most Interesting and Inspiring in the History of
the Land we live in

INTRODUCTION.

THIS book is designed to impress upon the mind of American youth the principal great events in our history; to acquaint them with the manners and customs of different periods and in different sections, and to stimulate in them such a love for American history that they will seek its fuller details in the volumes of our great historians.

It was the custom among some nations of antiquity to repeat to each fresh generation the noble deeds of their ancestors, thus making history a great oral tradition, and turning it from a dead record into a living romance. The Athenian boys learned Homer by heart; the "Iliad" and "Odyssey" took the place of the pile of books which the schoolboy of to-day carries under his arm when he sets his "morning face" schoolward. In this way boys learned beauty and eloquence of speech, and imbibed the spirit of art while they were yet at their games. But they learned even greater things than these; they grew up with the heroes of their race and took part in their great deeds. The bravest and most poetic things which their race had done were familiar and became dear to them while their natures were most receptive and responsive. The past was not dim and obscure to them as it is to too many Americans; it was a living past, full of splendid figures and heroic deeds. To boys so bred in the very arms and at the very heart of their race it was a glorious privilege to be an Athenian; to share in a noble history, to be a citizen of a beautiful city, to have the proud consciousness of such place and fame among men. It is not surprising that as the result of such an education the small city of Athens produced more great men in all departments in the brief limits of a century than most other cities have bred in the long course of history. There was a vital inspiring education behind that splendid flowering of art, literature, philosophy, and statesmanship.

This book endeavors to do for American boys and girls what such training

o c

as the above did for the young Athenian, by setting before them in true but glowing narrative the most heroic and most interesting things in the history of our grand and glorious country.

It is doubtful if any country has ever developed greater energy of spirit or greater variety of character than this; and this is the chief reason why our history has such significance and such fruitage of achievement.

To know this history is a duty and a delight. A man whose brave ancestors have carried the name he bears far, and made it a synonym for courage and honor, is rightly proud of his descent and gets from it a new impulse to bear as brave a part in his own day. Americans can honestly cherish such pride; it is justified by what lies behind them. No man can be truly patriotic who does not know something of the nation to which he belongs, and of the country in which he lives. Such knowledge is a part of intelligent citizenship. In this country, where the government rests on the intelligence and virtue of the entire population, such a knowledge is a duty and a necessity. Not to know these things is to miss a noble and inspiring landscape which we might see simply by the lifting up of the eyes.

The American boy and girl ought to have the same education, and this book is for them both. Too many women and almost as many men grow up with the most indefinite ideas of their own country. They do not know what has been done here; they do not even know how people live in other parts of the broad land. They know something of their own communities, but they are ignorant of the greater community to which they belong. The story of the country's birth and growth, of its struggles and achievements, of its wonderfully diversified life, of its heroic men and noble women, ought to be familiar to every boy and girl from earliest childhood. This knowledge is the A B C of real education, and to furnish this knowledge was an object in the preparation of this volume.

It is a book for the family and for fireside reading. America is pre-eminently the country of homes; that is, the country which, by its free institutions and its large social and industrial conditions, makes comfortable homes possible to its entire population. These homes are not only the sources of happiness and the nurseries of purity and prosperity, they are also the schools of citizenship. From these schools are graduated year after year, in unbroken and never-ending classes, the men and women who continue and enlarge the work and the influence of the nation. The Bible has been and will remain the great text-book in these schools; but other books are needed, and this book aims to take its place as an indispensable book of instruction and entertainment. The history of a race is the best possible material for the education of the children of that race.

There is no romance so marvelous as this record of fact; none so full of incident, adventure, heroism, and human vicissitude. From the voyages of the earliest Spanish, French, and English explorers to the inventions and discoveries of modern times; from the struggles for our own freedom in 1776 to our heroic battle for Cuban liberty from Spanish oppression in 1898, the story never fails of thrilling interest. It is a romance of humanity written by the hand of Providence on the clean, broad page of a new continent. It is a Bible for new illustration of the old laws of right and wrong which underlie all history; but it is a modern version of The Arabian Nights for marvels and miracles of human skill and achievements. The building of Aladdin's palace was a small affair compared with the building of some of our States; and the rubbing of Aladdin's lamp was but a faint burnishing compared with the glow of prosperity which hard work has brought out on the face of this continent. There is no romance so wonderful as the story of life told, not by novelists of varying degrees of skill, but acted out by great multitudes of eager, energetic men and women as recorded in this volume, for the education and inspiration of the boys and girls, young men and women of America.

America! What heart does not thrill with patriotic pride at the mention of the word? Of her glorious history how truly has the poet sung:

> "Land of the West, though passing brief
> The record of thine age,
> Thou hast a name that darkens all
> On history's wide page."

Yet, if we may dare to prophesy, the past with all its achievements is not to be compared to the future greatness of our country, from whose fires on freedom's altar the torch of liberty is being lighted throughout the world, and

> "We behold, as in a vision, stern Columbia, sword in hand,
> And we hear the tramp of legions marshaling at her command;
> Listen to the ringing challenge that she sends across the sea,
> 'They that wield the rod oppression must account for it to me.'
> We behold her, God commissioned, striking ancient error down,
> Wresting from the cruel despot sword and sceptre, throne and crown;
> All the watching world applauds her when she cuts the captive's thongs
> And, full fortified by justice, rights the martyred nation's wrongs."

LIST OF CHAPTERS AND SUBJECTS.

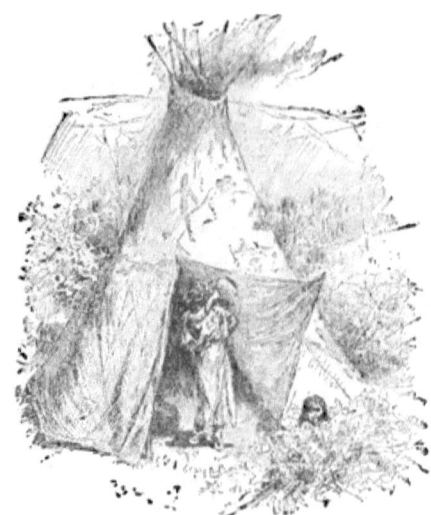

AN APACHE HOME.

The Story of Christopher Columbus and What He Did.

CHRISTOPHER COLUMBUS.

WHEN civilization had grown hoary with age in the orient, there still remained in the western hemisphere a vast land of marvelous wealth and resources—a continent undiscovered and undreamed of. True, three hundred years before Christ Aristotle had said the world was round, and that by sailing west from Athens one might touch the shores of eastern Asia. Nearly four hundred years later, Seneca, the philosopher of Rome, under Nero, made a similar affirmation. Fully nine hundred years further down the vistas of time the Norsemen first planted foot upon American soil, and they claim to have done so more than once again during the next three hundred years. But they either lacked the intelligence or the enterprise to make their discoveries known, and America lay in oblivious darkness until Columbus came.

It was the glory of Italy to furnish the greatest of the discoverers of the New World. Not only Columbus, but Vespucci (or Vespucius), the Cabots, and Verazzani were born under Italian skies; yet singularly enough the country of the Cæsars was to gain not a square foot of territory for herself where other nations divided majestic continents between them. So, too, in the matter of Columbus biography and investigation, up to the present time but one Italian, Professor Francesco Tarducci, has materially added to the sum of the world's knowledge in a field pre-eminently occupied by Washington Irving, Henry Harrisse, and Roselly de Lorgues, a Frenchman—these comprising the powerful original writers in Columbian biography.

In treating our subject we naturally begin at the starting point of biography, the birthplace. The generally accepted statement has been that Columbus was born at Genoa, especially as Columbus begins his will with the well-known declaration, "I, being born in Genoa."

But it has been asserted by numerous writers that in this Columbus was mistaken, just as for a long time General Sheridan was mistaken in supposing himself to have been born in a little Ohio town, when he learned,

MONUMENT TO COLUMBUS AT GENOA.

within a year or two of his death, that he was born in Albany, N. Y. But passing this, it remains to be said that the evidence of the Genoese birth of Columbus may now be considered as fully established. As to the time of his birth there has been not a little question. Henry Harrisse, the American scholar already referred to, placed it between March 25th, 1446, and March 20th, 1447. This, however, we can hardly accept, especially as it would make Columbus at the time of his first naval venture only thirteen years of age. Tarducci gives 1435 or 1436 as the year of his birth. This is also the date given by Irving, and it would seem to be the most probable. This is the almost decisive testimony of Andres Bernaldez, better known as the Curate of Los Palacios, who was most intimate with Columbus and had him a great deal in his house. He says the death of Columbus took place in his seventieth year. His death occurred May 20th, 1506, which would make the year of his birth probably about 1436. And now starting with Genoa as the birthplace of Columbus and about the year 1435 or 1436 as the time of his birth, we proceed with our story.

Christopher Columbus (or Columbo in Italian) was the son of Dominico Columbo and Susannah Fontanarossa his wife. The father was a wool carder, a business which seems to have been followed by the family through several generations. He was the oldest of four children, having two brothers,

Bartholomew and Giacomo (James in English, in Spanish, Diego), and one sister. Of the early years of Columbus little is known. It is asserted by some that Columbus was a wool comber—no mean occupation in that day—and did not follow the sea. On the other hand, it is insisted—and Tarducci and Harrisse hold to that view—that, whether or not he enlisted in expeditions against the Venetians and Neapolitans (and the whole record is misty and uncertain), Columbus at an early age showed a marked inclination for the sea, and his education was largely directed along the lines of his tastes, and included such studies as geography, astronomy, and navigation. Certain it is that when Columbus arrived at Lisbon he was one of the best geographers and cosmographers of his age, and was accustomed to the sea from infancy.[*] Happily his was an age favorable for discovery. The works of travel were brought to the front. Pliny and Strabo, sometime forgotten names, were more than Sappho and Catullus, which a later but not a better age affected. The closing decade of the fifteenth century was a time of heroism, of deeds of daring, and discovery. Rude and unlettered to some extent, it may be conceded it was; yet it was far more fruitful, and brought greater blessings to the world than are bestowed by the effeminate luxury which often characterizes a civilization too daintily pampered, too tenderly reared. Life then was at least serious.

Right here it may be in place to state how invention promoted Columbian discovery. The compass had been known for six hundred years. But at this time the quadrant and sextant were unknown; it became necessary to discover some means for finding the altitude of the sun, to ascertain one's distance from the equator. This was accomplished by utilizing the Astrolabe, an instrument only lately used by astronomers in their stellar work. This invention gave an entirely new direction to navigation, delivering seamen from the necessity of always keeping near the shore, and permitting the little ships—small vessels they were—to sail free amidst the immensity of the sea, so that a ship that had lost its course, formerly obliged to grope its way back by the uncertain guidance of the stars, could now, by aid of compass and astralobe, retrace its course with ease. Much has justly been ascribed to the compass as a promoter of navigation; but it is a question if the astralobe has not played quite as important a part.

The best authorities place the arrival of Columbus at Lisbon about the year 1470. It is probable Columbus was known by reputation to Alfonso V, King of Portugal. It is unquestionable that Columbus was attracted to Portugal by the spirit of discovery which prevailed throughout the Iberian peninsula, fruits of which were just beginning to be gathered. Prince Henry of Portugal

---

[*] Tarducci, I, 41.

who was one of the very first of navigators, if not the foremost explorer of his day, had established a Naval College and Observatory, to which the most learned men were invited, while under the Portuguese flag the greater part of the African coast had been already explored.   Having settled in Lisbon, at the Convent of All Saints, Columbus formed an acquaintance with Felipa Moñis de Perestrello, daughter of Bartholomew de Perestrello, an able navigator but poor, with whom and two others Prince Henry had made his first discovery.   The acquaintance soon ripened into love, and Columbus made her his wife.   Felipa's father

COLUMBUS IN IRONS.

his brothers, Bartholomew and Diego, left Isabella.   On the 25th of November, after an unusually comfortable passage, the vessels entered the harbor of Cadiz. The sight of the venerable form of Columbus in chains as he passed through the streets of Cadiz, where he had been greeted with all the applause of a conqueror, was more than the public would suffer.   Long and loud were the indignant protests that voiced the popular feeling.   The news of the state of affairs coming to Isabella, a messenger was dispatched with all haste to Cadiz, commanding his instant release.   When the poor broken-hearted admiral came into the queen's presence Isabella could not keep the tears back—while he,

Meanwhile Columbus was imbibing to the full the spirit of discovery so widely prevalent. It was not his wife who materially helped him at this time, as has been asserted, but his mother-in-law, who, observing the deep interest that Columbus took in all matters of exploration and discovery, gave him all the manuscripts and charts which her husband had made, which, with his own voyages to some recently discovered places, only renewed the burning desire for exploration and discovery. The leaven was rapidly working.

But the sojourn at Portugal must be briefly passed over. The reports that came to his ears while living at Porto Santo only intensified his convictions of the existence of an empire to the West. He heard of great reeds and a bit of curiously carved wood seen at sea, floating from the West; and vague rumors reached him at different times, of "strange lands" in the Atlantic—most if not all of them mythical. But they continued to stimulate interest as they show the state of public thought at that time respecting the Atlantic, whose western regions were all unknown. All the reports and all the utterances of the day Columbus watched with closest scrutiny. He secured old tomes for fullest information as to what the ancients had written or the moderns discovered. All this served to keep the subject fresh in his mind, nor would it "down," for his convictions were constantly ministered to by contemporary speculators. Toscanelli, an Italian mathematician, had written, at the instance of King Alfonso, instructions for a western route to Asia. With him Columbus entered into correspondence, which greatly strengthened his theories.

Now they came to a head. Constant thought and reflection resulted in his conception of an especial course to take, which, followed for a specific time, would result in the discovery of an empire. And the end! He would subdue a great trans-Atlantic empire, and from its riches he would secure the wealth to devote to expeditions for recovering the Holy Land, and so he would pay the Moors dearly for their invasion of the Iberian peninsula,—a truly fanciful but not a wholly unreasonable conception, as the times were.

COLUMBUS AND THE KING OF PORTUGAL.

At last he found means to lay his project before the King of Portugal. But the royal councillors treated the attempt to cross the Atlantic as rash and dangerous, and the conditions required by Columbus as exorbitant. The adventurous King, John II.—Alfonso had died in 1481—had more faith in his scheme than his wise men, and, with a dishonesty not creditable to him attempted at this time to reap the benefit of Columbus' studies and plans by sending out an expedition of his own in the direction and by the way traced in his charts. But the skill and daring of Columbus were wanting, and at the first mutterings of the sea the expedition sought safety in flight. It turned back to the Cape de Verde islands, and the officers took revenge for their disappointment by ridiculing the project of Columbus as the vision of a day dreamer. O, valiant voyagers!—New Worlds are not discovered by such men as you!

Columbus's brother Bartholomew had endeavored about this time to interest the British monarch in the project, but the first of the Tudors had too much to do in quelling insurrection at home, and in raising revenues by illegal means, to spend any moneys on visionary projects. Henry III would have none of him.

Meantime, indignant at the infamous treatment accorded him, and with his ties to Portugal already sundered by the death of his wife, he determined to shake the dust of Portugal off his feet, and seek the Court of Spain. He would start at once for Cordova, where the Spanish Court then was. Leaving Lisbon secretly, near the close of 1484, he chose to follow the sea coast to Palos, instead of taking the direct inland route, and most happily so; for, in so doing he was to gain a friend and a most important ally; this circumstance the unthinking man will ascribe to chance, but the believer to Providence. Weary and foot-sore, on his journey, he finally arrived at Palos, then a small port on the Atlantic, at the mouth of the Tinto, in Andalusia; here hunger and want drove him to seek assistance from the charity of the Monks, and ascending the steep mountain road to the Franciscan monastery of Santa Maria de La Rabida, he met the pious prior, Father Juan Perez, who, struck with his imposing presence, despite his sorry appearance, entered into conversation with him.

As the interview grew in interest to both the parties, Columbus was led to impart to the prior his great project, to the prior's increasing wonder, for in Palos the spirit of exploration was as regnant as in Lisbon. Columbus was invited to make the Convent his place of sojourn, an invitation he was only too glad to accept. Then Father Perez sent for his friend, a well known geographer of Palos, and, deeply interested in all that related to exploration and the discovery of new lands, the three took the subject into earnest consideration, thorough discussion of the question being had. It was not long before Father Perez—all honor to his name!—became deeply interested in the plans of Columbus. To glorify God is the highest aim to which one can address himself; of that feeling Father Perez was thoroughly possessed; and how could he more fully glorify him than by aiding in the discovery of new lands and the spreading of Christianity there? Impelled by this feeling, he urged Columbus to proceed at once to Cordova, where the Spanish Court then was, giving him money for his journey, and a letter of commendation to his friend, the father prior of the monastery of El Prado Fernando de Talavera, the queen's Confessor, and a person of great influence at Court. There was hope, and there was a period of long and weary waiting yet before him.

Arriving at Cordova, Columbus found the city a great military camp, and all Spain aroused in a final effort to expel the Moors. Fernando, the Confessor, was a very different man from Perez, and instead of treating Columbus kindly, received him coolly, and for a long while actively prevented him from meeting the king. The Copernican theory, though held by some, was not at this time established, and the chief reason why the Confessor opposed Columbus's plan was unquestionably because he measured a scientific theory by appeal to the Scriptures—just as the Sacred Congregation did in Galileo's case a century and a half later—just as some well-meaning but mistaken souls do to-day.

At length, through the friendship of de Quintanilla, Comptroller of the Castilian Treasury, Geraldini, the Pope's nuncio, and his brother, Allessandro, tutor of the children of Ferdinand and Isabella, Columbus was made known to Cardinal Mendoza, who introduced him to the king. Ferdinand listened to him patiently, and referred the whole matter to a council of learned men, mostly composed of ecclesiastics, under the presidency of the Confessor. Here again dogma supplanted science, and controverted Columbus's theories by Scriptural texts, and caused delay, so it was not till 1491—Columbus had now been residing in Spain six years—that the Commission reported the project "vain and impossible, and not becoming great princes to engage in on such slender grounds as had been adduced."

The report of the Commission seemed a death-blow to the hopes of Columbus. Disappointed and sick at heart, and disgusted at six years of delay, Columbus turned his back on Spain, "indignant at the thought of having been beguiled out of so many precious years of waning existence." Determined to lay his project before Charles VIII. of France, he departed, and stopped over at the little Monastery of La Rabida, from whose Prior, Juan Perez, six years before, he had departed with such sanguine hopes, for Cordova.

The good friar was greatly moved. Finally he concluded to make another and final effort. Presuming upon his position as the queen's Confessor, Perez made an appeal direct to Isabella, and this time with the result that an interview was arranged, at which Isabella was present. His proposals would have at once been accepted but that Columbus demanded powers * which even

---

* His principal stipulations were (1) that he should have, for himself during his life, and his heirs and successors forever, the office of admiral in all the lands and continents which he might discover or acquire in the ocean, with similar honors and prerogatives to those enjoyed by the high admiral of Castile in his district. (2) That he should be viceroy and governor-general over all the said lands and continents, with the privilege of nominating three candidates for the government of each island or province, one of whom should be selected by the sovereigns. (3) That he should be entitled to reserve for himself one-tenth of all pearls, precious stones, gold, silver,

de Talavera pronounced "arbitrary and presumptuous," though they were of like character with those conceded by Portugal to Vasco de Gamba. Angered and indignant at the rejection of his terms, which were conditioned only upon his success, Columbus impulsively left the royal presence, and taking leave of his friends, set out for France, determined to offer his services to Louis XII.

ISABELLA HAS A SOBER SECOND THOUGHT.

But no sooner had Columbus gone, than the queen, who we may believe regretted the loss of possible glory of discovery, hastily despatched a messenger after him, who overtook him when two leagues away and brought him back.

Although Ferdinand

spices, and all other articles and merchandises, in whatever manner found, bought, bartered, or gained within his admiralty, the cost being first deducted. (4) That he, or his lieutenant, should be the sole judge in all causes and disputes arising out of traffic between those countries and Spain, provided the high admiral of Castile had similar jurisdiction in his district.

COLUMBUS AND THE MESSENGER.

was opposed to the project, Isabella concluded to yield to Columbus his terms and agreed to advance the cost, 14,000 florins, about $7,000, from her own revenues, and so to Spain was saved the empire of a New World. On May 12 Columbus took leave of the king and queen to superintend the fitting out of the expedition at the port of Palos. The hour and the man had at last met.

FITTING OUT THE EXPEDITION.

What thoughts and apprehensions filled the heart and mind of Columbus as he at last saw the yearning desires of years about to be met, may be to some extent conceived; they certainly cannot be expressed. Not a general at the head of his great army who, at a critical moment in battle, sees the enemy make the false move which insures him the victory, could feel more exultant than Columbus must have felt when he left the presence of the Spanish Court, and, after seven years of weary and all but hopeless waiting at last saw the possibilities of the great unknown opening up before him, and beheld, in a vision to him as clear and radiant as the sun shining in the heavens, a New World extending its arms and welcoming him to her embrace. It would seem as if everything now conspired to atone for the disappointing past. His old tried friend, Perez, prior of the La Rabida monastery, near Palos, received him with open arms, and well he might, for had not his kind offices made success possible? And the authorities, as if to make good the disappointments of seven years, could not now do too much. All public officials, of all ranks and conditions in the maritime borders of Andalusia were commanded to furnish supplies and

CARAVELS OF CHRISTOPHER COLUMBUS.
(After an engraving published in 1584)

assistance of all kinds. Not only so, but as superstition and fear made ship owners reluctant to send their vessels on the expedition, the necessary ships and men were to be provided, if need be, by impressment, and it was in this way vessels and men were secured.

In three months the expedition was ready to sail. The courage of Columbus in setting sail in untried waters becomes more evident when we consider the size of the ships comprising the little expedition. They were three in number; the largest of them, the Santa Maria, was only ninety feet long, being about the size of our modern racing yachts. Her smaller consorts, the Pinta and the Nina, were little caravels, very like our fishing smacks, without any deck to keep the water out. The Santa Maria had four masts, of which two were square rigged, and two fitted with lateen sails like those

2

used on the Nile boats; this vessel Columbus commanded. Martin Alonzo
Pinzon commanded the Pinta, and his brother, Vincente Yañez Pinzon, the
Nina. The fleet was now all ready for sea; but before setting sail Columbus
and most of his officers and crew confessed to Friar Juan Perez, and partook
of the Sacrament. Surely such an enterprise needed the blessing of heaven,
if any did!

It was before sunrise on Friday morning, August 3, 1492, that Columbus
with 30 officers and adventurers and 90 seamen, in all 120 souls, set sail, "in
the name of Christ," from behind the little island of Saltes. Those inclined to
be superstitious regarding Friday will do well to note that it was on a Friday
Columbus set sail from Palos; it was on Friday, the 12th of October, that he
landed in the New World; on a Friday he set sail homeward; on a Friday,
again, the 15th of February, 1493, land was sighted on his return to Europe,
and that on Friday, the 15th of March, he returned to Palos. The story of that
eventful trip has never ceased to charm the world, nor ever will so long as
the triumphs of genius, the incentives of religion, and the achievements of
courage have interest for mankind.

It was Columbus's intention to steer southwesterly for the Canary Islands,
and thence to strike due west—due to misconception occasioned by the very
incorrect maps of that period. On the third day out the Pinta's rudder was
found to be disabled and the vessel leaking, caused, doubtless, by her owner,
who did not wish his vessel to go,—the ship having been impressed—and
thinking to secure her return. Instead of this, Columbus continued on his
course and decided to touch at the Canaries, which he reached on the 9th.
Here he was detained for some weeks, till he learned from a friendly sail that
three Portuguese war vessels had been seen hovering off the island Gomera,
where he was taking in wood, water, and provisions. Apprehensive, and
probably rightly so, that the object was to capture his fleet, Columbus lost
no time in putting to sea.

AND NOW FOR THE NEW WORLD.

It was early morning on the 6th of September that Columbus again set
sail, steering due west, on an unknown sea. He need fear no hostile fleets,
and he was beyond the hindrance of plotting enemies on shore; and yet so far
from escaping trouble it seemed as if he had but plunged into deeper tribulations
and trials than ever.

As the last trace of land faded from view the hearts of the crews failed
them. They were going they knew not where; would they ever return?
Tears and loud lamentings followed, and Columbus and his officers had all they
could do to calm the men. After leaving the Canaries the winds were light and
baffling, but always from the East. On the 11th of September, when about

450 miles west of Ferro, they saw part of a mast floating by, which, from its size, appeared to have belonged to a vessel of about 120 tons burden. To the crew this meant the story of wreck; why not prophetic of their own? The discovery only added to their fears. And now a remarkable and unprecedented phenomenon pre-

THE ECLIPSE OF THE SUN, AS PREDICTED BY COLUMBUS

sented itself. "As true as the needle to the pole" may be a pretty simile, but it is false in fact. For, on the 13th of September, at nightfall, Columbus, for the first time in all his experience, discovered that the needle did not point to the North star, but varied about half a point, or five and a half degrees to the northwest. As he gave the matter close attention Columbus found the variation to increase with every day's advance. This discovery, at first kept secret, was early noticed by the pilots, and soon the news spread among the crews, exciting their alarm. If the compass was to lose its virtues, what was to become of them on a trackless sea? Columbus invented a theory which was ingenious but failed wholly to allay the terror. He told them that the needle pointed to an exact point, but that the star Polaris revolved, and described a circle around the pole. Polaris *does* revolve around a given point, but its apparent motion is slow, while the needle does not point to a definite fixed point. The true explanation of the needle variations —sometimes it fluctuates thirty or forty degrees— is to be found in the flowing of the electrical currents through the earth in different directions, upon which the sun seems to have an effect.

Columbus took observations of the sun every day, with an Astrolabe, and shrewdly kept two logs every day. One of these, prepared in secret, contained the true record of the daily advance ; the other, showing smaller progress, was for the crew, by which means they were kept in ignorance of the great distance they were from Spain.

INDICATIONS OF LAND.

On the 14th of September the voyagers discovered a water-wagtail and a heron hovering about the ships, signs which were taken as indicating the nearness of land, and which greatly rejoiced the sailors. On the night of the 15th a meteor fell within five lengths of the Santa Maria. On the 16th the ships entered the region of the trade winds ; with this propitious breeze, directly aft, the three vessels sailed gently but quickly over a tranquil sea, so that for many days not a sail was shifted. This balmy weather Columbus constantly refers to in his diary, and observes that "the air was so mild that it wanted but the song of nightingales to make it like the month of April in Andalusia." On the 18th of September the sea, as Columbus tells us, was "as calm as the Guadalquiver at Seville." Air and sea alike continued to furnish evidences of life and indications of land, and Pinzon, on the Pinta, which, being the fastest sailer, generally kept the lead, assured the admiral that indications pointed to land the following day. On the 19th, soundings were taken and no bottom found at two hundred fathoms. On the 20th, several birds visited the ships ; they were small song birds, showing they could not have come a very long distance ; all of which furnished cause for encouragement.

But still discontent was growing. Gradually the minds of the men were becoming diseased through terror, even the calmness of the weather increasing their fears, for with such light winds, and from the east, too, how were they ever to get back? However, as if to allay their feelings, the wind soon shifted to the southwest.

A little after sunset on the 25th, Columbus and his officers were examining

GALLUP'S RECAPTURE OF OLDHAM'S BOAT

which had been taken by the Indians from the Puritan exiles in 1636. "Steer straight for the vessel," cried Gallup, and stationing himself at the bow he opened fire on the Indians. Every time he aimed and fired some one was hit. This incident was the beginning of the Pequot War.

POCAHONTAS SAVING THE LIFE OF JOHN SMITH

their charts and discussing the probable location of the island Cipango,* which the admiral had placed on his map, when from the deck of the Pinta arose the cry of "Land! Land!" At once Columbus fell on his knees and gave thanks to Heaven. Martin Alonzo and his crew of the Pinta broke out into the "Gloria in Excelsis," in which the crew of the Santa Maria joined, while the men of the Nina scrambled up to the masthead and declared that they, too, saw land. At once Columbus ordered the course of the vessels to be changed toward the supposed land. In impatience the men waited for the dawn, and when the morning appeared, lo! the insubstantial pageant had faded, the cloud-vision, for such it was, had vanished into thin air. The disappointment was as keen as the enthusiasm had been intense : silently they obeyed the admiral's order, and turned the prows of their vessels to the west again.

A week passed, marked by further variations of the needle and flights of birds. The first day of October dawned with such amber weather as is common on the Atlantic coast in the month of "mists and yellow fruitfulness." The pilot on Columbus's ship announced sorrowfully that they were then 520 leagues, or 1560 miles, from Ferro. He and the crew were little aware that they had accomplished 707 leagues, or nearly 2200 miles. And Columbus had a strong incentive for this deception ; for, had he not often told them that the length of his voyage would be 700 leagues?—and had they known that this distance had already been made, what might they not have done! On the 7th of October the Nina gave the signal for land, but instead of land, as they advanced the vision melted and their hopes were again dissipated.

The ship had now made 750 leagues and no land appeared. Possibly he had made a mistake in his latitude ; and so it was that, observing birds flying to the southward, Columbus changed his course and followed the birds, recalling, as he says in his journal, that by following the flight of birds going to their nesting and feeding grounds the Portuguese had been so successful in their discoveries. On Monday, the 8th, the sea was calm, with fish sporting everywhere in great abundance ; flocks of birds and wild ducks passed by. Tuesday and Wednesday there was a continual passage of birds. On the evening of this day, while the vessels were sailing close together, mutiny suddenly broke out. The men could trust to signs no longer. With cursing and imprecation

---

* Cipango was an imaginative island based upon the incorrect cosmography of Toscanelli, whose map was accepted in Columbus's time as the most nearly correct chart of any extant. The Ptolemaic theory of 20,400 geographical miles as the Equatorial girth was accepted by Columbus, which lessened his degrees of latitude and shortened the distance he would have to sail to reach Asia. The island Cipango was supposed to be over 1000 miles long, running north and south, and the distance placed at 52 degrees instead of the 230 degrees which actually separates the coast of Spain from the eastern coast of Asia. The island was placed in about the latitude of the Gulf of Mexico.

they declared they would not run on to destruction, and insisted upon returning
to Spain. Then Columbus showed the stuff he was made of. He and they, he
said, were there to obey the commands of their Sovereigns; they must find the
Indies. With unruffled calmness he ordered the voyage continued.

On Thursday, the 11th, the spirit of mutiny gave way to a very different
feeling, for the signs of the nearness of land multiplied rapidly. They saw a
green fish known to feed on the rocks, then a branch with berries on it,
evidently recently separated from a tree, floated by them, and above all, a
rudely carved staff was seen. Once more gloom and mutiny gave way to
sanguine expectation. All the indications pointing to land in the evening, the
ships stood to the west, and Columbus, assembling his men, addressed them.
He thought land might be made that night, and enjoined that a vigilant lookout
be kept, and ordered a double watch set. He promised a silken doublet, in
addition to the pension guaranteed by the Crown, to the one first seeing land.

LAND, HO!

That night, the ever memorable night of Thursday, opening into the
morning of Friday, the 12th of October, not a soul slept on any vessel. The
sea was calm and a good breeze filled the sails, moving the ships along at
twelve miles an hour; they were on the eve of an event such as the world had
never seen, could never see again. The musical rippling of the waves and the
creaking of the cordage were all the sounds that were audible, for the birds
had retired to rest. The hours passed slowly by. It was just past midnight
when the admiral, with restless eye, sought to penetrate the darkness. Then a
far-off light came to his vision. Calling Guiterrez, a court officer, he also saw
it. At two in the morning a gun from the Pinta, which led the other boats,
gave notice that land was at last found. A New World had indeed been
discovered. The hopes of years had attained their fruition. It was Rodrigo de
Triana, a seaman, who first saw land—though, alas! he received neither promised
doublet nor pension. Friday, the 12th of October, 1492, corresponding to the
21st of October, 1492, of the present calendar, was the ever memorable day.

The morning light came, and, lifting the veil that had concealed the
supreme object of their hopes, revealed a low, beautiful island, not fifty miles
long, and scarcely two leagues away. Columbus gave the signal to cast anchor
and lower the boats, the men to carry arms. Dressed in a rich costume of
scarlet, and bearing the royal standard, upon which was painted the image of
the crucified Christ, he took the lead, followed by the other captains, Pinzon and
Yañez. Columbus was the first to land; and as soon as he touched the shore
he fell down upon his knees and fervently kissed "the blessed ground" three
times, returning thanks to God for the great favor bestowed upon him. The
others followed his example; and then, recognizing the Providence which had

crowned his efforts with success, he gave the name of the Redeemer—San Salvador—to the discovered island, which was called by the natives "Guanahani."[*] And now the crews, who but a few days previously had reviled and cursed Columbus, gathered around, asking pardon for their conduct and promising complete submission in future.

Columbus supposed at last he had reached the opulent land of the Indies, and so called the natives Indians. But it was an island, not a continent or an Asiatic empire, he had found; an island "very large and level, clad with the freshest trees, with much water in it, a vast lake in the middle, and no mountains."

The natives dwelling on the island were found to be a well-proportioned people with fine bodies, simple in their habits and customs, friendly, though shy in manner, and they were perfectly naked. They thought the huge ships to be monsters risen from the sea or gods come down from heaven. Presents were exchanged with them, including gold bracelets worn by the natives. Inquiry was made as to where the gold came from. For answer the natives pointed by gestures to the southwest. Columbus tried to induce some of the natives to go with him and show where the land of gold was to be found. But this they refused to do; so on the next day (Sunday, the 14th), taking along by force seven natives, that he might instruct them in Spanish and make interpreters of them, he set sail to discover, if possible, where gold was to be had in such abundance, and which, he thought, must be Cipango.

---

[*] It is simply impossible to say which one of that long stretch of islands, some 3000 in number, extending from the coast of Florida to Haïti, as if forming a breakwater for the island of Cuba, Guanahani is. Opinion greatly varies. San Salvador, or Cat Island, was in early favor; Humboldt and Irving—the latter having the problem worked out for him by Captain A. S. Mackenzie, U. S. N.—favored that view. The objections are that it is not "a small island" as Columbus called it, and it does not answer to the description of having "a vast lake in the middle" as Columbus says of Guanahani in his journal. Navette advocates the Grand Turk Island which has the lake. Watling's Island was first advocated by Muñoz and accepted by Captain Beecher, R. N., in 1856, and Oscar Perchel in 1858. Major, of the British Museum, has taken up with Watling's Island, as did Lieutenant J. B. Murdoch, U. S. N., after a careful examination in 1884. This view is accepted by C. A. Schott of the U. S. Coast Survey. On the other hand, Captain G. V. Fox, U. S. N., in 1880, put forth an elaborate claim for Samana, based upon a very careful examination of the route as given in Columbus's journal. This claim, with careful consideration of other conditions, has been very carefully examined by Mr. Charles H. Rockwell, an astronomer, of Tarrytown, N. Y. Mr. Rockwell assents to Captain Fox's view, which he finds confirmed by the course Columbus took in bringing his ship to land. He also traverses Captain Beecher's claim for Watling's Island, which he finds to be inconsistent with Columbus's narrative. As we have said, the problem is beset with difficulties, both as relates to the sailing course, and the extent and topography of the island; and at the present time it appears to be well-nigh insoluble. Where the external conditions are met, the internal conditions, including the large lake, seem wanting; the difficulties in the case seem to be irresistible.

He was, of course, in the midst of the Bahama group, and did not have to sail far to discover an island. On the 15th he discovered the island Conception. On the third day he repeated the forms of landing and took possession, as he did also on the 16th, when he discovered an island which he called Fernandina, known to be the island at present called Exuma. On the 19th another island was discovered, which Columbus named Isabella, and which he declared to be "the most beautiful of all the islands" he had seen. The breezes brought odors as spicy as those from Araby the Blest; palm trees waved their fringed banners to the wind, and flocks of parrots obscured the sky. It was a land where every prospect pleased and Nature bestowed her largesse, from no stinted hand.

But no—it was not a land of gold. Leaving Isabella after a five days' sojourn, on Friday, the 26th of October, he entered the mouth of a beautiful river on the northeast terminus of the island of Cuba, where sky and sea seem to conspire to produce endless halcyon days, for the air was a continual balm and the sea bathes the grasses, which grow to the water's edge, whose tendrils and roots are undisturbed by the sweep of the tides. Upon the delights that came to Columbus in this new-found paradise we cannot dwell; admiration and rapture mingled with the sensations that swept over the soul of the great navigator as he contemplated the virgin charms of a new world won by his valor.

But the survey of succeeding events must be rapid. From the 28th of October till November 12th Columbus explored the island, skirting the shore in a westerly direction. He discovered during that time tobacco, of which he thought little, but which, singularly enough, proved more productive to the Spanish Crown than the gold which he sought but did not find.

On the 20th of November Columbus was deserted by Martin Pinzon, whose ship, the Pinta, could outsail all the others. Martin would find gold for himself. This was a kind of treachery which too often marred the story of Spanish exploration in the New World.

For two weeks after the Pinta's desertion Columbus skirted slowly along the coast of Cuba eastwardly till he doubled the cape. Had he only kept on what was now a westerly course he would have discovered Mexico. But it was not to be. Before sailing he lured on board six men, seven women, and three children, a proceeding which nothing can justify. Taking a southwesterly course, on Wednesday, December 5th, Columbus discovered Haiti and San Domingo, which he called Hispaniola, or Little Spain. The next day he discovered the island Tortuga, and at once returned to Haiti, exploring the island; there, owing to disobedience of orders, on Christmas morning, between midnight and dawn, the Santa Maria was wrecked upon a sand-bank, near the present site of Port au Paix. A sorry Christmas for Columbus, indeed!

The situation was now critical. The Pinta, with her mutinous commander and crew, was gone; the Santa Maria was a wreck. But one little vessel remained, the little, undecked Nina. Suppose she should be lost, too?—how would Spain ever know of his grand discoveries? Two things were necessary: he must at once set out on his return voyage, and some men must be left behind. The first thing he did was to build, on a bay now known as Caracola, a fort, using the timbers of the wrecked Santa Maria. In this he placed thirty-nine men. Nature would surely give them all the shelter and provisions they needed.

COLUMBUS RETURNS TO SPAIN.

It was not until Friday, January 4, 1493, that the weather was sufficiently favorable so that Columbus could hoist sail and stand out of the harbor of the Villa de Navidad, as he named the fort, because of his shipwreck, which occurred on the day of the Nativity. Two days later the ship Pinta was encountered. Pinzon on the first opportunity boarded the Nina, and endeavored, but unsuccessfully, to explain his desertion and satisfy the admiral. The two vessels put into a harbor on the island of Cuba for repairs, and continued to sail along the coast, now and then making a harbor. On Wednesday, the 16th day of January, 1493, they bade farewell to the Queen of the Antilles, and then the prows of the Nina and the Pinta, the latter the slower sailer because of an unsound mast, were turned toward Spain, 1450 leagues away.

It is not possible within the limits of this chapter to follow Columbus from day to day as he sails a sea now turbulent and tempestuous, as if to show its other side, in marked contrast to the soft airs and smooth waters that had greeted the voyagers when their purpose held—

> " To sail beyond the sunset and the baths
> Of all the western stars."

Nor can we follow with minuteness Columbus in his subsequent career. He had made the greatest discovery of his or any other age; he had found the New World, and this, more than anything else, has to do with "The Story of America."

It was on Friday, March 15, 1493, just seven months and twelve days after leaving Palos, that Columbus dropped anchor near the island of Saltes. It was not until the middle of April that he reached Barcelona, where the Spanish Court was sitting. As he journeyed to Court his procession was a most imposing one as it thronged the streets, his Indians leading the line, with birds of brilliant plumage, the skins of unknown animals, strange plants and ornaments from the persons of the dusky natives shimmering in the air. When he reached the Alcazar or palace of the Moorish Kings, where Ferdinand and Isabella were seated on thrones, the sovereigns rose and received him standing. Then they commanded him to sit, and learned from him the story of his discovery. Then and there the sovereigns confirmed all the dignities previously bestowed.

The rejoicing over, the good news spread everywhere, and Columbus was the hero of the civilized world. Ferdinand and Isabella at once addressed themselves to the task of preserving and extending their conquests, and a fleet of seventeen vessels and fifteen hundred men was organized to prosecute further discovery. It was on September 25, 1493, that Columbus set sail with his fleet. On the 3d of November he sighted land, a small, mountainous island, which Columbus called Dominica, after Sunday, the day of discovery. Then again they set sail, and in two weeks discovered several islands in the Caribbean waters. It was not till November 27th that Columbus arrived in the harbor of La Navidad. He fired a salute, but there was no response. On landing the next morning, he found the fortress gone to pieces and the tools scattered, with evidences of fire. Buried bodies were discovered—twelve corpses—those of white men. Of the forty who had been left there, not one was present to tell the tale. But all was soon revealed, and a harrowing, sorrowful tale it was. From a friendly chief, Guacanagari—whom Columbus at first suspected of treachery, and was never quite satisfied of his innocence—it was learned that mutiny, perfidy, and lust had aroused resentments and produced quarrels, resulting in a division into two parties, who, separating and wandering off, were easily overwhelmed by the superior numbers of the incensed natives.

Having discovered the Windward Islands, Jamaica, and Porto Rico, he founded a new colony in Hispaniola (Haïti or San Domingo), which he named Isabella, in honor of his queen. The place had a finer harbor than the ill-fated port of the Nativity. He named his brother Bartolommeo lieutenant governor, to govern when he should be absent on his explorations. On February 2, 1494, Columbus sent back to Spain twelve caravels under the command of Antonio de Torres, retaining the other five for the use of the colony, with which he remained. The vessels carried specimens of gold and samples of the rarest and most notable plants.

Besides these, the ships carried to Spain five hundred Indian prisoners, who, the admiral wrote, might be sold as slaves at Seville—an act which places an indelible stain upon the brilliant renown of the great admiral: that one inhuman act admits of no palliation whatever.

Of the troubles that ensued it is impossible to give any account in detail. Men returning disappointed at not finding themselves enriched, complained of Columbus as a deceiver, and he was charged with cruelty, and, indeed, there was scarcely a crime that presumably was not laid at his door. Then troubles broke out in the colony; the friar, incensed at Columbus, excommunicated him, and the admiral, in return, cut off his rations. Then the men, in the absence of Columbus, off on trips of exploration, gave way to rapine and passion, and the poor natives had no other means than flight to save their wives and daughters. Matters proceeded from bad to worse, the colony growing weaker through dissension.

Finally four vessels from Spain arrived at Isabella, in October, 1495, laden with welcome supplies. These were in charge of Torres, who was accompanied by a royal commissioner, Aquado, who was empowered to make full investigation of the charges brought against Columbus. It was evident to the admiral that he should take early occasion to return to Spain and make explanation to his sovereigns. Accordingly, in the spring of 1496, Columbus set sail for Cadiz, where he arrived on June 11, 1496. He was well received, and was successful in defending himself against the many charges and the clamor raised against

him. Ships for a third voyage were promised him, but it was not until the late spring of 1498 that the expedition was ready for sailing.

COLUMBUS SETS FORTH ON A THIRD EXPEDITION.

On May 30, 1498, with six ships, carrying two hundred men, besides sailors, Columbus set out on his third expedition. Taking a more southerly course, Columbus discovered the mouth of the Orinoco, which he imagined to be the great river Gihon, mentioned in the Bible (Genesis ii. 13) as the second river of Paradise; so sadly were our admiral's geography and topography awry! Columbus also discovered the coast of Para and the islands of Trinidad, Margarita, and Cabaqua, and then bore away for Hispaniola.

HAYTIAN INDIAN GIRL SPINNING

It was the old story told over again, with sickening disappointment. He found the colony was more disorganized than ever. For more than two years Columbus did his best to remedy the fortunes of the colony. At last an insurrection broke out. It was necessary to act promptly and decisively. Seven ringleaders were hanged and five more were sentenced to death. At this time the whole colony was surprised by the arrival at St. Domingo of Francisco de Bobadilla, sent out by Ferdinand and Isabella as governor, and bearing authority to receive from Columbus the surrender of all fortresses and public property. Calumny had done its work! Bobadilla then released the five

men under sentence of death, and finally, when Columbus and Bartholomew arrived at St. Domingo, Bobadilla caused them both to be put in
chains, to be sent to Spain. Seldom has a more touching, more cruel, more
pathetic picture been presented in the world's sad history of cruelty and
wrong!

Shocked as the master of the ship was at the spectacle of Columbus in
irons, he would have taken them off, but Columbus would not allow it; those
bracelets should never come off but at the command of his Sovereigns! It was
early in October, 1500, that the ships with the three prisoners, Columbus and

COLUMBUS'S ARRIVAL AT THE CONVENT OF LA RABIDA.

soon died, and then with his wife and her mother Columbus moved to Porto
Santo, where a son was born to them, whom they named Diego. Felipa hence
forth disappears from history; there is no further record of her. At Porto
Santo Columbus supported his family and helped sustain his aged father, who
was living poorly enough off at Savona, and who was forced to sell the little
property he had, and whose precarious living led him to make new loans and
incur new debts.

THE WOUNDING OF THORVALD THE NORTHMAN

Who with his comrades had may be reached the shores of America as far south as New York, but ... was afterwards killed by the Indians

SEARCH FOR THE FOUNTAIN OF YOUTH

The rest is soon told. The acts of the miserable creature, Bobadilla, were instantly disapproved, and he was recalled, but was drowned on his way home. Columbus, however, was not allowed to return to Hispaniola, but after two years' waiting sailed from Cadiz, May 9, 1502, with four vessels and a hundred and fifty men, to search for a passage through the sea now known as the Gulf of Mexico. It was the middle of June when Columbus touched at San Domingo, where he was not permitted to land. He set sail, and was dragged by the currents near Cuba. Here he reached the little island of Guanaja, opposite Honduras, and voyaged along the Mosquito coast, having discovered the mainland, of which he took possession. After suffering from famine and many other forms of hardship, he went to Jamaica and passed a terrible year upon that wild coast. In June, 1504, provision was made for returning to Spain, and on November 7th of that year, after a stormy voyage and narrow escape from shipwreck, Columbus landed at San Lucar de Barrameda, and made his way to Seville. He found himself without his best friend and protector, for Isabella was then on her death-bed. Nineteen days later she breathed her last. Ferdinand would do nothing for him. A year and a half of poverty and disappointment followed, and then his kindliest friend, Death, came to his relief, and his sorrows were at an end. Columbus died on Ascension Day, May 20, 1506, at Valladolid, in the act of repeating, *Pater, in manus tuas depono spiritum meum,*—"Lord, into Thy hands I commit my spirit." Death did not end his voyages. His remains, first deposited in the Monastery of St. Francis, were transferred, in 1513, to the Carthusian Monastery, of Las Cuevas. In 1536 his body, with that of his son, Diego, was removed to Hispaniola and placed in the cathedral of San Domingo, where it is believed, and pretty nearly certain, they were recently discovered. There seems no sufficient evidence that they were ever taken to Havana.

Thus passed away the greatest of all discoverers, a man noble in purpose, daring in action, not without serious faults, but one inspired by deep religious feeling, and whose character must be leniently measured by the spirit of the age in which he lived. He received from his country not even the reward of the flattering courtier, for he was deprived of the honors his due, and for which the royal word had gone forth; and in the end, when the weight of years was upon him and there was nothing more he could discover, he was allowed by Ferdinand to die in poverty, "with no place to repair to except an inn." But if Ferdinand was not a royal giver Columbus was more than one. For the world will never forget the inscription that, for very shame, was placed upon a marble tomb over his remains—he was now seven years dead—and which reads :—

> " A Castilla y á Leon
> Nuevo mundo dio Colon."
> To Castile and Leon Columbus gave a new world.

As to the character of Columbus, there is wanting space here for considering the subject at any length ; nor does it at all seem necessary. Time has given the great navigator a character for courage, daring, and endurance, which no modern historian can take from him—least of all can the statement, that the falsification of the record of his voyage was reprehensible, stand. It was no more reprehensible than the act of Washington in deceiving the enemy at Princeton ; and in Columbus's case his foes were the scriptural ones " of his own household." Living in an age when buccaneering was honorable and piracy reputable, it will not do to gauge Columbus by the standard of our day. It is sufficient to say that he was great, in the fact that he put in practice what others had only dreamed of. Aristotle was sure of the spheroidicity of the earth, and was certain that " strange lands " lay to the west : Columbus sailed and *found* ; —he went, he saw, he conquered. And these pages cannot better be brought to a close than by quoting what one of the most thoughtful of recent poets, Arthur Hugh Clough, has expressed in his lines, prompted no doubt by his visit to this country :—

> " What if wise men had, as far back as PTOLEMY,
>   Judged that the earth like an orange was round,
> None of them ever said, ' Come along, follow me,
>   Sail to the West and the East will be found '
>   Many a day before
>   Ever they'd come ashore,
>   From the ' San Salvador,'
>   Sadder and wiser men,
>   They'd have turned back again ;
> And that *he* did not, but did cross the sea,
> Is a pure wonder, I must say, to me."

                                                                M. H. B.

Great Discoverers and Explorers Who Followed Columbus.

SEBASTIAN CABOT

No sooner had the news of the successful results achieved by Columbus reached Spain than it spread like wild-fire through the then civilized world. The three other great maritime powers—Portugal, England, and France—were especially aroused to discover, if possible, lands for themselves. On the one side were Ferdinand and Isabella, who were determined to acquire and hold "the strange lands to the west," the possession of which had been guaranteed them by the Pope. On the other hand, there were the three other great powers, with whom desire of conquest and dominion existed no less strongly than with Spain. These nations were resolved to do all that lay in their power to acquire dominion; whatever difficulty might arise with Spain could be settled later.

The first country to compete with Spain in western discovery was England, and the first one to follow in the footsteps of Columbus was John Cabot, who, with his son Sebastian, was destined to make important discoveries which would hand the name of Cabot down to history as surely as that of the great pioneer discoverer, Columbus, himself.

It was as early as 1492 that Señor Puebla, then the Spanish Ambassador to the Court of England, wrote to his Sovereigns that "a person had come, like Columbus, to propose to the King of England an enterprise like that of the Indies." The Spanish King immediately instructed his minister that he should inform Henry VII. that the prior claims of Spain and Portugal would be interfered with if he commissioned any such adventurer. But the warning came too late.

It is possible that the unsuccessful mission of Bartholomew Columbus to England, while the future Admiral was besieging the Spanish Court, may have been the means of arousing in John Cabot's mind a desire to test the truth of the new theory of a westward path to the Indies. When the accomplished feat of the first voyage to the West Indies fired the imagination of Europe and became the chief topic of interest among the maritime nations, even cool-

blooded England was measurably excited, and her parsimonious King yielded
to the urgent prayers of a Genoese navigator, and authorized John Cabot and his
three sons "to sail to the East, West, or North, with five ships, carrying the
English flag, to seek and discover all the islands, countries, regions, or provinces
of pagans in whatever part of the world." We do not learn that this generous
permission to sail and discover unknown countries was accompanied by anything
more than a meagre provision for carrying it out, although the King in return
for the commission given and the single vessel equipped was to have one-fifth
of the profits of the voyage. According to at least one authority, Cabot had a
little fleet of three or four vessels fitted out by private enterprise, "wheryn
dyvers merchaunts as well of London as Bristowe aventured goodes and
sleight merchaundise wh departed from the West cuntrey in the begynnyng
of somer—." We are only sure, however, of one vessel, the Matthews, which
left Bristol in May of 1497.

Choosing the most probable of several vague accounts of Cabot's course in
starting out, we find the sturdy adventurer, with his son and eighteen followers,
standing to the northward, after leaving the Irish coast, and then westerly into
the unknown sea. The plan was that which Columbus followed, when he sailed
from the Island of Ferro in the Canaries, of striking a certain parallel of latitude
and sticking to it. The transatlantic liners of to-day call that "great-circle
sailing."

We have absolutely no record of the month or more spent upon the
outward course. What strange experiences the Gulf Stream or the Labrador
current presented to Cabot we can only surmise. There were no summer isles
and turquoise seas for him. Instead of the song birds, the spicy breezes and
silver sands that Columbus found, his less fortunate countryman came upon the
forbidding coast of Labrador, bleak even in the summer time, where he saw no
human beings.

It was on the 24th of June, 1497, that those on board of the Matthews
unexpectedly caught sight of that strange, unknown land. They had no more
notion than had Columbus of the magnitude of the discovery. This was to their
appreciation no new world, but rather the extreme coast of the kingdom of the
Grand Khan—a remote and desolate shore of India. But their imagination
peopled it with strange beings; demons, griffins, and all the uncouth creatures
of mediæval mythology dwelt there with the bear and the walrus. If the South
was the scene of brighter illusions, of kingdoms where the rulers lived in golden
halls and fountains which could confer upon the bather the gift of perpetual
youth, the glamour and legend which the cold crags of the North conjured up
were not less characteristic. Haunted islands and capes, where the clamor of
men's voices were heard at night, were known to all the sailors and pilots that
followed after the Cabots.

The land that John Cabot first reached, wherever it was, he called "Terra Firma." There he planted the royal standard of England, after which he seems to have sailed southward; presumably to reverse the course by which he came over. Peter Martyr, in relating the wonders that Cabot discovered, recounts that "in the seas thereabouts he found so great multitudes of certain Bigge fishes much like unto Tunies (which the inhabitants called baccalaos) that they

sometimes stayed his shippes." Another writer stated that the "Beares also be as bold which will not spare at mid-day to take your fish before your face." Coasting probably for three hundred leagues, with the land to starboard, Cabot seems to have discovered New-foundland on the mainland side and to have passed through the Gulf of St. Lawrence. He named several islands and prominent points, but the names are uncertain and the localities problematical. We only know that in his opinion England would no longer have to go to Iceland for her fish, and that he relied upon his crew to corroborate his state-ments when he returned to England, because his unsup-ported word would not have established the fact of his dis-coveries. Royalty is not al-ways liberal, despite the phrase "a royal giver"; for we learn

CABOT ON THE SHORES OF LABRADOR.

right here of the munificence of the English King, who gave this intrepid sailor and discoverer ten pounds as a reward for his labor, and afterwards added a yearly pension of twenty pounds, or $100. There is something pathetic in this fragmentary story of the second continent-finder. The little spasm of approval and excitement which his success occasioned soon died away, and even at its height was utterly inadequate to the magnitude of his work. The simple sailor must have made as great a show as possible upon the stipend granted by the

3

king, for we read in a letter of the Venetian, Pasqualigo, that "he is dressed in silk and the English run after him like a madman."

A second voyage of John and Sebastian Cabot to discover the island of Cipango,—that illusory land that Columbus had so hopefully sought,—was undertaken; but a storm came up and one of the vessels was much damaged, finally seeking refuge in an Irish port. The others sailed into a fog of tradition and mystery as dense as that which wrapped the new-found land. We read that the expedition returned and that Sebastian Cabot lived to engage in further adventures, but of his father we know nothing further, the supposition being that he died upon this second expedition. Whether the third traditional voyage of Sebastian Cabot in the fifteenth century is fact or fable is not known. His subsequent career was mainly in the service of other sovereigns.

The profits of the second voyage of the Cabots were so meagre as to fail to arouse any enthusiasm; they were so small, in fact, that almost all interest died out in England. We read of one or two minor adventures, as those of Rut and Grube, the former of whom went to find the northern passage to Cathay, in which voyage his two ships encountered vast icebergs, by which one of them was lost and the other "durst go no further," and after visiting Cape Race returned to England. With these few exceptions England took no part in the great work of discovery, by which, little by little, with here an island and there a headland, now a river and then a bit of coast, the results of that great discovery were combined into that which came to be known, though not at first, as the New World.

Yet Newfoundland was not deserted. Almost from the first the Breton and Basque fishermen, hardy and adventurous, frequented its shores. The Isle of Demons and other uncanny places in the new country were visited by fleets of French fishermen's boats, and plenteous cargoes of "Baccalois," or cod-fish, were taken eastward yearly for the Lenten market.

AMERICUS VESPUCIUS AND HIS VOYAGES.

The year 1500 was one of extreme importance in the making of New World history. The Spanish and Portuguese had already settled their dispute over the division of territory, the Pope's decision, to which all good Catholics in that day yielded unhesitating obedience, having given to Spain all land discovered west of a certain meridian line, and to Portugal whatever lay to the eastward. In this way Portugal acquired her right to the Brazils; and she also laid claim to Newfoundland. But the great element, time, had just begun to work. It was destined, under the ordering of Providence, that Spain and Portugal should make conquests, but not hold them. The Anglo-Saxon was only then a potentiality; his greatness was becoming recognized: he was yet to sweep the Atlantic, and, finally, settling on the stormy coast to the west, was to lay the foundations of a great empire, which was to make it possible to tell the inspiring and unique Story of America.

We now come to Americus Vespucius, who was, singularly enough, and through no scheming of his own, to give his name to a country that should rightly have borne the name Columbia. And he was to do this though he headed but one expedition. The story must necessarily be brief.

Vespucius was a Florentine—another conspicuous illustration of the fact that he was to discover even as Columbus had discovered, but Italy was to reap no benefit. He was, indeed, to sow the seed, but the strong arms of others were to reap the harvest. On the 9th day of March, 1451, Vespucius was born, in the city of Florence. Of a noble but not at all wealthy family, he received a liberal education, devoting himself to astronomy and cosmography. The fortunes of business took him to Seville, where he became the agent of the powerful Medici family. It was in 1490 that he became acquainted with Columbus, and was concerned in fitting out four caravels for voyages of discovery; he took an active part in assisting Columbus in preparing for his second voyage. Vespucius makes the statement, which we are prepared to accept, that in 1497 he sailed, and probably as astronomer, with one of the numerous expeditions that the success of Columbus had called into existence, leaving Cadiz on the 10th of May of that year. After twenty-seven days of sailing, the fleet, consisting of four vessels, reached "a coast which we thought to be that of a continent," traversing which they found themselves in "the finest harbor in the world." Just what that harbor is it is impossible to say. Some writers have placed it as far south as Campeachy Bay; Chesapeake Bay has also been designated, Cape Charles being the point of entering. It is impossible, however, owing to Vespucius's loose manner of writing, to fix the place with any certainty. But he states that he doubled Cape Sable, the southernmost point on the peninsula of Florida. Vespucius tells us that while in "the finest harbor" mentioned the natives were very friendly, and implored the aid of the whites in an expedition against a fierce race of cannibals who had invaded at different times their coasts, carrying away human victims whom they sacrificed by the score. The island in question was one of the Bahamas, one hundred leagues away. The fleet accordingly bore away, the Spaniards being piloted by seven friendly Indians. The Spaniards arrived off an island called Iti, and landed.

Here they encountered fierce cannibals, who fought bravely but unsuccessfully against firearms. More than two hundred prisoners were made captive, seven of them being presented to the seven Indian guides. But nearly a year had passed since they had left Cadiz. The vessels were leaky; it was time to return. Accordingly, leaving some point of the coast line of the United States, the fleet reached Cadiz on the 15th of October, 1498, with two hundred and

AN ITZAN CANNIBAL CHIEF OFFERING A HUMAN SACRIFICE TO THE SUN.

twenty-two cannibal prisoners as slaves, where they were well received and sold their slaves for a good sum.

Still following Vespucius's statement, on the 16th of May, 1499, he started on a second voyage in a fleet of three ships, under Alonzo de Ojeda. In this voyage Ojeda reached the coast of Brazil, and being compelled to turn to the north because of the strong equatorial current, they went as far as Cayenne, thence to Para, Maracaibo, and Cape de la Vela. They also touched at Saint Domingo. The expedition returned to Cadiz on the 8th of September, 1500. Three months later Yañez Pinzon, taking a like course, discovered the greatest river on the earth, the Amazon, as will be seen a little further on in this chapter. Ojeda just missed that discovery. A year later, for some reason dissatisfied with his position—and Vespucius seems to have passed at pleasure from one command to another—he entered the service of Emanuel, King of Portugal, and took part in an expedition to the coast of Brazil. He wrote a careful account of this voyage, which he addressed to some member of the Medici family, to whom, in 1504, he sent a fuller narrative of his expedition, which was published at Strasbourg. This gave him high reputation as a navigator and original discoverer.

Under the command of Coelho, a Portuguese navigator, on either May 10th or June 10th, 1503, a little squadron, with Vespucius, left the Tagus to discover, if possible, Malacca somewhere on the South American coast; but through mishap the fleet was separated, and Vespucius, with his own vessel, and later joined by another, proceeded to Bahia. Thence they sailed for Lisbon, arriving there, after about a year's absence, on the 18th of June, 1504.

HOW AMERICA CAME TO BE NAMED.

In a letter written from Lisbon, in 1504, to René, Duke of Lorraine, Vespucius gives an account of four voyages to the Indies, and says that the first expedition in which he took part sailed from Cadiz May 20, 1497, and returned in October, 1498. This letter has provoked endless discussions among historians as to the first discovery of the mainland of America, and it has been charged against Vespucius that after his return from his first voyage to Brazil he prepared a chart, giving his own name to that part of the country. It is high time the name of Vespucius was rid of this stain. It seems to be established that at this time the Duke René, of Lorraine, a scholar, and one deeply interested in the discoveries of the age, caused a map to be prepared for him by an energetic young student of geography, a young man named Waldsee-Müller, who innocently affixed the name America to the Brazil country. In this way the name became fixed, and was eventually taken up by others. It was not till nearly thirty years afterward—in 1535—that the charge of discrediting Columbus by affixing his own name was brought, and most unjustly so, against Vespucius. **Latter-day opinion acquits Vespucius of this charge,** and now with the fact established, at this time of our Columbian anniversary, it should no more be brought against the distinguished navigator, whose discoveries were important, if he did not accomplish all that was expected, and that through no fault of his.

Vespucius died in Seville, February 2, 1512—six years after his predecessor, the first Admiral, had passed away.

YAÑEZ PINZON AS A VOYAGER.

The first man of importance to sail after Ojeda and Vespucci was Vincent Yeñez Pinzon, who with his brother Ariez Pinzon, built four caravels, little deck-less or half-decked yachts, with which he sailed from Palos in the month of December, 1499. Going further south than his predecessors, Pinzon bore away toward the coast of Brazil, his first land being discovered at a point eight degrees north of the equator, near where the town of Pernambuco was afterwards built: he was the first Spaniard to cross the equinoctial line. We read that he lost sight of the pole-star, a circumstance which must have alarmed his sailors. More wonderful still,—most miraculous it must have seemed,—was the finding of a great flood of fresh water, at the Equator, out of sight of land, which induced the navigator to seek for a very large river, and he found it !—for there was the mighty Amazon with its mouth a hundred miles wide and sending a great tide of fresh water a hundred miles out to sea. At their first landing Pinzon's sailors cut the names of their ships and of their sovereign on the trees and the rocks, while he took possession of the land in behalf of Spain. Here Pinzon seized some thirty Indians as slaves. The mighty Amazon, with its hundred-mile wide mouth, filled the explorers with wonder, as well it might. But the capturing of the Indians had created difficulties which endangered the safety of the fleet, so that Pinzon deemed it prudent to shorten his stay. Accordingly he set sail, and skirting along the coast discovered the Orinoco River and Trinidad; after which they stood across to Hispaniola. A hurricane overtaking the little fleet nearly put an end to Pinzon's adventure, but he finally escaped with the loss of two of his vessels. With the others he returned to Spain, only to find that Diego de Lépe had sailed after him and returned before him, with a report of the continuance of the South American continent far to the southward.

Rightly Da Gama has no place here, save as a discoverer in times of discovery. A skilled Portuguese mariner, he coasted the eastern shores of Africa and visited India. In a second voyage he became involved in hostilities with the towns of the Malabar coast. In 1499 he was made Admiral of the Indies. He died at Cochin, India, Christmas Day, 1524.

In 1499, the same year that the Pinzons and Lépe sailed, Pedro Alvarez de Cabral was commissioned by the Portuguese King, Emanuel, to follow Vasco da

Gama's course and establish a trading station on the Malabar coast. Gomez, for some reason unknown, sailed by the way of the Cape Verde Islands, and taking from thence a much more westerly course than he intended, came, quite by accident, upon the Continent that Pinzon and Lépe had so lately left. Probably the real cause of Cabral's deflection from his original course was to avoid the calms of the Guinea shore. He had no sooner made the strange land than he resolved to cruise along it, and concluded that this wonderful coast was a continent. Despatching a ship home to Portugal with the news—

with Gaspar de Lemos in command—he pursued his voyage.
When Pinzon returned, therefore,
he not only found that Lépe had
been there before, but ascertained
that Portugal pressed its prior
claim to the coast he had discovered, based on the Pope's edict as
well as the voyage of Cabral.
The King of Portugal, on receiving Cabral's message, soon despatched a fleet to discover new
territory for his crown; and
Americus Vespucius, till then in
the Spanish service, accepted his
overtures and went with the expedition. When Gaspar de
Lemos started for Portugal with
the news of the discovery of the
southern continent, Cabral waited
only a few days and then sailed
southward.

The result of this second part
of his voyage was the discovery

VASCO DA GAMA.
(From the MS. of Lelio Barretti de Rezenda.)

of the Cape of Good Hope. There the fleet, heretofore so successful, was overtaken by a terrific storm, in the course of which four of his vessels went down, among them being one which was commanded by the navigator Bartholomew Diaz. The name which Cabral gave to this new country was Vera Cruz. The appellation by which it was afterwards known, of "Brazil" or "the Brazils," was taken from the dye wood found there; an Arabic word being borrowed for the purpose. Columbus discovered the new world without knowing he had done so, although his work was in pursuance of carefully laid plans. Cabral however, like Vespucius off the North American coast,

was aware from the first that the land he accidentally discovered was the mainland of a great continent.

After his adventure at the Cape of Good Hope Cabral went as far as
Hindostan and returned with laden ships, in which were immense quantities of
spices, jewels and rare merchandise. "Verily," said Vespucius, who met him in
the Cape Verde Islands upon his return voyage, "God has prospered King
Emanuel." The same year [1500] that the Pinzons and Cabral sailed from
their respective countries, Portugal sent the brothers Gaspar and Miguel
Cortereal on the first of a series of new expeditions to explore the Northwest.
The papal line of demarcation between Spanish and Portuguese possessions was
called Borgia's meridian, and the suspicion that Cabot's discoveries lay to the
eastward of this was sufficient cause for an expedition from Lisbon. These were
unfortunate voyages, for although the region already explored by the Cabots
was revisited and the flag of Portugal planted in the chill domain of the griffins
and demons of Breton fancy, yet the wild men and curiosities which they brought
home were but a sorry exchange for the lives that they cost. From Gaspar
Cortereal's second voyage he never returned. Two of his ships came home,
and when his brother Miguel went in search of him his flag-ship also was lost,
with all on board.

OTHER DISCOVERERS.

Rodigero de Bastidas and John de la Cosa, sailing with two ships from
Cadiz, in 1502, discovered the Gulf of Darien, which point Ojeda on his
second voyage also touched, thence proceeding to the West Indies. Following
these, after a number of smaller adventurers that tried their fortune upon
the Atlantic, Juan de Solis and Vincent Yañez Pinzon sailed from the Port
of Saville, six years later. They directed their two caravels toward the
coast of Brazil, going to the thirty-fifth degree south latitude, where they
discovered the Rio de la Plata,—the River of Silver,—which they at first
called Paranaguaza. To them also is due the credit for the discovery of
Yucatan, on this same voyage. De Solis was by some considered the very
ablest navigator of his time, and his fame at last induced the King of Spain to
appoint him to the command of two ships fitted out to discover a passage to the
Spice Islands, or Moluccas, for which he sailed in October, five years after he
and Pinzon had made the trip just alluded to. He returned to the la Plata
River, which stream he entered in January, 1516, but a tragic fate awaited him.
Attempting to ascend the river and explore its banks, de Solis and a number of
his crew were surprised and overpowered by the savages, who with barbaric
heartlessness roasted and ate the unfortunate Spaniards in the sight of their
companions on the vessels. The survivors, sickened and terrified by such a
spectacle, lost no time in escaping from the land of these cannibals. They
stopped only at Cape San Augustin, where they loaded their vessels with Brazil

wood, and made the best of their way back to Europe with the sad news. In the following year Charles V. sent Cordova, with a command of 110 men in three caravels, into that distant but no longer dreaded West, which still had its rewards for the adventurer.

Upon the shore of Yucatan, where he first landed, at Cape Catoche, the Spaniards saw with surprise people who in one respect differed very greatly from the natives who had so far been met with in the western voyages, inasmuch as they dressed in cotton and other fabrics, instead of going naked and painting their bodies. Not only in their dress but in their houses they exhibited signs of civilization that excited the wonder of Cordova and his men.

PONCE DE LEON DISCOVERS FLORIDA.

Six years had passed after the death of Columbus, when, in 1512, Juan Ponce de Leon sailed from Puerto Rico in a northerly direction and discovered the peninsula which the Admiral had so nearly found upon his first voyage. De Leon first sighted land at about the boundary line separating Florida from Georgia. Landing, he took possession in the name of his sovereign, calling the new country Florida ; for it was in April, when the Cherokee roses, the wild jessamine, and all the multitudinous blossoms of a Floridian spring-time were filling the air with their fragrance. The discoverer of this paradise returned to Spain, and, obtaining the governorship of the new coast, undertook to enter upon its possession. But the savages were otherwise minded. The followers of Ponce de Leon were hunted through the tangled growth of the luxuriant forests or harassed in their defences behind the sand-dunes, till many of them had been killed, and their leader was glad to escape with the little remnant of his force. So he re-embarked, abandoning the country ; but the Spaniards claimed Florida from that day, in spite of a counter-claim which England presented in virtue of the discoveries of the Cabots.

Later, in 1527, Pamphilo de Narvaes repeated Ponce de Leon's experiment, with a similar result. Then Ferdinand de Soto, who had been Governor of Cuba, obtained the title of Marquis of Florida, and, with nearly a thousand men and ten ships, he landed, in 1539, on the west coast of the peninsula. Five years later a little handful of broken, impoverished, beaten, disheartened Spaniards, less than a third of the number that had sailed so proudly to the conquest of Florida, left its shores to the sole occupancy of the jealous natives who inhabited it. There was no perpetual "fountain of youth" there for de Soto, but ageing, weariness, and disaster instead.

When Charles V., of Spain, was beginning to feel the benefit of the con quest in the New World, and Cortez and the Spanish captains and adventurers were planting the standard of Spain in rich territory, Francis the First, of France, chafed at the necessity of acknowledging the success of his rival. Francis was one of the most curious characters of European history, a combination of good and evil traits. Vanity, culture, sensibility to the influences of art and literature, hatred, malice, and all uncharitableness distinguished him. He was the friend of philosophers and of those who were far from being philosophers.

From Florence came Verazzano, a navigator of repute who, unlike most of the new world-finders, was by birth a gentleman, descended from men who had been prominent in Florentine history. He was appointed to sail westward from Dieppe with four ships, in the year 1523, to seek a new passage to that Cathay which still lured the hopes of Christendom; and in passing we may remark upon the curious irony of fortune which permitted Italy to lend to other nations the men who should win the greenest laurels as discoverers, when she herself was unable to claim a foot of territory in the new world. The beginning of Verazzano's voyage was puzzling enough. He had not proceeded far from Dieppe when a storm overtook him and he escaped with two of his vessels to Brittany; thence he cruised against the Spaniards and finally, having but one vessel left out of the four with which he started, he set sail for the island of Madeira, and on the 17th of January, 1524, turned the prow of his caravel, the Dolphin, westward, to cross the Atlantic. After a passage of forty-five days, during which the strange experiences common to such an adventure were not lacking, he sighted a low shore where vast forests of pine and cypress rose from the sandy soil. This was not far from the present site of Wilmington, North Carolina. Among other things the Florentine noticed the presence of many fragrant plants "which yeeld most sweete savours farr from the shore." The savages who appeared on shore attracted the greatest attention from the voyagers since they were not at all sure what their reception might be when they landed for the supply of water of which they stood in need. A boat approached as near as possible to the beach, when one of the sailors, taking some gifts as a propitiatory offering, jumped overboard and swam through the surf. But as he neared the beach and saw the throng of screeching red men who awaited him his courage failed, and flinging his presents among them he endeavored to return; but the savages succeeded in capturing him and returned to the sand, where in the sight of the terrified captive they built a great fire. Instead, however, of cooking him, as he expected, they warmed and dried him, showed him every mark of affection, and then led him to the shore and let him go. At the next place they touched, the crew of the Dolphin showed their appreciation of the courtesy of the Indians by stealing one of their children.

From the Carolinas Verazzano's course was northward along the coast, his first anchorage being in the bay of New York. Into that beautiful harbor, through the Narrows and under the green and tree-covered banks of Staten Island, he rowed, being met by numerous canoes filled with Indians who came out to welcome him. From New York the Dolphin followed the Long Island coast as far as Block Island, and from there to the harbor of Newport, where for fifteen days they rested, being entertained by two savage chiefs, who did all that lay in their power to dazzle the eyes of their white visitors with the signs of opulence, as evidenced by copper bracelets, wampum belts, the skins of wild beasts, etc.

From here the little vessel steered along the New England coast, neither officers nor seamen finding much to attract them. The Indians were suspicious and inhospitable, driving them back with shouts and showers of arrows when they ventured ashore in their boats. The seaboard of Maine was visited, and then the banks of Newfoundland, from which last point Verazzano, whose expedition was for us, perhaps, the most significant of all, sailed back for France, having explored the American coast from Hatteras to Newfoundland.

In the following year Verazzano sailed again from France with a fleet, but no news of that expedition ever came back, and the mystery of its loss chilled the ardor for discovery in that country, so that for several years we hear of no further adventures to the new world. But in 1534 the persuasions of Admiral Chabot led to the issuing of a commission to Jacques Cartier, of St. Malo, who sailed from that port in the same year with two ships and one hundred and twenty-two men. ' He circumnavigated Newfoundland and explored the Gulf of St. Lawrence, and upon a second voyage sailed up the river of the same name for three hundred leagues, as far as the "great and swift Fall." On the site of Montreal he visited an Indian town. Having attempted the settlement for which he had been sent out, Cartier went back to France only to return with a larger expedition to Canada five years later.

Half a century of discovery and adventure had elapsed. The map-makers of Europe during that time were kept busy by the changes made necessary from fresh data requiring the readjustment of old lines. From Columbus to Verazzano and Cartier, the whole coast, with a few exceptions, had been discovered, from the stony crags of Labrador to the Cape of Good Hope. It only remained now for the round-up of this magnificent hunt, which was accomplished by the intrepid Magellan, prince of navigators, who, first turning westwardly across the Pacific found the true path to far-off Cathay, which the mighty Genoese had sought so patiently, so grandly, so mistakenly, among the isles of June and the pearl banks of the Caribbean Sea.

More than ordinary romance and interest attend the story of Vasco Nunez de Balboa. His appearance in the story of Spanish conquest in America, if not dignified, is captivating to the imagination. Martin Fernandez de Enciso, the geographer, sailed from St. Domingo to go to the relief of the explorer, Ojeda, who was dying of famine at San Sebastian. Among the stores in his vessel was a cask which contained something more valuable than the bread which it was invoiced as containing. When Enciso's ships had got fairly out to sea, Balboa crept out of his cask and presented himself to the commander, who could, after all, do nothing but scold, as it was then too late to return the fugitive to the creditors from whom he had taken that means of escaping. There were some threats of putting the culprit ashore on a small desert island, but that was not done, or one of the most popular stories of the New World would have been unwritten.

But by the time the expedition in search of Ojeda had been abandoned and the followers of Enciso, reinforced by the haggard remnant of Ojeda's force, had reached the Gulf of Urabá, Balboa was no inconsiderable figure in that company.

When the building of Santa Maria del Darien had commenced and Enciso's temper provoked an insurrection, the stowaway, Balboa, was spoken of as his successor. The new-comers had encroached on the province of Nicuesa, who had been given a province in Darien, of which he was Governor, at the same time that Ojeda was similarly favored by King Ferdinand. Some of them, therefore, were for giving their allegiance to that Governor. The matter was settled by giving Balboa charge till Nicuesa should come.

Nicuesa, embittered by famine and all manner of hardship, was rejected by the men of Darien when he finally came to them, and, turning his poor little brigantine seaward, was never heard from again. The cruelty shown to him at this time was afterward charged upon Balboa, but he was cleared by the court. He, however, showed little kindness to the irate Enciso, who went home to Spain an avowed enemy, complaining bitterly of the treatment he had received at the hands of the stowaway, whom, doubtless, he regretted not having "marooned," i. e., cast on a desert island, when he had the chance.

Balboa next explored Darien. He married a native princess, thus making the old chief Comogre, her father, his firm friend. The first evidence which the Spaniards had of the superior claims of the people of Central America to civilization was at Comogre's house, where "finely wrought floors and ceilings," a chapel occupied by ancestral mummies, and other signs of ease and leisure, appeared. But dearer than anything else was the sight of ornaments and flakes of virgin gold. This the Spaniards, with their usual propensity, acquired, and marveled at the strange tales which were told them of a land further to the westward where the people made bowls and cups of the yellow metal. This was the first news they had received of the kingdom of Peru. Balboa sent the whole of the story and a fifth of the gold to Spain as Ferdinand's share, but the ship went down on the voyage. Its arrival at Court would have done more than anything else to check the legal proceedings which were being commenced against him at home. However, Balboa was appointed Captain-General of Darien by the Government of Hispaniola, which was some little comfort to him.

Balboa next advanced across the Isthmus to find "the great sea" of which he had heard. On the twenty-fifth of September, in 1513, after some trouble with the Indians, Vasco Nuñez de Balboa stood where the poet Keats has made Cortez stand for some years past, on a peak in Darien, a mountain in the country of Quarequa, and looked with the glad eyes of a discoverer on the blue waters of the mighty Pa-

BALBOA DISCOVERS THE PACIFIC.

cific Ocean, that till then had had no herald in the Eastern world. Having shortly after this gained the Pacific coast, Balboa returned to Darien with the news of his great discovery, which might have gained him the gratitude and reward it merited had not Pedrarias Davila succeeded in gaining the royal ear, and with a band of cavaliers, lured to new fields by the golden rumors of Peru, started for Darien. By his commission Davila was Admiral and Governor; he was a leading figure on the Isthmus for sixteen years, and during that time committed so many crimes that the historian Oviedo computes that he would have to face two million souls at the judgment day! Oviedo, like the humane Las Casas, believed that the Indians possessed souls; and though we know how given the Spanish chroniclers were to exaggeration and even downright mendacity, still we cannot doubt that enough murders were committed during the governorship of Davila to make even the conscience of a Spaniard feel uncomfortable. With the cavaliers who came over with Davila were Oviedo, the historian already named, and Enciso, Balboa's old commander. The first thing that the jealous Davila did was to arrest Balboa on trumped-up charges, but they did not suffice to insure his conviction, and about this time the news of his great discoveries was beginning to turn the tide in Spain in his favor. It is to be said to Balboa's credit that he was very politic in his treatment of the Indians, using kindness where the new Governor practiced the utmost cruelty. As a result Balboa was regarded with friendly feelings and his rival hated—a condition of affairs that could not fail to engender jealousy and danger.

The Spanish Bishop, who had come with the expedition, strove to patch up matters by suggesting a betrothal between Balboa and the daughter of the Governor. As the daughter was in Spain, and the alliance could not be consummated for some time, Balboa consented, though we have no evidence that he really contemplated abandoning his beloved Indian wife. The proposed marriage was but one article in an important treaty, without which the younger man would have been crushed by the elder.

Before long, however, Balboa again incurred the hatred of his enemy, and accepting a treacherous invitation to visit him, was arrested by his old comrade, Pizarro, and beheaded, at the age of forty-two, in the land with which his name and fame are indissolubly connected. It was just before his last quarrel with Davila, which resulted in his untimely end, that Balboa performed one of the most astonishing feats in Spanish-American annals; having taken his ships apart, he transported them across the Sierras, and launched them on the Pacific.

Ferdinand de Soto was born in Xeres, Spain, in 1500. We first meet with him, so far as American exploration is concerned, on accompanying his friend and patron Davila [previously referred to in the account of Balboa], on his expedition to Darien, of which Davila was Governor, and whose offensive administration De Soto was the first to resist. He supported Hernandez in Nicaragua in 1527, who perished by the hand of Davila for not obeying his instructions. Withdrawing from the service of Davila, in 1528 he explored the coasts of Guatemala and Yucatan for 700 miles, in search of the strait which was supposed to connect the two oceans. In 1532, by special request of Pizarro, he joined him in his enterprise of conquering Peru. He was present at the seizure of the Peruvian Inca, and took part in the massacre which followed, serving the usual apprenticeship in butchery which hardened the hearts and made callous the nerves of those who followed the Spanish conquerors; but we are told he condemned the murder of the Inca Atahualpa, as well he might!—Prescott has pictured the infamy of this crime in indelible colors.

In 1537, De Soto was appointed Governor of Cuba, and two years later he crossed the Gulf of Mexico to attempt the conquest of Florida at his own expense, believing it to be the richest province yet discovered. Anchoring in Tampa Bay, May 25th, 1539, his route was through a country made hostile by the violence of the Spanish in-

BURIAL OF DE SOTA.

vader, Navarez. It was fighting all the time, but it was not conquest. He continued to march northward, reaching, October 18th, 1540, the present site of Mobile, Alabama, and finally arriving at the mouth of the Savannah river. That country was then, as it is now, flat and sandy, its low forests of pine interspersed with cypress swamps and knolls where the live-oaks flourished. Frequent streams intersect portions of it. Traveling with such means as De Soto had at his disposal was very slow and troublesome. From the Savannah he turned inland, fighting the Indians at most every step, and overcoming mighty obstacles. With nearly a third of his men slain or lost, after a winter spent on the Yazoo, and disappointment following disappointment as he searched in vain, in his westward course, for the cities of gold which he saw in glowing but illusory vision, after a year and a half of unparalleled hardships and constant marching, in April, 1542, he discovered the Mississippi, that mighty stream whose current flows for four thousand miles, upon which the eyes of a white man had never before rested. This he explored for a short distance above and below Chickasaw Bluffs. Here his great career ended, for he died of malignant fever. To conceal his death from the Indians, his body was wrapped in a mantle, and in the stillness of midnight was silently sunk in the middle of the stream. His soldiers pronounced his eulogy by grieving for their loss, while the priests chanted the first requiem ever heard on the waters of the Mississippi.

WASHINGTON'S FIRST VICTORY

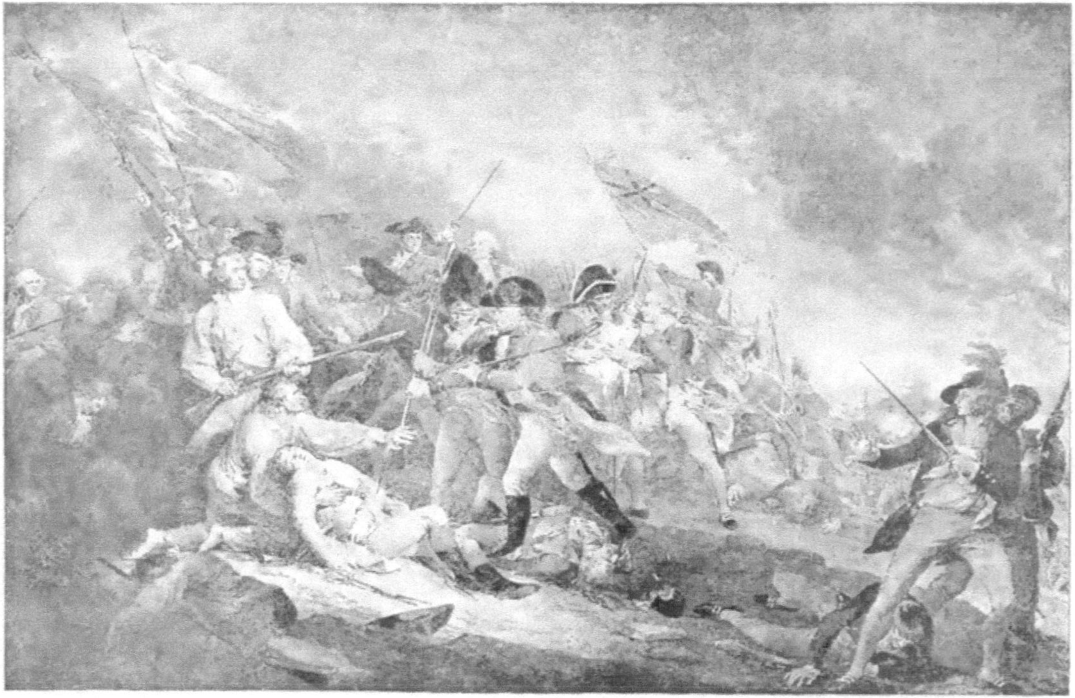

THE BATTLE OF BUNKER HILL

Thrilling Experiences of our Forefathers in the Early Days.

THE MARIGNY HOUSE, NEW ORLEANS, WHERE LOUIS PHILIPPE STOPPED IN 1798.

A few years cover the beginnings of westward migration from Europe and the British Isles. Great impulses seem to be epidemic. The variety of causes which led to the planting of the American colonies became operative under diverse national and race conditions, so that they appear in history as the synchronous details of a common plan. As the reader follows these pages and appropriates all the wonderful and inspiring details of this unequaled record of four centuries, his interest will deepen and his amazement will keep pace with his interest. Finding a barren shore, broken only by the roar of the surf, the cries of birds and animals, and the whoop of the Indian, he will lay down the volume, having discovered that civilization has followed the sun until the two oceans have met—connected by an unbroken tide of humanity ebbing and flowing from the Atlantic to the Pacific; and westward the Star of Empire still takes its way!

A minute account of the social and political situations in the various kingdoms of Europe during the sixteenth century is not within the scope of this work, but it will be well to make a very brief statement of the questions that agitated Christendom at this time, and to notice the temper of the times.

Cupidity and a love of adventure led the Spaniard to the conquest of the New World. Spain was then paramount in Europe, most powerful as well as most Catholic; and the controlling motive of her sovereigns was conquest. It was not reformation nor revolution that sent her people over seas, but

the love of power and wealth. In France, on the contrary, the spirit of
revolt against established dogmas had led to persecution, so that the Hugue-
nots were glad to find an asylum in the wilderness of the New World.
Under these conditions the first colonies were attempted in the middle of
the sixteenth century. Thirty years later a second planting, more general and
more effectual, was begun.

At that time Protestant England had a Catholic king. Henry of Navarre
was upon the throne of France, which he had gained by his apostacy. Holland,
the mighty little republic, was, under the wise leadership of John of Barne-
veld and the States General, keeping Catholic Europe in check. Spain
had been for years planning the conquest of England "as a stepping-
stone to the recovery of the Netherlands." It will be seen that the very
causes which led emigrants to colonize the new continent forbade friendship
or common interests between those of different races, the animosities of the
Old World being very carefully transplanted to the new along with other
possessions.

France made the first attempt at colonization in 1555. One of the leaders
in the enterprise was Coligny, the Huguenot admiral; John Ribault and
Laudoniere were masters of successive expeditions, seeking first the Florida
coast and afterward establishing a settlement in Carolina. The French have
seldom made good colonists, and those of Carolina were no exception to the
general rule. It is probable that their quarrelsome dispositions would have
destroyed them in time had not the Spanish claimants of the country, led by
Menendez, hastened the event. This expedition of the Spaniards was not
only noteworthy because of the cruel massacre of Ribault and his Huguenot
followers, but also as the occasion of the founding of the most ancient of
North American cities, St. Augustine. This occurred in 1564.

The settlement of St. Augustine was followed by a hiatus in which nothing
was done toward the colonization of America. This was due to the great
religious war which was then raging in Europe. But in the interval the missionary expeditions of the Spanish Franciscans, Ruyz and Espejio, in 1582,
resulted in the building of Santa Fé in New Mexico. There had also been the
establishment by adventurers of various fishing and trading stations, notably
the one on the island of New Foundland.

During the interval England had been steadily growing as a marine power,
and her navigators had directed men's eyes anew towards the land where so
many of their countrymen should find refuge. Finally Raleigh, following in
the footsteps of his famous half-brother, Sir Humphrey Gilbert, obtained a
patent from Queen Elizabeth, by the terms of which he should become pro-
prietor of six hundred miles ra   "   any point which he might discover
or take, provided he did not ca   territory otherwise granted by any

AN INDIAN ATTACK ON BROOKFIELD.

Christian sovereign. As an auxiliary to this grant the queen gave her favorite a monopoly of the sale of sweet wines, by the profits of which business he was soon enabled to fit out what was known as the Lane expedition, that sailed under the command of Grenville in 1585, and landed at Roanoke, in Virginia.

THE ROANOKE COLONY.

Grenville's first act upon landing was to rouse the animosity of the Indians by burning one of their villages and some cornfields, after which he left Lane, the Governor, with only an hundred and ten men and returned to England. Scarcity of provisions, a constant quarrel with their Indian neighbors, and a

general feeling of discouragement led these first Virginia colonists to hail the navigator, Drake, who appeared on the coast a few months after, as a deliverer, and rejecting his offers of a vessel and provisions, they insisted upon returning with him to the mother country. Their departure was almost immediately followed by the arrival of reinforcements and supplies from Raleigh, brought by Grenville, who, when he found the place deserted, left fifteen men to guard it and himself proceeded southward to pillage the Spaniards of the West Indies.

A second expedition, dispatched by Raleigh, included many women, that families might be formed on the new soil and the colonists be satisfied to remain. This enterprise was led by John White and eleven others, having a company charter. Upon arrival in Virginia White found only a skeleton to show where the former settlement had been. Indian treachery was assigned as the reason for its disappearance. Actuated probably by a nervous anxiety, White massacred some friendly Indians, under the impression that they were hostiles, and in August of 1587 returned to England for supplies, leaving behind him eighty-nine men, seventeen women, and eleven children, the youngest being his own granddaughter, Virginia Dare, the first white child born in America.

White arrived in England to find the nation preparing for a struggle with Spain. His return to the colonies was therefore delayed. Raleigh, finding himself impoverished by the former expeditions, which had cost him $200,000, made an assignment, under his patent, to a company which included White and one Thomas Smith. A new fleet was procured, though with considerable trouble, and again the adventurers sought the Virginia coast, in 1590, only to find that the unfortunate settlement of three years before had been utterly wiped out of existence. So ended the first English attempt to settle America.

THE FRENCH ATTEMPT COLONIZATION.

About the same time de La Roche, a Marquis of Brittany, obtained from Henry IV of France a commission to take Canada. His company consisted largely of convicts and criminals. Following him came Chauvin de Chatte, but he accomplished little of permanent value.

For some years following the last attempt of Raleigh to colonize Virginia, a desultory trade with the Indians of the coast was pursued, the staples being sassafras, tobacco, and furs. Richard Hakluyt, one of the assignees of Raleigh, was most active in promoting this traffic; and among others employed was Bartholomew Gosnold, who, taking a more northerly course than the one usually followed, discovered Cape Cod, Nantucket, and Martha's Vineyard, and the Elizabeth Islands. Following Gosnold, in 1603, came Martin Pring, exploring Penobscot Bay, tracing the coast thence as far south as Martha's Vineyard.

A French grant of the same year gave to Sieur de Monts, a Protestant, the whole of North America between the 40th and 46th parallels of north latitude. This domain was named Acadie. De Monts looked for a monopoly of the fur trade on what is now the New England and Canadian coast. His Lieutenants in the expeditions which he soon commenced, were Poutrincourt and Champlain, of whom the latter became famous for several discoveries, but in particular for the lake which bears his name.

So it will be noticed that both the French and English were stretching out their hands to acquire the same territory. De Monts and Champlain settled their colony at St. Croix, but soon shifted, trying various points along the coast, and even attempted to inhabit Cape Cod, but were driven away by the savages. At last they transferred the settlement to Port Royal (Annapolis), where it endured for about a year. De Monts' commission or patent was recalled in 1606, and but a little while previously Raleigh's grant was forfeited by attainder, he having been imprisoned by King James on a charge of treason.

The frequent failures to effect a permanent settlement in America did not discourage adventurers, whose desire to possess the new world seemed to grow stronger every year. Soon two new companies were incorporated under Royal charter, to be known as the First and Second Colonies of Virginia. The former was composed of London men, and the latter of Plymouth people principally.

The charter authorized the Companies to recruit and ship colonists, to engage in mining operations and the like, and to trade ; their exports to be free of duties for seven years and duties to be levied by themselves for their own use for a period of twenty years. They might also coin money and protect themselves against invasion. Their lands were held of the King.

HARD TIMES COME AGAIN.

Hardly had the charter been granted when James began to make regulations or instructions for the government of the colonies, which gave a shadow of self rule, established the church of England, and decreed, among other things, that the fruits of their industries were to be held in common stock by the colonists for five years.

These instructions, along with the names of the "Council" appointed by James for the government of the settlement, were carried, sealed in a tin box, by Captain Christopher Newport, who commanded the three vessels which constituted the initial venture of the London Company. An ill chosen band landed at last at Old Point Comfort, after a stormy voyage. Of the one hundred and five men there were forty three "gentlemen", twelve laborers, half a dozen mechanics and a number of soldiers. These quarreled during the voyage, so that John Smith, who it afterward appeared was one of the Councillors appointed by the Crown, entered Chesapeake Bay a prisoner, charged with conspiracy. As might have been expected, this company did not fare well. They were consumed with laziness and jealousy ; there were cabals in the council and bickerings outside of it. Repeatedly the men tried to desert ; deaths were frequent and want stared them in the face. During this time it is hardly too much to say that the energy and wisdom of John Smith held the discouraged adventurers together. New arrivals of the same sort as the first added to, rather than diminished, the difficulties of the situation, so that at length Smith wrote that thirty workmen would be worth more than a thousand of such people as were being sent out. Not till the third lot of emigrants arrived did any women visit the new settlement, and then only two. The Indians became more and more troublesome, and the London Company, dissatisfied at receiving no returns from their investment, threatened to leave the settlers to shift for themselves.

In 1609 the London Company succeeded in obtaining a new charter, by the terms of which it organized as a stock company, with officers chosen for life, a governor appointed by the Company's Council in England, and a territory extending from the Atlantic to the Pacific in a strip four hundred miles in width.

During the interval between the granting of the charter and the organization of the new government anarchy reigned in Virginia. Smith did everything possible to restore order, but was at last wounded by an accidental explosion of powder and forced to return to England. At this time Jamestown, which was the name of the settlement, contained five hundred men, sixty dwellings, a fort, store and church. The people possessed a little live stock and about thirty acres of cultivated land, but as this was all

AN INDIAN COUNCIL OF WAR.

inadequate to their support there followed what is known in the annals of the colony as the "Starving time."

These earlier days in Virginia, while historically valuable only as a warning, have afforded an unusual share of romance, much of which centres about the unromantic name of Smith. The historian gladly concedes to this remarkable man his full share of credit for the survival of one of the most ill assorted parties that ever attempted to settle a new land. But, added to what is known of Smith's adventures, struggles and escapes, is a great deal that rests solely upon his own authority, and much of this is probably apocryphal. One hesitates, for instance, to examine the Pocahontas legend too closely. There is no doubt of the existence of that aboriginal princess, of her marriage to the Englishman, Rolfe, of her enthusiastic reception by English society, or of the fact that some of her proud descendants live to-day in Virginia. But the pretty story of her devotion in saving the life of John Smith by protecting him with her own person when the club of the executioner was raised by chief Powhatan's order may be questioned. The account was not given in Smith's first narratives, and was subsequently written by him several years after the death of the lady in question. The multitude of hairbreadth escapes and marvelous adventures of which Smith made himself the centre, have laid him open to the suspicion of drawing a longer bow than Powhatan himself.

JOHN SMITH.

Clearing away the romance, and allowing all that is necessary to one who is so often the hero of his own narrative, it may not be uninteresting to briefly note some of the unquestioned services that John Smith performed for the struggling colony. We have seen how he arrived under suspicion and arrest, landing on the site of the little settlement which was destined to owe so much to him, like a felon. The opening of the hitherto secret instructions given under the broad seal of England, disclosed the fact that he was one of the Councillors named in that document. But it was his own clear head and strong courage rather than any royal appointment which won him the leadership in the affairs of the settlement. The quarrels and incompetency of the two governors, Wingfield and Ratcliffe, acted as a foil to display his superior quality. Although believing to the full in the common creed of his time, that the inducements of wealth were the only ones which would lead men to sacrifice home and comfort for the wilderness, yet he evinced a genius for hard work and a contempt for hard knocks worthy of a nobler purpose.

It was in his first extended exploration of the Chickahominy that the Pocahontas affair is supposed to have occurred. That he was taken prisoner then, and by some means escaped from his captors, is undeniable. And in passing, we may observe the curious misapprehension regarding the width of the American continent which Smith's journey up the Chickahominy betrayed. He was actually looking for the Pacific ocean! In keeping with this error is that clause in the American charters which would make the land grants like long, narrow ribbons reaching from ocean to ocean.

In 1608 Smith ascended Chesapeake Bay and explored the larger rivers emptying into it. In an open boat, he traveled over two thousand miles on fresh

BACON DEMANDING HIS COMMISSION OF GOVERNOR BERKELEY.

water. He parleyed with the Mohawks, and returned to subdue the much more unmanageable colonists at Jamestown. When the half-starved and wholly discouraged adventurers became mutinous, his methods of dealing with them were dictatorial and effectual.

As already stated, Smith, upon his departure from Virginia, left nearly five hundred people there. In six months there remained only sixty. Many had died, some thirty or more seized a small vessel and sailed South on a piratical expedition, and a number wandered into the Indian country and never came back. Sick and disheartened, the remainder resolved to abandon Virginia and seek Newfoundland. Indeed, they had actually made all preparations and were starting upon their voyage, when they were met by the new governor from England, Lord De La War, with ships, recruits and provisions.

The charter under which De La War assumed the government of Virginia was sufficiently liberal. It was that granted to Raleigh. But in the years that followed, the colony began to be prosperous and to excite the jealousy of the king—the same base, faithless king that had beheaded Raleigh. James began to conspire against the Virginia charter. It was too liberal: he dreaded the power it conferred. By 1620 colonists were pouring into Jamestown at the rate of a thousand a year, and thence being distributed through the country.

To try to condense the early colonial history of Virginia to the limits of our space would result in a bare recital of names, or a repetition of the narrative of ignorance, vice, and want, occasionally relieved by some deed of devotion or daring. At first, in spite of the liberal provisions of the charter, the conditions were, to a large extent, those of vassalage. In 1623 James ordered the Company's directors to surrender their charter, a demand which they naturally refused. He then brought suit against the Company, seized their papers so that they should have no defence, and finally, through foul means obtained a decision dissolving the Company. After that the government of the colony consisted in a governor and two councils, one of which sat in Virginia and the other in London. The governor and councils were by royal appointment.

BACON'S REBELLION.

Here we must be allowed to digress a little, to give the part played by one Nathaniel Bacon in the affairs of Virginia. It was the year 1676, when Bacon became the leader of a popular movement instituted by the people of Kent County, whose purpose was twofold—first, to protect themselves against the Indians, which the Government failed to do; and, secondly, to resist the unjust taxes and the oppressive laws enacted by the existing legislative assembly, and also to recover their liberties lost under the arbitrary proceedings of Sir William Berkeley, then Governor. Bacon, a popular, quiet man, who had come over from England a year before, was selected as their leader by the people, who, enrolling themselves 300 strong, were led by Bacon against the Indians. Bacon's success increased the jealousy of Sir William, who, because of Bacon's irregular leadership,—he having no proper commission,—proclaimed Bacon a rebel. Finally, the people rose *en masse*, and demanded the dissolution of the old assembly, whose acts had caused so much trouble. Berkeley was forced to yield, and a new assembly was elected, who, condoning Bacon's irregular leadership, promised him a regular commission as General. This commission Berkeley refused to issue, whereupon Bacon, assembling his forces, at the head of 500 men, appeared before

BURNING OF JAMESTOWN

Berkeley and demanded his commission, which Berkeley, who was a real coward, made haste to grant. But, as if repenting of his concession, Berkeley determined to oppose Bacon by force. In this he was unsuccessful, and in July of that year, Bacon entered Jamestown, the Capital, and burned the town. A little later, in October, Bacon died, and with him the "rebellion," or "popular uprising" as it had been variously called, subsided. Shortly afterward Berkeley was removed, for oppression and cruelty—a cruel, bloodthirsty man he was—and, sailing for England, died soon after his arrival, and the world's population of scoundrels was lessened by just one.

While the curious mixture of cavalier and criminal was working out the early destinies of Virginia, a deeply religious element in Nottinghamshire and Yorkshire, England, were being educated by adversity for an adventure of a very different sort. At Scrooby, in 1606, a congregation of Separatists or Brownists, who were ultra Puritans, used to meet secretly for worship at the house of their elder, William Brewster. King James, like most renegades, was a good persecutor, and he finally drove the Scrooby church to flee. Led by their pastor, that wisest and gentlest of the Puritans, John Robinson, the little company escaped to Holland. The history of their ten years of sorrow and hardship in Amsterdam and Leyden is too well known to require repetition here. It is impossible to overestimate the influence of such a man as Robinson, or to question the permanency of the impression which his character and teaching made upon his flock.

Procuring a patent from the London company, the Scrooby-Leyden Separatists prepared for their adventure. Only about half the Holland company could get ready, and it fell to the pastor's lot to stay with those who were left behind. Embarking on the Speedwell, at Delft Haven, the colonists bade good-by to their friends and directed their course to England, where they were joined by the Mayflower.

ARRIVAL OF THE MAYFLOWER.

The Speedwell was found to be unseaworthy, so at length most of her passengers were transferred to the Mayflower, which proceeded on the voyage. To those who know how small a vessel of 180 tons is, the fact that one hundred souls, besides the crew, were upon a stormy ocean in her for more than sixty days, will be as eloquent as any description of their discomforts could be. The objective point was far to the southward of the land that they finally fell upon, which was not within the limits of their patent from the Virginia Company. But they dropped anchor in Cape Cod harbor, sick and weary with the voyage, and landed, giving thanks for their deliverance. With wisdom and frugality the plans for the home in the wilderness were made.

Being too far North to be bound or protected by the provisions of the Virginia charter, the Pilgrims, as they called themselves, made a compact which was mutually protective. The terms of the contract foreshadowed republican institutions. Thus in character, purpose and outward surroundings the Puritan of Plymouth and the Cavalier of Jamestown differed essentially. The after development of the two settlements followed logically along these lines, emphasizing these differences.

Of the hundred souls left in Plymouth only fifty per cent. remained alive when the supplies from England came, a year later. Scurvy, famine and exposure to the severe climate had killed most of the weakest of them. Not a household but had suffered loss. Yet not one offered to go back. Men and women alike stood to their posts with a heroism that has never been excelled in the world's history. We read how they planted their corn in the graveyard when planting time came, so that the Indians might not discover the greatness of their loss. Cotton Mather, in writing of this dark time says, with that provoking, cold-blooded philosophy that can bear other people's troubles with equanimity: "If disease had not more easily fetched so many away to heaven,"

all must have died for lack of provisions. The Indians were at first very hostile, owing to depredations committed by a previous navigator, but they were too few in number to be very troublesome. Squanto, who became the interpreter, and Samoset, a sagamore from the eastern coast, were their first friends among the red men. Squanto was their tutor in husbandry and fishing. Then, too, came Hobbamock, whom Longfellow has immortalized as the "friend of the white man." The names of those who formed this little colony have become household words all over the land. Miles Standish, John Alden, Priscilla, Elder Brewster, Bradford,— where are these names not known?

Frugal as the Pilgrims were, and industrious, they

ARMOR WORN BY THE PILGRIMS IN 1620.

found that their inexperience in planting maize, together with other drawbacks, kept them on the edge of starvation for several years. Clams became at one time the staple diet, and were about all that the settlers had to regale their friends with, when a new ship-load of those that had been left behind in Leyden, arrived.

A description of Plymouth, given in 1626, shows the situation of the town: A broad street, "about a cannon shot of eight hundred yards long," bordered by the houses of hewn planks, followed by a brook down the hillside. A second road crossed the first, and at the intersection stood the Governor's house. Upon

MILES STANDISH HOLDS A COUNCIL WITH THE INDIANS.

the mound known as "burial hill" was a building which served the double purpose of a fort and a church. A stockade surrounded the whole. At first the agricultural and other labors of the people had been communistic, in accordance with the conditions of the London Company's charter. But in 1624 this plan was done away with and the lands thereafter held separately. Still the people, unlike those of Virginia, continued to dwell in towns, and their habits in this respect descended to their children.

The second New England colony was that of Massachusetts Bay, which was sent out by a company provided with a charter very much like that of Virginia. The provisions of this patent allowed for the appointment of officers by the company, but it was not stated where the headquarters of the company were to be. This important oversight allowed the transplanting of the company, with officers, elective power, and other democratic rights, to New England. The company, which pretended to be a commercial organization, was really composed of Puritans, who, though not Separatists, were strict to the point of fanaticism. The leader of the first emigrants was John Endicott. His followers numbered less than a hundred souls, with which little force he planted Salem. The Salem colonists, though they had known less persecution and hardship than those of Plymouth, or perhaps for that reason, yet were more intolerant and Quixotic in their rules for self government, in social observances, and especially in their dealings with people of other religious sects. The transference of the government of the company, together with the addition of over eight hundred new colonists, was made in 1630.

As the Massachusetts colonies grew they excited the jealousy or animosity of two very different classes of people. These were their

A PIONEER FLEEING FROM ENRAGED PEQUOTS.

Dutch neighbors and the Indians. The most serious of the early difficulties with the aborigines was, in fact, the effect of Dutch interference. These people had purchased the Connecticut river lands from the Pequots. The Pequots only held the territory by usurpation and the original owners obtained the Puritan protection, giving them a rival title. The enraged Pequots commenced hostilities which were promptly resented by the Puritan Governor, Endicott, who led his men into the Indian country, punishing the assailants severely. This act, however necessary it may have been, laid the colony open to all the cruelty of a long-continued war, which lasted until the final remnant of the Pequot tribe had been extinguished.

A PEQUOT MASSACRE.

The war with Philip, Massasoit's son, occurred in 1675, when the colony was stronger and better able to bear the tax upon its vigor, but during the year in which it lasted the settlements were frightfully crippled. Six hundred houses had been burned, the fighting force of the English had been decimated, and the fruits of years of labor wasted. The whole difficulty arose from the Puritans' "lust for inflicting justice," and might have been avoided.

One of the most significant, as well as beneficial, of early New England institutions was the "town meeting," which ranked next to "the meeting house worship" in importance to the colonist ; for while in one he indulged liberty of conscience, the other allowed him liberty of speech. Having both his speech and his conscience under control, the Puritan took a sober delight in their indulgence. The town meeting was in the New Englander's blood, and it needed only the peculiar conditions of his new life to bring it out. His ancestors had had their Folkmotes where all questions of public policy and government were freely discussed. So it came natural to him to gather in unsmiling earnestness with his neighbors, and attend to their plans or suggest others for their mutual guidance and safety. This ventilation of grievances and expression of views did more, in all probability, to prepare for the part which New England should take in future political movements than any other one agency.

HENDRICK HUDSON.

The discovery of the Hudson River, and that of Lake Champlain occurred at nearly the same time, each discoverer immortalizing himself by the exploit. That of Hudson has, however, been of vastly more importance to America and the world than that of his French contemporary.

Hudson was known as a great Arctic explorer prior to his discovery of the site of America's metropolis. He had previously sailed under English patronage, but now he and his little "Half-Moon" were in the service of the Dutch East India Company, and in search of a northwest passage, which he essayed to find by way of Albany, but failed. At the same time Smith was searching the waters of the Chesapeake. In 1614, the charter granting all of America between Virginia and Canada was received by the "Company of the New Netherlands ' from the lately formed States General of Holland. The command of so magnificent a river system as that of the Hudson and its tributaries established almost at once the status and success of the Dutch colony.

The States General held complete control of their American dependency They appointed governors and councillors and provided them with laws, Ordinarily, the people seemed to care as little to mix with politics as does the modern average New Yorker, a good deal of bad government being considered better than a little trouble.

Once in a while a governor got in some difficulty over the Indian question, and called a council of citizens to help him, but ordinarily he was despotic

5

The colonists were content to wax fat without kicking. They were honest, shrewd, good-natured, tolerant bodies, as different from the New Englander as from the Virginian, or as either of these neighbors was from the other. Primarily traders, they found themselves in one of the best trading grounds in the world, with nothing serious to prevent them from growing rich and multiplying. This they proceeded to do with less noise and more success than either of the other contemporary settlements. In the fifty years of Dutch rule, the population of New Amsterdam reached eight thousand souls. The character of the city was so cosmopolitan that it has been estimated that no less than twelve languages were spoken there. Free trade obtained, in contrast to the policy of New England and Virginia. The boundary difficulties with the Puritan colonies were a constant irritation, but were allowed to slumber when it was necessary to make common cause against the Indians.

THE DUTCH LOSE NEW AMSTERDAM.

In the time of Petrus Stuyvesant, the last of the Dutch governors, the rivalry which existed between the English and Dutch nations regarding the trade of the new world led the treacherous Charles II of England to send an armament in a time of profound peace to take the colony of a friendly nation.

Colonel Richard Nichols commanded the expedition. His orders caused him to stop at the Massachusetts Bay for reinforcements. The colonists there were reluctant to aid him, but those of Connecticut joined eagerly with the expedition, and Governor Winthrop took part in it. The colony passed, without a blow, with hardly a murmur on the part of the people, though considerably to the rage of Governor Stuyvesant, into the hands of the English, to be known thenceforth as New York. Notwithstanding the success of the Dutch colony of New Amsterdam, it was unquestionably a most important advantage in the after history of America that it should have fallen into the hands of the English.

As a conservative element, the peaceful, prosperous Friend was of immense value in colonial development. The grant which William Penn obtained in 1681 gave him a tract of forty thousand square miles between the estates of York and Baltimore. Penn's charter was in imitation of that granted to Maryland, with important differences. With the approval of Lord Baltimore, laws passed by the Maryland Assembly were valid, but the king reserved the right to approve the laws of Pennsylvania. The same principle was applied to the right of taxation. There was about fifty years between the two charters.

The settlement of New Jersey by Quakers was that which first drew Penn's attention to America. In drawing up the plans for his projected State he did so in accordance with Quaker ideas, which in point of humanity were far in advance of the times. The declaration that governments exist for the sake of the

governed, that the purpose of punishment is reformation, that justice to Indians as well as to white men should be considered, were startling in their novelty.

The success of this enterprise was instant and remarkable. In three years the colony numbered eight thousand people. The applications for land poured in and the affairs of the colonists were wisely administered, and before the death of her great founder, Pennsylvania was firmly established. Education was a matter of care from the very start in Philadelphia, although throughout the rest of the state it was neglected for many years. Indian troubles were scarcely known. The great blot on the scutcheon of the Quaker colony was the use of white slaves, for whom Philadelphia became the chief market in the new world. Not less remarkable than the unity of time which characterized the planting of several American settlements was the unity of race into which they all finally merged, with few and slight exceptions, so that in after years all of the various lines of development which have been indicated in this chapter should combine to form a more complete national life. Penn made a treaty with the Indians, *and kept it;* and herein lies the secret of his success. If only all treaties had been kept, what bloodshed might not have been avoided !

PAUL REVERE'S RIDE

KING PHILIP'S WAR DEATH OF THE KING

Curious Manners and Customs in Colonial Times.

A CHAISE OF THE EIGHTEENTH CENTURY.
(From " L'Art du Menuisier-Carrossier" 1771.)

MANY were the varieties of New England life before the American Revolution. Each township maintained its own peculiar laws; clung to its own peculiar customs; cherished its own peculiar traditions. Never, perhaps, except in Greece, were local self-government and local patriotism pushed to such an extreme. Not only did commonwealth hold itself separate from commonwealth, but township from township, and often village from village. Long stretches of uninhabited land effectively divided these self-reliant communities from one another. "The road to Boston," says one of the most graphic of New England's local historians,[*] when speaking of the route from Buzzard's Bay, in 1743, "was narrow and tortuous—a lane through a forest—having rocks and quagmires and long reaches of sand, which made it almost impassable to wheels, if any there were to be ventured upon it. Branches of large trees were stretched over it, so that it was unvisited by sunlight, except at those places where it crossed the clearings on which a solitary husbandman had established his homestead, or where it followed the sandy shores of some of those picturesque ponds which feed the rivers emptying into Buzzard's Bay. Occasionally a deer bounded across the path, and foxes were seen running into the thickets." Such roads, picturesque as they were, naturally discouraged travel. Occasionally a Congregational council called together the ministers of several towns at an installation or an ordination. Once a year the meeting of the General Court tempted the rural authorities up to the capital; during a week's time a few travelers may have

* Mr. W. R. Bliss, in his "Colonial Times on Buzzard's Bay," an excellent depiction of early New England life, from which other quotations will appear later in this chapter.

ridden by on horseback and baited at the village inn ; now and then a visitor
came to town, making no little stir, or perhaps a new immigrant settled on the
confines of the parish. But there were then no Methodist preachers, with short
and frequent pastorates, and no commercial travelers, with boxes of the latest
goods, who could serve as conductors of thought and gossip from village to
village and make them homogeneous.

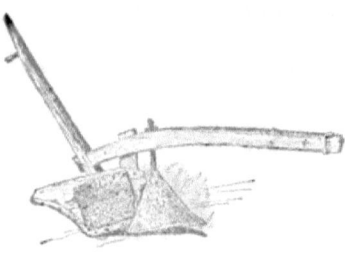

COLONIAL PLOW WITH WOODEN MOLD-BOARD.   1706.
(State Agricultural Museum, Albany, N. Y.)

America was not then a land of travelers
What little travel there might have been,
was often still further discouraged by
local ordinances, and in many a town,
a citizen had to have a special permit
from the Selectmen before he could enter-
tain a guest for anything over a fortnight. Thus one father was fined ten
shillings for showing hospitality to his
daughter beyond the legal period. In
many a spot in early New England the
protectionist principle was so thoroughly
localized that the importation of labor, as well as of merchandise, was
rigorously restricted. Towns so insulated naturally took on distinctive traits.
Even religious customs, literal scripturalists as these people were, differed in
different places. The Puritan Sabbath began on Saturday night in one
commonwealth, on Sunday morning in another. In brief, no picture of any
one town can serve as a picture of any other.

To describe a typical Puritan home, therefore, is
not easy. Yet it is not impossible. For the New
England Puritans were a peculiar and easily distinguished people. The fundamental differences in
character which set them off from the rest of the
world, are far more prominent to the eye than are the
local differences which divided town from town. A
Connecticut settler, or even a Rhode Island Baptist,
might be taken for a Massachusetts Puritan, but a
Knickerbocker could be mistaken for neither.

ANCIENT HAND-MADE SPADE.
(State Agricultural Museum, Albany,
N. Y.)

To begin with, the New Englanders were the
most truly benevolent and unselfish people of their
time. They had hardly set foot on New England's shore before their history
was marked by a magnanimous act of genuine forgiveness of injuries. It
was in the middle of the landing at Plymouth Rock, when the colony was
prostrated by illness and was exposed to the worst inclemencies of a
new and inclement climate. "Destitute of every provision which the weak-

ness and daintiness of the invalid require," so runs the description of a
well-known historian, " the sick lay crowded in the unwholesome vessel or in
half-built cabins, heaped around with snow-drifts.   The rude sailors refused

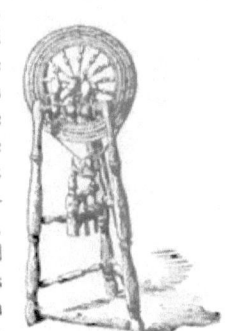

IRISH IMMIGRANT'S FLAX
WHEEL.

them even a share of those coarse sea-stores which would
have given a little variety to their diet, till disease spread
among the crew and the kind ministrations of those
whom they had neglected and affronted brought them
to a better temper."   There could be no better example
of Christian forbearance than this.   At the start the
Indians also came within the scope of the Puritan's
charity.   He nursed them assiduously in times of small-
pox, rescued many a child from a plague-stricken wigwam,
helped them through times of famine, Christianized and
partially civilized some of them, and in business dealings
treated them not only justly but with a sincere though
tactless kindness.   The Puritan's home life was unselfish ;
he was profoundly regardful of his children, though he
evinced that regard not by indulging them, but by pains-

taking discipline and a rigorous thrift, the better to provide for their future.
It was a French Jesuit of the last century who testified that the New Englander,
unlike the Canadian, labored for his heirs.   These early settlers made staunch

A COLONIAL FLAX WHEEL.

neighbors.   They were ready at almost any
time to leave their work to drive a pin
or nail in a young home-maker's new
dwelling-house as a token of their good
will, while they found their greatest pleasures in such means of mutual helpfulness
as corn huskings, quilting-bees, and barn-
raisings.   They were, no doubt, exacting
and unsympathetic masters, but in the
commands which they enjoined they kept
in view the moral welfare of their slaves
and servants as of far greater importance
than their own material prosperity.   Never
were slaves better treated than in New
England.

The Puritans were strenuously intent
on making the world, not only better,
but, as they thought, happier.   It was to guard the more solid pleasures of a
pure home-life and of an honest pride in one's country, that they bulwarked
themselves against the encroachments of sordid self-indulgences.   But they went

about their task in crude fashion. They recognized, for instance, quite wisely, that there is no more insidious enemy of happiness than vanity, which makes a man utterly miserable whenever he is ignored and only uneasily pleased even

A COMFORTIER, OR CHAFING-DISH.
(New York State Cabinet of Natural History, Albany.)

when he is admired the most, but they tried to eradicate vanity from the human heart not by planting something better in its place, but by such petty sumptuary laws as prohibiting the wearing of lace. They simply attempted to cut off whatever might minister to vanity's indulgence. Their chief reliance for improving the condition of the world was in a countless number of minute restrictions and self-limitations. The more law there is, however, the more there needs to be, for prohibit nine-pins and soon there will be a new game of ten-pins to prohibit also. So it was with the Puritans. Restriction was placed here and restriction was placed there, until restriction became constriction and grew intolerable. The children were never allowed to lose sight of parental regulations, the parents of township ordinances, the town of state laws. But it was in the number and pettiness of these laws, not any cruelty in them, which made them intolerable, for the humanity of New England's legislators is evinced in the fact that there were only ten crimes punishable with death in New England when there were one hundred and sixty in Old England. The New Englanders were swaddled, not chained. The best that was in them did not have full play, but it had more play than it could have had in any other country, except Great Britain and Holland.

From the start New England was a country of homes. The typical New England dwelling was the work of several generations. It had begun perhaps as a solidly built but plain rectangular house

DUTCH HOUSE IN ALBANY, N. Y.
(From an Old Print.)

of one story and two rooms. In one of them the good wife cooked the meals on the hearth—and simple cooking was never better done—laid the table, as meal-time approached, with the neat wooden bowls, plates, platters, and spoons and primitive knives of the time, or, the meal over, received a neighbor dropping in on a friendly errand, or perhaps the minister gravely making the rounds of his parish. This was the living room, the centre of the family life. The other room contained two great bedsteads with their puffy feather-beds, while the trundle-bed in the corner betrayed the presence of little children in the household. If the family was large, a rude ladder led the way to a sleeping-place in the garret, the very spot for a boy with a romantic turn.

Slowly but faithfully the farmer added to the size and to the comforts of his home. What a place the hearth soon became! "In the wide fireplace and over the massive back-log, crane, jack, spit and pot-hook did substantial work,

PRIMITIVE MODE OF GRINDING CORN

while the embers kept bake-kettle and frying-pan in hospitable exercise." Here was the place for the iron, copper or brass andirons, often wrought into curious devices and religiously kept bright and polished. In front of the fire was the broad wooden seat for four or five occupants, with its generously high back to keep off the cold. This was the famous New England settle, making an inviting and cozy retreat for the parents in their brief rests from labor, or perhaps for lovers when the rest of the house was still. On each side of the hearth, in lieu of better seats were wooden blocks on which the children sat as they drew close to the fire on winter evenings to work or read by its blaze. Perhaps, in some corner of the room could be seen the brass warming-pan, which every winter's evening

was filled with embers and carried to the sleeping chambers to give a temporary
warmth to the great feather-beds. There was a place near at hand for the
snow-shoes, while matchlocks, swords, pikes, halbert, and some pieces of
armor fixed against the wall showed that the farmer obeyed the town
ordinances and kept himself prepared against Indian raids.

For like all frontiersmen, these farmers never felt secure. The Indians,
instigated by the French, and exasperated by the cheating and bullying English
adventurers, who had crept into New England against the colonists' will, were
not only the cruelest of foes, they were the most treacherous of friends. They
had pillaged and destroyed more than one secluded and unsuspecting settlement, murdering, torturing, or carrying into captivity, as they pleased, the

OLD FRENCH HOUSE.

peaceful inhabitants. The big,
vague rumors of such midnight
raids exercised their uncanny spell
over many a household as it
gathered about the hearth of a
winter's evening. There was the
Deerfield massacre, for instance.
Just before the dawn of a cold
winter's night the Indians fell
upon the fated village. They
spent twenty-four hours in wanton
destruction, slaughtered sixty helpless prisoners, and carried a hundred back with them for an eight
weeks' cruel march to the north,
during which nineteen victims were
murdered on the way and two
were starved to death.

Such was the story associated with the arms upon the wall; but a happier
story was told by the ears of corn, the crooknecks, the dried fruit, and the flitches
of bacon hanging from the beams and ceiling of the room. They were a
perpetual reminder of Thanksgiving Day. If the Puritan discountenanced
Christmas observances as smacking of "papishness"—such was the narrow-
mindedness of the times—he showed by this feast-day, his appreciation of the
good things of earth. It was characteristic of the early New Englanders to
make much of little things. The housewife was rightfully proud of her simple
but nice cooking, and her husband of his plain but substantial produce. There
is something appetizing in the very thought of their homely but choice dishes,
their hasty-pudding, their Yankee breads, their pumpkin and mince pies. These
simple people cultivated to an unsurpassed extent the wholesome pleasure

which comes from a full appreciation of nature's wealth of gifts. They were lovers and cultivators of the wholesome fruits. It was a custom often observed in New England to give a favorite tree or bush a special and appropriate name, as a token of affection and so to make it seem the more companionable. The Puritan, indeed, had strong local affections and attachments. He found his pleasures in what came to his hand and made pleasures often out of the work he had to do. He provided little that was even amusement for his children, but this misfortune was alleviated by the abundant outlet for youthful energies which they found in the activities of the household. There was little time which could be spent in mere amusement. The home was a hive of busy workers. The planting, cultivating and harvesting of his crops consumed perhaps the smaller portion of the farmer's time. Cattle raising for the West Indies and

sheep growing took much of his attention. He was something of a lumberman, as well, and still more of a mechanic. Perhaps he bought iron rods and, when debarred from outdoor labor, hammered them into nails at the kitchen fireside. It was much more important, however, that he should have some skill at carpentry. Often too, he carved out of wood his table dishes. In the diverse industries of his house was the germ of many a nucleus factory. From his wife's busy loom came home-

SILK WINDING.
(Facsimile of a Picture in Edward Williams's "Virginia Truly Valued." 1650)

spun cloth for the family. In the kitchen were distilled her favorite remedies. The children of the family were not only kept busy; they were kept thinking; their inventive faculties were constantly on the alert. Hardly a week passed but a new device was needed. Early in the history of New England, to be sure, there were tanners who would keep half the skins they received and return the other half in leather, brickmakers, masons, carpenters, millers with very busy wind-mills, curriers, sawyers, smiths, fullers, malsters, shoe-makers, wheelwrights, weavers and other artisans to do the work of specialists in the community, yet the farmer did not a little for himself in every one of these trades. His home was an industrial community in and of itself.

The fisherman who dwelt upon the sea-coast needed quite as active and versatile a family as did his inland brother. He left them to build the boats, hoop the casks, forge the irons, and manage the many other industries pre-

requisite to the complete outfit of a vessel for a long and hazardous voyage.
At any time they might be obliged to support themselves entirely or be thrown
upon the town, for all fishing out at sea is a dangerous vocation, and whaling had
its peculiar perils. Occasionally a boat and crew were sunk by the tremendous
blows with which some great whale lashed the sea in his death agony. Now and
then one of these tormented giants would turn madly upon his pursuers. Then,
so says one careful historian, "he attacked boats, deliberately, crushing them
like egg-shells, killing and destroying whatever his massive jaws seized in their
horrid nip. His rage was as tremendous as his bulk ; when will brought a purpose
to his movement, the art of man was no match for the erratic creature." One
such fighting monster attacked the good ship "Essex," striking with his head
just forward of her fore-chains. The ship, says the mate, "brought up as suddenly and violently as if she had struck a rock, and trembled for a few seconds
like a leaf." She had already begun to settle when the whale came again,
crashing with his head through her bows. There was bare time to provision and
man the small boats before the vessel sank. The crew suffered from long
exposure and severe privations, and only a part of them were ever saved.

Such tales as this reached inland and attracted boyish lovers of adventure
to the sea. There were other and different tales of the sea, as well, to allure
them—tales of great wealth amassed in the India trade, of prizes captured from
the French by audacious privateersmen, or of pirates, then scourging the sea, or,
more boldly still, entering Boston harbor and squandering their ill-gotten gains
at the Boston taverns. The ocean was then the place for the brave and the
ambitious. It is a significant fact that probably the first book of original fiction
ever published in New England was "The Algerine Captive," a story of a
sailor's slavery among the Moors. Yet this story was long in coming. New
England produced no fiction of its own and reprinted little of old England's
until ten years after the close of the American Revolution. In the early farm-
houses, the library consisted of two or three shelves of Puritan theology. As
time went on Bunyan's Pilgrim's Progress, a few ecclesiastical and local histories,
one or more records of witchcraft trials, and some doggerel verse from the New
England poets were added to the dry and scant supply of reading. Yet the
enterprising and imaginative reader, though a child, could ferret out not a few
exciting episodes from such uninviting volumes as Josephus's "History of the
Jews," or Rev. Mr. Williams's record of Indian Captivity, while by 1720 a few
of the more fortunate little ones had a printed copy of Mother Goose jingles
for their amusement. But, although this was all the reading the farmer had--
for the newspapers were wretched and were seldom seen fifty miles from Boston—it must not be supposed that he underestimated the value of books. He
read far more than the modern farmer does—indeed all he could afford to get
and had the time for ; the clergy of the time often had substantial libraries of

"I AM READY FOR ANY SERVICE THAT I CAN GIVE MY COUNTRY"

In 1798 our Government was about to declare war against France. Congress appointed Washington commander-in-chief
of the American Army. The Secretary of War carried the commission in person to Mt. Vernon. The old
hero, sitting on his horse in the harvest field, accepted in the above patriotic words.

BATTLE OF RESACA DE LA PALMA

Captain May leaped his steed over the parapets, followed by those of his men whose horses could do a like feat, and was among the
gunners the next moment, sabering right and left. General La Vega and a hundred of his men were
made prisoners and borne back to the American lines.

one or two or even three hundred volumes ; while in the Revolutionary period, any young lady in a well-to-do family could easily obtain the best writings of Dryden, Pope, Addison, Swift, Thomson, and the other classic writers of the eighteenth century.

NIAGARA AND THE BEAVER DAMS.
(*From Moll's "New and Exact Map" 1715.*)

Indeed, the "young lady," as the feature of human society, was not altogether neglected, even in earlier times. To be sure, she could not dance without shocking most, if not all, of the community ; she could not act in church charades—for all dramatic exhibitions were forbidden by law ; but in the inter-

vals between her sewing and her housekeeping cares, she played battledore
and shuttlecock with her sister or friends, or practised the meeting-house
tunes on the old-fashioned and quaint spinet or virginal. If she were so
fortunate as to be born in the eighteenth century instead of the seventeenth,
she was regularly escorted by her swain to the singing-school, which not
only furnished training in psalmody, but was the occasion of much social
companionship among the young people of the village, and of not a little
match-making.

These gatherings often started incidentally other intellectual interests
besides those of music, and books were discussed and recommended.   Here was

FROZEN NIAGARA.

the birth-place of the reading circle and the modern lecture system.   Awkward
and restrained as their society manners were, the Puritans were a social people ;
jealously as they preserved their home-life, they joined quite as readily as do
modern farmers in general village pleasures.   The barn raisings for men, the
quilting-bees for women and the merry corn-huskings and house-warmings for
both, were not the only social gatherings of young and old.   Every ordination
or installation of a new minister—it came seldom, to be sure,—was the occasion
of feasting and a sociable assembling by the congregation.   Training day was
another time when the township was agog with excitement.   Every male citizen of the village, from the boy of sixteen to the man of sixty, was compelled on
these occasions to shoulder his musket and march in the militia.   An awkward

squad of amateur soldiers they were, as they paraded the village, complacent and valiant in fair weather, but bedraggled, crestfallen and wofully diminished in numbers in wet. Yet the women and children were proud of them and followed along the route. In honor of the occasion special booths were erected for the sale of gingerbread and harmless drinks to the on-lookers. The tavern too was kept busy, for every settlement of any pretensions had a tavern, where the passing traveler might get refreshment for himself and his horse. Here the selectmen planned the village policy for the consideration of the town-meeting. Here too were held public debates between rival theological disputants, sitting over their mild spirituous beverages. Here too was disseminated the latest news from Boston and the old world.

The two other public buildings of the place were the school-house and the meeting-house. As early as 1647, every Massachusetts village of fifty householders was required by state law to maintain a school, in which the catechism and the rudiments of reading, writing and arithmetic should be taught, while every town which boasted a hundred householders was obliged to establish a grammar school. But New England was not dependent upon these schools alone for her education. Massachusetts and Connecticut each had its college, in which learned and often eminent men trained the more ambitious youth of the land. One hundred thousand graduates were among the early emigrants from England and mingled with the people, while in the first days of the church, the pulpits even in the smaller towns, were almost without exception filled with men accomplished in the best learning of the time.

The church was the centre of the community's social and political life. Attendance on public worship was enforced, during many decades and in many places, by village ordinance. Church and state were curiously confused. Only church members were allowed to vote at town-meetings, and the selectmen of the village assigned the seats to the congregation, according to the peculiar regulations of the town-meeting. Customs differed in different places. In some villages, just before service began, the men would file in on one side of the church and the women on the other, while the boys and girls, separated from each other as scrupulously, were uncomfortably fixed in the gallery, or placed on the gallery stairs, or on the steps leading up to the pulpit. It was in one of these churches that the following ordinance was enforced :—

"Ordered that all ye boys of ye town are and shall be appointed to sitt upon ye three pair of stairs in ye meeting-house on the Lord's day, and Wm. Lord is appointed to look to the boys yt sit upon ye pulpit stairs, and ye other stairs Reuben Guppy is to look to."

In other meeting-houses, each household had a curious box pew of its own, fashioned according to the peculiar tastes of its occupants. The assignment of pew room in these places of worship was determined by the most careful class distinctions, for democratic as the Puritans were in their political institutions and commercial methods, each family jealously guarded whatever aristocratic pretensions it might have inherited. To the plain seats in the gallery were relegated the humbler members of the parish; a few young couples had pews of their own set off for them there, while a special gallery was occasionally provided for the negro slaves. There was no method of heating the edifice; to warm their feet the women had recourse to foot-stoves, carried to the meeting-house by the children or apprentices; the men to the more primitive method of pinching their shins together. When the hour-glass in the pulpit had marked the passage of an hour and a half, the sermon usually came to a close, and the people in the

CHAMPLAIN'S FORTIFIED CAMP; THE FIRST HOUSE ERECTED IN QUEBEC.

gallery descended and marched two abreast up one aisle and past the long pew which directly faced the pulpit and in which the elders and deacons sat. Here was the money-box, into which each person dropped his shilling or more, as the case might be, while the line was turning down the other aisle. There was an intermission of service at noon, when the people ate their luncheon in the adjacent school-house, where a wood-stove could be found, and discussed the village gossip and the public notices posted on the meeting-house door.

In every family the minister of the parish was received with an awe and reverence which seemed suitable not only to the dignity of his calling, but to the extreme gravity of his deportment and the impressive character of his learning. In weight and authority he was the peer of the village officials. Only the squire, the appointee of the Crown, was his superior; for he held his office as representative of the Crown. If offenders did not pay the fines imposed upon them, this village dignitary could place them in the stocks, or order them to be whipped. Persons who lived disorderly, "misspending their precious time, he could send to work house, to the stocks, or to the whipping-post, at his discretion. He could break open doors where liquors were concealed to defraud His Majesty's excise. He could issue hue-and-cries for runaway servants and thieves. There are instances on record in which a justice of the peace issued

COLONIAL MANSION   RESIDENCE OF THE LATE WILLIAM BULL PRINGLE, ESQ., CHARLESTON, S. C.

his warrant to arrest the town minister, about whose orthodoxy there were distressing rumors, and required him to be examined upon matters of doctrine and faith. But a more pleasing function of his office was to marry those who came to him for marriage, bringing the town clerk's certificate that their nuptial intentions had been proclaimed at three religious meetings in the parish during the preceding fortnight."

The Squire's office, however, was an English, not an American institution, and did not long survive on our soil. What was peculiar to New England public life was the town meeting, held in the parish church. Every freeman of the

6

township was obliged to attend it, under penalty of a fine. It distributed in early days the land among the settlers; it regulated, often according to communistic and often according to protectionist principles, the industries of the community; and it repressed gay fashions and undue liberties in speech and deportment. Its representatives were the selectmen and town-clerk, and were held in high esteem, from the respect due to their office.

Yet none of these dignitaries, much as they were held in awe, could permanently suppress the instincts of youth for gayer fashions and happier times. It is impossible on any rational basis to explain the inconsistent Puritan standards of right and wrong amusements. The most conscientious of Puritans would go, merely out of curiosity, to a hanging, and see no harm in it, but he looked with grave suspicion on church chimes as a worldly frivolity. Feasting he encouraged and religious services he discouraged at a funeral. Marriage he made a secular function; the franchise religious. To dancing he objected as improper and to card-playing as dangerous, but he saw no harm in kissing-games and lotteries. Finally the influence of the city proved too much for him. Boston customs were imitated in the provincial towns. Young and old indulged in the fashionable disfigurements of the day. The women wore black patches on their faces to set off their complexions and the men slashed the sleeves of their coats to show the fine quality of their underclothes, and even funeral services became occasions for display. Sumptuary laws were ignored or repealed. The country towns became social centres. By the time of the American Revolution, New England was already merging from Puritanism, with its virtues and limitations, into a new Americanism, with its new merits and its new defects.

The Romantic Story of Captain Kidd and Other Buccaneers and Pirates.

To the north of Cuba, between that island and the Great Bahama banks, is a navigable channel known as the old Bahama passage. Three centuries ago it had its day, a rich day, when freighted Spanish merchantmen and galleons, seeking in the new world the riches which impoverished Spain grasped so eagerly for, "dropped down with costly bales" from Cuba and the American coast, finding their way by the Caicos passage to the ocean.

Between Cuba and Haïti, or Hispaniola, is what is known as "the windward passage," almost at the intersection of which with the Bahama channel, at the northest end of Haïti, is Tortuga del Mar—the sea tortoise.

As it was described in the sixteenth century, so it is to-day—a wooded, rocky island, with few inhabitants and much game. Its only good harbor is on the south, and the blue water that surrounds it is as clear as a mountain spring and deeper than the mountain itself. It covers the entrance to the little fortified Haïtian town of Port au Paix, with a strait ten miles wide between them. With its beauty of foliage, mild, sea-tempered, tropical climate, and advantage of position, nature evidently intended Tortuga for a little insular heaven, but man succeeded in making quite the reverse of it. On Tortuga the Buccaneers (formerly known as Boucaniers and Buccaniers) started and developed, till Spain rang with the terror and fame of their achievements, and throughout the Antilles and the Spanish Main they enacted one of the most terrific romances of history.

Boucaning, from which we get Buccanier, originally meant to prepare beef in a peculiar way, by smoking; and the Buccaneers were cow-boys, who were a part of the French settlement that had driven the Spanish owners from Tortuga. The horses and cattle of the latter, running wild in large droves, afforded the material for their adventurous trade. It was not long before these old-time "cowpunchers" became a separate and peculiar people, living much of their lives in camp, and returning to town only to dispose of their spoils and to commit untold debaucheries. Spain, in possession of Hispaniola, naturally was

jealous of her interloping French neighbors. France disclaimed any responsibility for their acts, on the ground that she neither governed nor received
tribute in Tortuga. Then the Spaniards tried to eject the Buccaneers, and only
succeeded in incurring their undying enmity. At last a destruction of cattle
drove the Frenchmen to more desperate adventures.

The first departure was that of Pierre Le Grand, who, tired of the waning
activity of the beef business, took a small vessel, and with twenty-eight men
cruised towards Caicos, with the purpose of surprising some Spanish merchantman. Finally discovering a war vessel, instead of such game as he was in
search of, this Peter the Great approached to examine his prey more closely,
and succeeded in exciting the suspicions of some of the Spaniards on board of
the stranger, who told their captain that they believed the little vessel to be a
pirate; but the commander, who was vice-admiral of the Spanish fleet, laughed
at their anxiety, replying that even if the Frenchman was near their own
vessel's size they would have nothing to fear.

Waiting till cover of evening, the Buccaneers approached so close to the
Spaniard that they could not have withdrawn without discovery and suspicion.
In order to insure success, Pierre made the pirates' chances desperate by
scuttling his own vessel; thereupon they closed with the man-of-war and
boarded her with such adroitness and celerity that they succeeded in surprising
the captain and some of his officers in the cabin, and, after a short struggle,
shooting down those that opposed them, possessed themselves of the gun
room. It was an easy but brilliant victory, an achievement that set the hot
blood of the Tortuga Buccaneers in a sudden blaze, and freebooting on the
high seas became at once a fashionable and much-followed profession. As for
Pierre le Grand, the pioneer in piracy, he was content with his first venture,
and, having taken his rich prize to France, remained there, never revisiting the
Western World. Doubtless the Spaniards passing Cape de Alvarez in their
little tobacco boats, or hide-laden vessels from Havana, were surprised and,
not pleasantly so, by the sudden appearance and activity of canoes and small
boats manned with murderous Frenchmen from Tortuga.

The Buccaneer was beginning his trade of piracy in a small way,
industriously accumulating the capital with which to venture on greater
enterprises. The small vessels he converted into little freebooting ships; the
small cargoes he took home and sold in Tortuga, till he had enough saved to
equip them properly. When everything was ready, and agreements as to the
share of each man had been entered into, and every man had chosen his side-
partner, who should share his good and evil fortune and stand by him in a
fracas, the notice was given to assemble. Whereupon every pirate brought
his powder and arms to the appointed place, and off they went. That was the
fashion of it. As we would plan a little jaunt down the river, or across the

ke, or up to the top of a mountain to see the moon rise, these jolly
uccaneers got ready and went a-pirating.

Let us not be misled at the outset by a glamour of romance which time and
partial historian have thrown about the deeds of the buccaneers. No more
terly debased, bestial, merciless, and bloodthirsty set of fiends ever figured
history; but it is no less true that their physical fearlessness led them to deeds
hich, by their audacity and atrocity, set the world ringing with their fame.

The first four great prizes were made within a month. Two of these were
anish merchantmen and two were vessels loaded with plate at Campéche.
ccess so great, the proofs of which were at once brought to Tortuga, as to
ouse the wildest enthusiasm. In a little time there were twenty vessels in
e buccaneer fleet. Spain, disgusted at this new state of affairs, sent two
en-of-war to guard her shipping. It is impossible to say how much more
ischief might have been done had it not been for this precaution. As it was,
e commerce of His Most Catholic Majesty suffered frightfully.

A second Pierre, called François, led a crew of twenty-six men in a little
ssel against the pearl fleet, near the river De La Plata where they lay at work
der the protection of a gun-boat. The man-of-war was barely half a league
ay from the fleet, but François resolved to attempt a swoop. He feigned to
a Spanish vessel coming up the coast from Maracaibo. On reaching the fleet
assaulted the vessel of the vice-admiral, of eight guns and sixty men, and
ced a surrender. He then resolved to take the man-of-war. So he sunk his
n boat and, compelling the Spaniards to assist him, set sail in the prize, with
anish colors flying. Thinking that some of the sailors were trying to run
ay with what they had got, the man-of-war gave chase. This did not suit
ançois at all. It is one thing to fight a surprised and unsuspecting enemy and
ite another to combat a foe that greatly outweighs and outmeasures one's self
en he is suspicious and advancing. François tried to get away. That he
uld have succeeded in escaping had his rigging stood, there is little doubt.
s it was the mainmast gave way under the sudden strain of canvas, and the
ebooters were at the mercy of their enemy. On being overhauled François
d his men—twenty-two of whom could fight—made a fierce resistance, but
re at length overcome, but only yielded on favorable terms, which were that
y were to be put, uninjured, on shore, on free land.

It is estimated that the booty which they obtained and lost that day was
rth about 100,000 pistoles, or about $400,000.

In course of time, and no very long time, Port Royal, in Jamaica, became
e chief rendezvous for the pirates. On the harbor where Kingston now
nds there is a little town to remind one of the city that was engulfed by the
eat earthquake—a city said to be the wickedest in the world. Near Port
yal, upon the same harbor, is a landing by which one could go, and still

can, by a short cut of half a dozen miles, to the capital city, Santiago de la Vega, now known as Spanish-Town. Near this landing there are large caverns and fissures of enormous depth, into which one may cast a stone and hear it bound and rebound, till the sound is lost in the distance. These caverns, tradition says, were the hiding places and silent accomplices in murder of the Buccaneers when they were hard pressed. Some are still supposed to contain vast treasure.

BARTHOLOMEUS de PORTUGEES.
Hooft van een party Fransc
en Engelse Roovers.

(From the Portrait in "De Americaensche Zee Rovers.")

Attracted by the great success of the Frenchmen, accessions from English, Portuguese, and Dutch mariners joined the ranks of those who preyed upon Spanish commerce. Nearly always the buccaneers appear to have sailed under some semi-official letters of marque granted by the colonial governors.

Bartholomew Portugues, a man of cat-like cunning, courage, and ferocity, was among the first to arrive. He had been a noted desperado in the old world before he ventured his fortunes in the new. With a small vessel, about thirty men, and four small cannon, he attacked a large Spaniard running from Maracaibo to Havana, and after being once repulsed succeeded in taking her. Her force of men was more than double his own, and her armament vastly larger, but she finally struck her flag to the pirate, who had lost ten or twelve men. Being bothered by head winds, Portugues sailed for a cape on the west end of Cuba, to repair and take in supplies. Just as he rounded the cape, he ran into the midst of three large Spanish vessels, by whom he was taken. Shortly afterward a storm arose and separated the ships, but the one which bore the desperado put into Campéche, where he was recognized by some

Spaniards who had suffered at his hands in other waters. He was condemned without trial, to be hung at daybreak, and for safe keeping was confined that night on the ship; but having a friend and accomplice near, he procured a knife, murdered his guard and escaped to land, floating on earthen wine jars, for he could not swim. Hiding in the woods for three days without food other than that the forest afforded, the pirate saw the parties sent in search of him, and afterward traveled nearly forty leagues, living on what he could glean on the shore, and exposed to all the discomforts, which only those who have traveled in a tropical country can at all appreciate. On his journey he performed, it is said, a remarkable feat which illustrated his tenacity of purpose, and power of will. Coming to a considerable river and being unable to cross it by swimming, he shaped rude knives from some great nails which he found attached to a piece of wreckage on the shore, and with no other instrument, cut branches with which he constructed a sort of boat. When he reached Golfo Triste and found there others of his own kidney, he told them of his sufferings and adventures and begged a small boat and twenty men with which to return to Campéche.

In the meantime the Spaniards, having supposed their foe dead, made a great rejoicing, which was summarily cut short by his unexpected return. In the dead of night he encountered the very vessel which had lately captured him, and from which he had escaped. She was lying in the mouth of the river.

Softly the pirates steal across the starlit water, slipping from shadow to shadow along the shore, starting at the whistle of the duck or the hoarse cry of the flamingo, till they are in position to pounce upon their prey. Then a sudden dash, a few shots and groans, and Portugues is again the successful Buccaneer, the master of a rich prize.

But he did not keep it long. He was wrecked on his way to Jamaica, and returned to that evil place as empty as when he started out, and although he engaged in several expeditions and made brilliant efforts to regain his advantages he never did so, but was always followed by the ill fortune he so richly deserved.

Braziliano—a Dutchman, long resident in Brazil—had his share of notoriety. He won a rich prize or two and spent his money so recklessly that a fortune slipped through his fingers in three months. At this time Port Royal was so choicely wicked that only the quaint chronicler of three hundred years ago would dare to put in words the details of its debauchery, and only in the old fashioned style of that early day would the account be readable. Literally, wine flowed in the streets like water, was thrown over the persons of passers by, who were ordered, at the pistol mouth, to partake. Murder, lust, and drunkenness, in forms indescribably beyond all precedent or comparison, were the order of the day. And this tremendous reputation for crime and debauchery, that is pre-eminent after the lapse of centuries, was won in less than half a generation.

After a little the Spaniards, grown wary, were too well convoyed and armed to be easy conquests, and a new era was inaugurated. Lewis Scott was the first of the Buccaneers to attempt the adventures upon land which added so greatly to the fame of the freebooters. He attacked and almost destroyed the town of Campêche. His example incited the Dutchman, Mansvelt, who invaded Grenada, the island of St. Catherine, which he took, and which was for some time a pirate rendezvous, and Carthagena.

Nor must we forget John Davis, whose fame is only second to that of Morgan himself. Davis was a Jamaican by birth. His first great exploit was the sack of Nicaragua. He had in all forty men, of whom he left ten to guard the vessel, and with the remainder, in three boats, approached the city.

Sending a captive Indian slave in advance to murder the sentry, the party landed and went from house to house, knocking and entering, putting the inmates to death and looting all they could lay their hands on. They pillaged the churches and took prisoners for ransom, escaping when the hue and cry was raised, and the uproar in the suddenly awakened city taught them that it was time to retreat. The Spaniards followed them to the seashore, but too late to recover their townsmen or treasure, though not too late to receive a warm parting salute from the guns of the pirate. The value of booty acquired on this raid is said to have exceeded $300,000 in gold, besides much plate and jewels—probably all told reaching $75,000 more. We next learn of Davis as the commander of a fleet of half a dozen or more pirate vessels, and among other adventures is that of the capture of St. Augustine, Florida.

LOLONOIS AND HIS ADVENTURES.

The plans and exploits of the pirates continued to grow in magnitude. Their vessels became fleets and their fleets almost navies. One of the great leaders was Lolonois, who began in the early days of buccaneering on Tortuga, and rose to be a freebooter of great prominence and reputation. The Governor of Tortuga, Monsieur de la Place, was so struck with his qualities that he gave him his first ship. He so beset the Spaniards in her that it is said by his biographer that "the Spaniards, in his time, would rather die fighting than surrender, knowing they should have no mercy at his hands."

He gained great wealth, but after awhile lost his ship on the coast of Campêche, where he and his crew, after escaping from the wreck, were beset and almost destroyed by the Spaniards. Lolonois himself, being wounded, feigned death and was passed over by his foes. Afterwards escaping, by the aid of some negroes to whom he made great promises, the captain got back to Tortuga, and after some trouble succeeded in getting another vessel and crew

With these he put into the port of Cayos, and learning the channel from some captive fishermen, lay in wait for a vessel which the governor of Cuba sent to capture him. After nightfall, while the vessel lay at anchor, several boats approached her, and were hailed with the inquiry whether they had seen any pirates. The fishermen in the boat replied that they had not. But beside the fishermen were pirates, compelling them to answer so. Thereupon the boats drew nearer, and presently the Buccaneers assaulted, swarming up both sides of the great vessel and forced the Spaniards below hatches. From below decks they were ordered out one by one and decapitated at Lolonois' order. One man alone was saved, to bear a message back to the governor, to the effect that the pirate captain would never spare any Spaniard thereafter, and hoped shortly to make an end of the governor himself.

FRANCOIS LOLONOIS.
geboeren in Olenne in Vranckryck
Generael van de Fransse Roovers in Tortuga

(From the Portrait in "De Americaensche Zee Roovers.")

While cruising in this ship, another vessel was taken near Maracaibo—a ship loaded with plate and merchandise. With this Lolonois returned to Tortuga to receive the congratulations and praise that usually await the successful.

His next venture was with eight vessels, ten guns and nearly seven hundred men. His first prize was a ship of sixteen guns with fifty fighting men on board. She yielded after hot fighting for three hours, the flag-ship of the pirate fleet having engaged her singly without assistance from the others. She contained, besides a rich cargo, a treasure of over fifty thousand pistoles, of $200,000 in value. Other prizes soon put the fleet in a position to attempt more extensive operations.

The Gulf of Venezuela or Bay of Maracaibo, as it was called, afforded a peculiarly tempting field for the freebooter, Lolonois. Its narrow channel, protected by the watch tower and fortress on the islands at its mouth, led to a lake near which the Spaniards had settled several towns and cities, whose wealth came to be quite disproportioned to their size or populations. Maracaibo, Gibralter, Merida—all had much to recommend them to the hungry pirate. One can hardly understand at first how so much silver and other valuable booty could have been gathered from the insignificant settlements of the Spanish Main ; but when we consider that from Peru and the Pacific settlements to the islands of the Caribbean there was almost constant communication, that the inhabitants of all were reaping the full advantage of being first in a rich treasure field, and that there were no banks, each man holding or hoarding his own gains and keeping his capital under his own roof, the mystery grows less.

To Maracaibo Lolonois shaped his fleet's course. Arriving at the entrance, he landed and took the fort or earthworks by storm, in a fight which lasted for several hours, then, sailing through the passage, brought his whole fleet into the lake and towards Maracaibo, which lay about six leagues beyond. Becalmed in sight of the town, the inhabitants saw the fleet and had time to flee with much of their treasure towards Gibralter. But on the following day the invaders landed and Lolonois sent a company of men into the woods to follow the fugitives, whose houses, with stores of food and drink, stood open. By the time the search party returned with such prisoners and booty as they could recover, the remainder of the crews were not of the soberest, as might be imagined. Then began one of those revolting scenes of cruelty and crime, the details of which we follow shudderingly. Men were tortured in every conceivable way, their limbs broken, their bodies mutilated, their most sacred feelings outraged, to force them to a confession of hidden riches. Many a poor wretch died under the torments inflicted, protesting with his dying breath that he could not reveal what he had never known. For fifteen days Maracaibo was occupied, till like a lemon whose juice is exhausted and the rind flung away, it was abandoned and the murderers proceeded towards Gibralter, which was a smaller town than Maracaibo, but in communication with Merida, to which place the pirates advanced last, after having treated Gibralter as they had Maracaibo. The governor of Merida, who had been a soldier in Flanders and who made no doubt that he could hold his own in a fight with the freebooters, barricaded the roads, felled trees in the passages through the swamps and planted batteries where they would be of most avail. Over these obstructions Lolonois and his men were obliged to fight their way step by step, now taking the woods and anon the road, but swearing with curses loud and deep that the Spaniards would have to pay for their discomfiture. It came near being a defeat for the buccaneers, as they were outnumbered and overmatched, and would probably have been totally destroyed, or at least have escaped only with severe loss, but for a very old stratagem. Pretending to flee, they drew the enemy from one of his strongest batteries, and then turning, overpowered and defeated him.

After Merida had been taken and new cruelties devised for its suffering inhabitants the captors rested there four weeks, until the increasing death-rate among them warned them to escape from a climate to which their excesses made them easy victims. Sending parties then into the woods for those who had still preserved their lives there, the pirate captain demanded a ransom for the town, promising to burn it to the ground if 10,000 pistoles were not immediately forthcoming. Finally this sum was secured, but only after part of Merida had been consumed with fire. A similar ransom was extorted from the already exhausted Maracaibo as the fleet passed out of the gulf, and then the buccaneers sailed away, having 260,000 pistoles in ready money and an immense booty in merchandise.

It would be impossible and not very instructive to follow Lolonois through his further adventures. He sacked many cities, killed and tortured numberless Spaniards, won and wasted an almost countless treasure, and at last died a miserable death of lingering torture at the hands of some enraged Indians.

Following Lolonois came Henry Morgan, the last and greatest of the Buccaneers, whose crimes and adventures have made him, in the popular conception a sort of nautical demi-god; only second in fame to Sir Francis Drake, and much greater in exploits.

Without question, Morgan was a remarkable man. A Welsh boy, sold for his passage to the New World, after the fashion of those days, he was a naval commander who belonged to no navy, a conqueror to whom conquest and pillage were equal terms, a genius in murder and robbery. He commanded at times many ships and hundreds of pirates, yet was one of those instrumental in putting down piracy. He was utterly lawless, yet always claimed that he sailed under commission from the Governor of Jamaica. He was knighted for one of his most outrageous acts of piracy at a time when the Governor who had given him his commission was in prison for doing so. He was Acting-Governor of the very island where most of the fruits of his lawlessness had been exhibited, and where he was said to have wisely maintained the laws. He became a planter of wealth and repute, and finally languished in an English prison for the crimes so long condoned. Certainly, romance need not seek further than this for material.

One of Morgan's earliest exploits was the taking of Puerto Bello, in Costa Rica. This he effected partly by stratagem, causing the sentry to be seized and approaching the strong walls of the city under cover of darkness. He also managed to surprise the inmates of some religious houses, priests and nuns, whom he afterwards put forward as a defense to his soldiers when scaling ladders were brought into use. But never was a more obstinate defense made and never was Henry Morgan more nearly defeated than that day at Puerto Bello. The Spaniards fought with fury, the Governor especially showing no mercy and finally refusing all quarter, dying with his sword in his hand, crying that he would rather fall a soldier than live a coward.

St. Catherine's Island was taken by Morgan, to be used as a pirate rendezvous, but the Governor of that place, while agreeing to capitulate before a blow had been struck, insisted on a sham battle to save his credit. To this Morgan good-naturedly acceded. Following the example of Lolonois and others, he attacked ill-fated Maracaibo and put the inhabitants to torture worse than that which they had before suffered. We will not go into details, having already supped on horrors. More interesting is the account of the dilemma in which the buccaneer found himself upon seeking to leave the Gulf of Venezuela with his ships loaded with booty and prisoners. He had eight little vessels. He found opposing him several war ships in the narrow passage already so well guarded by the guns of the fortress on the island. The Admiral of the Spanish fleet sent a letter to Morgan telling him that he might be allowed to escape on condition of leaving all his plunder behind, but that otherwise he would be treated without mercy.

The Buccaneer might have said, as General Sheridan is reported to have said on a much later occasion, "I am in a bottle and the enemy have the neck of it." However, he made a bold front and resolved to perish in fighting his way out rather than abandon his ill-gotten gains. By means of a fire ship, cunningly manned and armed with dummies, he managed to deceive and destroy the largest of the Spanish ships and then defeated the others. This accomplished, he waited for a favorable opportunity to pass the fort, the guns of which still pointed too ominously across the exit.

The question was how to turn those guns the other way. Finally he hit upon a scheme. Sending boat after boat to the shore filled with men and returning apparently empty to the ships, but in reality with their crews lying covered in the bottoms, he deceived the Spaniards into believing that he meditated a night attack on the fort from the landward side. In consequence all the great guns were turned that way, in expectation. Then the crafty captain stood out to sea, firing a salute of bullets, to which the disgusted garrison did not attempt to reply.

When Morgan had reduced Puerto Bello he had a passage of arms with the Governor of Panama, who had come vainly to the relief of that place. A little bit of theatrical civility or courtesy took place at the time, the Governor sending a message to Morgan, to know by what arms he had succeeded in overcoming so strong a fortress; and the captain politely returning a pistol and bullets with a message to the effect that he would come for them in a year.

After a while Morgan went for that pistol. This was in 1670. Sending some vessels in advance, which took the town of Chagres, the leader presently came and led them across the Isthmus, where they met with almost unbearable hardships on the march. It was the month of August. A little army of twelve hundred men, with artillery and ammunition, pushed on foot across a country where men have since ridden and thought it hardship. They had no food ; the fatigue was great ; hostile Indians added their unwelcome addresses to the pangs of starvation ; yet the intrepid pirates kept on as though they expected in some way to be miraculously saved from the death that in different disguises peered at them from the ambushes along the way. One would suppose that their ardor would have been tamed ; but on the contrary, when they came in sight of Panama, these irrepressible freebooters cheered and threw up their hats as though they had been out for a holiday. This was on the ninth or tenth day of the march. Almost within sight of the city they found food, which they devoured like wild beasts. They had one or two skirmishes, and at last were rejoiced to see

BLACKBEARD, THE PIRATE.

a company of the Spaniards coming to meet them. These men, who were mounted, came near enough to call names and shout unpleasant things to them, but soon retired and left the way clear to the city. But Morgan, a schemer himself, feared an ambuscade. He made a detour to avoid the batteries which he judged rightly, the enemy had put in the way. Then the Spaniards left

these works and came to meet him. There were four regiments of foot, a
body of horse and a large number of wild bulls that were driven by Indians.
There was something humorous in the idea of
sending cattle against buccaneers ; but there was

DIGGING FOR KIDD'S TREASURES.

very little military judgment in it, as
the sequel showed. The bulls ran away. The Spanish forces, nearly if not
quite three thousand strong, were vanquished after a sanguinary battle, and the

ity of Panama was taken and looted, after which Captain Morgan put it to he torch.

Two churches, eight monasteries, two hundred warehouses, and a great number of residences were the prizes which this richest of American cities offered. They were all utterly stripped, and the usual tortures resorted to in order to extort confessions concerning the treasure which might possibly be idden. People were burned alive, eyes dug out, ears and noses cut off, arms islocated, and all imagined or unheard-of barbarities practiced. Then the reatest of all pirates and freebooters went away with a hundred and seventy easts laden with precious metals and jewels and merchandise of value, besides ix hundred prisoners. He made, when he reached the coast, a false division f spoils among his men, and escaping with the lion's share abjured piracy nd became, as has been before said, a knight of Charles the Second's creation, nd an exemplary planter and Governor of the island of Jamaica !

We have dwelt long,—too long,—with the Buccaneers. There were other irates of a later time whose names are not less familiar, and one at least of the umber whose fame is world wide. I mean Captain Kidd, who stood upon sort of middle ground between the buccaneers and the marooners proper. each, or Blackbeard, made his headquarters among the Bahama Islands and as a past-master of claptrap. He created theatrical effects with burned brimtone and paint, and not only tortured others but himself as well, giving us very reason to believe him an insane man. That he took and buried treasure t different points is certain, and probably the half of his villanies have never een told. But of Blackbeard and Avery and Roberts we can say very little ; ney were roaring, ranting, raving pirates, *per se*. Their stories lack the flavor f courage and dash of romance that make us willing to endure the recital of ne crimes of Morgan, Lolonois or the rest of the Buccaneers.

But we may not leave Kidd so. Along every mile of Atlantic coast in the Inited States his money has been dreamed about and often searched for. The tory of how he

> " Murdered William More
> And left him in his gore
> As he sailed,"

part of our nursery education.

There were pirates troubling the shipping of the very good Dutch-English own of New York long ago, and some very good and very rich merchants btained a commission from Lord Bellamont for William Kidd to go out and ok for pirates, which he did, and found one.

It was a little hard on the respectable merchants aforementioned, that they hould have been suspected by an envious world of sharing in the profits of the iratical voyages. More was a gunner, or gunner's mate, whom Captain Kidd put to death; and it is one of the curious examples of the working of law that Kidd after his capture would have escaped under a general amnesty to pirates had he not been held on the charge of murder. He enjoyed the unenviable distinction of being the one of very few pirates who have been hung.

But, nevertheless, though the fame of Kidd and Morgan is so pre-eminent,

there are others only second to them in renown—others whose names and deeds have also been chronicled by Captain Johnson, the famous historian of scoundreldom. Captain Bartholomew Roberts, for instance, if he may not have had the fortune to be so famous as the two above-mentioned worthies, yet in his marvelous escapes and deeds of daring, he well deserves to stand upon the same pedestal of renown. And Captain Avery, though his history is, perhaps, more apocryphal in its nature, nevertheless there is sufficient stamina of trust in the account of his exploits to grant him also a place with his more famous brothers, for the four together—Blackbeard, Kidd, Roberts, and Avery—form a galaxy the like of which is indeed hard to match in its own peculiar brilliancy.

Through circumstances the hunter name of buccaneers was given to the seventeenth century pirates and freebooters; the term "marooners" was bestowed upon those who followed the same trade

CAPTAIN BARTHOLOMEW ROBERTS.

in the century succeeding. The name has in itself a terrible significance. The dictionary tells us that to maroon is to put ashore as upon a desert island, and it was from this that the title was derived.

These later pirates, the marooners, not being under the protection of the West Indian Governors, and having no such harbor for retreat as that, for instance, of Port Royal, were compelled to adopt some means for the disposal of prisoners captured with their prizes other than taking them into a friendly port

Occasionally such unhappy captives were set adrift in the ship's boats—with or without provisions, as the case might be. A method of disposing of them, maybe more convenient, certainly more often used, was to set them ashore upon some desert coast or uninhabited island, with a supply of water perhaps, and perhaps a gun, a pinch of powder, and a few bullets—there to meet their fate, either in the slim chance of a passing vessel or more probably in death.

Nor was marooning the fate alone of the wretched captives of their piracy; sometimes it was resorted to as a punishment among themselves. Many a mutinous pirate sailor and not a few pirate captains have been left to the horrors of such a fate, either to die under the shriveling glare of the tropical sun upon some naked sand-spit or to consume in the burning of a tropical fever amid the rank wilderness of mangroves upon some desert coast.

Hence the name marooners.

The Tudor sea-captains were little else than legalized pirates, and in them we may see that first small step that leads so quickly into the smooth downward path. The buccaneers, in their semi-legalized piracy, succeeded them as effect follows cause. Then, as the ultimate result, followed the marooners—fierce, bloody, rapacious, human wild beasts, lusting for blood and plunder, godless, lawless, the enemy of all men but their own wicked kind.

Is there not a profitable lesson to be learned in the history of such a human extreme of evil—all the more wicked from being the rebound from civilization?

Even to this day imaginative fishermen and oystermen on Connecticut and Long Island shores occasionally see a phantom ship sailing, with all sail set, across some neck of land; and more than one will tell how he started to dig for a treasure, and was driven away by having the pirate vessel bear down upon him, which goes to show that once in awhile fiction is stranger than fact.

7

The Story of the Revolution==Its Battles and Heroes.

A WITTY foreigner, watching the course of the American Revolution, wrote to Benjamin Franklin that Great Britain was undertaking the task " of catching two millions of people in a boundless desert with fifty thousand men." This was a crude and inaccurate way of putting it, but it expresses succinctly the magnitude and difficulty of the campaign that lay before the British generals. When Parliament rather reluctantly authorized the raising of twenty-five thousand men for the war, Great Britain was still forced to obtain most of this number by subsidizing German mercenaries from the small principalities, who were indiscriminately called Hessians by the colonists, and the employment of whom did much to still further provoke bitterness of feeling. At one time in the Revolution Great Britain had over three hundred thousand men in arms, the world over, but of this number not more than one-tenth could be sent to America. But the greatest obstacle to British success lay in the fact that the English leaders, military and civil, constantly underrated the courage, endurance, and earnestness of their opponents. That raw militia could stand their ground against regulars was a hard lesson for the British to learn; that men from civil life could show such aptitude for strategy, as did Washington, Schuyler, and Greene, was a revelation to the professional military men, the significance of which they grasped only when it was too late.

Above all, the one thing that made the colonists the victors was the indomitable energy, self-renunciation, and strategic ability of George Washington. We are so accustomed to think of Washington's moral qualities, that it is only

when we come close to the history of the war that we fully recognize how great
was his military genius—a genius which justly entitles him to rank with the few

CORNWALLIS

truly great soldiers of history, such as Alexander,
Cæsar, Napoleon, and Von
Moltke. Almost alone
among the American gen-
erals of the Revolution, he
was always willing to subordinate his own personal
glory to the final success
of his deep laid and com-
prehensive plans. Again
and again he risked his
standing with Congress,
and ran the danger of
being superseded by one
or another jealous general
of lower rank, rather than
yield in a particle his deliberate scheme of cam-
paign. Others received
the popular honors for brilliant single movements
while he waited and plan-
ned for the final result.
What the main lines of his
strategy were we shall endeavor to make clear in
the following sketch :—

When the news of the
running fight from Con-
cord to Lexington spread
through the country, the
militia hurried from every
direction toward Boston.
Israel Putnam literally left
his plough in the field ;
John Stark, with his sturdy

New Hampshire volunteers, reached the spot in three days ; Nathaniel Greene
headed fifteen hundred men from Rhode Island ; Benedict Arnold led a band

WASHINGTON'S RECEPTION AT TRENTON

of patriots from Connecticut; the more distant colonies showed equal eagerness to aid in the defense of American liberties. Congress displayed deep
wisdom in appointing George Washington Commander in Chief, not only
because of his personal ability and the trust all men had in him, but because
it was politically an astute measure to choose the leader from some other
State than Massachusetts. But before Washington could reach the Continental forces, as they soon began to be called, the battle of Bunker Hill
had been fought. And before that, even, Ethan Allen, with his Green Mountain Boys, had seized Fort Ticonderoga "in the name of Jehovah and the Continental Congress"—which Congress, by the way, showed momentarily some
reluctance to sanction this first step of aggressive warfare. The occupation by
Allen and Arnold of Ticonderoga and Crown Point, at the southern end of
Lake Champlain, was of great military importance, both because of the large
quantities of ammunition stored there, and because these places defended the
line of the Hudson River valley against an attack from Canada.

The battle of Bunker Hill, looked at from the strictly military point of
view, was a blunder on both sides, astonishing as was its moral effect. The
hill, properly named Breed's Hill, but to which the name of Bunker Hill is
now forever attached, rises directly back of Charlestown, on a peninsula connected with the main land by a narrow isthmus. The American forces seized
this on the night of June 16th, 1775, and worked the night through intrenching
themselves as well as they could. With the morning came the British attack.
The position might easily have been reduced by seizing the isthmus, and for this
reason the Americans had hardly shown military sagacity in their occupation of
the hill. But the British chose rather to storm the works from the front.
Three times the flower of the English army in battle line swept up the hill;
twice they were swept back with terrible loss, repulsed by a fire which was
reserved until they were close at hand; the third time they seized the position,
but only when the Americans had exhausted their ammunition, and even then
only after a severe hand to hand fight. The British loss was over a thousand
men; the American loss about four hundred and fifty. When Washington
heard of the battle he instantly asked if the New England militia had stood
the fire of the British regulars, and when the whole story was told him he
exclaimed, "The liberties of the country are safe." The spirit shown then and
thereafter by our sturdy patriots is well illustrated by the story (chosen as the
subject of one of our pictures) of the minister, who when in one battle there
was a lack of wadding for the guns, brought out an armful of hymn books and
exclaimed "Give them Watts, boys!"

The next clash of arms came from Canada. General Montgomery led two
thousand of the militia against Montreal, by way of Lake Champlain, and easily
captured it (November 12, 1775). Thence he descended the St. Lawrence to

Quebec, where he joined forces with Benedict Arnold, who had brought twelve hundred men through the Maine wilderness, and the two Generals attacked the British stronghold of Quebec. The attempt was a failure; Arnold was wounded, Montgomery was killed, and though the Americans fought gallantly they were driven back from Canada by

"GIVE THEM WATTS, BOYS!"

superior forces. Meanwhile the siege of Boston was systematically carried on by Washington, and in the spring of 1776 the American General gained a commanding position by seizing Dorchester Heights (which bore much the same relation to Boston on the South that Breed's Hill did on the North) and General Howe found himself forced to evacuate the city. He sailed with his whole force for Halifax, taking with him great numbers of American sympathizers with British rule, together with their property.

The new Congress met at Philadelphia in May. During the first month of its sessions it became evident that there had been an immense advance in public opinion as to the real issue to be maintained. Several of the colonies had expressed a positive conviction that National independence must be demanded. Virginia had formally instructed her delegates to take that ground, and it was, on the motion of Richard Henry Lee, of Virginia, seconded by John Adams, of Massachusetts, that Congress proceeded to consider the resolution "That these united colonies are and of right ought to be free and independent States; that they are absolved from all allegiance to the British Crown, and that all political connection between them and the State of Great Britain is and ought to be totally dissolved." This bold utterance was adopted on July 2d by all the colonies except New York. The opposition came mainly from Pennsylvania and New York, and was based, not on lack of patriotism, but on a feeling that the time for such an assertion had not yet come, that a stronger central government should first be established, and that attempts should be made to secure a foreign alliance. It should be noticed that the strongest opponents of the measure, John Dickinson and Robert Morris, of Pennsylvania, were among the most patriotic supporters of the Union. To Robert Morris in particular, whose skill as a financier steered the young Nation through many a difficulty, the country owes a special debt of gratitude. The Declaration of Independence, formally adopted two days later, was written mainly by the pen of Thomas Jefferson. It is unique among State papers—a dignified though impassioned, a calm though eloquent, recital of injuries inflicted, demand for redress, and avowal of liberties to be maintained with the sword. Its adoption was hailed, the country through, as the birth of a new Nation. Never before has a country about to appeal to war to decide its fate put upon record so clear-toned and deliberate an assertion of its purposes and its reasons, and thus summoned the world and posterity to witness the justice and righteousness of its cause.

Thus far in the war the engagements between the opposing forces had been of a detached kind—not related, that is, to any broad plan of attack or defense. Of the same nature also was the British expedition against South Carolina, led by Sir Henry Clinton and Lord Cornwallis. Their fleet attacked Charleston, but the fort was so bravely defended by Colonel Moultrie, from his palmetto-log fortifications on Sullivan's Island, that the fleet was forced to abandon the attempt and to return to New York. But the British now saw that it was imperative to enter upon a distinct and extensive plan of campaign. That adopted was sagacious and logical; its failure was due, not to any inherent defect in itself, but to lack of persistency in adhering to it. Washington understood it thoroughly from the first, and bent all his energies to tempting the enemy to diverge from the main object in view. The plan, in brief, was this: New York City was to be seized and held as a base of supplies and centre of operations; from it a stretch of country to the west was to be occupied and held, thus cutting off communication between New York and the New England States on the one side and Pennsylvania and the Southern States on the other. Meanwhile a force was to be pushed down from Canada to the head of the Hudson River, to be met by another force pushed northward up the Hudson. In this way New England would be practically surrounded, and it was thought that its colonies could be reduced one by one, while simultaneously or later an army could march southward upon Philadelphia. The plan was quite feasible, but probably at no time did the British have sufficient force to carry it out in detail. They wofully over-estimated, also, the assistance they might receive from the Tories in New York State. And they still more wofully under-estimated Washington's ability as a strategist in blocking their schemes.

General Howe, who was now Commander-in-Chief of the British army, drew his forces to a head upon Staten Island, combining there the troops which had sailed from Boston to Halifax, with Clinton's forces which had failed at Charleston, and the Hessians newly arrived. In all he had over thirty thousand soldiers. Washington, who had transferred his headquarters from Boston to the vicinity of New York after the former city had been evacuated by the British, occupied the Brooklyn Heights with about twenty thousand poorly equipped and undrilled colonial troops. To hold that position against the larger forces of regulars seemed a hopeless task; but every point was to be contested. In point of fact, only five thousand of the Americans were engaged in the battle of Long Island (August 27, 1776) against twenty thousand men brought by General Howe from Staten Island. The Americans were driven back after a hotly contested fight. Before Howe could follow up his victory Washington planned and executed one of those extraordinary, rapid movements which so often amazed his enemy; in a single night he withdrew his entire army across the East River into New York in boats, moving so secretly and swiftly that the British first found out what had happened when they saw the deserted camps before them on the following morning. Drawing back through the city Washington made his next stand at Harlem Heights, occupying Fort Washington on the east and Fort Lee on the west side of the Hudson, thus guarding the line of the river while prepared to move southward toward Philadelphia if occasion should require. In the battle of White Plains the Americans suffered a repulse, but much more dispiriting to Washington was the disarrangement of his plans caused by the interference of Congress. That over-prudent body sent special orders to General Greene, at Fort Washington, to hold it at all odds, while Washington had directed Greene to be ready on the first attack to fall back upon the main army in New Jersey. The result was the capture of Fort Washington, with a loss of three thousand prisoners. To add to the misfortune, General Charles Lee, who commanded a wing of the American

WASHINGTON CROSSING THE DELAWARE

rmy on the east side of the river, absolutely ignored Washington's orders to
oin him. Lee was a soldier of fortune, vain, ambitious, and volatile, and there
s little doubt that his disobedience was due to his hope that Washington was
retrievably ruined and that he might succeed to the command. Gathering his
cattered troops together as well as he could, Washington retreated through
few Jersey, meeting everywhere with reports that the colonists were in despair,
nat many had given in their allegiance to the British, that Congress had fled to
laltimore, and that the war was looked on as almost over. In this crisis it was
n actual piece of rare good fortune that Charles Lee should be captured by
oldiers while spending the night at a tavern away from his camp, for the result
as that Lee's forces were free to join Washington's command, and at once
id so. Altogether some six thousand men were left in the army, and
ere drawn into something like coherence on the other side of the Delaware
liver. General Howe announced that he had now nothing to do but wait the
eezing of the Delaware, and then to cross over and "catch Washington and
nd the war."

But he reckoned without his host. Choosing, as the best time for his bold
nd sudden movement, Christmas night, when revelry in the camp of the
nemy might be hoped to make them careless, Washington crossed the river.
eading in person the division of twenty-five hundred men, which alone suc-
eeded in making the passage over the river, impeded as it was with great
locks of ice, he marched straight upon the Hessian outposts at Trenton and
aptured them with ease. Still his position was a most precarious one. Corn-
allis was at Princeton with the main British army, and marching directly upon
le Americans, penned them up, as he thought, between Trenton and the
Delaware. It is related that Cornwallis remarked, "At last we have run down
ne old fox, and we will bag him in the morning." But before morning came
Vashington had executed another surprising and decisive manœuvre. Main-
aining a great show of activity at his intrenchments, and keeping camp-fires
rightly burning, he noiselessly led the main body of his army round the flank
f the British force and marched straight northward upon Princeton, capturing
s he went the British rear guard on its way to Trenton, seizing the British
ost of supplies at New Brunswick, and in the end securing a strong position
n the hills in Northern New Jersey, with Morristown as his headquarters.
here he could at last rest for a time, strengthen his army, and take advantage
f the prestige which his recent operations had brought him.

Let us turn our attention now to the situation further north. General
urgoyne had advanced southward from Canada through Lake Champlain and
ad easily captured Ticonderoga. His object was, of course, to advance in the
ıme line to the south until he reached the Hudson River; but this was a very
ifferent matter from what he had supposed it. General Schuyler was in com-

mand of the Americans, and showed the highest military skill in opposing Burgoyne's progress, cutting off his sup-
plies and harassing him generally. An
expedition to assist Burgoyne had been
sent down the St. Lawrence to Lake
Ontario, thence to march eastward to
the head of the Hudson, gathering aid
as it went from the Indians and Tories.

SURRENDER OF BURGOYNE.

This expedi-
tion was an
utter failure;
a t Oriskany
the Tories and

British were defeated in a fiercely fought battle, in which a greater proportion of those engaged were killed than in any other battle of the war. Disheartened at this, and at the near approach of Benedict Arnold, St. Leger, who was at the head of the expedition, fled in confusion back to Canada. Meanwhile Burgoyne had sent out a detachment to gather supplies. This was utterly routed at Bennington by the Vermont farmers under General Stark. Through all the country round about the Americans were flocking to arms, their patriotism enforced by their horror at the atrocities committed by Burgoyne's Indian allies and by the danger to their own homes. Practically Burgoyne was surrounded, and though he fought bravely in the battles of Stillwater (September 19, 1777) and Bemis's Heights (October 7th), he was overmatched. Ten days after the last-named battle he surrendered with all his forces to General Gates, who was now at the head of the American forces in that vicinity and thus received the nominal honor of the result, although it was really due rather to the skill and courage of General Schuyler and General Arnold. Almost six thousand soldiers laid down their arms, and the artillery, small arms, ammunition, clothing, and other military stores which fell into General Gates's hands were immensely valuable. Almost greater than the practical gain of this splendid triumph was that of the respect at once accorded throughout the world to American courage and military capacity.

General Burgoyne had every right to lay the blame for the mortifying failure of his expedition upon Howe, who had totally failed to carry out his part of the plan of campaign. It was essential to the success of this plan that Howe should have pushed an army up the Hudson to support Burgoyne. In leaving this undone he committed the greatest blunder of the war. Why he acted as he did was for a long while a mystery, but letters brought to light eighty years after the war was over show that he was strongly influenced by the traitorous arguments of his prisoner, Charles Lee, who for a time, at least, had decided to desert the American cause. While in this frame of mind he convinced Howe that there was plenty of time to move upon and seize Philadelphia and still come to Burgoyne's aid in season. Howe should have known Washington's methods better by this time. At first the British General attempted a march through New Jersey, but for nearly three weeks Washington blocked his movements, out-manœuvred him in the fencing for advantage of position, and finally compelled him to withdraw, baffled, to New York. Though no fighting of consequence occurred in this period, it is, from the military standpoint, one of the most interesting of the entire war. The result was that Howe, unwilling to give up his original design, transported his army to the south of the Delaware by sea, then decided to make his attempt by way of Chesapeake Bay, and finally, after great delay, landed his forces at the head of that bay, fifty miles from Philadelphia. Washington interposed his army between the enemy and the city and for several weeks delayed its inevitable capture. In the Battle of Brandywine the Americans put eleven thousand troops in the field against eighteen thousand of the British, and were defeated though by no means routed (September 11, 1777). After Howe had seized the city he found it necessary to send part of his army to capture the forts on the Delaware River, and this gave the Americans the opportunity of an attack with evenly balanced forces. Unfortunately, the battle of Germantown was, by reason of a heavy fog, changed into a confused conflict, in which some American regiments fired into others, and which ended in the retreat of our forces. Washington drew back and went into winter quarters at Valley Forge. Congress, on the approach of the enemy, had fled to York. Howe had accomplished his immediate object, but at what a cost! The possession of Philadelphia had not appreciably brought nearer the subjugation of the former colonies, while the opportunity to co operate with Burgoyne had been irretrievably lost, and as we have seen, a great and notable triumph had been gained by the American in his surrender.

The memorable winter which Washington spent at Valley Forge he often described as the darkest of his life. The course of the war had not been altogether discouraging, but he had to contend with the inaction of Congress, with cabals of envious rivals, and with the wretched lack of supplies and food. He writes to Congress that when he wished to draw up his troops to fight, the men were unable to stir on account of hunger, that 2898 men were unfit for duty because they were barefooted and half naked, that "for seven days past there has been little else than a famine in the camp." Meanwhile an intrigue to supersede Washington by Gates was on foot and nearly succeeded. The whole country also was suffering from the depreciated Continental currency and from the lack of power in the general government to lay taxes. What a contrast is there between Washington's position at this time and the enthusiasm with which the whole country flocked to honor him in the autumn of the first year of his Presidency (1789), when he made a journey which was one long series of ovations. An idea of the character of these is given in the accompanying picture of his reception at Trenton, where the date on the triumphal arch recalled that famous Christmas night when he outwitted the British.

But encouragement from abroad was at hand. Perhaps the most important result of Burgoyne's surrender was its influence in procuring us the French Alliance. Already a strong sympathy had been aroused for the American cause in France. The nobility were influenced in no small degree by the sentimental and philosophical agitation for ideal liberty which preceded the brutal reality of the French Revolution. Lafayette, then a mere boy of eighteen, had fitted out a ship with supplies at his own expense, and had laid his services at Washington's command. Our Commissioners to France —John Adams, Arthur Lee, and Benjamin Franklin—had labored night and day for the alliance. Franklin, in particular, had, by his shrewd and homely wit, his honesty of purpose and his high patriotism, made a profound impression upon the French people. We read that on one occasion he was made to embrace the rôle of an Apostle of Liberty at an elegant *fête* where the most beautiful of three hundred women was designated to go and place on the philosopher's white locks a crown of laurel, and to give the old man two kisses on his cheeks." Very "French" this, but not without its significance. But after all, the thing which turned the scale with the French Government was the partial success of our armies. France was only too willing, under favoring circumstances, to obtain its revenge upon Great Britain for many recent defeats and slights. So it was that in the beginning of 1778 the independence of the United States was recognized by France and a fleet was sent to our assistance. During the winter, meanwhile, the thirteen States had adopted in Congress articles of confederation and perpetual union, which were slowly and hesitatingly ratified by the legislatures of the several States.

The news of the reinforcements on their way from France, led Sir Henry Clinton, who had now succeeded Howe in the chief command of the British, to abandon Philadelphia, and mass his forces at New York. This he did in June, 1778, sending part of the troops by sea and the rest northward, through New Jersey. Washington instantly broke camp, followed the enemy, and overtook him at Monmouth Court House. In the battle which followed the forces were equally balanced, each having about fifteen thousand men. The American attack was entrusted to Charles Lee, who had been exchanged, and whose treachery was not suspected. Again Lee disobeyed orders, and directed a retreat at the critical minute of the fight. Had Washington not arrived, the retreat would have been a rout; as it was he turned it into a victory, driving the British from their position, and gained the honors of the day. But had it not been for Lee, this victory might have easily been made a crushing and final defeat for the British army. A court-martial held upon Lee's conduct expelled him from the army. Years later he died a disgraced man, though it is only in our time that the full extent of his dishonor has been understood.

The scene of the most important military operations now changes from the Northern to the Southern States. But before speaking of the campaign which ended with Cornwallis's surrender, we may characterize the fighting in the North, which went on in the latter half of the war, as desultory and unsystematic in its nature. The French fleet under Count d'Estaing was unable to cross the New York bar on account of the depth of draught of its greatest ships; and for that reason the attempt to capture New York City was abandoned. Its next attempt was to wrest Rhode Island from the British. This also was defeated, partly because of a storm at a critical moment, partly through a misunderstanding with the American allies. After these two failures, the French fleet sailed to the West Indies to injure British interests there. The assault on the fort at Stony Point by "Mad Anthony" Wayne has importance as a brilliant and thrilling episode, and was of value in strengthening our position on the Hudson River. All along the border the Tories were inciting the Indians to barbarous attacks. The most important and deplorable of these at-

WASHINGTON APPEARING 124 AT MONMOUTH.

tacks were those which ended in the massacres at Wyoming and Cherry Valley. Reprisals for these atrocities were taken by General Sullivan's expedition, which defeated the Tories and Indians combined, near Elmira, with great slaughter. But all these events, like the British sudden attacks on the Connecticut ports of New Haven,

Fairfield, and Norwalk, were, as we have said, rather detached episodes than related parts of a campaign.

We should also note before entering upon the final chapter of the war, that Great Britain had politically receded from her position. Of her own accord she had offered to abrogate the offensive legislation which had provoked the colonies to war. But it was too late; the proposition of peace commissioners sent to America to acknowledge the principle of taxation by colonial assemblies

NEGRO VILLAGE IN GEORGIA.

was not for a moment considered. The watchword of America was now Independence, and there was no disposition in any quarter to accept anything less than full recognition of the rights of the United States as a Nation.

The second and last serious and concerted effort by the British to subjugate the American States had as its scene of operations our Southern territory. At first it seemed to succeed. A long series of reverses to the cause of independence were reported from Georgia and South Carolina. The plan formed by

5

Sir Henry Clinton and Cornwallis was, in effect, to begin at the extreme South and overpower one State after another until the army held in reserve about New York could co-operate with that advancing victoriously from the South. Savannah had been captured in 1778, while General Lincoln, who commanded our forces, was twice defeated with great loss—once at Brier Creek, in an advance upon Savannah, when his lieutenant, General Ashe, was actually routed with very heavy loss; and once when Savannah had been invested by General Lincoln himself by land, while the French fleet under d'Estaing besieged the city by sea. In a short time Georgia was entirely occupied by the British. They were soon reinforced by Sir Henry Clinton in person, with an army, and the united forces moved upward into South Carolina with thirteen thousand men. Lincoln was driven into Charleston, was there besieged, and (May 12, 1780) was forced to surrender not only the city but his entire army. A desultory but brilliant guerrilla warfare was carried on at this time by the Southern militia and light cavalry under the dashing leadership of Francis Marion, "the Swamp Fox," and the partisan, Thomas Sumter.

These men were privateers on horseback. Familiar with the tangled swamps and always well mounted, even though in rags themselves, they were the terror of the invaders. At the crack of their rifles the pickets of Cornwallis fled, leaving a score of dead behind. The dreaded cavalry of Tarleton often came back from their raids with many a saddle emptied by the invisible foes. They were here, they were everywhere. Their blows were swift and sure; their vigilance sleepless. Tarleton had been sent by Cornwallis with a force of seven hundred cavalry to destroy a patriot force in North Carolina, under Buford, which resulted in his utterly destroying about four hundred of the patriots at Waxhaw, the affair being more of a massacre than a battle. Thus the name of Tarleton came to be hated in the South as that of Benedict Arnold was in the North. He was dreaded for his celerity and cruelty. As illustrative of the spirit of the Southern colonists, we may be pardoned for the digression of the following anecdote. The fighting of Marion and his men was much like that of the wild Apaches of the southwest. When hotly pursued by the enemy his command would break up into small parties, and these as they were hard pressed would subdivide, until nearly every patriot was fleeing alone. There could be no successful pursuit, therefore, since the subdivision of the pursuing party weakened it too much.

"We will give fifty pounds to get within reach of the scamp that galloped by here, just ahead of us," exclaimed a lieutenant of Tarleton's cavalry, as he and three other troopers drew up before a farmer, who was hoeing in the field by the roadside.

The farmer looked up, leaned on his hoe, took off his old hat and mopping his forehead with his handkerchief looked at the angry soldier and said:—

"Fifty pounds is a big lot of money."

"So it is in these times, but we'll give it to you in gold, if you'll show
us where we can get
a chance at the rebel;
did you see him?"

"He was all
alone, was
he? And

TARLETON'S LIEUTENANT AND THE FARMER (BY K. DAVIS).

he was mounted on a black horse with a white star in his forehead, and he
was going like a streak of lightning, wasn't he?"

"That's the fellow!" exclaimed the questioners, hoping they were about to get the knowledge they wanted.

"It looked to me like Jack Davis, though he went by so fast that I couldn' get a square look at his face, but he was one of Marion's men, and if I ain' greatly mistaken it was Jack Davis himself."

Then looking up at the four British horsemen, the farmer added, with quizzical expression :—

"I reckon that ere Jack Davis has hit you chaps pretty hard, ain't he?"

"Never mind about *that*," replied the lieutenant ; "what we want to know is where we can get a chance at him for just about five minutes."

The farmer put his cotton handkerchief into his hat, which he now slowly replaced, and shook his head : "I don't think he's hiding round here," he said ; "when he shot by Jack was going so fast that it didn't look as if he could stop under four or five miles. Strangers, I'd like powerful well to earn that fifty pounds, but I don't think you'll get a chance to squander it on me."

After some further questioning, the lieutenant and his men wheeled their horses and trotted back toward the main body of Tarleton's cavalry. The farmer plied his hoe for several minutes, gradually working his way toward the stretch of woods some fifty yards from the roadside. Reaching the margin of the field, he stepped in among the trees, hastily took off his clothing, tied it up in a bundle, shoved it under a flat rock from beneath which he drew a suit no better in quality, but showing a faint semblance to a uniform. Putting it on and then plunging still deeper into the woods, he soon reached a dimly-marked track, which he followed only a short distance, when a gentle whinney fell upon his ear. The next moment he vaulted on the back of a bony but blooded horse, marked by a beautiful star in his forehead. The satin skin of the steed shone as though he had been traveling hard, and his rider allowed him to walk along the path for a couple of miles, when he entered an open space where, near a spring, Francis Marion and fully two hundred men were encamped. They were eating, smoking and chatting as though no such horror as war was known.

You understand, of course, that the farmer that leaned on his hoe by the roadside and talked to Tarleton's lieutenant about Jack Davis and his exploits was Jack Davis himself.

Marion and his men had many stirring adventures. A British officer, sent to settle some business with Marion, was asked by him to stay to dinner Marion was always a charming gentleman, and the visitor accepted the invitation, but he was astonished to find that the meal consisted only of baked sweet potatoes served on bark. No apology was made, but the guest could not help asking his host whether that dinner was a specimen of his regular bill of fare. "It is," replied Marion, "except that to-day, in honor of your presence, we have more than the usual allowance."

North Carolina was now in danger, and it was to be defended by the overrated General Gates, whose campaign was marked by every indication of military incapacity. His attacks were invariably made recklessly, and his positions were illchosen. At Camden he

ESCAPE OF BENEDICT ARNOLD.

was utterly and disgracefully defeated by Lord Cornwallis (August 16, 1780). It seemed now as if the British forces could easily hold the territory already won and could advance safely into Virginia. This was, indeed, one of the darkest periods in the history of our war, and even Washington was inclined to despair.

To add to the feeling of despondency came the news of Benedict Arnold's infamous treachery. In the early part of the war he had served, not merely with credit but with the highest distinction. Ambitious and passionate by temper, he had justly been indignant at the slights put upon him by the promotion over his head of several officers who were far less entitled than he to such a reward. He had also, perhaps, been treated with undue severity in his trial by court martial on charges relating to his accounts and matters of discipline. No doubt he was greatly influenced by his marriage to a lady of great beauty, who was in intimate relations with many of the leading Tories. It is more than probable, still further, that he believed the cause of American independence could never be won. But neither explanations nor fancied wrongs in the least mitigate the baseness of his conduct. He deliberately planned to be put in command of West Point, with the distinct intention of handing it over to the British in return for thirty thousand dollars in money and a command in the British army. It was almost an accident that the emissary between Arnold and Clinton, Major André, was captured by Paulding and his rough but incorruptible fellows. André's personal charm and youth created a feeling of sympathy for him, but it cannot be for a moment denied that he was justly tried and executed, in accordance with the law of nations. Had Arnold's attempt succeeded, it is more than likely that the blow dealt our cause would have been fatal. His subsequent service in the British army only deepened the feeling of loathing with which his name was heard by Americans; while even his new allies distrusted and despised him, and at one time Cornwallis positively refused to act in concert with him.

A bright and cheering contrast to this dark episode is that of the glorious victories at sea won by John Paul Jones, who not only devastated British commerce, but, in a desperately fought naval battle, captured two British men-of-war, the "Serapis" and the "Countess of Scarborough," and carried the new American flag into foreign ports with the prestige of having swept everything before him on the high seas. Here was laid the foundation of that reputation for intrepidity and gallantry at sea which the American navy so well sustained in our second war with Great Britain.

As the year 1780 advanced, the campaign in the South began to assume a more favorable aspect. General Greene was placed in command of the American army and at once began a series of rapid and confusing movements, now attacking the enemy in front, now cutting off his communications in the rear, but always scheming for the advantage of position, and usually obtaining it. He was aided ably by "Light Horse Harry" Lee and by General Morgan. Even before his campaign began the British had suffered a serious defeat at King's Mountain, just over the line between North and South Carolina, where a body of southern and western backwoodsmen had cut to pieces and finally captured a British detachment of twelve hundred men. Greene followed up this victory by sending Morgan to attack one wing of Cornwallis's army at Cowpens, near by King's Mountain, where again a large body of the enemy were captured with a very slight loss on the part of the Americans. Less decisive was the battle of Guilford Court House (March 15, 1781), which was contested with great persistency and courage by both armies. At the end of the day the British held the field, but the position was too perilous for Cornwallis to maintain long, and he retreated forthwith to the coast. General Greene continued to seize one position after another, driving the scattered bodies of the British through South Carolina and finally meeting them face to face at Eutaw Springs, where another equally contested battle took place; in which, as at Guilford, the British claimed the honors of the day, but which also resulted in their ultimately giving away before the Americans and intrenching themselves in Charleston. Now, indeed, the British were to move into Virginia, not as they had originally planned, but because the more southern States were no longer tenable. It seemed almost as if Greene were deliberately driving them northward, so that in the end they might lie between two American armies. But they made a strong stand at Yorktown, in which a small British army under Benedict Arnold was already in possession and had been opposed by Lafayette.

Washington, who had been watching the course of events with the keen eye of the master strategist, saw that the time had come for a decisive blow. The French fleet was sent to the Chesapeake, and found little difficulty in reducing the British force and approaching Yorktown by sea. Washington's own army had been lying along the Hudson, centered at West Point, ready to meet any movement by Sir Henry Clinton's army at New York. Now Washington moved southward down the Hudson into the upper part of New Jersey. It was universally believed that he was about to attack the British at New York. Even his own officers shared this belief. But with a rapidity that seems astonishing, and with the utmost skill in handling his forces, Washington led them swiftly on, still in the line toward the south, and before Clinton had grasped his intention he was well on his way to Virginia. Cornwallis was now assailed both by land and by sea; he occupied a peninsula, from which he could not escape except by forcing a road through Washington's united army of sixteen thousand men. The city of Yorktown was bombarded for three weeks. An American officer writes: "The whole peninsula trembles under the incessant thunderings of our infernal machines." General Rochambeau who had been placed in command of the French forces in America, actively co-operated with Washington. The meeting of the two great commanders forms the subject of one of our illustrations. Good soldier and good general as Cornwallis was, escape was impossible. On October 19, 1781, he suffered the humiliation of a formal sur render of his army of over seven thousand men, with two hundred and forty cannon, twenty-eight regimental standards, and vast quantities of military stores and provisions. When Lord North, the English Minister, heard of the surrender, we are told, he paced the floor in deep distress, and cried, "O God, it is all over!"

And so it was, in fact. The cause of American independence had practically been won. Hostilities, it is true, continued in a feeble and half-hearted way, and it was not until September, 1783, that the Treaty of Peace secured by John Jay, John Adams, and Benjamin Franklin was actually signed—a treaty which was not only honorable to us, but which, in the frontier boundaries adopted, was more advantageous than even our French allies were inclined to approve, giving us as it did the territory westward to the Mississippi and southward to Florida. Great Britain as a nation had become heartily sick and tired of her attempt to coerce her former colonies. As the war progressed she had managed to involve herself in hostilities not only with France, but with Spain and Holland, and even with the native princes of India. Lord North's Ministry fell, the star of the younger Pitt arose into the ascendency, and George the Third's attempt to establish a purely personal rule at home and abroad was defeated beyond redemption.

As we read of the scanty recognition given by the American States to the soldiers who had fought their battles; as we learn that it was only Washington's commanding influence that restrained these soldiers, half starved and half paid, from compelling that recognition from Congress by force; as we perceive how many and serious were the problems of finance and of government distracting the State Legislatures; as, in short, we see the political disintegration and chaotic condition of affairs in the newly born Nation, we recognize the fact that the struggle which had just ended so triumphantly was but the prelude to another, more peaceful but not less vital, struggle—that for the founding of a strong, coherent, and truly National Government. The latter struggle began before the Revolution was over and lasted until, in 1787, by mutual concession and mutual compromise was formed the Constitution of the United States.

The Eventful Story of Daniel Boone, Fremont, and Other Pathfinders and Pioneers.

BOONE'S name was among the most prominent and his life one of the most exciting as well as useful of the early pioneers. His name is indissolubly connected with Kentucky. Boone's father emigrated from Bucks County, Pennsylvania, to North Carolina when Daniel was a boy. Grown to manhood, here the future pioneer married Rebecca Bryan, their life being such as was common in the backwoods settlements of that time. Boone, like David Crockett, thought that when he had offered his broad hand and stout heart to the girl of his choice he had given her property enough to start with. Household furniture was of such simple pattern as could be made with an axe and a saw, while clothes were homespun or shaped from the dressed skins of animals, and dyed by utilizing the butternut and goldenrod.

The political troubles in North Carolina, the imposition of illegal fines and taxes, no doubt made many settlers besides the Boones anxious to escape to some more favored region.

Boone had a fore-runner, who was Dr. Thomas Walker, of Virginia. This gentleman, fired by hunters' accounts of Western lands, now the State of Tennessee, started in company with Colonels Woods, Patton, and Buchanan, and a number of hunters and others, on an exploring tour. To them are due the names of the Cumberland Mountains, Gap, and River, which with one single exception are the only names of purely English origin in earlier Tennessee geography.

At that time Tennessee was claimed as part of Virginia, which State made grants of its territories. Twelve years later Dr. Walker again passed over Clinch and Powell's Rivers and penetrated into what is now Kentucky. Others followed in his footsteps as far as Tennessee and some probably into Kentucky. That Daniel Boone was with one of these expeditions as far back as 1760 is considered to have been proven by the discovery of his name carved, with a date, upon an old tree near the stage road between Jonesboro and Blountsville, in the valley of Boone's Creek, which is a tributary of the Watauga. The legend inscribed on the tree runs thus: "D. BOON cilled a BAR on tree in THE year 1760."

A MUSK OX HUNT.

A hunter named John Finley penetrated into Kentucky some time after this and brought back marvelous accounts of the hunter's paradise he found there. Boone resolved to go into this new country. The preparations for his departure took time. Even homespun and deerskin had to be gotten ready; the necessary money for the maintenance of his family had to be provided; and when, finally, all was ready, Boone shouldered his rifle and started with John Finley, John Stewart, Joseph Holden, James Moncey, and William Cool, to traverse a mountainous wilderness for several hundred miles. Our pioneer's physique at this time was perfect. He is described as being of full size, hardy, robust, and sinewy, with mild, hazel eyes.

After numerous hardships, which we have not space to chronicle, the explorers finally stood on a mountain crest overlooking the fertile valleys watered by the Kentucky River. There were herds of buffalo and of deer in sight, and evidences of game were everywhere plenty. The country was luxuriant almost beyond description in its vegetation, and it seemed indeed, as Finley had described it, "a hunter's paradise." From the cane-brakes in the river bottoms to the forest trees that crowned the wooded hills, it appeared to be a land of peace and plenty. And yet this very territory had among the Indians a

DANIEL BOONE AND HIS BROTHER IN "HUNTERS' PARADISE."

name of ominous import; it was called "The dark and bloody ground." No one tribe made these valleys their home, although they were claimed by the Cherokees; but both Cherokee, Shawnee, and Chickasaw bands occasionally hunted over them, and they were the scene of many bloody feuds and forest encounters.

Boone and his party encamped within view of all this beauty and wealth of nature, in a rock-cleft over which had fallen a giant tree. This camp from time to time they improved and enlarged, as it remained their headquarters during the succeeding summer and autumn. In all that time they roamed and hunted freely, finding abundance of game, exploring the country thoroughly, but meeting with none of the red men.

In the autumn of 1760 Boone and John Steuart one day left their companions and plunged into the forest for a little longer excursion than usual. One cannot but imagine what the scene must have been at that season of the year in the forest primeval. The rich luxuriance of vegetable life and the plentiful supply of game must have appealed strongly to the feelings of these hunters, whose sense of security had not yet been disturbed by any encounters. Of all this domain they had literally been in peaceful possession until then. Suddenly the feeling of safety was rudely dissipated by the appearance of a band of Indians, who surprised Boone and Steuart so completely that resistance was out of the question, and they were taken prisoners.

On the seventh night after the capture the Indians encamped in a cane-brake and built their fire. Perhaps the fatigue of a long march made them abate something of their customary caution; at all events, as they slept by the fire, Boone, who was always on the alert, saw his opportunity to extricate himself from among them and escape. Refusing, however, to abandon his companion, although knowing that the risk of waking him was very great, as the slightest noise would alarm their captors, he went to where Steuart was sleeping, and taking hold of him, succeeded in rousing him without noise. By morning the hunters were far away on their return to camp, where they arrived without being overtaken, only to find that Finley and the others had disappeared. They were never heard of again.

Early in the next year Squire Boone, Daniel's brother, arrived with a companion. On their approach to camp they were sharply challenged, not being at once recognized; but the meeting was naturally one of great rejoicing when the hermits found who their visitors were. Now, for the first time during his long banishment from home, Boone heard from his family, received messages from his wife, and learned how his boys were progressing with the little farm. It was not long after the arrival of Squire Boone that Boone and Steuart were again attacked by the Indians, and this time Steuart was killed. Following this, Squire Boone's companion strayed from camp and never returned. That left the two brothers entirely alone, and as ammunition was running low the later comer decided to return home and get the necessary supplies. We hardly know which to admire most, the courage of the man who would face the perils of that return journey by himself, or the fortitude of the other who remained alone in that wild country, infested by his enemies, where for three months he constantly shifted his camp to avoid discovery. From his own account of this part of his life we find, however, that those days which he passed alone in the wild woods of Kentucky, depending upon his own skill and vigilance, eluding his enemies and tracking his game, were far from being the least pleasant in his life. After three months Squire Boone returned, and together the brothers pursued their calling once more, until finally, with a very thorough knowledge of the country and its capabilities, Daniel Boone returned to his family in North Carolina.

Boone's account of what he had seen, of the game, the fertility of the country, the beauty of the mountains and rivers, and of all that had so impressed his own imagination, is said to have set North Carolina on fire.

DEATH OF JOHN STEUART, BOONE'S FAITHFUL COMPANION.

And now, while the discoverer is preparing for still another start, we may explain the purpose of these several expeditions. As we have said, Kentucky,— that is, the southern part of it,—nominally belonged to the Cherokee Indians. It was claimed by Virginia and North Carolina and afterwards by Tennessee. A noted character of the day, Colonel Henderson, with several other gentlemen, concerted a scheme for the purchase of all that country from the Cherokees and the founding of an independent State or Republic, which should be called Transylvania. There is hardly a question that Boone's first expedition to

Kentucky and long sojourn there was undertaken in the employ of Colonel Henderson and his Land Company.

The second journey was unquestionably for the purpose of negotiating with the Cherokees, and making all the preliminary arrangements for the purchase of the tract. If his report of the nature of the land induced the formation of the Company, he was no less successful in conducting the second part of the business. When he had arranged terms with the Cherokees, Colonel Henderson joined him on the Watauga to conclude the bargain. There he met the Indians in solemn conclave, took part in their council, smoked the pipe, and paid in merchandise the purchase-money for Kentucky, receiving from the Indians a deed for the same.

Colonization was next in order, and Boone undertook with a party to open a road from the Holston River to the Kentucky River, and to erect stations or forts. Gathering a party for the purpose, on April 1st they succeeded, after a laborious march through the wilderness, in the course of which they lost several men, in arriving at the spot where Boonesborough now stands. There they fixed their camp and built the foundations for a fort. Near this place was a salt lick. A few days after the commencement of the fort another of the party was killed during an attack by Indians, but after that there was no disturbance for some time. This was the beginning of colonization in Kentucky. It was, of course, commenced under the impression that the Cherokee purchase was good, but the validity of the deed was at once denied by the Governor of North Carolina and also by the Government of Virginia as well as that of Tennessee. Each State, however, granted to the Land Company large tracts of land on the same territory, so that while unsuccessful in founding an independent Republic, Colonel Henderson and his associates became very wealthy. For a long time those who were doing the actual work on the frontier, bearing the hardships and the brunt of battle, did not know that any question had been raised as to the validity of the title under the Indian purchase, and still supposed themselves to be engaged in the founding of a Commonwealth.

A KENTUCKY FORT.

A fort at that day meant a structure of a very primitive kind. Butler, in his History of Kentucky, says: "A fort in those times consisted of pieces of timber sharpened at the ends and firmly lodged in the ground. Rows of these pickets enclosed the desired space which embraced the cabins of the inhabitants. One or more block houses, of superior care and strength, commanding the sides of the ditch, completed the fortifications or stations, as they were called. Generally, the sides of the interior cabins formed the sides of the fort."

About thirty or forty new settlers came to Boonesborough with Colonel Henderson, to whom Boone had written. So far the new-comers were all men. Before long, however, the leader returned for his own family, and others, to **the** number of twenty-six men, four women, and half a dozen boys and girls, accompanied him back through the Cumberland Gap. Before arriving at Boonesborough the little caravan separated, part of them settling at another point, where they built a fort of their own. Mrs. Boone and her daughters were the first white women to arrive at Boonesborough to settle there. Other settlers followed with new colonies, and these began to make Kentucky their home. One of the stations was called Harrod's Old Cabin ; another was Logan. Among the men of prominence were Simon Kenton, John Floyd, Colonel Richard Callaway, and other names that appear again and again in the early annals of the country.

INDIAN CAPTURES.

At the breaking out of the Revolutionary War, the Indians, excited by the British, greatly disturbed and harassed the new settlers, and many of the latter, becoming frightened or discouraged, abandoned the promised land and went back to North Carolina. In 1775 the settlers still kept their faith in the Cherokee purchase, and holding this view, took leases from the Company, established courts of justice, and, through a Convention or Congress which met at Boonesborough made laws and provided for a militia organization. This Convention was the first of its kind ever held in the West.

Among the exciting episodes of the first years in Kentucky was the capture of one of Boone's daughters and two of Callaway's daughters by the Indians. The eldest of these girls was about twenty and the youngest fourteen years of age. They were sitting in a canoe under the trees which overhung the opposite bank of the river. There they were surprised by the Indians and taken away before their friends at the Fort discovered their peril. This happened so near nightfall that pursuit was impossible, but in the morning Boone and Floyd started in pursuit. They surprised the Indians that day as they halted to cook, and killing one or two, drove the rest away. Feeling their own force too weak for pursuit, they were glad to return with the almost heart-broken girls. The account of this, affording, as it did, evidence of the renewed hostility of the savages, induced nearly three hundred people to return to their homes during the next few months.

We cannot follow the fluctuating fortunes of the colonists or give a detailed account, interesting as that would be, of the incidents of border warfare. For a long time Kentucky was not recognized as a free State, and its people not acknowledged as citizens. Virginia still made claim to the territory, and yet when General George Clark was sent as a Representative to the Virginia House his claim was rejected by that party. Failing to receive recognition, Clark labored to obtain the independence of Kentucky as a State. This he finally succeeded in doing, in opposition to Colonel Henderson and others. The formation of Kentucky politically was first as a county of Virginia. It was the bulwark of

Virginia during the Indian troubles, and General Clark was nicknamed the Hannibal of the West.   In 1786 the Virginia Legislature enacted the necessary provisions for permitting Kentucky to assume the position of a separate State on condition that the United States would admit her to the sisterhood, which was accomplished June 1, 1792.

Daniel Boone lost all his Kentucky property through carelessness or ignorance of legal forms, and after the prosperity and growth of the new State was fully assured he went to Virginia to begin life over again.   There he stayed until the accounts brought from Missouri of the rich land and good hunting there aroused his pioneer spirit once more, and he again emigrated to settle in Spanish territory.   He made his home in the Femme Osage district, over which, before long, he became military commander with a commission from the Spanish governor.   Upon the acquisition of Missouri by the United States our backwoodsman again found himself stripped of his property.   The Government under which he had been lately serving had presented him with ten thousand arpents of land (an arpent is eighty-five one-hundredths of an acre) to which he had neglected to secure or record his title.   Through the intervention of the Kentucky Legislature in the Congress of the United States by a strong memorial, Boone was finally put in legal possession of the land.

Only once did the great Kentucky pioneer return to the country that he had explored and settled, where, according to his own account, he had lost so much.   He says: "I may say that I have verified the words of the old Indian who signed Colonel Henderson's deed.   Taking me by the hand at the delivery thereof, 'Brother,' he said, 'we have given you a fine land, but I believe you will have much difficulty in settling it.'   My footsteps have often been marked by blood, and therefore I can truly subscribe to its original name.   Two darling sons and a brother have I lost by savage hands, which have also taken from me forty valuable horses and abundance of cattle.   Many dark and sleepless nights have I been a companion for owls, separated from the cheerful society of men, scorched by the summer's sun and pinched by the winter's cold, an instrument to settle the wilderness."

Boone's death occurred in 1820 at his home in Missouri.   He was then in the eighty-sixth year of his age.

DAVID CROCKETT.

David Crockett, who died the last of those who were defenders of the Alamo in Texas, is one of the picturesque figures in American history.   David, or, as he is familiarly called, "Davy" Crockett was born in 1786, of Irish-American parentage.   His boyhood was spent in his father's cabin in Tennessee, from which he ran away, and, after various vicissitudes, took service with a Quaker, where he remained until his marriage.   Then, after several years of hardship, he moved to

the Elk River country, and when the Creek War broke out he was living near
Winchester, Tennessee. He became well known as an Indian fighter, one of
his earliest services being in 1813, when at Beatty's Spring he was chosen by his
captain to act as a scout with Major Gibson to go into the Creek country and re-
connoitre. On the first day of his journey he lost the Major, but pushed on
with five companions for sixty-five miles into the enemy's country, bringing back
news of an important nature. The garrison was hastily fortified and General

EXPLORING THE ECHO RIVER, MAMMOTH CAVE, KENTUCKY.

Jackson summoned by express. We will not attempt to follow the details of this
war. Crockett saw much vigorous fighting, was present at the burning of an
Indian village (of the horrors of which he tells in his autobiography without
the slightest apparent compunction), acted with Major Russell's "spies," and
when he returned to his Tennessee home had quite a reputation as an Indian
fighter.

After the Creek War Crockett was one of those who tried to bring order out of the chaotic state in which Tennessee society was at that time. His home was among a reckless set, and the organization of a temporary government was imperative. Upon its formation Crockett was made Magistrate. Afterwards he became a member of the Legislature, although one of his biographers states that at this time he could hardly read a newspaper. Later in life he showed the acquisition of more "book learning," and the best account of his life and adventures is found in the autobiography which he left. His early success as a politician was due principally to his qualities of humor, good story-telling, hard sense, and true marksmanship with a rifle, a combination that is sure to win favor among backwoodsmen.

Crockett served in Congress two terms, and won national reputation and popularity as one of the "half horse, half alligator" class. His career in Washington was brought to an end by his quarrel with General Jackson, to whose party he had at first been an adherent. He then cast his lot with those who were battling for Texan independence, and died, as we have already noticed, with Travis and Bowie, at the Alamo.

Equally important with the exploration, settlement, and conquest of Kentucky and the Southwest were the expeditions of those who found a path through the great mountain divide and were the forerunners of those that should afterwards settle the Pacific slope.

LEWIS AND CLARK.

Among the earliest explorers of Rocky Mountain fame were Lewis and Clark, who, in 1804, were sent to command the expedition in search of the headwaters of the Columbia River and to mark its course. General Clark was the brother of George R. Clark, of whom mention has been made in an earlier part of this chapter. The family were from Virginia, but had become identified with the early history of Kentucky, and William Clark was known from his youth as an Indian fighter. At eighteen years of age he was made ensign, and in 1792 became a lieutenant of infantry, being appointed in the following year adjutant and quartermaster. He served on the frontier until 1796, when he resigned on account of ill health and went to reside in St. Louis. Seven years later President Jefferson offered him the rank of second lieutenant of artillery, to assume with Merriwether Lewis the command of the exploring expedition to the Columbia River.

Lieutenant Lewis was also a Virginian, whose first service had been in quelling the whiskey insurrection in Western Pennsylvania, in 1794. Afterward entering the regular army he rose to the rank of captain, was then private secretary to President Jefferson, and so won the President's respect and favor by his superior qualities of mind that he was appointed to the scientific and general command of the expedition of which we have just spoken.

Lewis and Clark left St. Louis in the summer of 1803. They encamped for the winter on the bank of the Mississippi opposite the mouth of the Missouri River. The company included nine Kentuckians, who were used to Indian ways and frontier life, fourteen soldiers, two Canadian boatmen, an interpreter, a hunter, and negro boatman. Besides this, a corporal and guard with nine boatmen, were engaged to accompany the expedition as far as the territory of the Mandans.

The party carried with it the usual goods for trading with the Indians, looking glasses, beads, trinkets, hatchets, etc., and such provision as were necessary for the sustenance of its members. While the greater part of the command embarked in a fleet of three large canoes, the hunters and pack-horses paralleled

THE FAR WEST—YELLOWSTONE NATIONAL PARK.

their course along the shore. In this way, in the spring of 1804, the ascent of the Mississippi was commenced. In June the country of the Osages was reached, then the lands occupied by the Ottawa tribes, and finally, in the fall, the hunting grounds of the Sioux. Here the leaders of the expedition ordered cabins to be constructed, and camped for the winter among the Mandans, in latitude 27° 21' north. They found in that country plenty of game, buffalo and deer being abundant ; but the weather was intensely cold and the expedition was hardly prepared for the severity of the climate, so that its members suffered greatly.

In April a fresh start was made and they ascended the Missouri, reaching the great falls by June. Here they named the tributary waters and ascended the Northernmost, which they called the Jefferson River, until further navigation was impossible ; then Captain Lewis with three companions left the expedition in camp and started out on foot toward the mountains, in search of the friendly Shoshoné Indians, from whom he expected assistance in his projected journey across the mountains.

A RIVER WHICH RAN TO THE WEST.

On the twelfth of August he discovered the source of the Jefferson River in a defile of the Rocky Mountains and crossed the dividing ridge, upon the other side of which his eyes were gladdened by the discovery of a small rivulet which flowed toward the west. Here was proof irrefutable "that the great backbone of earth" had been passed. The intrepid explorer saw with joy that this little stream danced out toward the setting sun—toward the Pacific Ocean. Meeting a force of Shoshonés and persuading them to accompany him on his return to the main body of the expedition, Captain Lewis sought his companions once more. Captain Clark then went forward to determine their future course, and coming to the river which his companion had discovered he called it the Lewis River.

A number of Indian horses were procured from their red-skinned friends and the explorers pushed on to the broad plains of the western slope. The latter part of their progress in the mountains had been slow and painful, because of the early fall of snow, but the plains presented all the charm of early autumn. In October the Kaskaskia River was reached, and leaving the horses and whatever baggage could be dispensed with in charge of the Indians, the command embarked in canoes and descended to the Columbia River, upon the south bank of which, four hundred miles from their starting point, they passed the second winter. Much of the return journey was a fight with hostile Indians, and the way was much more difficult than it had been found while advancing toward the West. Lewis was wounded before reaching home, by the accidental discharge of a gun in the hands of one of his force.

Finally, after an absence of two years, the expedition returned, the leaders reaching Washington while Congress was in session, and grants of land were immediately made to them and to their subordinates. Captain Lewis was rewarded also with the governorship of Missouri. Clark was appointed briga-

FREMONT, THE GREAT PATHFINDER, ADDRESSING THE INDIANS AT FORT LARAMIE.

145

dier general for the territory of upper Louisiana, and in 1813 was appointed governor of Missouri, holding office till that territory became a state, after which he retired into private life till 1822, when Mr. Monroe made him Superintendent of Indian Affairs, which office he successfully filled until his death. Lewis's end was a sad one. An inherited tendency to melancholia developed itself and led him, after a long and useful career, to take his own life.

THE FAR WEST—GYSER, YELLOWSTONE NATIONAL PARK, IDAHO AND MONTANA.

Of later, though not less fame, were the successors of Lewis and Clark in the exploration of the Rocky Mountains and the plains beyond. We refer to General Fremont and his famous scout, Kit Carson. It may be said without exaggeration that in all human probability the reputation achieved by the young lieutenant and his subordinate in the South Pass was based upon a love adventure.

When in 1840 General Fremont was a second lieutenant, he was called to Washington, and while there met and fell in love with Jessie, the daughter of Thomas H. Benton. Colonel Benton liked the young Lieutenant, but thought that a fifteen-year-old daughter was altogether too young to contract an engagement, and failing in other efforts, he is thought to have procured the imperative order from the War Department which sent Fremont to explore the Rocky Mountains. Colonel Benton's influence at that time was paramount in Washington. The duty assigned was finished by Lieutenant Fremont, perhaps more speedily than would have been the case under other circumstances, and upon his return the lovers were secretly married; but the love for adventure and exploration had been fully kindled, and a plan was forming in the brain of the future Pathfinder to explore the whole Western country, to study its topography, facilities, etc. As a part of this general scheme he was ordered, at his own request, to make a geographical survey of the Rocky Mountains, especially the South Pass.

While engaged in this work the explorer met Kit Carson, a professional hunter and trapper, who had been for eight years regular hunter for Bent's Fort. Fremont at once engaged him as hunter and scout. Many of those who are inclined to detract from the reputation belonging to the former have averred that the credit of the discoveries made was mainly due to Carson; but a knowledge of the fact that barometric observations, topographical data, and other scientific records beyond Carson's capacity were made, and not only so, but excited the admiration and attention of foreign as well as American authorities, shows such a charge to be without foundation. Yet the fame of the subsequent candidate for the Presidency will always be linked with that of the humbler companion whose

SHAWANGH, THE UTE CHIEF WHO WAS SENT TO WASHINGTON IN 1863 TO TREAT WITH THE UNITED STATES GOVERNMENT.

knowledge of the frontier made so much success possible.

Carson was sent to Washington as a bearer of dispatches in 1847, and there received an appointment as lieutenant in the United States Rifle Corps. He was afterward appointed Indian agent, a post for which his experience admirably fitted him.

Of other Western explorers, discoverers, and pioneers we have not space to speak in this chapter. We have sketched the lives and deeds of a few of the more prominent only, indicating how the West was opened for the march of the millions that have come after. We honor the brave men who risked everything and sacrificed everything to open the way, and cannot but believe, in the words of Daniel Boone, that they were " instruments to settle the wilderness."

VOLCANIC REEFS OF ARIZONA.

The Burning of Washington City and the Story of the War of 1812.

By their first war with Great Britain our forefathers asserted and maintained their right to independent national existence; by their second war with Great Britain they claimed and obtained equal consideration in international affairs. The War of 1812 was not based on a single cause; it was rather undertaken from mixed motives—partly political, partly commercial, partly patriotic. It was always unpopular with a great number of the American people; it was far from logical in some of its positions; it was perhaps precipitated by party clamor. But, despite all these facts, it remains true that this war established once for all the position of the United States as an equal power among the powers.

The cause of the War of 1812, which appealed most strongly to the patriotic feelings of the common people (though the violation of the principle of the rights of neutrals was the prime cause), was unquestionably the impressment by Great Britain of sailors from American ships. No doubt great numbers of English sailors did desert from their naval vessels and take refuge in the easier service and better treatment of the American merchant ships. Great Britain was straining every nerve to strengthen her already powerful navy, and the press-gang was constantly at work in English sea-ports. Once on board a British man-of-war, the impressed sailor was subject to overwork, bad rations, and the lash. That British sailors fought as gallantly as they did under this régime will always remain a wonder. But it is certain that they deserted in considerable numbers, and that they found in the rapidly-growing commercial prosperity of our carrying trade a tempting chance of employment. Now, Great Britain, with a large contempt for the naval weakness of the United States, assumed, rather than claimed, the right to stop our merchant vessels on the high seas, to examine the crews, and to claim as her own any British sailors among them. This was bad enough in itself, but the way in which the search was carried out was worse. Every form of insolence and overbearing was exhibited. The pretense of claiming British deserters covered what was sometimes barefaced and outrageous kidnaping of Americans. The British officers went so far as to lay the burden of proof of nationality in each case upon the sailor himself; if he were without papers proving his identity he was at once assumed to be a British subject. To such an extent was this insult to our flag carried that our Government had the record of about forty-five hundred cases of impressment from our ships between the years of 1803 and 1810; and when the War of 1812 broke out the number of American sailors serving against their will in British war vessels was variously computed to be from six to fourteen thousand. It is even recorded that in some cases American ships were obliged to return home in the middle of their voyages because their crews had been so diminished in number by the seizures made by British officers that they were too short-handed to proceed. In not a few cases these depredations led to bloodshed. The greatest outrage of all, and one which stirred the blood of Americans to the fighting point, was the capture of an American war vessel, the "Chesapeake," by the British man-of-war, the "Leopard." The latter was by far the more powerful vessel, and the "Chesapeake" was quite unprepared for action; nevertheless, her commander refused to accede to a demand that his crew be overhauled in search for British deserters. Thereupon the "Leopard" poured broadside after broadside into her until the flag was struck. Three Americans were killed and eighteen wounded; four were taken away as alleged deserters; of these, three were afterwards returned, while in one case the charge was satisfactorily proved and the man was hanged. The whole affair was without the slightest justification under the law of nations and was in itself ample ground for war. Great Britain, however, in a quite ungraceful and tardy way, apologized and offered reparation. This incident took place six years before the actual declaration of war. But the outrage rankled all that time, and nothing did more to fan the anti-British feeling which was already so strong in the rank and file, especially in the Democratic (or, as it was often called then, Republican) party. It was such deeds as this that led Henry Clay to exclaim, "Not content with seizing upon all our property which falls within her rapacious grasp, the personal rights of our countrymen—rights which must forever be sacred—are trampled on and violated by the impressment of our seamen. What are we to gain by war? What are we not to lose by peace? Commerce, character, a nation's best treasure, honor!"

VIEW OF A COTTON-CHUTE.

considered blockaded, whereupon Napoleon, not to be outdone, declared the entire Islands of Great Britain to be under blockade. Up to a certain point the interruption of the neutral trade relations between the countries of Europe was to the commercial advantage of America. Our carrying trade grew and prospered wonderfully. Much of this trade consisted in taking goods from the colonies of European nations, bringing them to the United States, then trans-shipping them and conveying them to the parent nation. This was allowable under the international law of the time, although the direct carrying of goods by the neutral ship from the colony to the parent nation (the latter, of course, being at war) was forbidden. But by her famous "Orders in Council" Great Britain absolutely forbade this system of trans-shipment as to nations with whom she was at war. American vessels engaged in this form of trade were seized and condemned by English prize courts. Naturally, France followed Great Britain's example and even went further. Our merchants, who had actually been earning double freights under the old system, now found that their commerce was wofully restricted. At first it was thought that the unfair restriction might be punished by retaliatory measures, and a quite illogical analogy was drawn from the effect produced on Great Britain before the Revolution by the refusal of the colonies to receive goods on which a tax had been imposed. So President Jefferson's Administration resorted to the most unwise measure that could be thought of—an absolute embargo on our own ships. This measure was passed in 1807, and its immediate result was to reduce the exports of the country from nearly fifty million dollars' worth to nine million dollars' worth in a single year. This was evidently anything but profitable, and the act was changed so as to forbid only commercial intercourse with Great Britain and France and their colonies, with a proviso that the law should be abandoned as regards either of these countries which should repeal its objectionable decrees. The French Government moved in the matter first, but only conditionally. Our non-intercourse act, however, was after 1810 in force only against Great Britain. That our claims of wrong were equally or nearly equally as great against France in this matter cannot be doubted. But the popular feeling was stronger against Great Britain; a war with England was popular with the mass of the Democrats; and it was the refusal of England to finally accept our conditions which led to the declaration of war. By a curious chain of circumstances it happened, however, that between the time when Congress declared war (June 18, 1812) and the date when the news of this declaration was received in England, the latter country had already revoked her famous "orders in council." In point of fact, President Madison was very reluctant to declare war, though the Federalists always took great pleasure in speaking of this as "Mr. Madison's war." The Federalists throughout considered the war unnecessary and the result of partisan feeling and unreasonable prejudice.

It is peculiarly grateful to American pride that this war, undertaken in defense of our maritime interests and to uphold the honor of our flag upon the high seas, resulted in a series of naval victories brilliant in the extreme. It was not, indeed, at first thought that this would be chiefly a naval war. President Madison was at one time greatly inclined to keep strictly in port our war vessels; but, happily, other counsels prevailed. The disparity between the American and British navies was certainly disheartening. The United States had

seven or eight frigates and a few sloops, brigs, and gunboats, while the sails of
England's navy whitened every sea, and her ships certainly outnumbered ours
by fifty to one. On the other hand, her hands were tied to a great extent by the
European wars of magnitude in which she was involved. She had to defend her
commerce from formidable enemies in many seas, and could give but a small
part of her naval strength to the new foe. That this new foe was despised by

LOADING A COTTON STEAMER.

the great power which claimed, not without reason, to be the mistress of the seas
was not unnatural. But soon we find a lament raised in Parliament about the
reverses, "which English officers and English sailors had not before been used
to, and that from such a contemptible navy as that of America had always been
held." The fact is that the restriction of our commerce had made it possible for
our navy officers to take their pick of a remarkably fine body of native American
seamen, naturally brave and intelligent, and thoroughly well trained in all sea-

manlike experiences. These men were in many instances filled with a spirit of resentment at British insolence, having either themselves been the victims of the aggressions which we have described, or having seen their friends compelled to submit to these insolent acts. The very smallness of our navy, too, was in a measure its strength; the competition for active service among those bearing commissions was great, and there was never any trouble in finding officers of proved sagacity and courage.

At the outset, however, the policy determined on by the Administration was not one of naval aggression. It was decided to attack England from her Canadian colonies. This plan of campaign, however reasonable it might seem to a strategist, failed wretchedly in execution. The first year of the war, so far as regards the land campaigns, showed nothing but reverses and fiascoes. There was a long and thinly settled border country, in which our slender forces struggled to hold their own against the barbarous Indian onslaughts, making futile expeditions across the border into Canada and resisting with some success the similar expeditions by the Canadian troops. It was one of the complaints which led to the war that the Indian tribes had been incited against our settlers by the Canadian authorities and had been promised aid from Canada. It is certain that after war was declared English officers not only employed Indians as their allies, but in some instances, at least, paid bounties for the scalps of American settlers. The Indian war planned by Tecumseh had just been put down by General, afterward President, Harrison. No doubt Tecumseh was a man of more elevated ambition and more humane instincts than one often finds in an Indian chief. His hope to unite the tribes and to drive the whites out of his country has a certain nobility of purpose and breadth of view. But this scheme had failed, and the Indian warriors, still inflamed for war, were only too eager to assist the Canadian forces in a desultory but bloody border war. The strength of our campaign against Canada was dissipated in an attempt to hold Fort Wayne, Fort Harrison, and other garrisons against Indian attacks. Still more disappointing was the complete failure of the attempt, under the command of General Hull, to advance from Detroit as an outpost, into Canada. He was easily driven back to Detroit, and when the nation was confidently waiting to hear of a bold defense of that place it was startled by the news of Hull's surrender without firing a gun, and under circumstances which seemed to indicate either cowardice or treachery. Hull was, in fact, court-martialed, condemned to death, and only pardoned on account of his services in the war of 1776.

The mortification that followed the land campaign of 1812 was forgotten in joy at the splendid naval victories of that year. Pre-eminent among these was the famous sea-duel between the frigates "Constitution" and "Guerrière." Every one knows of the glory of "Old Ironsides," and this, though the greatest, was only one of many victories by which the name of the "Constitution" became the most famed and beloved of all that have been associated with American ships. She was a fine frigate, carrying forty-four guns, and though English journals had ridiculed her as "a bunch of pine boards under a bit of striped bunting," it was not long before they were busily engaged in trying to prove that she was too large a vessel to be properly called a frigate, and that she greatly out-classed her opponent in metal and

BURNING OF WASHINGTON.

men. It is true that the "Constitution" carried six more guns and a few more men than the "Guerrière," but, all allowances being made, her victory was yet a naval triumph of the first magnitude. Captain Isaac Hull, who commanded her, had just before the engagement proved his superior

amanship by escaping from a whole squadron of British vessels, out-sailing d out-manœuvring them at every point. It was on August 19 when he descried the "Guerrière." Both vessels at once cleared for action and came together with the greatest eagerness on both sides for the engagement. Though the battle lasted but half an hour, it was one of the hottest in naval annals. At one time the "Constitution" was on fire, and both ships were soon seriously crippled by injury to their spars. Attempts to board each other were thwarted on both sides by the close fire of small arms. Here, as in later sea-fights of this war, the accuracy and skill of the American gunners were something marvelous. At the end of half an hour the "Guerrière" had lost both mainmast and foremast and floated helplessly in the open sea. Her surrender was no discredit to her officers, as she was almost in a sinking condition. It was hopeless to attempt to tow her into port, and Captain Hull transferred his prisoners to his own vessel and set fire to his prize. In the fight the American frigate had only seven men killed and an equal number wounded, while the British vessel had as many as seventy-nine men killed or wounded. The conduct of the American seamen was throughout gallant in the highest degree. Captain Hull put it on record that "From the smallest boy in the ship to the oldest seaman not a look of fear was seen. They all went into action giving three cheers and requesting to be laid close alongside the enemy." The effect of this victory in both America and England was extraordinary. English papers long refused to believe in the possibility of the well-proved facts, while in America the whole country joined in a triumphal shout of joy, and loaded well-deserved honors on vessel, captain, officers, and men.

The chagrin of the English public at the unexpected result of this sea battle was changed to amazement when one after another there followed no less than six combats of the same duel-like character, in which the American vessels were invariably victorious. The first was between our sloop, the "Wasp," and the English brig, the "Frolic," which was convoying a fleet of merchantmen. The fight was one of the most desperate in the war; the two ships were brought so close together that their gunners could touch the sides of the opposing vessels with their rammers. Broadside after broadside was poured into the "Frolic" by the "Wasp," which obtained the superior position, but her sailors, unable to await the victory which was sure to come from the continued raking of the enemy's vessel, rushed upon her decks without orders and soon overpowered her. Again the British loss in killed and wounded was large; that of the Americans very small. It in no wise detracted from the glory of this victory that both victor and prize were soon captured by a British man-of-war of immensely superior strength. Following this action, Commodore Stephen Decatur, in our frigate, the "United States," attacked the "Macedonian," a British vessel of the same kind, and easily defeated her, bringing her into New York harbor on New Year's Day, 1813, where he received an ovation equal to that offered Captain Hull. The same result followed the attack of the "Constitution," now under the command

f Commodore Bain-
'Java;" the latter had her
bout one hundred wound-
hat it was decided to blow
ion" suffered so little that
ronsides," a name now
een in every school-boy's
esulted, in the great ma-
jority of cases in the same
vay—in all unstinted
raise was awarded by the

bridge, upon the English
captain and fifty men killed and
ed, and was left such a wreck
her up, while the "Constitu-
she was in sport dubbed "Old
ennobled by a poem which has
mouth. Other naval combats

STATUE OF COMMODORE PERRY.

whole world, even including
England herself, to the admirable seamanship, the wonderful
gunnery, and the constant personal intrepitude of our naval
forces. When the second year
of the war closed our little navy

had captured twenty-six war-ships, armed with 560 guns, while it had lost only seven ships, carrying 119 guns.

But, if the highest honors of the war were thus won by our navy, the most serious injury materially to Great Britain was in the devastation of her commerce by American privateers. No less than two hundred and fifty of these sea guerrillas were afloat, and in the first year of the war they captured over three hundred merchant vessels, sometimes even attacking and overcoming the smaller class of war-ships. The privateers were usually schooners armed with a few small guns, but carrying one long cannon mounted on a swivel so that it could be turned to any point of the horizon, and familiarly known as Long Tom. Of course, the crews were influenced by greed as well as by patriotism. Privateering is a somewhat doubtful mode of warfare at the best; but international law permits it; and though it is hard to dissociate from it a certain odor, as of legalized piracy, it is legitimate to this day. And surely if it were ever justifiable it was at that time. As Jefferson said, there were then tens of thousands of seamen forced by war from their natural means of support and useless to their country in any other way, while by "licensing private armed vessels the whole naval force of the nation was truly brought to bear on the foe." The havoc wrought on British trade was widespread indeed; altogether between fifteen hundred and two thousand prizes were taken by the privateers. To compute the value of these prizes is impossible, but some idea may be gained from the single fact that one privateer, the "Yankee," in a cruise of less than two months captured five brigs and four schooners with cargoes valued at over half a million dollars. The men engaged in this form of warfare were bold to recklessness, and their exploits have furnished many a tale to American writers of romance.

The naval combats thus far mentioned were almost always of single vessels. For battles of fleets we must turn from the salt water to the fresh, from the ocean to the great lakes. The control of the waters of Lake Erie, Lake Ontario, and Lake Champlain was obviously of vast importance, in view of the continued land-fighting in the West and of the attempted invasion of Canada and the threatened counter-invasions. The British had the great advantage of being able to reach the lakes by the St. Lawrence, while our lake navies had to be constructed after the war began. One such little navy had been built at Presque Isle, now Erie, on Lake Erie. It comprised two brigs of twenty guns and several schooners and gunboats. It must be remembered that everything but the lumber needed for the vessels had to be brought through the forests by land from the eastern seaports, and the mere problem of transportation was a serious one. When finished, the fleet was put in command of Oliver Hazard Perry. Watching his time (and, it is said, taking advantage of the carelessness of the

British commander in going on shore to dinner one Sunday, when he should have been watching Perry's movements), the American commander drew his fleet over the bar which had protected it while in harbor from the onslaughts of the British fleet. To get the brigs over this bar was a work of time and great difficulty; an attack at that hour by the British would certainly have ended in the total destruction of the fleet. Once accomplished, Perry, in his flagship, the "Lawrence," headed a fleet of ten vessels, fifty-five guns, and four hundred men. Opposed to him was Captain Barclay with six ships, sixty-five guns, and also

VIEW ON LAKE ONTARIO.

about four hundred men. The British for several weeks avoided the conflict, but in the end were cornered and forced to fight. It was at the beginning of this battle that Perry displayed the flag bearing Lawrence's famous dying words, "Don't give up the ship!" No less famous is his dispatch announcing the result in the words, "We have met the enemy and they are ours." The victory was indeed a complete and decisive one; all six of the enemy's ships were captured, and their loss was nearly double that of Perry's forces. The complete control of Lake Erie was assured; that of Lake Ontario had already been gained by Commodore Chauncey.

Perry's memorable victory opened the way for important land operations by General Harrison, who now marched from Detroit with the design of invading Canada. He engaged with Proctor's mingled body of British troops and Indians, and by the Battle of the Thames drove back the British from that part of Canada and restored matters to the position in which they stood before Hull's deplorable surrender of Detroit—and, indeed, of all Michigan—to the British. In this battle of the Thames the Indian chief, Tecumseh, fell, and about three hundred of the British and Indians were killed on the field. The hold of our enemies on the Indian tribes was greatly broken by this defeat. Previous to this the land campaigns had been marked by a succession of minor victories and defeats. In the West a force of Americans under General Winchester had been captured at the River Raisin; and there took place an atrocious massacre of large numbers of prisoners by the Indians, who were quite beyond restraint from their white allies. On the other hand, the Americans had captured the city of York, now Toronto, though at the cost of their leader, General Pike, who, with two hundred of his men, was destroyed by the explosion of a magazine. Fort George had also been captured by the Americans and an attack on Sackett's Harbor had been gallantly repulsed. Following the battle of the Thames, extensive operations of an aggressive kind had been planned looking toward the capture of Montreal and the invasion of Canada by way of Lakes Ontario and Champlain. Unhappily, jealousy between the American Generals Wilkinson and Hampton resulted in a lack of concert in their military operations, and the expedition was a complete fiasco.

One turns for consolation from the mortifying record of Wilkinson's expedition to the story of the continuous successes which had accompanied the naval operations of 1813. Captain Lawrence, in the "Hornet," won a complete victory over the English brig "Peacock;" our brig, the "Enterprise," captured the "Boxer," and other equally welcome victories were reported. One distinct defeat had marred the record—that of our fine brig, the "Chesapeake," commanded by Captain Lawrence, which had been captured after one of the most hard-fought contests of the war by the British brig, the "Shannon." Lawrence himself fell mortally wounded, exclaiming as he was carried away, "Tell the men not to give up the ship but fight her till she sinks." It was a paraphrase of this exclamation which Perry used as a rallying signal in the battle on Lake Erie. Despite his one defeat, Captain Lawrence's fame as a gallant seaman and high-minded patriot was untarnished, and his death was more deplored throughout the country than was the loss of his ship.

In the latter part of the war England was enabled to send large reinforcements both to her army and navy engaged in the American campaigns. Events in Europe seemed in 1814 to insure peace for at least a time. Napoleon's power was broken; the Emperor himself was exiled at Elba; and Great Britain at last

BATTLE OF MOBILE BAY, AUGUST 5TH, 1864

ATTACK ON CHARLESTON, AUGUST 23d TO SEPTEMBER 29, 1863

After a mongly kept in frail in front of Fort Sumter, at a distance varying from a third to half a mile. This placed them in direct range of our heavy guns, which concentrated their appalling fire upon them, the tools following our attacks to rapidly as to be notorized as such it

had her hands free. But before the reinforcements reached this country, our army had won greater credit and had shown more military skill by far than were evinced in its earlier operations. Along the line of the Niagara River active

WEATHERSFORD AND GENERAL JACKSON.

fighting had been going on. In the battle of Chippewa, the capture of Fort Erie, the engagement at Lundy's Lane, and the defense of Fort Erie the troops, under the command of Winfield Scott and General Brown, had held their own, and more, against superior forces, and had won from British officers the admission that they fought as well under fire as regular troops. More encouraging still was the total defeat of the plan of invasion from Canada undertaken by the now greatly strengthened British forces. These numbered twelve thousand men and were supported by a fleet on Lake Champlain. Their operations were directed against Plattsburg, and in the battle on the lake, usually called by the name of that town, the American flotilla under the command of Commodore Macdonough completely routed the British fleet. As a result the English army also beat a rapid and undignified retreat to Canada. This was the last important engagement to take place in the North.

Meanwhile expeditions of considerable size were directed by the British against our principal Southern cities. One of these brought General Ross with five thousand men, chiefly the pick of the Duke of Wellington's army, into the Bay of Chesapeake. Nothing was more discreditable in the military strategy of our Administration than the fact that at this time Washington was left unprotected, though in evident danger. General Ross marched straight upon the Capital, easily defeated at Bladensburg an inferior force of raw militia—who yet fought with intrepidity for the most part—seized the city, and carried out his intention of destroying the public buildings and a great part of the town. Most of the public archives had been removed. Ross' conduct in the burning of Washington was probably within the limits of legitimate warfare but has been condemned as semi-barbarous by many writers. The achievement gave great joy to the English papers, but was really of less importance than was supposed. Washington at that time was a straggling town of only eight thousand inhabitants; its public buildings were not at all adequate to the demands of the future; and an optimist might even consider the destruction of the old city as a public benefit, for it enabled Congress to adopt the plans which have since led to the making of perhaps the most beautiful city of the country.

A similar attempt upon Baltimore was less successful. The people of that city made a brave defense and hastily threw up extensive fortifications. In the end the British fleet, after a severe bombardment of Fort McHenry, were driven off. The British Admiral had boasted that Fort McHenry would yield in a few hours; and two days after, when its flag was still flying, Francis S. Key was inspired by its sight to compose the "Star Spangled Banner."

A still larger expedition of British troops landed on the Louisiana coast and marched to the attack of New Orleans. Here General Andrew Jackson was in command. He had already distinguished himself in this war by putting down with a strong hand the hostile Creek Indians of the then Spanish territory of Florida, who had been incited by English envoys to warfare against our Southern settlers; and in April, 1814, William Weathersford, the half-breed chief, had surrendered in person to Jackson (see illustration). General Packenham, who commanded the five thousand British soldiers sent against

New Orleans, expected as easy a victory as that of General Ross at Washington. But Jackson had summoned to his aid the stalwart frontiersmen of Kentucky and Tennessee—men used from boyhood to the rifle, and who made up what was in effect a splendid force of sharp-shooters. Both armies threw up rough fortifications; General Jackson made great use for that purpose of cotton bales, Packenham employing the still less solid material of sugar barrels. Oddly enough, the final battle, and really the most important of the war, took place after the treaty of peace between the two countries had already been signed. The British were repulsed again and again in persistent and gallant attacks on our fortifications. General Packenham himself was killed, together with many officers and seven hundred of his men. One British officer pushed to the top of our earthworks and demanded their surrender, whereupon he was smilingly asked to look behind him, and turning saw, as he afterward said, that the men he supposed to be supporting him "had vanished as if the earth had swallowed them up." The American losses were inconsiderable.

The treaty of peace, signed at Ghent, December 24, 1814, has been ridiculed because it contained no positive agreement as to many of the questions in dispute. Not a word did it say about the impressment of American sailors or the rights of neutral ships. Its chief stipulations were the mutual restoration of territory and the appointing of a commission to determine our northern boundary line. The truth is that both nations were tired of the war; the circumstances that had led to England's aggressions no longer existed; both countries were suffering enormous commercial loss to no avail; and, above all, the United States had emphatically justified by its deeds its claim to an equal place in the council of nations. Politically and materially, further warfare was illogical. If the two nations had understood each other better in the first place; if Great Britain had treated our demands with courtesy and justice instead of insolence; if, in short, international comity had taken the place of international ill-temper, the war might have been avoided altogether. Its undoubted benefits to us were incidental rather than direct. But though not formally recognized by treaty, the rights of American seamen and of American ships were in fact no longer infringed upon by Great Britain.

One political outcome of the war must not be overlooked. The New England Federalists had opposed it from the beginning, had naturally fretted at their loss of commerce, and had bitterly upbraided the Democratic administration for currying popularity by a war carried on mainly at New England's expense. When in the latter days of the war New England ports were closed, Stonington bombarded, Castine in Maine seized, and serious depredations threatened everywhere along the northeastern coast, the Federalists complained that the administration taxed them for the war but did not protect them. The outcome of all this discontent was the Hartford Convention. In point of fact it was a quite harmless conference which proposed some constitutional amendments, protested against too great centralization of power, and urged the desirability of peace with honor. But the most absurd rumors were prevalent about its intentions ; a regiment of troops was actually sent to Hartford to anticipate treasonable outbreaks ; and for many years good Democrats religiously believed that there had been a plot to set up a monarchy in New England with the Duke of Kent as king. Harmless as it was, the Hartford Convention proved the death of the Federalist party. Its mild debates were distorted into secret conclaves plotting treason, and, though the news of peace followed close upon it, the Convention was long an object of opprobrium and a political bugbear.

A PLANTER'S HOUSE IN GEORGIA.

The Story of the Indian from the Coming of the White Man to the Present Time.

BY HONORABLE HENRY L. DAWES,

Chairman Committee on Indian Affairs, United States Senate.

INDIAN MOTHER AND INFANT.

At the time when our forefathers first landed on these shores, they found the Indian here. Whether at Plymouth or Jamestown, at the mouth of the Hudson or in Florida, their first welcome was from the red man. To him the country belonged, and from him the white man secured it, sometimes by form of purchase, sometimes as conqueror, more often by the simpler process of taking possession as a settler. For the most part the Indian acquiesced at first. The white man and his ways were new and strange and somewhat fearful to the child of the forest, and it seemed best to propitiate so formidable an antagonist. But the early settlers were men of blood and iron, and both in theory and practice their tender mercies were cruel. On the part of the settlers the Indian was everywhere so treated that friendship turned to enmity, and on both sides fear became an ally of hate. Now and then a leader, broader minded than his fellows, like Standish or John Smith, met the red man with justice, and cemented bonds that stood the strain of battle; but at the beginning, as truly as to-day, the white settler coveted land and pushed the Indian off it that he might dwell thereon in peace. And it must be said that in the seventeenth century he violated no tradition, set himself against no law, human or divine, when he did this. Possession was still the right of the stronger, the world over, and the conquest of new countries the chief glory of king and commons alike. To flee away from oppression was the only refuge, and to oppressor as well as oppressed it seemed a natural resort. The country was broad enough for both, thought the white man. If the red man could not live with the new comers on the coast, let him fly to the fresh wilderness of the interior; and so he did, year after year, until one day there was no more wilderness. Then the nation

OLD MISSION INDIAN OF SOUTHERN CALIFORNIA.

which in the nineteenth century still kept up the habits of the seventeenth, found that the weapons of that old time were two-edged; we could not conquer without fighting, nor oppress without revolt; and we learned at last that a new day must have new deeds.

Our early relations with the Indian may be roughly divided into different periods, covering the time from the first landing on our shores until somewhere about 1830; and then again into other periods, from that time until now. In the first or early chapter of our Indian experiences we find the period of discovery, when the savage met the new comer with wonder and welcome, and the invader plundered and enslaved the savage; the colonial period, when the savage had grown wiser and more cunning and waited for knowledge of the settler's purpose before treating with him, sometimes living peaceably by his side, or sometimes uniting in the vain effort to drive him away, but always baffled, defeated and conquered; and the national period, when the Indian was the accepted enemy of the young nation, or temporarily its ally; but always their relations were those of fighting and destruction. From the year 1830 onward, we were dictating the terms of those relations and changing them to suit the mood of the hour. It is necessary, however, to first consider the early relations of the two peoples.

When the Pilgrims landed at Plymouth, in 1620, or Captain John Smith and his followers settled Jamestown, in 1607, they were by no means the first to hold relations with the red men. More than one hundred years had elapsed since Columbus, mistaking our shores for the East Indies, had named the wild inhabitants Indians. In that time one explorer after another had landed on our shores and had taken possession of one tract or another for himself or his king and held it, or forgotten it, as the case might be. But whether French or English, Spanish or Dutch, these men were invariably met with kindness, hospitality, friendship; and invariably they had returned cruelty. The Indians lived in scattered villages in much quiet and friendliness. Game, fish, a few simple vegetables, including maize and wild roots, made up their living. Hospitality to friend and stranger was a duty, and to refuse succor a crime. They were nowise anxious to take on the white man's ways, which seemed to them inferior in all that was manly. Nor was it much wonder, for the new comers deceived and cheated the simple Indian, or when occasion offered—sometimes without—burned his villages, and killed the inhabitants; and never a ship sailed away from the new world without its quota of kidnapped red men, carried over seas for trophies and slaves. The Spanish and Portuguese in the South, under Cortereal and Coronado and De Soto and others, the French and English in the north, under Cartier and Cabot and their companions, all came on the same search for gold, and all treated the Indian after the same fashion.

When the year 1600 came in, it beheld a new era in America—the era of settlement—the day of homes and villages, and the new question arose whether the two races could live together in peace and quietness. All the experience of the past was against it in the long memory of the red man. In North Carolina, Sir Walter Raleigh's romantic experiment at colonizing Roanoke Island had come to nothing, and left behind it the memory of an unprovoked and treacherous massacre by the suspicious English. Yet notwithstanding this, the Indian still tried the vain experiment of kindness. When in 1607 a colony appeared at Jamestown, the great warrior Powhatan, whose realms had been invaded by the Carolina colony, "kindly entertained" the Englishmen, feeding them with bread and berries and fish, while his people danced for their entertainment. Shortly becoming convinced, however, that the English occupation boded ill for his people, finding that "the rights of the Indian were little respected, and the English did not disdain to appropriate by conquest the soil, the cabins, and the granaries of the tribe of the Appomattox," Powhatan determined to protect his people, and strove in every way to dispossess the English. The skill and courage of the redoubtable Captain John Smith were too much for him, and an outward peace was maintained, although with some difficulty, by that warrior. At one time Captain Smith was himself taken prisoner and his life threatened, and the romantic story is told that his life was preserved by the Princess Pocahontas. It is more probable, however, that he owed his life to his native wit, although such a rescue had been the happy fate of a much earlier explorer years before. The beautiful Pocahontas married John Rolfe, and thus helped greatly to bind together the colonists and the Indians. But even this outward kindliness was not of long duration, for the death of Powhatan was shortly followed by a dreadful massacre of the whites, and for twenty years both races in that region rivaled each other in destruction.

T MASSASOIT AND HIS NEPHEW
(from a print after the painting by William Verelst)

In New England the story was much the same. Before the Pilgrims reached New England the Indians of Maine had suffered much, and the name of the Englishman was already feared and hated. Thus it was that a shower of arrows was the first welcome Massachusetts gave the white man. But a few months later an Indian, Samoset, walked into Plymouth, saying, "Welcome, Englishmen!" and was the first of a group of famous red men who became the friends of the settlers. Squanto, Hobamok, Massasoit, Canonicus, Uncas, Miantonomah, are names well known to New England annals, names of great warriors most of them, men who kept faith with their allies. But as time went on, and the inevitable results of the new occupation appeared, the Indians grew more and more unwilling to give up their lands, and now and again made a brave stand for their own. Then occurred awful wars, bloody and terrible as only savage wars could be, complicated oftentimes by the jealousies and hereditary enmities of the different tribes. Thus if Miantonomah and the Narragansetts were friendly to the settler, Uncas and his Mohicans were their enemies. Early in sixteen hundred, Sassacus and the proud tribe of the Pequots made an unavailing attempt to destroy the invader, and were utterly exterminated. It is hard to tell which were the more barbarous, the colonists or the Indians; alike they burned defenseless villages, alike they murdered women and children. Fifty years later one of the greatest of all the Indian warriors, King

"DONT GIVE UP THE SHIP"

Capt. Lawrence, War of 1812

THE "OREGON," A TYPE OF THE MODERN BATTLESHIP

One of the most renowned ships of the American Navy is the mighty Battleship "Oregon." Her famous run from San Francisco around Cape Horn to take part in the Battle of Santiago has never been equalled by any battleship in the world's history. After she won fame in this development of Cervera's fleet she was ordered to Manila for political reasons "for political reasons" and remained there through the Philippine War

Philip, made one more last effort for his country. For a year and a half he kept the English at bay, appearing and reappearing all over Massachusetts, Rhode Island, and Connecticut, fighting with musket and fire as well as with tomahawk and scalping-knife, brave beyond the telling, and as cruel. The colonists suffered untold horrors, and the Indian endured still more, for in the end he saw his power depart and his race disappear from the soil he had loved so long.

Meanwhile in New York and west of it, the great confederated tribes of the Iroquois or the "Six Nations" ruled over all the surrounding country. Northward to Quebec, southward to Maryland, westward to Illinois and Michigan, they controlled the tributary tribes, and by their political ability, their courage

AN OLD INDIAN FARM HOUSE.

and their power, they daily established themselves more and more firmly. Mohawks, Onondagas, Cayugas, Oneidas, Senecas and Tuscaroras, they founded a federation or league, and with an elaborate polity and much advancement in the arts of life, with strong towns and stockaded forts, they thought themselves invincible. The towns were well fortified, and their palisades proved sure defenses even against the dreaded powder and balls. For more than a hundred years the Iroquois fought the French in Canada, or defended themselves against the French invasions in New York. The fingers of a single hand will suffice for the victories of the white man, yet in the end the Iroquois were so weakened and decimated by Frontenac, that their power was broken. Partly they owed this result, however, to the extraordinary diplomatic ability of the chief of the Hurons, their hereditary enemies, who with the skill of a Talleyrand so manipulated both French and Indians as to greatly prolong the war.

In Pennsylvania alone was there peace. Coming over in the last half of the seventeenth century, William Penn brought with him Quaker principles and Quaker methods. For the first time in the history of our dealings with the aborigines we not only began with justice but maintained it. Penn bought the land with much merchandise, and thereafter held the red man as of one blood with the white man. There were neither wars nor massacres, and in the dark

COURTSHIP AMONG THE INDIANS.

story of the Indian this treaty shines with the light of righteousness. On the Pacific coast, too, was a brief brightness. There Sir Francis Drake landed in the "fair and good bay" of San Francisco, in 1579, and so won the hearts of the natives that they made him king, and wept sore for his departure; but this was only an episode, and not the long test of daily contact which the Pennsylvania Quakers bore so serenely. Other and smaller points of light there were; stars in the dark night. It was not until 1528 that any man remembered that these savages had souls, but thereafter there were never wanting brave and holy priests who dared unknown dangers and endured all things to teach here and there a few. Franciscans, Dominicans, and Jesuits, equaled each other in labors and martyrdoms in Florida and New Mexico, while the story of the Jesuits in the North and West is the very romance of heroism. The grants under which the Protestant English took possession of their lands had much to say of the noble work of bringing civilization and Christianity to the "infidels and savages living in these parts," and Virginia early made some efforts to establish schools and induce "the children of those barbarians" to learn the "elements of literature" and "the Christian religion," but we hear little of practical results until the day when that apostle to the red men, John Eliot, first taught the Indians of Massachusetts and Connecticut. For thirty years he

BURYING THE SACRED PLUME-STICKS IN THE OCEAN—A CURIOUS RELIGIOUS CEREMONY.

lived among them and taught them to read, to work, to pray. He gave them a Bible in their own tongue, and amid labors many and perils more, he and his faithful follower, Thomas Mayhew, gathered from among those hunted and fighting savages six Indian churches, whose more than a thousand "praying Indians" once and again stood firm against fearful odds, and became a bulwark of safety to their pale-faced neighbors.

While the colonists were growing strong in the North, and circumstances were speedily to change the Indian problem, the red men of the South were beginning a career unusual in our annals, since it continues in unbroken sequence unto this day. The Indian has gone from New England and the middle West;

the great league of the Iroquois survives only in the legal privileges still accorded the poor remnants of the Six Nations ; the warrior of the plains has hardly a link with Powhatan or Pontiac ; but the Cherokee and the Seminole are still Indian nations, and still treat with us and still keep to their proud isolation, as their forefathers did. Cherokees, Chickasaws, Seminoles, Creeks and Choctaws, in the early days they spread over the South from the hills of Carolina to the plains of Texas. The Spaniards found them there and so did the French. The Choctaws joined themselves to the French to massacre and exterminate their neighbors, the splendid Natchez ; the Chickasaws beat back the invading Frenchmen allied with the Choctaws, and owned no masters. The Cherokees met the friendship of Gov. Oglethorpe in Georgia with like fidelity and friendship, but met treachery and blood in the Carolinas with like treachery and blood, until much fighting and many troops were spent in conquering them. The Creeks and Seminoles kept proud state along the Ohio, in Georgia and in Florida, and during the vicissitudes of their northern brethren, their lives went on more nearly as of old than was possible in the North.

The wars between France and England for the possession of the New World in America, brought about new conditions for the Indian. It is no longer conflicts between separate tribes and their white neighbors we have to consider, but battles which were part of a larger plan and attacks inspired from a different motive. The chronicle becomes no longer so much the story of great chiefs, and struggles for tribal existence, but the Indians "were tossed upon the bayonets of the contending parties, courted no allies, used as scourges, and at all times disdained as equals." For nearly fifty years the French and their allies, the Algonquin tribes, made constant and bloody forays all along the English frontier defended by the Iroquois. Through central New York, Massachusetts, southern New Hampshire and Maine, there was no rest to the settler. At any moment the dreaded war-whoop might be heard, and an awful death awaited him, while worse captivity was the certain fate of the women and children. The familiar story of Deerfield, Massachusetts, was a twice-told tale all through this wide and thickly-settled region. A remote little town, it was marked for attack because of its unhappy possession of a church bell intended for an Indian village in Canada. To rescue this bell, the ever-ready Indians joined the French soldiers, and amidst the snows of February, the town was burned to the ground, and one hundred and twelve inhabitants all killed or carried in cruel captivity in the eight weeks' march through the deep snows and bitter cold to Canada. Death brought welcome release to many of the party. Thus did the whole country suffer, and thus did the red man make his name feared above all things else.

The varying fortunes of France and England, constantly brought similar fluctuations to the peace of the New World, in the fifty years before the treaties f Utrecht and Aix la Chapelle; but that famous peace scarcely more than ltered the scene of the fighting on this side the water. English and French like claimed the country west of the Alleghanies, and the French, with their

THE INDIAN'S DECLARATION OF WAR.

ndian allies, lost no time in asserting neir claims and defending their rights.
'hen it was, that in the spring of 1754, one George Washington, the young djutant general of the Virginia militia, scarcely come to his majority, won his purs in the unavailing campaign against Fort Duquesne. For more than five

years the desultory war went on. Braddock's defeat was followed by many another French success, with its horrid accompaniment of savage warfare. Under Montcalm still more of the Indians joined the French, even the Iroquois uniting with the other tribes against the English, and it was not until 1760, that Canada was finally surrendered to the British. At last the harassed colonists hoped for peace, and dreamed that the scalping knife was thrown away.

Shortly enough it proved a vain dream. As the plantations and towns crowded the hunting grounds farther and farther back, it "threw the Indian who had become possessed of habits modified by contact with the whites, upon the tribes living in the ancient manner, and bred tribal jealousies." The fierce struggle between French and English for the possession of the Mississippi Valley, made a new opportunity, and once more a great warrior arose, determined to make a desperate effort to free his people from the white man. We have hardly given enough credit to the military capacity and the genius for governing, of these great chiefs. They played French against English, Spanish against French, tribe against tribe; they conspired, manipulated men and armies, fought or covenanted, with the skill and insight and courage of great commanders. What was known as "Pontiac's War" was in its inception and development a revolution worthy to rank with the great uprisings of the old world. The Indian is always and everywhere possessed of the genius of ruling. State-craft is his birthright equally with wood craft. Pontiac, leader of the Ottawas, Ojibways, and Pottawatomies, inspired by the French to take revenge, and eager to free his people from the hated dominion of the English, dreamed a dream of patriotism. To more than usual ability in many directions, he joined the imperious will and high ambition which mark the conqueror. He had ever been victorious, and he planned on a given day to sweep away the forts and crowd the invader into the sea; and not without a sense of what he was undertaking, he proposed to do this by bringing back the French. All along the Canadian frontier, and in Pennsylvania and Virginia as well, the war raged for more than three years, before the great chief finally surrendered the hope he so cherished, and in 1766 made a reluctant treaty with the English.

The hundred years which closed with the end of the Colonial period had not been altogether without effort to civilize and Christianize the red heathen. In Pennsylvania and Ohio the Moravians had won the hearts and lives of the Delawares until their towns blossomed with peace and prosperity, and the lives of the people gave goodly witness to the faith they professed. Beset by hostile Indians and worse beset by hostile whites, three times they were driven—these Christian Indians—from their beautiful homes into a new wilderness, and practising to the full the doctrine of love and forgiveness, these converted savages made no resistance. At last they were rewarded with the crown of martyrdom, when at Gnaden Huten, without pretext, ninety unresisting and Christian Indians were slaughtered in cold blood by the white men, and no voice of man, woman or child was left to tell the tale. Such instances are in striking contrast with the just dealings of Penn in Pennsylvania. Among the Iroquois the Church of England, the Moravians again, and the Presbyterians made much progress in teaching the children and spreading religion throughout the tribes. From one of their schools arose Hamilton College. In New England too, John Eliot had left worthy successors. The names of Brainard, Jonathan Edwards, Sergeant and

PENN'S RESIDENCE IN SECOND STREET, BELOW CHESTNUT STREET.

Wheelock are known to us still by their labors and their success in teaching the Indian youth; and from both sides the water came the money to carry on their work. It was the last named, Rev. Eleazar Wheelock, whose determination to start a boarding school for his wards resulted in the establishment of Dartmouth College, and among his pupils was the well known Chief of the Mohawks, Joseph Brant, who became such a figure in the Revolutionary War.

When the Colonies finally rebelled against the Mother Country, in 1775, the English had learned much from the French and Indian war as to the military value of the alliance with the Indians. In one way or another they had suc-

THE APACHE CHIEFS, GERONIMO, NATCHEZ.

ceeded in gaining the friendship of most of the tribes. The Iroquois confederation was their natural ally, through its able chief, Joseph Brant, whose sister had

married the famous governor, Sir William Johnson ; and thus the border line was always open to the British. As the French had thrown the Indian upon the settlers in the past, so the English now set their savage allies upon the defenseless towns and unprotected forts. The tomahawk and scalping knife were again the recognized weapons of warfare, and throughout New York and even in Pennsylvania terror was again abroad. It was in this struggle that the famous Seneca, Red Jacket, fought with desperation, and opposed to the last the treaty which buried the hatchet, with such eloquence that twenty-five years later Lafayette still remembered his words. In the Northwest, the French influence happily prevailed to prevent the Indian defection to any great extent, but in Kentucky and West Virginia there was desperate fighting in a sort of guerrilla warfare between the red braves and such backwoodsmen as Daniel Boone. In the South the warlike Creeks made haste to attack the whites, but met with short shrift. Meanwhile the Continental Congress had placed the affairs of the Indians in three departments, under direction of some of its most famous men, and even employed the Indians in its armies. But only an isolated few were actively on the side of the Colonists.

The close of the Revolutionary War brought only a partial cessation of the Indian warfare. The red man was by no means disposed to give up his country without a struggle, and all throughout the interior, in what is now Indiana, Illinois, and Wisconsin, and along the Ohio River, there were constant outbreaks, and battles of great severity. The conflict in Indiana brought forward the services of a young Lieutenant, William Henry Harrison, who for many years had much to do with Indians, both as officer and as Governor of the new Indian Territory. In 1811 appeared another of those great Indian chiefs whose abilities and influence are well worth attention and study. Tecumseh, a mighty warrior of mixed Creek and Shawnee blood, once more dreamt the old dream of freeing his people. With eloquence and courage he urged them on, by skill he combined the tribes in a new alliance, and, encouraged by British influence, he looked forward to a great success. While he sought to draw the Southern Indians into his scheme, his brother rashly joined battle with General Harrison, and was utterly defeated in the fight which gained for Harrison the title of Old Tippecanoe. Disappointed and disheartened at this destruction of his life-work, Tecumseh threw all his great influence on the British side in the War of 1812, where he dealt much destruction to the United States troops. At Sandusky and Detroit and Chicago, and at other less important forts, the Indian power was severely felt ; at Terre Haute the young Captain Zachary Taylor met them with such courage and readiness of resources that they were finally repulsed, but rarely did a similar good fortune befall our troops ; and it was more than a month after Commodore Perry won victory for us at Lake Erie, that Tecumseh himself was killed, and the twenty-five hundred Indians of his force were finally scattered in the great fight of the Thames River, where our troops were commanded by William Henry Harrison and Richard M. Johnson, afterward President and Vice-President of the United States. For a little time the Northwest had peace. But in the South the warfare was not over. Tecumseh had stirred up the Creeks and Seminoles against the whites, and throughout Alabama, Georgia, and Northern Florida the Creek War raged with all its horrid accompaniments until 1815; even the redoubtable Andrew Jackson could not conquer the brave Creeks until they were almost exterminated, and then a small remnant still remained in the swamps of Florida to be heard of at a later time.

Thus ends a brief and hasty chronicle of the American Indians in the early days of our Nation. Thereafter they were a subject race, and a new policy was adopted in which we fixed the terms, and they, rebelling or accepting our decision as it might be, in the end could only submit. But as from the beginning so it has gone on until now; as we pushed the frontier farther back, at every stage the Indian made one more effort for his home and his hunting-grounds.

Let us now consider how the United States has governed the Indian and some of our later difficulties with him. The Indian problem has been a perplexing one for our country. The red man had the first moral right to the land, and in occupying it we felt bound to provide for his maintenance. Before the new Government of the United States was fully upon its feet it recognized the necessity and duty of caring for its Indian population. In 1775, a year before the Declaration of Independence, the Continental Congress divided the Indians into three Departments, Northern, Middle, and Southern, each under the care of three or more Commissioners, among whom we find no less personages than Oliver Wolcott, Philip Schuyler, Patrick Henry, and Benjamin Franklin. As early as 1832 the young nation found itself confronted with an Indian problem, and created a separate Bureau for the charge of the red men, and inaugurated a policy in its treatment of them. Speaking in general, we have altered this policy three times.

As a matter of fact, we have certainly altered its details, changed its plans, and adopted a new point of view as changing Administrations have changed the administrators of our Indian affairs. But in the large, there have been three great steps in our Indian policy, and these have to some extent grown out of our changing conditions. The first plan was that of the reservations. Under that system, as the Indian land was wanted by the white population he was removed across the Mississippi and still further west, pushed step by step beyond and beyond; and as time went on and the population followed hard after, he was confined to designated tracts. It was no matter that these tracts were absolutely guaranteed to him, he was still driven off them again and again as the farmer or the miner demanded the land. In time a new policy was attempted, or, rather, an old policy was revived, that of concentrating the whole body of Indians in one State or Territory, but the obvious impossibility of that scheme soon wrought its own end. Less than twenty years ago the present plan took its place, that of education and eventual absorption.

In 1830 the country seemed to stretch beyond any possible need of the young nation, lusty as it was, and the wide wilderness of the Rocky Mountains to furnish hunting grounds for all time. The Mississippi Valley and the Northwest were still unsettled and uneasy, and in the South the Five Nations were greatly in the way of their white neighbors, and the scheme of removing the red inhabitants beyond the Mississippi was begun. The first removals were, like the last, times of trouble and disturbance, and then, as now, there were two parties in the tribes, those who saw there was no way but submission, and those who indulged the fruitless dream of revolt. Thus the Sac and Fox tribe of Wisconsin was divided, and although Keokuk and one band went peaceably to their new home among the Iowas, Black Hawk and his followers were slow to depart, and were removed by force. The Indian Department failed to furnish corn enough for the new settlement, and going to seek it among the Winnebagoes, the Indians came into collision with the Government. Thereafter ensued a series of misunderstandings, and consequent fights, and great alarm among the whites and the destruction of the Indians. The story is the same story, almost to details, that every year has seen from that day to this.

Under President Monroe several treaties were made with the Five Nations, by which, one after another, they ceded their Southern lands to the Government, and took in exchange the country now known as the Indian Territory. They were already far advanced in civilization, with leaders combining in blood and brain the Indian astuteness and the white man's experience and education. John Ross, a half-breed chief of the Cherokees, of extraordinary ability, brought about the removal under conditions more favorable than often occurred. He was bitterly opposed by full half the Indians, and it was not without sufferings and losses of more than one kind that the great Southern league was removed to the fair and fertile land they had chosen in the far-off West. It was owing to the sagacity of John Ross and his associates that this land was secured to them, as no other land has ever been secured to any Indian tribe. They hold it to-day by patent, as secure in the sight of the law as an old Dutch manor house or Virginia plantation, and all the learning of the highest tribunals has not yet found the way to evade or disregard these solemn obligations. To these men, too, and to the missionaries who had long taught these tribes, do they owe an elaborate and effective civilization, and a governmental polity which preserves for them alone, among all their red brethren, the title and the state of nations. The Seminoles, who were of the Creek blood, were divided, some of them going west with their brethren,

some of them, the larger part, remaining in Florida. With these, about four thousand in all, under Osceola, the Government fought a seven years' war, costing forty millions of dollars and untold lives. After like fashion have all our "removals" proceeded, and from like causes—the greed of the white man and the ferocity of the outraged Indian. It is useless and impossible to give the details of all the various tribes that have been pushed about, hither and yon. In 1830 the East was already crowding toward the West, and every decade saw the frontier moved onward with giant strides. Everywhere the Indian was an undesirable neighbor, and when, in 1849, the discovery of gold began to create a new nation on the Pacific slope, a pressure began from that side also, and the intervening deserts became a thoroughfare for the pilgrims of fortune and the many lovers of adventure. From year to year the United States made fresh

treaties with the innumerable tribes ; those in the East were gone already, those in the interior were following fast, and there had arisen the new necessity of dealing with those in the far West. One tribe after another would be planted on a reservation millions of acres in extent and apparently far beyond the home of civilization, and almost in a twelvemonth the settler would be upon its border demanding its broad acres. The reservations were altered, reduced, taken away altogether, at the pleasure of the Government, with little regard to the rights or wishes of the Indian. Usually this brought about fighting, and it produced a state of permanent discontent that wrought harm for both settler and savage. The Indian grew daily more and more treacherous and constantly more cruel. The white settler was daily in greater danger, and constantly more full of revenge.

PEDRO PINO, PALU'AH ISALELA, FORMERLY GOVERNOR OF ZUNI FOR THIRTY YEARS.

A new complication entered into the problem. The game was fast disappearing, and therewith the life of the Indian. It became necessary for the Government to furnish rations and clothes, lest he starve and freeze. Cheating was the rule and deception the every-day experience of these savages. In 1795 General Wayne gained the nickname of General To-morrow, so slow was the Government to fulfill his promises ; and thus for more than a hundred years it has always been to-morrow for the Indian. Exasperated beyond endurance, he was ever ready to retaliate, and the horrors of an Indian war constantly hung over the pioneer. During all this period we treated these Indians as if they were foreign nations, and made solemn treaties with them, agreeing to furnish them rations or marking the reservation bounds. We have made more than a thousand of these treaties, and General Sherman is the authority for the statement that we have broken every one ourselves. Day by day the gluttonous idleness, the loss of hope and future, the sense of wrong, and the bitter feeling of contempt united to degrade the red man as well as to madden him. The fighting did not cease, for all the promises or the threats of the Government. But always, it is credibly declared, the first cause of an Indian outbreak has been a wrong suffered. And always, in these latter days as in the earlier period, it has meant one more effort on the part of the old warriors to regain

the power they saw slipping away so fast. Both these causes entered into the awful Sioux War in Minnesota in 1862. Suffering from piled-up wrongs, smarting under the loss of power, and conscious that the Civil War was their opportunity, a party of one hundred and fifty Sioux began the most horrid massacre of the last fifty years; the beginning of a struggle which lasted more than a year, which was remarkable for the steadfast fidelity of the Christian Indians, to whose help and succor whole bodies of white men owed their lives. Four years later, in 1866, the discovery of gold in Montana caused the invasion of the Sioux reservation,

KON-IT'L, AN INDIAN CHIEF.

and Red Cloud set about defending it. Scarcely more than thirty years old, but no mean warrior, he fought the white man long and desperately and with the cunning of his race. This outbreak was scarcely quieted when another occurred. As was its wont, the Government forgot the promises of its treaty of peace, and a small band of the Cheyennes retaliated with a raid upon their white neighbors. General Sheridan made this the occasion he was seeking for a war of extermination, and in November, 1868, Lieutenant Custer fell upon Black Kettle's village and after a severe fight destroyed the village, killing more than a hundred warriors and capturing half as many women and children. The next year General Sheridan ordered the Sioux and Cheyennes off the hunting grounds the treaty had reserved to them, but these were the strongest and bravest of the tribes and they resisted the order. A list of heroes, Crook, Terry, Custer, Miles, and McKenzie, led our troops, and among the chiefs whom they met in a long and desperate struggle were Crazy Horse and Spotted Tail, notable warriors both. At the battle of the Big Horn, by some misunderstanding or mismanagement General Custer was left with only five companies to meet nearly three thousand savage Sioux. He fought desperately until the last but he himself was killed, and so utterly was his command destroyed that not a single man was left alive. The attempt to remove the Modocs from California to Oregon in 1872 was the signal for a new war; and a year or two afterward similar results followed when it was attempted to push the Nez Perces from the homes they had sought in Oregon to a new reservation in Idaho. This tribe under their famous leader, Chief Joseph, were hard to conquer. Their military organization, their civilized method of warfare, their courage and skill, were publicly complimented by General Sherman and General Howard and General Gibbons, who declared Chief Joseph to be one of the greatest of modern warriors.

In 1877, discouraged at all our efforts to hold the Indians in check, it was determined by Secretary Schurz, then in charge of the Department of the Interior, to remove them all to the western part of the Indian Territory, where the Five Nations would cede the necessary land, and there create an Indian State. Great trouble arose from the attempt to carry out this well-meant, but impossible, effort. A single story, the story of the Northern Cheyennes, will illustrate the wrongs the Indian suffered as well as those he inflicted. The Cheyennes, as has been seen, were a tribe of great warriors, some of them at home in the hills of the North, some in the hills of the South. Cheyennes and Arapahoes, Kiowas and Comanches, were banded together in a close and common bond, and at first the friends of the Government, had become frequently its enemies, by reason of broken faith, cruel treatment, injustice, and downright wrong. That chronicle of misery, "A Century of Dishonor," contains forty pages of facts taken from the Government records, which relate the inexcusable and indefensible treatment of this tribe by the Government and the vain effort for endurance of the Cheyennes, interspersed with frequent savage outbreaks when human nature could endure no longer. It includes the account of a massacre of helpless Indian women and children under a flag of truce; a war begun over ponies stolen from the Indians and sold in the open market by the whites in a land where the horse thief counts with the murderer; another incited by rage against a trader who paid one-dollar bills for ten-dollar bills; and tells of whole tracts of land seized without compensation by the United States itself. The Northern Cheyennes had been taken by force to the Indian Territory, and in its awful heat, with scant and poor rations, a pestilence came on. Two thousand were sick at once, and many died because there was not medicine enough. At last three hundred braves, old men and young, with their women and children, broke away and, making a raid through Western Kansas, sought their Nebraska home. This was not a mild and peaceable tribe. It was fierce and savage beyond most, and they were wild with long endured injustice and frantic with a nameless terror. Three times they drove back the troops who were sent to face them, and, living by plunder, they made a red trail all through Kansas, until they were finally captured in Nebraska in December. They refused to go back to the Indian Territory, and the Department ordered them starved into submission. Food and fuel were taken from those imprisoned Indians. Four days they had neither food nor fire—and the mercury froze at Fort Robinson in that month! And when at last two chiefs came out under a flag of truce, they were seized and imprisoned. Then pandemonium broke loose inside. The Indians broke up the useless stoves, and fought with the twisted iron. They brought out a few hidden arms, and howling like devils they rushed out into the night and the snow. Seven days later they were shot down like dogs.

Experiences like this soon ended the attempt to gather together all our Indian wards, and we returned to the old plan of the reservations, but with little more certainty of peace than before. Again and again starvation was followed by fighting, nameless outrages upon the Indian by cruel outrages upon the white man. Whether Apaches under Geronimo in New Mexico, or Sioux in Dakota, it was the old story over again. Thus with constant danger menacing the white settler from the infuriated and savage Indian, and constant outrage upon the red man by rapacious and cruel whites, the government found a new policy necessary. By a strange and unusual sequence of events this policy was inaugurated. In 1869 a sharp difference arose between the two Houses of Congress over the appropriations to pay for eleven treaties then just negotiated, and the session closed with no appropriation for the Indian service. The necessity for some measure was extreme; the plan was devised of a bill, which was passed at an extra session, putting two millions of dollars in the hands of President Grant, to be used as he saw fit, for the civilization and protection of the Indian. He immediately called to his aid a commission composed of nine philanthropic gentlemen to overlook the affairs of the Indian and advise him thereupon. This Commission served without salary and continues to this day its beneficent work. Another valuable measure resulted. At the next Congress a law was passed forbidding any more treaties with Indians, and thenceforth they became our wards, not our rivals.

The war of 1876 had indirectly another beneficent result of most far-reaching consequences. Among the brave men who had fought the Cheyennes and Kiowas and Comanches, was Captain Richard H. Pratt, who was put in charge of the prisoners sent to Fort Marion, Florida, as a punishment worse than death. They were the wildest and fiercest of warriors, who had fought long and desperately. On their long way to the East they had killed their guard, and repeatedly tried, one and another, to kill themselves. But Captain Pratt was a man of wonderful executive ability, of splendid courage and great faith in God and man. By firmness and patience and wondrous tact he gradually taught them to read and to work, and when after three years the Government offered to return them to their homes, twenty-three refused to go. Captain Pratt appealed to the Government to continue their education, and General Armstrong, with his undying faith in human beings as children of one Father, and with his sublime enthusiasm for humanity, took most of them at Hampton Institute, the rest being sent to the North under the care of Bishop Huntington of New York. In the end these men returned to their tribes Christian men, and with the seventy who returned directly from Florida, every one became a power for peace and industry in his tribe. Out of this small beginning grew the great policy of Indian education, and the long story of death and destruction began to change to the bright chronicle of peace and education.

What, then, is the condition of the Indian to-day? In number there are scarcely more than two hundred and forty thousand in the whole country. Of these less than one-fifth depend upon the Government for support. All told, they are less than the inhabitants of Buffalo or Cleveland or Pittsburgh, but they are *not* dying out, the rather steadily increasing. They are divided and subdivided into multitudinous tribes of different characteristics and widely different degrees of civilization. Some are Sioux—these are brave and able and intelligent ; they live in wigwams or tepees, and are dangerous and often hostile. Some are Zunis, and live in houses and make beautiful pottery, and are mild and peaceable, and do not question the ways of the Great Father at Washington. Some are roving bands of Shoshones, dirty, ignorant, and shiftless—the tramps of their race—who are on every man's side at once. Some are Chilcats or Klinkas, whose Alaskan homes offer new problems of new kinds for every day we know them. And some are Cherokees, living in fine houses, dressed in the latest fashion, and spending their winters in Washington or Saint Louis. Yet these, and many more of many kinds, are all alike Indians. They have their own governments, their own unwritten laws, their own customs. As a race they are neither worthless nor degraded. The Indian is not only brave, strong, able by inheritance and practice to endure beyond belief, but he is patient under wrong, ready and eager to learn, and willing to undergo much privation for that end ; usually affectionate in his family relations, grateful to a degree, pure and careful of the honor of his wife and daughter ; and he is also patriotic to a fault. He has a great genius for government, and an unusual interest in it. He is full of manly honor, and he is supremely religious. His history and traditions are but just now discovered, to the delight and the surprise of scientific students. His daily life is a thing of elaborate ceremonial, and his national existence is as carefully regulated as our own, and by an intricate code. It is true that our failure to comprehend his character and our neglect to study his customs have bred many faults in him and have fostered much evil. Our treatment of him, moreover, has produced and increased a hostility which has been manifested in savage methods for which we have had little mercy. But we have not always given the same admiration to warlike virtues when our enemy was an Indian that we have showered without stint upon ancient Gaul or modern German. The popular idea of the Indian not only misconceives his character, but to a large

UNHORSED—AN INCIDENT OF CUSTER'S FIGHT.

degree his habits also. Even the wildest tribes live for the most part in huts or cabins made of logs, with two windows and a door. In the middle is a fire, sometimes with a stovepipe and sometimes without. Here the food is cooked, mostly stewed, in a kettle hung gypsy-fashion, or laid on stones over the fire. Around this fire, each in a particular place of his own, lies or sits the whole family. Sometimes the cooking is done out of doors, and in summer the close cabin is exchanged for a tepee or tent. Here they live, night and day. At night a blanket is hung up, partitioning the tent for the younger women, and if the family is very large, there are often two tents, in the smaller of which sleep the young girls in charge of an old woman. These tents or cabins are clustered close together, and their inhabitants spend their days smoking, talking, eating, quarreling, as the case may be. Sometimes near them, sometimes miles away, is the agent's house and the Government buildings. These are usually a commissary building where the food for the Indians is kept, a blacksmith shop, the store of the trader, school buildings, and perhaps a saw-mill. To this place the Indians come week by week for their food. The amount and nature of the rations called for by the different treaties vary greatly among different tribes. But everywhere the Indian has come into some sort of contact with the whites, and usually he makes some shift to adopt the white man's ways. A few are rich, some own houses, and almost universally, now, Government schools teach

INDIAN AGENCY.

the children something of the elements of learning as well as the indispensable English.

The immediate control of the reservation Indian is in the hands of the agent, whose power is almost absolute, and, like all despotisms, is very good or intolerable, as the individual character of the man may be. The agencies are inspected from time to time by Inspectors, who report directly to the Commissioner [of Indian Affairs], who in his turn is an officer of the Interior Department and responsible to the Secretary, who is, of course, amenable to the President. In each house of Congress is a committee having charge of all legislation relating to Indian Affairs. Besides these officials there is the Indian Commission already mentioned. The National Indian Rights Association and the Women's National Indian Association are the unofficial and voluntary guardians of the Indian work. It is their task to spread correct information, to create intelligent interest, to set in motion public and private forces which will bring about legislation, and by public meetings and private labors to prevent wrongs against the Indian, and to further good work for him of many kinds. While the Indian Rights Association does the most public and official work for the race and has large influence over legislation, the Women's Indian Association concerns itself more largely with various philanthropic efforts in behalf of the individual, and thus the two bodies supplement each other.

Hopeless and impossible as it seemed twenty years ago to absorb the

Indian, to-day we see the process more than begun and in some cases half accomplished; and in this work the Government, philanthropy, education, religion, have all had their share, and so closely have these walked together that neither can be set above or before the others. We began to realize, it is true, that our duty and our safety alike lay in educating these Indians, as early as 1819, when Congress appropriated $10,000 for that purpose, and still earlier President Washington de-

ATTACK BY MODOCS ON THE PEACE COMMISSIONERS,
APRIL 11, 1873.

clared to a deputation of Indians his belief that industrial education was their greatest need; but it is only within fifteen years that determined efforts have been made or adequate provision afforded. Beginning with $10,000 in 1819, we had reached only $20,000 in 1877; but the appropriation for 1891 for Indian education was $2,291,000. With this money we support thirteen great industrial training schools established at various convenient points, and five more are about to be added. In them nearly 5000 children are learning not only books, but all manner of industries, and are adding to civilization the training of character. There are no less than seventy boarding schools on the various reservations teaching and training as many more of these children of the hills and plains, and half as many gather daily at the one hundred little day schools which dot the prairies, some of them appearing to the uninitiated to be miles away from any habitation. This does not include the more than thirty mission schools of the various Churches. But all together it is hoped that in the excellent Government schools now provided, in the splendid missionary seminaries, and in the great centres of light like Hampton and Carlisle and Haskell Institute, we shall in 1892 do something for the education of nearly or quite two-thirds of all the 30,000 Indian children who can be reached with schools.

The two great training schools at the East, Hampton and Carlisle, have proved object lessons for the white man as well as the Indian, and the opposition they constantly encounter from those who do not believe that the red man can ever receive civilization is in some sort a proof of their value. In the main, they and all their kind have one end—the thorough and careful training in books and work and home life of the Indian boy and girl, and their methods are much alike. Once a year the Superintendents or teachers of these schools go out among the Indians and bring back as many boys and girls as they can persuade the fathers and mothers to send. At first these children came in dirt and filth, and with little or no ideas of any regular or useful life, but of late many of them have learned some beginnings of civilization in the day schools. They are taught English first, and by degrees to make bread and sew and cook and wash and keep house if they are girls ; the trade of a printer, a blacksmith, a carpenter, etc., if they are boys. They study books, the boys are drilled, and from kind, strong men and gentle, patient women they learn to respect work and even to love it, to turn their hands to any needed effort, to adapt themselves to new situations, the meaning of civilization.

It is charged that the Indian educated in these schools does not remain civilized, but shortly returns to his old habits and customs. Can an Indian boy or girl be so far civilized in five years, it is asked, that he will withstand all the forces, personal and social, striving to draw him back to the easy ways of barbarism when he returns to his old associates ? A detailed examination into the lives of three hundred and eighteen Indian students who have gone out from Hampton Institute has shown that only thirty-five have in any way disappointed the expectations of their friends and teachers, and only twelve have failed altogether ; and the extraordinary test of the last Sioux war, in which only one of these students, and he a son-in-law of Sitting Bull, joined the hostiles, may well settle the question.

With the passage of the Severalty Law, in 1887, a new era opened before the Indian. Under it, if he will, there is secured to him and each member of his family a homestead of eighty acres, inalienable and exempt from taxation for twenty-five years. With this homestead comes citizenship and all its privileges and immunities, obligations and opportunities. All these are his, also, without allotment of any land in severalty, whenever he will abandon his tribe and take upon himself the ways of the white man. Nearly twenty thousand

GENERAL GEORGE CROOK

have already since the passage of this law taken their place in the citizenship of the nation. The transition from a state of dependent wards, whose dwelling place and manner of life, whose food and raiment and very being, were controlled by another, into the independence and responsibilities of United States citizenship, has been so sudden, and in some cases without due preparation for so great a change, as to prove a severe test of the manhood in the Indian. There have been failures, but they have been marvelously few, and this way out of barbarism to civilization is becoming plainer and surer every day.

The providing of an inalienable home for the Indian, and citizenship, with all that pertains to that royal title, to all who avail themselves of this grant, has brought along with it the necessity for new laws, almost a new code, for the government and protection of this race. Citizenship, provided in the Severalty Law, by its own force brought every one it reached at once into the same forum and under the same shield as every other citizen of the United States. It also defined and guarded the marriage relation and the descent of property, as well as other domestic relations, hitherto shadowy and but little regarded. But the reservation and wild Indian cannot appeal to this law for protection or assertion of his rights. It has been more difficult to bring him within the pale of legal enactment either for restraint or protection. Yet great progress has been made even here. The judicious expenditure of large appropriations for the education of the Indian has done much to clear the way and make the bringing of this class of Indians under the restraining and civilizing influence of law. It has not always been possible, among savages, to do this in strict conformity with the normal methods pointed out in the Constitution which governs the States and civilized people, but methods have been adopted suited to the conditions of the several tribes, and best adapted to the maintenance of peace, the protection of person and property, and the lesson of restraint which comes from familiarity with the administration of law in its various forms. This has been accomplished to a remarkable degree through the agency of the Indian himself. An Indian police selected from the most trustworthy and efficient Indians, paid and uniformed by the Government, patrol the reservations, preserving the peace and enforcing an observance of law. A "Court of Indian Offenses," presided over by three discreet and influential Indians appointed by and under the constant supervision of the Secretary of the Interior, try and punish those who are charged with the commission of minor offenses; while in the matter of the more serious crimes of murder, arson, robbery, and the like, perpetrated either by or upon an Indian, the offender is by law to be tried and punished in all respects as if both parties were white men. In this way substantial security to person and property prevails upon the reservation.

It has been said that religion and philanthropy and the Government have gone hand in hand in the work of educating the Indian to a new conception of manhood. Without the work done for him by the missionaries, no progress would have been possible. And if some of the work already described has been labeled philanthropic or legislative or educational, it has been as truly missionary work as any done on the frontier, and its motives and many times its methods have been the missionary zeal and the missionary teaching. Captain Pratt was by no means the first man who ever taught an Indian. The saintly Bishop Whipple had lived among the Minnesota Indians for years, and that other saint, Dr. Riggs, had given his life to the Dakotas long before, and a generation had passed since Samuel Wooster suffered in prison for teaching the Cherokees. The Congregationalists at Santee, at Hampton, the Episcopalian Bishop Hare's wonderful schools in Dakota, the Presbyterians in Nebraska and Alaska, the Unitarians among the Crows, the Friends with the Sacs and Foxes in the South, and each of these and others in many other places dotted all over the land, are teaching the Indians of the Great Father, of Him who is the light and life of the world, of the salvation and brotherhood of men; and they are eager to hear it. Our duty and our interest go hand in hand and the pathway is becoming plainer every day.

The irresistible growth of the nation in the increase of its population demanding homes, in the reaching out after every element of wealth and power lying within its utmost confines, is absorbing, with everything else material, the last unoccupied acre of the heritage of the Indian. Shall it also absorb the race itself, and make it part of its citizenship and body politic? Either this, or what is left of the Indian race, two hundred and fifty thousand, must be soon turned out, a homeless, penniless band of wandering, savage tramps, the terror of the land. There is no alternative to this outcome but absorption or extermination. The latter being impossible, the former alone is left us. We have wisely accepted it, and the success which has thus far attended the undertaking to fit the race for absorption attests its wisdom. As an Indian of the old time and character he is fast disappearing, and a new strain of blood, relatively slight and not void of good elements, is being safely injected into national citizenship. If the work be persisted in patiently and kindly it will soon be ended. But it cannot be accomplished by enactment alone, nor, without that, by educational or missionary effort. All these in harmonious endeavor, with self-supporting citizenship as the end in view, bent on the lift, will surely and speedily raise him from the low condition of helpless and aimless and worse than useless barbarism, to the plane where he can, according to the measure of an ever-increasing capacity, contribute to the wealth of citizenship in the land. This is no small labor lightly turned off. It is changing into civilized life the barbarism of centuries. The savage must be inspired with new thoughts and aspirations, and to make room for these the passions and tendencies of ages and generations must be driven out. It is not beginning with the *tabula rasa* of an infant, but with life born and bred a savage life. The infant is to be taught to walk, not only as a white man walks, but to shun the slippery ways toward which all its surroundings, all its blood, and all the life which it inherits are drawing it. It is a great

GENERAL CROOK'S APACHE GUIDE.

THE PEACE COMMISSIONERS

Three commissioners from the Confederacy suggesting terms of Peace to President Lincoln and Secretary Seward at Fortress Monroe, January, 1865

PICKETT'S RETURN FROM HIS FAMOUS CHARGE

undertaking, and will cost much in time and money; but it is also a necessity, and in the end will bring full recompense.

The Indian race is worthy of our deepest interest. Here is a people full of natural pride and bound together in a national feeling much stronger than we ourselves know anything about, crushed down by the power of a Government which seems to them always their enemy but always professing to be their protector; full of despair that sees no hope in the future; perplexed with the present, that seems to their direct ways and simple thought to have no explanation, but is always in some manner to be full of sorrow and trouble; without occupation, with no one to understand their past or care for their heroes and their history; shot down like dogs for disobeying law they do not comprehend, and execrated for the bravery that all men elsewhere are wont to admire; losing at once their children and their customs; these uncomprehended statesmen, these despised knights, this people, who can find no common ground with their destroyers, ask of us at least to know who they are, what they want, why they are as they are, to see where the fault lies, to know what it means when a war arises;—to put ourselves in their place, and at least to pay attention. A tragedy of nations is going on in our midst and we sit calmly by, never giving it even the idle attention of our leisure. And some of the woes of this tragedy are also the birth-pangs of a new nation. If the sorrows of the past and the present do not affect us, let us at least sympathize with the hopes of the present and the future. We are given the unusual privilege to see a nation born in our midst. Out of the darkness of the past, its ignorance, its custom-bound barbarism, its wild and splendid bravery of battle, a nation is coming into the light, is beginning to know knowledge, to feel the freedom of life under law, to show the less splendid but all-requiring bravery of the new manhood, the every-day fortitude of the new womanhood.

EXECUTING NEGROES IN NEW YORK.

The Story of the Black Man in Slavery and in Freedom.

WHEN, over two hundred and seventy years ago (it is in doubt whether the correct date is 1619 or 1620) a few wretched negroes, some say fourteen, some say twenty, were bartered for provisions by the crew of a Dutch man-of-war, then lying off the Virginia coast, it would have seemed incredible that in 1890 the negro population of the Southern States alone should almost reach a total of seven million souls. African negroes had, indeed, been sold into slavery among many nations for perhaps three thousand years; but in its earlier periods slavery was rather the outcome of war than the deliberate subject of trade, and white captives no less than black were ruthlessly thrown into servitude. It has been estimated that in historical times some forty million Africans have been enslaved. The Spaniards found the Indian an intractable slave, and for the arduous labors of colonization soon began to make use of negro slaves, importing them in great numbers and declaring that one negro was worth, as a human beast of burden, four Indians. Soon the English adventurers took up the traffic. It is to Sir John Hawkins, the ardent discoverer, that the English-speaking peoples owe their participation in the slave trade. He has put it on record, as the result of one of his famous voyages, that he found "that negroes were very good merchandise in Hispaniola and might easily be had on the coast of Guinea." For his early adventures of this kind he was roundly taken to task by Queen Elizabeth. But tradition says that he boldly faced her with the argument that the Africans were an inferior race, and ended by convincing the Virgin Queen that the slave trade was not merely a lucrative but a perfectly philanthropic undertaking.

Certain it is that she acquiesced in future slave trading, while her successors, Charles II and James II, chartered four slave trading companies and received a share in their profits. It is noteworthy that both Great Britain and the United States recognized the horrors of the slave trade as regards the seizing and transportation from Africa of the unhappy negroes, long before they could bring themselves to deal with the problem of slavery as a domestic institution. Of those horrors nothing can be said in exaggeration. They exist to-day in the interior of Africa, in no less terrible form than a hundred years ago; and the year 1891 has seen the Great Powers combining in the attempt to eradicate an evil of enormous and growing proportions. The peculiar atrocities attending the exportation of slaves from Africa to other countries have, however, happily become a thing of the past. What those atrocities were even in our day may be judged from one of many accounts given by a no means squeamish or over sensitive sailor, Admiral Hobart. He thus describes the appearance of a slaver just captured by a British ship: "There were four hundred and sixty Africans on board, and what a sight it was! The schooner had been eighty-five days at sea. They were short of water and provisions; three distinct diseases—namely, small-pox, ophthalmia, and diarrhœa in its worst form—had broken out, while coming across, among the poor, doomed wretches. On opening the hold we saw a mass of arms, legs, and bodies, all crushed together. Many of the bodies to whom these limbs belonged were dead or dying. In fact, when we had made some sort of clearance among them we found in that fearful hold eleven bodies lying among the living freight. Water! Water! was the cry. Many of them as soon as free jumped into the sea, partly from the delirious state they were in, partly because they had been told that if taken by the English they would be tortured and eaten."

The institution of slavery, introduced as we have seen into Virginia, grew at first very slowly. Twenty-five years after the first slaves were landed the negro population of the colony was only three hundred. But the conditions of agriculture and of climate were such, that once slavery obtained a fair start, it spread with continually increasing rapidity. We find the Colonial Assembly passing one after another a series of laws defining the condition of the negro slave more and more clearly, and more and more pitilessly. Thus, a distinction was soon made between them and Indians held in servitude. It was enacted, "that all servants not being Christians imported into this colony by shipping, shall be slaves for their lives; but what shall come by land shall serve, if boyes or girles until thirty years of age, if men or women twelve years and no longer." And before the end of the century a long series of laws so encompassed the negro with limitations and prohibitions, that he almost ceased to have any criminal or civil rights and became a mere personal chattel.

In some of the Northern colonies slavery seemed to take root as readily and to flourish as rapidly as in the South. It was only after a considerable time that social and commercial conditions arose which led to its gradual abandonment. In New York a mild type of negro slavery was introduced by the Dutch. The relation of master and slave seems in the period of the Dutch rule, to have been free from great severity or cruelty. After the seizure of the government by the English, however, the institution was officially recognized and even encouraged. The slave trade grew in magnitude; and here

INTRODUCTION OF SLAVERY.

again we find a series of oppressive laws forbidding the meeting of negroes together, laying down penalties for concealing slaves, and the like. In the early years of the eighteenth century fears of insurrection became prevalent, and these fears culminated in 1741 in the episode of the so-called Negro Plot. Very briefly stated, this plot grew out of a succession of fires supposed to have been the work of negro incendiaries. The most astonishing contradictions and self-inculpations

are to be found in the involved mass of testimony taken at the different trials.
It is certain that the perjury and incoherent accusations of these trials can
only be equaled by those of the alleged witches at Salem, or of the famous
Popish plot of Titus Oates. The result is summed up in the bare statement
that in three months one hundred and fifty negroes were imprisoned, of
whom fourteen were burned at the stake, eighteen hanged, and seventy-one
were transported. Another result was the passing of even more stringent
legislation, curtailing the rights and defining the legal status of the slave.
When the Revolution broke out there were not less than fifteen thousand
slaves in New York, a number greatly in excess of that held by any other
Northern colony.

Massachusetts, the home in later days of so many of the most eloquent
abolition agitators, was from the very first, until after the war with Great Britain
was well under way, a stronghold of slavery. The records of 1633 tell of the
fright of Indians who saw a "Blackamoor" in a tree top whom they took for
the devil in person, but who turned out to be an escaped slave. A few years
later the authorities of the colony officially recognized the institution. It is true
that in 1645 the general court of Massachusetts ordered certain kidnapped
negroes to be returned to their native country, but this was not because they
were slaves but because their holders had stolen them away from other masters.
Despite specious arguments to the contrary, it is certain that, to quote Chief
Justice Parsons, "Slavery was introduced into Massachusetts soon after its first
settlement, and was tolerated until the ratification of the present constitution in
1780." The curious may find in ancient Boston newspapers no lack of such
advertisements as that, in 1728, of the sale of "two very likely negro girls"
and of "A likely negro woman of about nineteen years and a child about seven
months of age, to be sold together or apart." A Tory writer before the outbreak of the Revolution, sneers at the Bostonians for their talk about freedom
when they possessed two thousand negro slaves. Even Peter Faneuil, who
built the famous "Cradle of Liberty," was himself, at that very time, actively
engaged in the slave trade. There is some truth in the once common taunt of
the pro-slavery orators that the North imported slaves, the South only bought
them. Certainly there was no more active centre of the slave trade than Bristol Bay, whence cargoes of rum and iron goods were sent to the African coast
and exchanged for human cargoes. These slaves were, however, usually taken,
not to Massachusetts, but to the West Indies or to Virginia. One curious outcome of slavery in Massachusetts was that from the gross superstition of a
negro slave, Tituba, first sprang the hideous delusions of the Salem witchcraft
trials. The negro, it may be here noted, played a not insignificant part in
Massachusetts Revolutionary annals. Of negro blood was Crispus Attucks,
one of the "martyrs" of the Boston riot; it was a negro whose shot killed the

British General Pitcairn at Bunker Hill; and it was a negro also who planned the attack on Percy's supply train.

As with New York and Massachusetts, so with the other colonies. Either slavery was introduced by greedy speculators from abroad or it spread easily from adjoining colonies. In 1776 the slave population of the thirteen colonies was almost exactly half a million, nine-tenths of whom were to be found in the Southern States. In the War of the Revolution the question of arming the negroes raised bitter opposition. In the end a comparatively few were enrolled, and it is admitted that they served faithfully and with courage. Rhode Island even formed a regiment of blacks, and at the siege of Newport and afterwards at Point's Bridge, New York, this body of soldiers fought not only without reproach but with positive heroism.

With the debates preceding the adoption of the present Constitution of the United States the political problem of slavery as a national question began. Under the colonial system the responsibility for the traffic might be charged, with some justice, to the mother country. But from the day when the Declaration of Independence asserted "That all men are created equal, that they are endowed by their Creator with certain inalienable rights ; that among these are life, liberty and the pursuit of happiness," the peoples of the new, self-governing States could not but have seen that with them lay the responsibility. There is ample evidence that the fixing of the popular mind on liberty as an ideal bore results immediately in arousing anti-slavery sentiment. Such sentiment existed in the South as well as in the North. Even North Carolina in 1786 declared the slave trade of "evil consequences and highly impolitic." All the Northern States abolished slavery, beginning with Vermont, in 1777 and ending with New Jersey in 1804. It should be added, however, that many of the Northern slaves were not freed, but sold to the South. As we have already intimated, also, the agricultural and commercial conditions in the North were such as to make slave labor less and less profitable, while in the South the social order of things, agricultural conditions, and the climate, were gradually making it seemingly indispensable.

When the Constitutional debates began the trend of opinion seemed strongly against slavery. Many delegates thought that the evil would die out of itself. One thought the abolition of slavery already rapidly going on and soon to be completed. Another asserted that "slavery in time will not be a speck in our country." Mr. Jefferson, on the other hand, in view of the retention of slavery, declared roundly that he trembled for his country when he remembered that God was just. And John Adams urged again and again that "every measure of prudence ought to be assumed for the eventual total extirpation of slavery from the United States." The obstinate States in the convention were South Carolina and Georgia. Their delegates declared that their States would absolutely refuse ratification to the Constitution unless slavery were recognized. The compromise sections finally agreed upon avoided the use of the words slave and slavery but clearly recognized the institution and even gave the slave States the advantage of sending representatives to Congress on a basis of population determined by adding to the whole number of free persons, "three-fifths of all other persons." The other persons thus referred to were, it is needless to add, negro slaves.

The entire dealing with the question of slavery, at the framing of the Constitution, was a series of compromises. This is seen again in the postponement of forbidding the slave trade from abroad. Some of the Southern States had absolutely declined to listen to any proposition which would restrict their freedom of action in this matter, and they were yielded to so far that Congress was forbidden to make the traffic unlawful before the year 1808. As that time approached, President Jefferson urged Congress to withdraw the country from all "further participation in those violations of human rights which have so long been continued on the unoffending inhabitants of Africa." Such an act was at once adopted, and by it heavy fines were imposed on all persons fitting out vessels for the slave trade and also upon all actually engaged in the trade, while vessels so employed became absolutely forfeited. Twelve years later another act was passed declaring the importation of slaves to be actual piracy. This latter law, however, was of little practical value, as it was not until 1861 that a conviction was obtained under it. Then, at last, when the whole slave question was about to be settled forever, a ship-master was convicted and hanged for piracy in New York for the crime of being engaged in the slave trade. In despite of all laws, however, the trade in slaves was continued secretly, and the profits were so enormous that the risks did not prevent continual attempts to smuggle slaves into the territory of the United States.

The first quarter of a century of our history, after the adoption of the Constitution, was marked by comparative quietude in regard to the future of slavery. In the North, as we have seen, the institution died a natural death, but there was no disposition evinced in the Northern States to interfere with it in the South. The first great battle took place in 1820 over the so-called Missouri Compromise. Now, for the first time, the country was divided, sectionally and in a strictly political way, upon issues which involved the future policy of the United States as to the extension or restriction of slave territory. State after State had been admitted into the Union, but there had been an alternation of slave and free States, so that the political balance was not disturbed. Thus, Virginia was balanced by Kentucky, Tennessee by Ohio, Louisiana by Indiana, and Mississippi by Illinois. The last State admitted had been Alabama, of course as a slaveholding State. Now it was proposed to admit Missouri, and, to still maintain the equality of political power, it was contended that slavery should be

JAMES G. BLAINE   McKINLEY

CLEVELAND   WILLIAM BRYAN

GREAT AMERICAN POLITICAL LEADERS, LAST QUARTER OF THE NINETEENTH CENTURY

ABRAHAM LINCOLN. (1809-1865.)

ULYSSES SIMPSON GRANT. (1822-1885.)

ROBERT EDWARD LEE. (1807-1870.)

WILLIAM T. SHERMAN. (1820-1891.)

THE GREAT LEADERS OF THE CIVIL WAR

prohibited within her borders. But the slave power had by this time acquired great strength, and was deeply impressed with the necessity of establishing itself in the vast territory west of the Mississippi. The Southern States would not tolerate for a moment the proposed prohibition of slavery in the new State of Missouri. On the other hand, the Middle and Eastern States were beginning to be aroused to the danger threatening public peace if slavery were to be allowed indefinite extension. They had believed that the Ordinance of 1787, adopted simultaneously with the Constitution, and which forbade slavery to be established in the territory northwest of the Ohio, had settled this question definitely. A fierce debate was waged through two sessions of Congress, and in the end it was agreed to withdraw the prohibition of slavery in Missouri, but absolutely prohibit it forever in all the territory lying north of 36° 30′ latitude. This was a compromise, satisfactory only because it seemed to dispose of the question of slavery in the territories once and forever. It was carried mainly by the great personal influence of Henry Clay. It did, indeed, dispose of slavery as a matter of national legislative discussion for thirty years.

But this interval was distinctively the period of agitation. Anti-slavery sentiment of a mild type had long existed. The Quakers had, since Revolutionary times held anti-slavery doctrines, had released their own servants from bondage, and had disfellowshiped members who refused to concur in the sacrifice. The very last public act of Benjamin Franklin was the framing of a memorial to Congress deprecating the existence of slavery in a free country. In New York the Manumission Society had been founded in 1785, with John Jay and Alexander Hamilton, in turn, as its presidents. But all the writing and speaking was directed against slavery as an institution and in a general way, and with no tone of aggression. Gradual emancipation or colonization were the only remedies suggested. It was with the founding of the "Liberator" by William Lloyd Garrison, in 1831, that the era of aggressive abolitionism began. Garrison and his society maintained that slavery was a sin against God and man ; that immediate emancipation was a duty ; that slave owners had no claim to compensation ; that all laws upholding slavery were, before God, null and void. Garrison exclaimed : "I am in earnest. I will not equivocate—I will not excuse—I will not retreat a single inch. And I will be heard." His paper bore conspicuously the motto "No union with slaveholders." The Abolitionists were, in numbers, a feeble band ; as a party they never acquired strength, nor were their tenets adopted strictly by any political party ; but they served the purpose of arousing the conscience of the nation. They were abused, vilified, mobbed, all but killed. Garrison was dragged through the streets of Boston with a rope around his neck—through those very streets which, in 1854, had their shops closed and hung in black, with flags Union down and a huge coffin suspended in mid-air, on the day when the fugitive slave, Anthony Burns, was marched through them on his way back to his master, under a guard of nearly two thousand men. Mr. Garrison's society soon took the ground that the union of States with slavery retained was "an agreement with hell and a covenant with death," and openly advocated secession of the non-slaveholding States. On this issue the Abolitionists split into two branches, and those who threw off Garrison's lead maintained that there was power enough under the Constitution to do away with slavery. To the fierce invective and constant agitation of Garrison were in time, added the splendid oratory of Wendell Phillips, the economic arguments of Horace Greeley, the wise statesmanship of Charles Sumner, the fervid writ-

A COTTON FIELD IN GEORGIA.

ings of Channing and Emerson, and the noble poetry of Whittier. All these and others, in varied ways and from different points of view, joined in educating the public opinion of the North to see that the permanent existence of slavery was incompatible with that of a free Republic.

In the South, meanwhile, the institution was intrenching itself more and more firmly. The invention of the cotton-gin and the beginning of the reign of Cotton as King made the great plantation system a seeming commercial necessity. From the deprecatory and half apologetic utterances of early Southern statesmen we come to Mr. Calhoun's declaration that slavery "now preserves in quiet and security more than six and a half million human beings, and that it could not be destroyed without destroying the peace and prosperity of nearly half the States in the Union." The Abolitionists were regarded in the South with the bitterest hatred. Attempts were even made to compel the Northern States to silence the anti-slavery orators, to prohibit the circulation through the mail of anti-slavery speeches, and to refuse a hearing in Congress to anti-slavery petitions. The influence of the South was still dominant in the North. Though the feeling against slavery spread, there co-existed with it the belief that an open quarrel with the South meant commercial ruin ; and the anti-slavery sentiment was also neutralized by the nobler feeling that the Union must be preserved at all hazards, and that there was no constitutional mode of interfering with the slave system. The annexation of Texas was a distinct gain to the slave power, and the Mexican war was undertaken, said John Quincy Adams, in order that "the slaveholding power in the Government shall be secured and riveted."

The actual condition of the negro over whom such a strife was being waged differed materially in different parts of the South, and under masters of different character, in the same locality. It had its side of cruelty, oppression, and atrocity ; it had also its side of kindness on the part of master and of devotion on the part of slave. Its dark side has been made familiar to readers by such books as " Uncle Tom's Cabin," as Dickens' " American Notes," and as Edmund Kirk's "Among the Pines ;" its brighter side has been charmingly depicted in the stories of Thomas Nelson Page, of Joel Chandler Harris, and of Harry Edwards. On the great cotton plantations of Mississippi and Alabama the slave was often overtaxed and harshly treated ; in the domestic life of Virginia, on the other hand, he was as a rule most kindly used, and often a relation of deep affection sprang up between him and his master. Of insurrections, such as those not uncommon in the West Indies, only one of any extent was ever planned in our slave territory—that of Nat Turner, in Southampton County, Virginia—and that was instantly suppressed.

With this state of public feeling North and South, it was with increased bitterness and increased sectionalism that the subject of slavery in new States was again debated in the Congress of 1850. The Liberty Party, which held that slavery might be abolished under the Constitution, had been merged in the Free Soil Party, whose cardinal principle was, "To secure free soil to a free people " without interfering with slavery in existing States, but insisting on its exclusion from territory so far free. The proposed admission of California was not affected by the Missouri Compromise. Its status as a future free or slave State was the turning point of the famous debates in the Senate of 1850, in which Webster, Calhoun, Douglas and Seward won fame—debates which have never been equaled in our history in eloquence and acerbity. It was in the course of these debates that Mr. Seward, while denying that the Constitution recognized property in man, struck out his famous dictum, "There is a higher law than the Constitution." The end reached was a compromise which allowed California to settle for itself the question of slavery, forbade the slave trade in the District of Columbia, but enacted a strict fugitive slave law. To the Abolitionists this fugitive slave law, sustained in its most extreme measures by the courts in the famous—or as they called it, infamous—Dred Scott case, was as fuel to fire. They defied it in every possible way. The Underground Railway was the outcome of this defiance. By it a chain of secret stations was

A NEGRO VILLAGE IN ALABAMA.

established, from one to the other of which the slave was guided at night until at last he reached the Canada border. The most used of these routes in the East was from Baltimore to New York, thence north through New England; that most employed in the West was from Cincinnati to Detroit. It has been estimated that not fewer than thirty thousand slaves were thus assisted to freedom.

Soon the struggle was changed to another part of the Western territory, now beginning to grow so rapidly as to demand the forming of new States. The Kansas-Nebraska Bill introduced by Douglas was in effect the repeal of the

Missouri Compromise in that it left the question as to whether slavery should be carried into the new territories to the decision of the settlers themselves. As a consequence immigration was directed by both the anti-slavery and the pro-slavery parties to Kansas, each determined on obtaining a majority to control the form of the proposed State Constitution. Then began a series of acts of violence which almost amounted to civil war. "Bleeding Kansas" became a phrase in almost every one's mouth. Border ruffians swaggered at the polls and attempted to drive out the assisted emigrants sent to Kansas by the Abolition societies. The result of the election of the Legislature on its face made Kansas a slave State, but a great part of the people refused to accept this result; and a convention was held at Topeka which resolved that Kansas should be free even if the laws formed by the Legislature should have to be "resisted to a bloody issue."

Prominent among the armed supporters of free State ideas in Kansas was Captain John Brown, a man whose watchword was at all times Action. "Talk," he said, "is a national institution: but it does no good for the slave." He believed that slavery could only be coped with by armed force. His theory was that the way to make free men of slaves was for the slaves themselves to resist any attempt to coerce them by their masters. He was undoubtedly a fanatic in that he did not stop to measure probabilities or to take account of the written law. His attempt at Harper's Ferry was without reasonable hope, and as the intended beginning of a great military movement was a ridiculous fiasco. But there was that about the man that none could call ridiculous. Rash and unreasoning as his action seemed, he was yet, even by his enemies, recognized as a man of unswerving conscience, of high ideals, of deep belief in the brotherhood of mankind. His offense against law and peace was cheerfully paid for by his death and that of others near and dear to him. Almost no one at that day could be found to applaud his plot, but the incident had an effect on the minds of the people altogether out of proportion to its intrinsic character. More and more as time went on he became recognized as a pro-martyr of a cause which could be achieved only by the most complete self-sacrifice of individuals.

Events of vast importance to the future of the negro in America now hurried fast upon each other's footsteps—the final settlement of the Kansas dispute by its becoming a free State; the forming and rapid growth of the Republican party; the division of the Democratic party into Northern and Southern factions; the election of Abraham Lincoln; the secession of South Carolina, and, finally, the greatest civil war the world has known. Though that war would never have been waged were it not for the negro, and though his fate was inevitably involved in its result, it must be remembered that it was not undertaken on his account. Before the struggle began Mr. Lincoln said: "If there be those who would not save the Union unless they could at the same time save slavery. I do not agree with them. If there be those who would not save the Union unless they could at the same time destroy slavery, I do not agree with them. My paramount object is to save the Union, and not either to destroy or to save slavery." And the Northern press emphasized over and over again the fact that this was "a white man's war." But the logic of events is inexorable. It seems amazing now that Union generals should have been puzzled as to the question whether they ought in duty to return runaway slaves to their masters. General Butler settled the controversy by one happy phrase when he called the fugitives "contraband of war." Soon it was deemed right

EARLY HOME OF ABRAHAM LINCOLN, GENTRYVILLE, INDIANA.

to use these contrabands, to employ the new-coined word, as the South was using the negroes still in bondage, to aid in the non-fighting work of the army —on fortification, team driving, cooking, and so on. From this it was but a step, though a step not taken without much perturbation, to employ them as soldiers. At Vicksburg, at Fort Pillow, and in many another battle, the negro showed beyond dispute that he could fight for his liberty. No fiercer or braver charge was made in the war than that upon the parapet of Fort Wagner by Colonel Shaw's gallant colored regiment, the Massachusetts Fifty-fourth.

In a thousand ways the negro figures in the history of the war. In its literature he everywhere stands out picturesquely. He sought the flag with the greatest avidity for freedom; flocking in crowds, old men and young, women and children, sometimes with quaint odds and ends of personal belongings, often empty-handed, always enthusiastic and hopeful, almost always densely ignorant of the meaning of freedom and of self support. But while the negro showed this avidity for liberty, his conduct toward his old masters was often generous, and almost never did he seize the opportunity to inflict vengeance for his past wrongs. The eloquent Southern orator and writer, Henry W. Grady, said: "History has no parallel to the faith kept by the negro in the South during the war. Often five hundred negroes to a single white man, and yet through these dusky throngs the women and children walked in safety and the unprotected homes rested in peace. . . A thousand torches would have disbanded every Southern army, but not one was lighted."

It was with conditions, and only after great hesitation, that the final step of emancipating the slaves was taken by President Lincoln in September, 1862. The proclamation was distinctly a war measure, but its reception by the North and by the foreign powers and its immediate effect upon the contest were such that its expediency was at once recognized. Thereafter there was possible no question as to the personal freedom of the negro in the United States of America. With the Confederacy, slavery went down once and forever. In the so-called reconstruction period which followed, the negro suffered almost as much from the over-zeal of his political friends as from the prejudice of his old masters. A negro writer, who is a historian of his race, has declared that the Government gave the negro the statute book when he should have had the spelling book; that it placed him in the legislature when he ought to have been in the school house, and that, so to speak, "the heels were put where the brains ought to have been." A quarter of a century and more has passed since that turbulent period began, and if the negro has become less prominent as a political factor, all the more for that reason has he been advancing steadily though slowly in the requisites of citizenship. He has learned that he must, by force of circumstances, turn his attention, for the time at least, rather to educational, industrial, and material progress than to political ambition. And the record of his advance on these lines is promising and hopeful. In Mississippi alone, for instance, the negroes own one-fifth of the entire property in the State. In all, the negroes of the South to-day possess two hundred and fifty million dollars' worth of property. Everywhere throughout the South white men and negroes may be found working together.

At the beginning of the war the negro population of the country was about four millions, to-day it is between seven and seven and a-half millions; in 1880, fifteen-sixteenths of the whole colored population belonged to the Southern States, and the census of 1890 shows that the proportion has not greatly changed.

This ratio in itself shows how absurdly trifling in results have been all the movements toward colonization or emigration to Northern States. The negro emphatically belongs to the Southern States, and in them and by them his future must be determined. Another point decided conclusively by the census of 1890 is seen in the refutation of an idea based, indeed, on the census of 1880, but due in its origin to the very faulty census of 1870. This idea was that the colored population had increased much more rapidly in proportion than the white population. The new census shows, on the contrary, that the whites in the Southern States increased during the last decade nearly twice as rapidly as the negroes, or, as the census bulletin puts it, in increase of population, " the colored race has not held its own against the white man in a region where the climate and conditions are, of all those which the country affords, the best suited to its development."

The promise of the negro race to-day is not so much in the development of men of exceptional talent, such as Frederick Douglas or Senator Bruce, as in the general spread of intelligence and knowledge. The Southern States have very generally given the negro equal educational opportunities with the whites, while the eagerness of the race to learn is shown in the recently ascertained fact that while the colored population has increased only twenty-seven per cent. the enrollment in the colored schools has increased one hundred and thirty-seven per cent. Fifty industrial schools are crowded by the colored youth of the South. Institutions of higher education, like the Atlanta University, and Hampton Institute of Virginia, and Tuskegee College, are doing admirable work in turning out hundreds of negroes fitted to educate their own race. Within a year or two honors and scholarships have been taken by half a dozen colored young men at Harvard, at Cornell, at Phillips Academy and at other Northern schools and colleges of the highest rank. The fact that a young negro, Mr. Morgan, was in 1890 elected by his classmates at Harvard as the class orator has a special significance. Yet there is greater significance, as a negro newspaper man writes, in the fact that the equatorial telescope now used by the Lawrence University of Wisconsin was made entirely by colored pupils in the School of Mechanical Arts of Nashville, Tenn. In other words, the Afro-American is finding his place as an intelligent worker, a property owner, and an independent citizen, rather than as an agitator, a politician or a race advocate. In religion, superstition and effusive sentiment are giving way to stricter morality. In educational matters, ambition for the high-sounding and the abstract is giving place to practical and industrial acquirements. It will be many years before the character of the negro, for centuries dwarfed and distorted by oppression and ignorance, reaches its normal growth, but that the race is now at last upon the right path and is being guided by the true principles cannot be doubted.

STATUE OF WASHINGTON IN THE GROUNDS OF THE STATE HOUSE, RICHMOND.

The Story of Our Great Civil War.

GENERAL ULYSSES S. GRANT.

It would be a mistake to suppose that secession sentiments originated and were exclusively maintained in the Southern States. Ideas of State sovereignty and of the consequent right of a State to withdraw from the Union, or at least to resist the acts and laws of Congress on adequate occasion, were held by many statesmen in the North as well as in the South. Thus the "Essex Junto," which had openly advocated a dissolution of the Union and the formation of an Eastern Confederacy, were foremost in assembling a convention of the Federalists on December 15, 1814, at Hartford, Connecticut, at which resolutions were passed recommending the State Legislatures to resist Congress in conscripting soldiers for carrying on the war then being waged against England. Threats of disunion were again heard in 1821, but this time from the South, in case Missouri should be denied admission to the Union on account of her unwillingness to surrender the institution of slavery. Once more, in 1832, a South Carolina convention proceeded to declare the tariff of the United States null and void within her own borders; but, owing to the decisive action of President Jackson, the State authorities did not venture into an actual collision with Congress.

But the agitation in favor of disunion reached culmination under the aggressive efforts by the South to extend slavery into new Territories, and the determination by the North to confine it strictly within the States where it already existed. With the formation of anti-slavery societies in the North, the nomination of anti-slavery candidates for the Presidency from 1840 onward, the passage of the "Wilmot Proviso" in 1846, the repeal of the Missouri compromise in 1854, the Dred-Scott decision by the United States Supreme Court in 1857, the adoption of the Lecompton Constitution in Kansas in 1859, and the raid by John Brown at Harper's Ferry in 1859, it became painfully evident that Mr. Seward's prediction of an "irrepressible conflict" between the North and South on the subject of slavery was becoming, had already become, a reality.

As to John Brown's raid we have only to recount that on the 16th of October, 1859, he took an armed force to Harper's Ferry, capturing the arsenal and armory and killing the men on guard. He was then endeavoring to secure arms for operating against the South. He was, however, captured and executed December 2, 1859. The expedition, it is unnecessary to say, was foolhardy and wholly without justification, and Brown paid for his misguided zeal with his life. But it must be said of him that he was conscientious, and that by his reckless daring he helped to crystallize sentiment on both sides of the slavery question.

The election in 1860 of Abraham Lincoln as President, on the platform of resistance to all further extension of slavery, was the signal for the previous disunion oratory and menaces to crystallize themselves into action. Seven States, in the following order, viz.: South Carolina, Mississippi, Florida, Alabama, Georgia, Louisiana, and Texas, seceded, and by a Congress held at Montgomery, Ala., February 4, 1861, formed a Confederacy with Jefferson Davis, of Mississippi, as President, and Alexander H. Stephens, of Georgia, as Vice-President.

The reasons avowed for this perilous course were, "the refusal of fifteen of the States for years past to fulfill their constitutional obligations, and the election of a man to the high office of President of the United States whose opinions and purposes are hostile to slavery."

After Mr. Lincoln's inauguration on March 4, 1861, the Confederacy was increased by the addition of Virginia, Arkansas, North Carolina, and Tennessee; Kentucky and Missouri, being divided in opinion, had representatives and armies in both sections.

The eleven "Confederate States of America" took from the Union nearly one-half of its inhabited area, and a population of between five and six millions of whites and about four millions of slaves. Their entire force capable of active service numbered 600,000 men. The twenty-four States remaining loyal to the Union had a population of 20,000,000, and the army at the close of the war numbered 1,050,000; but as the majority of these were scattered on guard duty over a vast region, only 262,000 were in fighting activity. Whilst the North was more rich and powerful, it was, nevertheless, more inclined to peace. The South was of a military spirit, accustomed to weapons, and altogether eager for

JOHN BROWN AFTER HIS CAPTURE.

the fray. The soldiers of both sides were equally brave, resolute, heroic, and devoted to what they respectively deemed a patriotic cause.

The Confederates had the advantage in the outset, because Mr. Floyd, the Secretary of War under President Buchanan, had dispersed the regular army, comprising 16,402 officers and men, to distant parts of the country where they were not available, and had sent off the vessels of the navy to foreign stations.

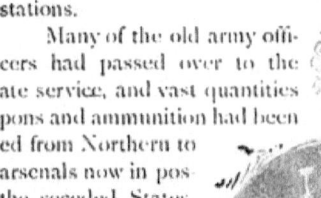

Many of the old army officers had passed over to the Confederate service, and vast quantities of weapons and ammunition had been transferred from Northern to Southern arsenals now in possession of the seceded States. A part of the army at Indianola had been surrendered on February 18, 1861, by General Twiggs, to the Confederates, and other soldiers guarding our Mexican and Indian frontiers were captured, besides several national vessels and fortresses. The South was, in short, much better prepared for the great conflict, and during the first year the preponderance of success was in its favor.

THE ARTS OF PEACE AND THE ART OF WAR.

The Confederates opened the war on April 12, 1861, by bombarding Fort Sumter, which had been occupied by Major Robert Anderson and a company of eighty men. This fort, although fiercely pounded by cannon balls and shells and set on fire several times, was gallantly held for two days, when it was obliged to surrender; but its brave defenders were allowed to march out saluting the old flag, and to depart for the North without being regarded as prisoners of war. The attack on Sumter created the wildest excitement throughout the entire land, and it opened the eyes of the North to the amazing fact of a civil war. A wave of patriotism, as mighty as it was sudden, swept over the United States. President Lincoln issued a call for 75,000 volunteers for three months, and soon after another call for 64,000 men for the army and 18,000 for the navy, to serve during the war. The need for these calls was urgent enough. On April 20th the Confederates easily captured the great Norfolk Navy Yard, with three or four national vessels, including the frigate "Merrimac," which subsequently wrought such fearful havoc at Hampton Roads, 2000 cannon, besides small arms, munitions, and stores of immense value, all of which were given up without a shot in defense. The arsenal at Harper's Ferry, with millions of dollars' worth of arms and ammunition, was also in their possession; and before the end of April 35,000 of their soldiers were already in the field, whilst 10,000 of these were rapidly marching northward. General R. E. Lee had been appointed Commander-in-chief of the army and navy of Virginia, and the 6th Regiment of Massachusetts militia had been savagely mobbed in the streets of Baltimore whilst going to the protection of Washington.

A Unionist attack on the Confederates at Big Bethel, Va., was repulsed, but the Confederates were driven out of Western Virginia by General G. B. McClellan. Then came, on July 21, the engagement at Bull Run, known also as that of Manassas Junction, one of the most significant battles of the war. General Irwin McDowell, acting under instructions of General Scott, marched against the Confederate army under General Beauregard, and in the outset met with encouraging success; but just as the Unionists imagined the victory theirs they were vigorously pressed by reinforcements that had come hurriedly up from Winchester under the leadership of General Johnston; and being exhausted from twelve hours of marching and fighting under a sultry sun, they began a retreat which was soon turned into a panic, attended with wild disorder and demoralization. Had the Confederates, among whom at the close of the day was President Davis himself, only known the extent of their triumph, they might have followed it and possibly have seized Washington. About 30,000 men fought on each side. The Confederate loss was 378 killed, 1489 wounded, and 30 missing. The Unionists lost 481 killed, 1011 wounded, and 1460 missing, with 20 cannon and large quantities of small arms.

From this moment it was understood that the struggle would be terrible, and that it might be long, not to say doubtful. Congress, then in extra session, authorized the enlistment of 500,000 men and the raising of $500,000,000.

Many of the States displayed intense patriotism. New York and Pennsylvania, for example, appropriating each $3,000,000, whilst Massachusetts and other New England States sent regiments fully equipped into the field. General McClellan was summoned to reorganize and discipline the multitudes of raw recruits that were thrown suddenly on his hands. His ability and thoroughness were of immense value in preparing them for their subsequent effective service, and he was soon after made Commander-in-chief in place of General Scott, retired. The South was also laboring with tremendous zeal and energy in the endeavor to enlist 400,000 men.

FORT MOULTRIE, CHARLESTON, WITH FORT SUMTER IN THE DISTANCE.

Early in August the death of General Nathaniel Lyon whilst attacking the Confederate General Ben. McCulloch at Wilson's Creek, and the retreat of his army, threw all Southern Missouri into the hands of the enemy. A few days after, General Butler took Forts Hatteras and Clark, with 700 prisoners, 1000 muskets, and other stores. But victories alternated, for now General Sterling Price surrounded and captured the Unionist Colonel Mulligan and his Irish brigade of 2780, at Lexington, Mo. Worse, however, than this was the near annihilation, October 21st, of a Unionist force of 1700 under General C. P. Stone and Colonel E. D. Baker at Ball's Bluff. The noble Baker and 300 of the men were slain and over 500 taken prisoners. Ten days later Commodore S. F. Dupont, aided by General T. W. Sherman with 10,000 men, reduced the Confederate forts on Hilton Head and Phillips' Island and seized the adjacent Sea Islands. General Fremont, unable to find and engage the Confederate General Price in the West, was relieved of his command of 30,000 men; but General U. S. Grant, by capturing the Confederate camp at Belmont, Mo., checked the advance of General Jeff. Thompson. On the next day, November 8th, occurred a memorable event which imperiled the peaceful relations between

BATTLE OF PITTSBURG LANDING.

the United States and Great Britain. Captain Wilkes of the United States frigate, "San Jacinto," compelled the British mail steamer, "Trent," to give up two of her passengers, the Confederate Commissioners, Mason and Slidell, who were on their way respectively to England and France in the interest of the South. A foreign war might have resulted had not Mr. William H. Seward, the astute Secretary of State, promptly disavowed the act and returned the Commissioners to English keeping. General E. O. C. Ord, commanding the Third Pennsylvania Brigade, gained a victory on December 20th at Dranesville over the Confederate brigade of General J. E. B. Stuart, who lost 230 soldiers, and during the same month General Pope reported the capture of 2500 prisoners in Central Missouri, with the loss of only 100 men : but 1000 of these were taken by Colonel Jeff. C. Davis by surprising the Confederate camp at Milford.

The year 1862 was marked by a series of bloody encounters. It opened with a Union army of 450,000 against a Confederate army of 350,000. The fighting began at Mill Spring, in Southern Kentucky, on January 19th, with an assault by the Confederates led by General F. K. Zollicoffer, acting under General G. B. Crittenden. They were routed by General George H. Thomas, Zollicoffer being killed and Crittenden flying across the Cumberland River, leaving ten guns and 1500 horses. This victory stirred the heart of the nation, and brought at once into brilliant prominence the great soldier and noble character whose greatnes blazed out like a sun at the close of the war.

Another blow was soon struck. Brigadier General Grant, with 15,000 troops, supported by Commodore A. H. Foote with seven gunboats, reduced Fort Henry on the Tennessee River and took its commander, General L. Tilghman, prisoner, but could not prevent the greater portion of the garrison from escaping to Fort Donelson, twelve miles to the east. This stronghold, commanding the navigation of the Cumberland River and containing 15,000 defenders under General J. B. Floyd, was regarded as impregnable. It fell, however, on February 16th, under a combined attack of Grant and Foote, surrendering 12,000 men and 40 cannon. Generals Floyd and Buckner, with a few of their command, managed to escape across the river by night, and General N. B. Forrest, with 800 cavalry, also got away. This splendid achievement threw Nashville and all Northern Tennessee into possession of the Unionists, and caused the immediate evacuation of the Confederate camp at Bowling Green, Kentucky.

In the East, about the same time, General Burnside and Commodore Goldsborough, with 11,500 men on 31 steamboats, captured, with a loss of 300, Roanoke Island, N. C., and 2500 Confederates. On March 14th they carried New Bern by assault, losing 600 but taking 2 steamboats, 69 cannon, and 500 prisoners ; and next they seized Fort Macon, with its garrison of 500 and stores. But the Unionist Generals Reno and Foster were repulsed, respectively, at South Mills and Goldsborough. One of the most notable of naval engagements took place on March 8th and 9th, when the Confederate ironclad, "Virginia," known better by her original name, the "Merrimac," steamed out from Norfolk attended by two gunboats. She plunged her iron ram into the Union frigate, "Cumberland," causing her to sink and to carry down part of her crew : she blew up the "Congress," another Union frigate, destroying more than half of her crew of 434, drove the frigate "Lawrence" under the guns of Fortress Monroe, and bombarded until dusk with terrific energy, aided also by her gunboats, the

Union steam frigate "Minnesota," which had got aground. She seemed destined on the next day to work immeasurable and unimpeded havoc. But, providentially, during the night the Union "Monitor," looking like "a cheese box on a raft," which had been built by Captain Ericsson and was commanded with consummate skill by Lieutenant J. L. Worden, steamed into the roadstead on her trial trip from New York. When, therefore, the "Merrimac" approached for new conquests the following morning her surprise was tremendous upon meeting such a strange craft. An unwonted and dramatic naval duel now

ANTIETAM BRIDGE.

occurred, from which the Confederate ram retired badly crippled and was soon afterward blown up to prevent her being captured. The "Monitor" was, unfortunately, lost some months afterward, in a storm off Hatteras.

The smoke had not vanished from Hampton Roads before news came of an assault at Pea Ridge by from 16,000 to 18,000 Confederates, including 5000 Indians, under General E. Van Dorn, on 10,500 Unionists under General S. R. Curtis, supported by Generals Asboth and Sigel. After three days of severe fighting, in which 1351 Unionists fell, the Confederates fled with precipitation, leaving Generals B. McCulloch and McIntosh dead and having Generals Price and Slack among their wounded.

General McClellan having raised his 200,000 or more men to a high degree of efficiency, transferred considerably more than half of them to Fortress Monroe for the purpose of advancing on Richmond by way of the peninsula between the York and James Rivers. He left General Banks with 7000 soldiers to guard the Virginia Valley. This force, at that time under the command of General James Shields, because Banks had gone temporarily to Washington, was fiercely assailed at Kernstown by "Stonewall" Jackson at the head of 4000 men. Jackson was repulsed with a loss of 1000, whilst Shields lost 600. McClellan's advance was checked for a month by Confederate batteries at Warwick Creek and again at Williamsburg by General Magruder's works. Here General Hooker's division fought well for nine hours with heavy losses. Magruder, flanked by Hancock, whose two brigades fought bravely, was obliged to retreat, leaving 700 of his wounded. The Unionists lost altogether 2228, whilst the Confederates lost not quite so many.

In the meantime, on April 6th, General Grant, with an army of 40,000, was surprised at Pittsburg Landing by 50,000 Confederates under General A. S. Johnson. General Grant, instead of being with his troops, was on a boat near Savannah, seven miles below. The Union forces were completely surprised. No intrenchments or earthworks of any kind had been erected—there were no abattis. The Union forces, surprised, were rapidly driven back with heavy loss in guns, killed, wounded, and prisoners, from Shiloh Church to the bluffs of the Tennessee, under which thousands of demoralized men took refuge. General Albert S. Johnson had been killed in the midst of the battle and General Beauregard succeeded to the command. Had General Johnson been alive the result might have been different; but Beauregard was in command, and he missed the one opportunity of his life in resting on his arms when he should have pressed the enemy to the river and forced a surrender. But relief was at hand, and under a leader who was a master general on the field. Sunday night General Don Carlos Buell arrived on the scene with a part of the Army of the Ohio. Moving General Nelson's division across the Tennessee in boats, he had them in position by seven o'clock in the evening, ready for the onset in the morning. Two more divisions were crossed early in the morning. At seven o'clock the attack was begun, General Buell leading his troops in person and General Grant advancing with his troops, yesterday overwhelmed by defeat, to-day hopeful and confident. The result is well known. Buell's fresh troops, handled in a masterly manner, were irresistible. By four o'clock the enemy lost all they had gained and were in full retreat, and the day was won, General Buell receiving unstinted praise for his victory. The Union loss was 1735 killed, 7882 wounded, and 3956 missing; total, 13,573.

The Confederates' loss was 1728 killed, 8012 wounded, 957 missing; total, 10,699.

About the same date General Pope and Commodore Foote captured Island No. 10, with 6700 Confederates under Brigadier General Makall; and soon after Memphis surrendered to the Unionists, and on April 11th Fort Pulaski fell before a bombardment by General Q. A. Gilmore. This same month was notable for naval victories. Admiral Farragut with a fleet of forty-seven armed vessels and 310 guns stormed the Confederate Forts St. Philip and Jackson, destroyed various fire-rafts and gunboats, and after a series of brilliant actions compelled the Confederate General Lovell with 3000 defenders to withdraw from New Orleans, leaving it to be occupied by 15,000 Unionists under General Butler. In the words of another, this "was a contest between iron hearts in wooden vessels, and iron clads with iron beaks, and the iron hearts prevailed."

McClellan's army—a part of which had been thrown across the Chickahominy—was savagely attacked on May 28th, at Fair Oaks, by General Joseph E. Johnston, now Commander-in-chief of the Confederate forces. Although Johnston was badly wounded and his troops after a day of hard fighting were obliged to retire, yet the Union loss was 5739, including five colonels killed and seven generals wounded. McClellan was now reinforced until he had altogether 156,828 men, of whom 115,162 were in good condition for effective service. Nothing, however, was accomplished until General Lee, who had succeeded the disabled Johnston, forced the fighting on June 26th that led to six horrible battles on as many successive days, known as those of Oak Grove, Mechanicsville, Gaines's Mills, Savage Station, White Oak Swamp, and Malvern Hill. In the last one the Confederates were signally defeated by McClellan with a loss of 10,000, while the Union loss was about 5000. During those six battles the Union loss was 1582 killed, 7709 wounded, and 5958 missing, making a total of 15,249. The Confederate loss was perhaps double; General Griffith and three colonels killed. Nevertheless, McClellan's campaign was unsuccessful; Richmond was not taken; and by order of the President he retreated to the Potomac.

General Halleck now became Commander-in-chief, and a vigorous campaign was opened by the Unionist General Pope. He was met in several stubbornly fought actions by the Confederates under Generals Lee, Jackson, and Longstreet, and was badly routed. * In this bloody affair, known as the second battle of Bull Run, the Unionists lost 25,000, including 9000 prisoners; the Con-

---

* In accounting for his defeat General Pope attempted to fix the blame upon General Fitz John Porter, a very able and successful commander, charging that he failed to support him, and a court-martial convened in the heat of the discussion cashiered the General. But later, in deference to public opinion, the case was reopened, the previous unjust verdict was set aside, and General Porter's good name was cleared, his conduct being fully justified—an acquittal in entire accord with the riper second thought of public opinion.

federates lost 15,000. General Lee, on September 8th, invaded Maryland, where at South Mountain he was worsted by McClellan, who lost heavily of his own men, but took 1500 prisoners.

A few days later Harper's Ferry, with 11,583 Unionists, 73 guns, and immense quantities of war munitions, was surrendered to Stonewall Jackson.

McClellan, with 80,000 men attacked Lee, posted with 70,000 on a ridge facing Antietam Creek. This determined battle ended in Lee's defeat and retreat. McClellan lost 2010 men killed, 9416 wounded, and 1043 missing; a total of 12,469. Lee lost 1842 killed, 9399 wounded, and 2292 missing; total, 13,533. This is regarded as the bloodiest day in the history of America. There is little doubt that had McClellan followed up his magnificent victory he could have entered Richmond. Here was his mistake; but this did not justify the Government in

GENERAL ROBERT EDMUND LEE.

retiring him as it did. Surely McClellan's great victory entitled him to the further command; but the opposition, especially that of Secretary Stanton, was too powerful, and he was retired.

General Burnside, having succeeded McClellan, assailed Lee at Fredericksburg, December 13th, but was disastrously beaten. His loss was 1152 killed.

14

9101 wounded, 3234 missing; total, 13,771. The Confederate loss was about 5000. General Burnside was relieved in favor of General Hooker in January, 1863, who—having received reinforcements until his army amounted to 100,000 infantry, 13,000 cavalry, and 10,000 artillery—assumed the offensive against Lee on May 2d, 1863, at Chancellorsville, but was terribly defeated. He lost 17,197 men. His defeat was due to a brilliant rear and flank movement executed by Stonewall Jackson, who thus demolished the Eleventh Corps but was himself slain. Jackson's death might well be regarded as an irreparable disaster to the Confederate cause.

Lee, with nearly 100,000 men, again marched northward, taking 4000 prisoners at Winchester. He was overtaken, July 1st, by the Union army, numbering 100,000, now under the command of General George G. Meade, at Gettysburg; where a gallant and bloody battle was fought, lasting three days and ending in a great victory for the Unionists. One of the features of the battle was a gallant charge of Pickett's Confederate Brigade, when they faced a battery of 100 guns and were nearly annihilated. But it was all American bravery. They lost 2834 killed, 13,709 wounded, 6643 missing; total, 23,186. The total Confederate loss was 36,000. Had Meade known the extent of his triumph he might have followed and destroyed the retreating Lee, whose army in this campaign dwindled from 100,000 to 40,000.

On the same memorable day, July 3d, Vicksburg, after having resisted many and determined assaults, and after finding its defenders on the south surprised and beaten in detail by Grant's army aided by Commodore Porter's naval operations, surrendered, closing a campaign in which Grant had taken 37,000 prisoners, with arms and munitions for 60,000 men. His own loss was 943 killed, 7095 wounded, and 537 missing; a total of 8515. These two notable victories were the turning points in the war.

Meantime, in the West the war had been pursued during the year with varying fortunes. The Confederate General Forrest had captured 1500 men at Murfreesboro, Tenn.; Kirby Smith had captured 5000 Unionists at Richmond, Ky.; General Bragg had captured 4000 prisoners at Mumfordsville, Tenn.; Generals McCook and Rousseau, having attacked the enemy without the orders of General Buell, and thinking, as General Buell said, to win a victory without his assistance, were defeated by General Bragg at Perryville, whose loss was 2300; our loss was 4340. General Rosecrans, with a loss of 782, whipped the Confederate General Price, at Iuka, Miss., whose loss was 1000 men. Rosecrans repulsed again the Confederates on September 17th at Corinth, inflicting a loss of 1423 killed and taking 2248 prisoners. His own loss was 2359 men. A brigade of 2000 Unionists was captured by John Morgan. A campaign of 46,010 men under Rosecrans culminated in the battle of Stone River, January 2d, 1863, against Bragg, who was beaten and forced to retreat. The Unionist

BATTLE OF CHANCELLORSVILLE. JACKSON'S ATTACK ON THE RIGHT WING.

losses were 1533 killed, 7245 wounded, 2800 missing; a total of 11,578. Bragg's loss was 9000 killed and wounded and over 1000 missing. The Confederate Van Dorn surprised and took prisoners 2000 men at Holly Springs, and at the same time took $4,000,000 worth of stores. General Sherman was repulsed at Chickasaw Bayou with a loss of 2000 men; but General J. A. McClernand reduced Fort Hindman, capturing 5000 prisoners and 17 guns, while his loss was only 977. Colonel Grierson made a famous raid with 1700 cavalry to Baton Rouge, cutting Confederate communications and taking 500 prisoners. At Milliken's Bend the Unionist General Dennis, having 1400, repelled an attack of the Confederate General H. McCulloch, the loss on either side being 500. At Helena, Arkansas, the Unionist General B. M. Prentiss, with 4000, also repulsed General Holmes with 3646, of whom 1636 were lost. The Confederate raider, Morgan, with a mounted force of 4000 men, invaded Ohio, July 7th, but was caught by gunboats and obliged to surrender.

General Burnside, early in September, at Cumberland Gap, captured General Frazier with fourteen guns and 2000 men. Then came, on September 19th, the great battle of Chickamauga, between Rosecrans and Thomas with 55,000 men on one side, and Bragg and Longstreet with about the same number on the other side. Longstreet annihilated Rosecrans' right wing; but Thomas by his firmness and skill saved the day. The Confederates lost 18,000, while the Union loss was 1644 killed, 9262 wounded, 4945 missing: total, 15,581. Our army fell back on Chattanooga. Longstreet's attempt, Nov. 28th, to dislodge Burnside from Knoxville resulted in his own loss of 800 and retreat. The Unionists lost 100 men.

On September 22d to 24th the forces of General George H. Thomas, reinforced by General Sherman, under the command of Grant, assaulted Bragg's army on Mission Ridge, facing Chattanooga. General Sherman crossed the Tennessee to attempt a flank movement but was repulsed. General Hooker moved up Lookout Mountain and drove the Confederates before him, capturing men and guns. Then General G. H. Thomas, in accordance with his original plan of battle, moved his army by the front directly up the heights of Mission Ridge, assailing the enemy in the very teeth of his batteries. The fight was desperate, but Thomas's forces won, driving the enemy, making many prisoners and capturing many guns. The Union losses were 757 killed, 4529 wounded, 330 missing; total, 5616. There were 6142 prisoners captured from the enemy.

During this time Charleston, which had inaugurated the Rebellion, pluckily resisted all attempts to take it. For example, her defenders beat back 6000 Unionists with a loss of 574 men at Secessionville June 16th. Again, they disabled two of the blockading gunboats on January 1st, 1863; again, they forced nine bombarding iron-clads under Commodore Dupont to retire; again, they repulsed from Fort Wagner a storming party under General Gilmore, inflicting a loss of 1500, while their loss was but 100 men; again, while obliged to evacuate

Fort Wagner, leaving 18 guns there, and seven guns in Battery Gregg, they repulsed the Unionists' attempt to scale Fort Sumter and slew 200 men.

Nor did the Unionists fare better in Florida. They lost under General T. Seymour 2000 of his 6000 troops at Olustee, where the Confederates lost but 730 men. The Unionists again lost 1600 out of 2000 men under Gen.

RETREAT OF LEE'S ARMY.

Wessels at Plymouth, North Carolina, when the Confederate General Hoke's loss was but 300 men.

In the Southwest, however, the Unionists' cause had gained considerable advantages under General Banks, having a command of 30,000 men. Aided by Commodore Farragut, at Alexandria, La., he drove General R. Taylor and captured 2000 prisoners, several steamboats, and 22 guns. His assault, however, on Port Hudson, in June, was repelled with a loss of 2000

men, while the Confederates lost but 300 men. But Port Hudson, as it was about to be cannonaded by the gunboats set free by the fall of Vicksburg, was surrendered, July 6th, by the Confederate General Gardener, with his garrison of 6408 men. Banks' effective force had been reduced to 10,000. His total captures during the campaign were 10,584 men, 73 guns, and 6000 small arms. But Brashear City had some days before been surprised and captured by General R. Taylor (Confederate) with a Union loss of 1000 men and 10 guns. The Unionist General Dudley lost near Donaldsonville 300 prisoners, and again, the Unionist General Franklin with a fleet and 4000 men was repelled with a loss of two gunboats, 15 guns, and 250 men, by less than that number within the fort at Sabine Pass, and at Teche Bayou the 67th Indiana Regiment was captured entire.

The Red River expeditions in March and April, 1864, toward Shreveport under General Banks, from New Orleans, with a force of 40,000, and under General Steel, from Little Rock, with 12,000, were disastrous failures. The former had to retreat with a loss of about 5000, and the latter was also beaten back with a loss of 2200; but at Jenkins Ferry he repulsed the Confederate attack led by General Kirby Smith, with a loss of 2300. In August of this year (1864) Commodore Farragut executed one of the fiercest and most heroic naval combats on record. Having lashed himself to the mast of the Hartford, he advanced with a fleet of 14 wooden steamers and gunboats and four iron-clad monitors against Forts Morgan and Gaines, at the entrance of Mobile Bay. He ran the bows of his wooden vessels full speed against the rebel iron-clad Tennessee, gaining a notable victory, which ended in the fall of the forts and the city of Mobile.

General Grant was appointed Commander-in-chief of all the Union armies on March 1, 1864. Having sent Sherman to conduct a campaign in the West, he himself, on May 4 and 5, crossed the Rapidan for a direct southerly advance to Richmond. A campaign of 43 days followed, in which more than 100,000 men, frequently reinforced, were engaged on either side. He was met by Lee in the Wilderness, where, after two days of terrible slaughter, the battle ended without decided advantage to either side. Among the Unionists, General J. S. Wadsworth was killed and seven generals were wounded, the entire loss amounting to 20,000 men. The Confederates lost 8000 men, with Longstreet badly wounded.

Finding Lee's position impregnable, Grant advanced by a flank movement to Spottsylvania Court House. Here, on May 11th, Hancock, by a desperate assault, captured Generals Johnson and E. H. Stewart, with 3000 men and 30 guns, while Lee himself barely escaped. But no fighting, however desperate, could carry Lee's works. Sheridan with his cavalry now made a dashing raid toward Richmond. He fought the Confederate cavalry, killed their General, J. E. B. Stuart, and returned, having suffered little damage, to Grant. General

Butler with 30,000 men steamed up the James River and seized City Point, with the view of seizing Petersburg. He was, however, too slow, and in a fight with Beauregard, near Proctor's Creek, lost 4000 men, while the Confederates lost but 3000.

General Grant reached, May 17th, the North Anna, where he gained some advantage, but as Lee was strongly intrenched, he moved on again to Cold Harbor. Here an assault on Lee ended with a Union loss of 1705 killed, 9072 wounded and 2406 missing. Sheridan again raided Lee's rear, tore up railroads, and burnt stores, and after having lost 735 men he returned to Grant with 370 prisoners. Grant now pressed on toward the James River; assaults were

ENTRANCE TO GETTYSBURG CEMETERY.

made on Petersburg with a loss of many killed and 5000 prisoners. The Unionist General Wilson, with 8000 cavalry, while tearing up the Danville railroad, lost 1000 prisoners.

Another attempt to take Petersburg by a mine explosion resulted in a Unionist loss of 4400 and Confederate loss of 1000. A series of gallant attacks by the Unionists were as gallantly repulsed. Thus Hancock assailed Lee's left wing below Richmond, losing 5000 men. Warren seized the Weldon Railroad, at the expense of 4450, while the Confederates lost but 1200. Hancock's attempt to seize Ream's Station ended in his being driven back and losing 2400 men. Warren grasped the Squirrel Level Road at a cost of 2500 men. Butler, however, took Port Harrison, with 115 guns, but failed to take Fort Gilmore after a loss of 300. The Confederates, attempting to retake Fort Harrison, were beaten back with a heavy loss. The Union cavalry under General Kautz advanced within five miles of Richmond, but were driven back with a loss of 9 guns and 500 men. Hancock tried to turn the Confederate flank and took 1000 prisoners, but had to retire with a loss of 1500.

Thus this campaign of 1864 closed with a loss in the aggregate of 87,387 men from the Army of the Potomac.

In West Virginia Sigel was routed at New Market by J. C. Breckinridge with a loss of six guns and 700 men. Hunter, succeeding Sigel, beat the Confederates, June 8th, at Piedmont, killing General Jones and taking 1500 men, but was himself, with 20,000 men, soon after beaten at Lynchburg, and forced to a disastrous retreat over the Alleghanies to the Potomac.

This opened the way for the Confederate, Early, with 20,000 veterans, to march northward. With a loss of but 600 he defeated General Lew Wallace near Frederick, killing and capturing 2000 men. After threatening Baltimore and Washington he retreated South with 2500 captured horses and 5000 cattle. He also defeated at Winchester General Crook, whose loss was 1200. Shortly after the Unionist General Averill defeated B. F. Johnson's cavalry and took 500 prisoners.

Not long after, on September 19, 1864, Early, after a brilliant attack by Sheridan at Winchester, was routed, losing 6000 men, while the Unionists lost 1000 less. At Fisher's Hill Sheridan again routed him, taking 16 guns and 1100 prisoners; at Cedar Creek, while Sheridan was absent at Washington, Early made a sudden and determined assault, throwing the Unionists into a panic-stricken mob, capturing 24 guns and 1200 prisoners. Sheridan, by his famous ride of twenty miles, met his beaten army. He reorganized it, inspired it to make a general and magnificent attack, and won a great victory, recapturing his 24 guns, taking 23 more, and 1500 prisoners. The loss on either side was about 3000.

In the Southwest General Sturgis (Union) with 12,000 men routed General Forrest at Guntown, Miss., killing and capturing 4000. In East Tennessee the Confederate raider Morgan captured 1600 Unionists at Licking River, but was himself soon after chased away with a loss of half his force. During these operations General Sherman advanced (May 18, 1864) with 100,000 men from Chattanooga. He was stubbornly resisted by General J. E. Johnston with an army of 54,000. At Kenesaw Mountain Sherman lost 3000 men while the Confederates lost 442. He, however, kept flanking and fighting the Confederates until he reached Atlanta, during which two months the enemy had lost 14,200 men; but reinforcements kept their numbers up to 51,000. During these movements the Confederate General Polk, who on accepting his commission in the army had not resigned his position as a Bishop of the Protestant Episcopal Church, was killed by a cannon ball while reconnoitring on Pine Mountain, a few miles north of Marietta. Hood succeeded Johnston, and aimed a heavy blow at Thomas, on Sherman's right, losing 4000 and inflicting

LONGSTREET AND GRANT AT LEWIS'S HEADQUARTERS.

a loss of but 1500. On the 22d occurred another great battle in which McPherson, a very superior Union general, was killed, and 4000 Unionists were lost. The Confederate loss was, however, not less than 8000. General Stoneman whilst raiding Hood's rear was captured, with 1000 of his cavalry. Hood, after suffering a heavy repulse by Logan, and another at Jonesboro by Howard, in the latter of which he lost 2000, and still another by J. C.

Davis, when Jonesboro and many guns and prisoners were taken from him, retreated eastward, leaving Atlanta, September 1st, to the Union victors. Being reinforced, however, so as to have about 55,000 troops, he returned for an invasion of Tennessee. At Franklin, November 30th, he made a desperate onset against Schofield, and was baffled, at an expense of 4500 men to himself and of 2320 to the Union. At Nashville, to which he laid siege, he was struck by Thomas, December 15th, with great skill and determination during a two days' battle, and broken to pieces, having lost more than 13,000, besides seventy-two pieces of artillery. The Union loss was 10,000 during the campaign. In November and December Sherman at the head of 65,500, including the cavalry protection of Kilpatrick, executed his famous march to the sea, *i.e.*, from Atlanta to Savannah. His reward was 167 guns and 1328 prisoners and a demoralized South. The Confederate General Hardee, who had already evacuated Savannah, was obliged by a new advance of Sherman northward, February, 1865, to evacuate Charleston also, with 12,000 men. A cavalry engagement took place near the north line of South Carolina, between Kilpatrick and Wade Hampton, in which the former was surprised, but the latter finally beat him. Near Fayetteville, North Carolina, March 15th, he was attacked without success by Hardee, now acting under Joseph Johnston, having 40,000 men under his command: and three days after at Bentonville by Johnston himself. Sherman lost 1643, but forced Johnston to retire, leaving 267 dead and 1625 prisoners and wounded.

Fort Fisher, that protected the blockade runners at Wilmington, N. C., was bombarded by Commodore Porter and carried by assault by General A. H. Terry, January 16, 1865. This victory, purchased at a cost of 410 killed and 536 wounded, threw into the Union hands 169 guns and 2083 prisoners. And Wilmington itself fell about one month later, under an attack by Schofield.

General James H. Wilson, with 15,000 cavalry from the armies of Grant and Thomas, routed General Forrest at Selma, Ala., April 2d, capturing 22 guns and 2700 prisoners and burning 125,000 bales of cotton. Soon after, he captured at Columbus, Ga., 52 guns and 1200 prisoners, besides burning a gunboat, 250 cars, and 115,000 cotton bales. He took Fort Tyler by assault, but ceased operations at Macon, Ga., because by that time the rebellion was crushed.

General Grant resumed operations February 6, 1865, when he repulsed at Hatcher's Run, at a cost of 2000 troops, the Confederates, who lost 1000. General Sheridan with 10,000 cavalry routed Early, on March 2d, from Waynesboro, taking 11 guns and 1600 prisoners, and joined Grant at Petersburg after having passed entirely around Lee's army. An attack by Lee against Fort Stedman was repelled with a loss of 2500 to the Unionists and 4500 to the Confederates.

Grant, fearing that Lee might attempt to evacuate Richmond, threw Warren's corps and Sheridan's cavalry to the southwest of Petersburg. Warren, after having his divisions broken by Lee but re-formed by the aid of Griffin, united with Sheridan, who had been foiled the day before, April 1st, at Five Forks. Warren and Sheridan now charged the Confederates' works, which were taken, along with 5000 prisoners. A general assault was made by the Union army at daylight, April 2d, when Ord's Corps (Union) carried Forts Gregg and Alexander by storm. A. P. Hill, a brilliant Confederate general, was shot dead. That night Lee evacuated Richmond, burning his warehouses filled with stores. General Weitzel, at 6 A.M. April 3d, entered the city with his men and was soon followed by President Lincoln. Petersburg was at the same time abandoned. Lee halted his army, now dwindled to 35,000 men, at Amelia Court House. Grant rapidly pursued. Ewell was severed from Lee's rear and became one among 6000 prisoners. Lee heroically pushed on to Appomattox Court House, where his flight was intercepted by Sherman marching from the South. Lee was inclined to renew the fighting against Sherman, but his weary and famished army stood no chance against the fearful odds around them. And Lee, to prevent further useless bloodshed, surrendered his army to Grant on April 9, 1865, within three days of four years after the rebellion had been opened by the bombardment of Fort Sumter. Bell ringing, triumphant salutes, and boundless joy throughout the United States hailed this event as the close of the war. Johnston surrendered his army to Sherman at Raleigh, N. C., April 26th, and Dick Taylor his, to Canby at Citronville, Ala., May 4th. The terms of the surrender were magnanimous : " Each officer and man was allowed to return to his home, not to be disturbed by the United States authority so long as they observed their paroles and the laws in force where they may reside."

Jefferson Davis, the president of the now destroyed Confederacy, fled from Richmond at the time of its evacuation. Attended at first with a cavalry escort of 2000, which soon dwindled mostly away, he was making his way toward the coast, with his family and "a few faithful followers" when he was captured near Irwinsville, Georgia. After an imprisonment of two years in Fortress Monroe, he was released, and allowed to live without molestation, mourning the lost cause, until he died, December 6, 1889.

The Union soldiers numbered during the war 2,666,999, of which 294,266 were drafted, the rest being volunteers. The deaths on the field or from wounds amounted to 5221 officers and 90,868 men, while 2321 officers 182,329 men died from disease or accident. The Confederate armies enrolled were 600,000 men, of whom they lost more than one-half. The Confederate cruisers, the "Alabama," "Florida," "Georgia," "Sumter," and "Tallahassee," most of which were fitted out in British ports, well nigh destroyed American commerce. The "Alabama," commanded by Raphael Semmes, went down off the French coast, June 19, 1864, in a memorable action with the U. S. S. "Kearsarge," commanded by Captain Winslow.

The greatest act of Abraham Lincoln was his Emancipation Proclamation, issued January 1, 1863, giving freedom to 4,000,000 of slaves.

And so ended the great internecine conflict, which has made us a strong, consolidated, free nation, never again, let us hope, to be given over to fraternal strife.

LINCOLN'S GRAVE.

Lessons and Recollections of the Civil War by the Old Soldier, Colonel A. K. McClure,

ABRAHAM LINCOLN.

BEFORE all those who more or less actively participated in the civil or military events of our Civil War shall have passed away, it might be well to crystallize into history some of its forgotten lessons. The young student of to-day, who must turn to history for all knowledge of the dark days of the bloodiest civil war of modern times, can be easily and fully informed as to all important political events and the many battles which were fought between the blue and the gray. But there are many facts and incidents connected with the origin and prosecution of that memorable conflict which have no place in the annals of history, but which exercised a very great, and at times a controlling, influence in shaping the policy of the Government, and even in deciding the issues of the war itself. It is to some of these apparently forgotten lessons of the great conflict I propose to give a chapter that I hope may be entertaining and instructive.

When we turn aside from the beaten historical paths to explore the forgotten issues and movements of more than thirty years ago, we are startled at the magnitude of questions in those days which seem now to be accepted as incapable of controversy. The student of to-day only sees the fact that the issues between slavery and freedom were natural and irrepressible, and that in such a contest, with a vast preponderance of numbers, wealth, and physical and moral power, there could be but one result from such a struggle; but there are few to-day who have knowledge of the intrenched power of slavery, not only in our commercial cities, but also throughout

e whole business interests of the country, and it will doubtless surprise many
aders when they are told that even as late as September, 1862, when the war
d been in progress for nearly two years, scores of thousands of thoroughly
yal supporters of the Government in every State shuddered at the idea of
mancipation. It will be equally sur-
rising to the students of American
story to-day to learn that the great
ass of the people of both sections
the country were so
rofoundly interested in

THE SWAMP ANGEL BATTERY BOMBARDING CHARLESTON.

averting fraternal conflict that only the
madness of the secession leaders forced
e North to unite in the support of the war by wantonly firing upon the
arving and helpless garrison of Fort Sumter when its peaceable surrender
uld have been accomplished within a few hours thereafter. So general and
ep-seated was the aversion to war in the North, that had the Government

commenced hostilities, even after the capture of the national forts and arsenals which had been seized by the insurgents, the North would have been hopelessly divided on the question of supporting the Government.

While it is probable that the slavery issue would have culminated in civil war some time during the present century, I feel entirely warranted in assuming

GENERAL SHERIDAN TURNING DEFEAT INTO VICTORY AT CEDAR CREEK.

that the sectional conflict begun in 1861 would not have reached an appeal to the sword but for the fact that both sections mutually believed the other incapable of accepting civil war. Had the Northern and Southern people understood each other then as well as they understood each other after the soldiers of the blue and gray had exhibited their matchless heroism on so many battlefields, the election and inauguration of Abraham Lincoln as President would not have precipitated war. Civil war had been threatened by alarmists and agitators in and out of Congress for many years, and many of the Southern leaders grew offensively arrogant in discussing sectional issues during the debates in Congress, for several years before the election of Lincoln. It was not uncommon for Northern men to be taunted as cowards because they refused to accept the code of honor, and finally, when the secession of States began, it was the almost universal belief throughout the South that the Northern people were mere money getters, and incapable of heroic action even in defense of their convictions. The South assumed that the North would not fight, because it was believed that the Northern people were so averse to fighting that they would submit even to dissolution of the government rather than risk their lives for its defense. On the other hand, the Northern people believed the Southerners to be led by bombasts who would take pause in their aggressive actions whenever compelled to face the fearful realities of actual war.

I have never forgotten an incident that occurred in a party caucus in the Pennsylvania Legislature, held on the night after the surrender of Sumter. I was then a Senator and in political accord with the majority of both branches of the Legislature that heartily sustained President Lincoln. The occasion was so grave that the caucus met in secret session, and the first half dozen speeches ridiculed the idea of actual war, because the Southern people were bombasts and cowards, and some of the speakers boldly declared that the Northern women could sweep away to the South of the Potomac, with their brooms, these blatant warriors. Having studied the situation both North and South, as Chairman of the Military Committee of the Senate, I ventured to correct the erroneous impressions created by the speakers, saying that the Southerners were of our own blood and lineage, had shared all our heroism in the achievements of the past, and that if we should become involved in civil war, it would be one of the most desperate and bloody wars of history. My declaration that the South would fight as heroically as the North was hissed from every section of the caucus. How fearfully true my statements and predictions were, was soon attested on the many battlefields, from the first Bull Run to Appomattox. No one then could have believed that the South would marshal and maintain an army of half a million men, to display the highest measure of heroism and sacrifice to overthrow the noblest government of the earth, and none could then have believed that the Northern people would furnish and maintain more than a million men during four long years of the bloodiest conflict, as the price of the perpetuity of the Republic. Had we known each other better then; had we known that the soldiers of both the North and the South would make Grecian and Roman story pale before their heroism in fraternal conflict, I doubt not that the Civil War begun in 1861 would have been postponed for a future generation.

The first gun fired against Sumter, on the 12th of April, 1861, sounded

15

the death knell of the Southern Confederacy and of slavery; and had the first gun of the war been fired by Major Anderson, the commander of Fort Sumter, against any of the Confederate batteries erected to bombard him and his little command, the North would have been divided on the vital issue of supporting the Government, and even revolution

DEATH OF GENERAL POLK.

in the North would have been more than possible. Mr. Lincoln was inaugurated on the 4th of March, and from that time until the bombardment of Sumter the provisional Confederate Government, then located at Montgomery, Alabama, committed acts of war against the National Government, by seizing forts and arsenals, and by erecting batteries at Charleston, within range of Major Anderson's guns, to make his fort defenseless. With all these preparations for war on the part of the South, begun during the last three months of

Buchanan's Administration and continued after Lincoln's inauguration, the Government was entirely helpless to defend its forts and property. The forts could not be reinforced because the small standing army at that day was utterly unequal to the task. Nine important forts in six Southern States were garrisoned by but a handful of men, without supplies in case of siege, or means of defense in case of assault from batteries whose construction could not be impeded, as to fire upon them would have been an act of war. The Government was not only unable to man its forts and defend them and the arsenals of the South, but neither President Buchanan nor President Lincoln dared to call for an increase of the army. Had either of them done so, it would have been an open menace of war to coerce the rebellious States back into the Union; it would have inflamed the South into precipitating the conflict, and would not have been sustained by the people in the North.

Thus was the Government utterly helpless to hinder preparations for war by the new Confederacy. Many of the ablest and most patriotic men of both parties of the North doubted the right of the Government to coerce a State by the bayonet, and had either Buchanan or Lincoln called for an increase of the army, or attempted to recapture forts and arsenals seized by the South, it would have been regarded as needlessly hastening a conflict that all hoped could be avoided. It was the midsummer madness of the Southern Confederacy in precipitating the war by firing upon the starved and feeble garrison of Sumter that obliterated the issue of "coercion," and that practically united the North in sustaining the Government in an aggressive war policy. So entirely were we unprepared for war, that the President had no authority to call out troops, even after Sumter had been fired upon, and the President's proclamation summoning 75,000 volunteers for three months' service had to be legalized by subsequent act of Congress. The discussion of the propriety or impropriety of war was summarily ended when war was actually declared by the Charleston batteries hurling their hot shot into Sumter; and from that day until the surrender of the Confederate armies, after the sacrifice of hundreds of thousands of lives and countless treasure, the North was inspired by its patriotism to prosecute the war until the Rebellion should be overthrown and the authority of the Government established in every State of the Union.

Had the Confederate Government been content to hold the forts and arsenals it had seized without bloodshed, and waited for the General Government to precipitate war, the conflict would have been indefinitely postponed and the Confederacy would have become so strong by the passive assent of the Government to its establishment that its overthrow might have been impossible. Certain it is that if President Lincoln had opened the war by firing upon the Southern forces, except in defense of assailed Government troops, he could not have commanded anything approaching a united support from the Northern people; he would have been fearfully censured as having wantonly engaged in a great war over issues that might have been adjusted peaceably by patience; and none can now assume to say what would have been the issue of such a conflict with the North bitterly divided because of a sectional war precipitated by the aggressive action of the Government. It was the first gun fired against Sumter that crystallized the North, that gave Lincoln the power to summon patriotic armies to defend the Republic, and that assured, in the fullness of time the utter overthrow of the Confederacy and the re-establishment of the great American Republic without the blot of slavery upon its escutcheon.

The naval warfare of the world was revolutionized in a single day by the battle between the " Merrimac " and the " Monitor " at Fortress Monroe, on the 9th of March, 1862. It was the most sudden and startling revolution ever attained in methods of warfare, and it was a revelation to every nation of the earth. The United States steam frigate " Merrimac " was set on fire at the Gosport Navy Yard at the outbreak of the war, when hastily abandoned by the Federal navy officers. It was burned to the water's edge and sunk, but soon after the Confederates raised the hull, which was not seriously damaged, and its engines in yet reasonably good condition, and they hurriedly undertook the then original conception of converting it into an iron-clad. A powerful prow of cast iron was attached to its stem, a few feet under water, and projecting sufficiently to enable it to break in the side of any wooden vessel. A low wooden roof two feet thick was built at an incline of about 36 degrees, and this was plated with double iron armor, making a four-inch iron plating. Under this protection were mounted two broadside batteries of four guns each, and a gun at the stem and stern. The Government was soon advised of the raising of the hull of the " Merrimac," and without having detailed information on the subject, knew that a powerful iron-clad was being constructed. A board of naval officers had been selected by the Government to consider the various suggestions for the construction of iron-clad vessels, and although, as a rule, naval officers had little faith in the experiment, Congress coerced them into action by the appropriation of half a million dollars for the work. The Naval Board recommended a trial of three of the most acceptable plans presented, and they were put under contract.

Among those who pressed the adoption of light iron-clads, capable of penetrating our shallow harbors, rivers, and bayous, was John Ericsson. He was a Swede by birth, but had long been an American citizen, and exhibited uncommon genius and scientific attainments in engineering. The vessel he proposed to build was to be only 127 feet in length, 27 feet in width, and 12 feet deep, to be covered by a flat deck rising only one or two feet above water. The only armament of the vessel was to be a revolving turret, about

20 feet in diameter and nine feet high, made of plated wrought iron aggregating eight inches in thickness, with two eleven-inch Dahlgren guns. The guns were so constructed that they could be fired as the turret revolved, and the port-hole would be closed immediately after firing. The size of the "Merrimac" was well known to the Government to be quite double the length and breadth of the "Monitor," but it had the disadvantage of requiring nearly double the depth of water in which to manœuvre it. Various sensational reports were received from time to time of the progress made on the "Merrimac," the name of which was changed by the Confederates to "Virginia," and as we had only wooden hulls at Fortress Monroe to resist it, great solicitude was felt for the safety of the fleet and the maintenance of the blockade. While the Government hurried the construction of the new iron-clads to the utmost, little faith was felt that such fragile vessels as the "Monitor" could cope with so powerful an engine of war as the "Merrimac." The most formidable vessels of the navy, including the "Minnesota," the twin ship of the original "Merrimac," the "St. Lawrence," the "Roanoke," the "Congress," and the "Cumberland," were all there waiting the advent of the "Merrimac."

On Saturday, the 8th of March, the "Merrimac" appeared at the mouth of the Elizabeth River and steamed directly for the Federal fleet. All the vessels slipped cable and started to enter the conflict, but the heavier ships soon ran aground and became helpless. The "Merrimac" hurried on, and after firing a broadside at the "Congress," crashed into the sides of the "Cumberland," whose brave men fired broadside after broadside at their assailant only to see their balls glance from its mailed roof. An immense hole had been broken into the hull by the prow of the "Merrimac," and in a very few minutes the "Cumberland" sank in fifty feet of water, her last gun being fired when the water had reached its muzzle, and the whole gallant crew went to the bottom with their flag still flying from the masthead. The "Merrimac" then turned upon the "Congress." It was compelled to flee from such a hopeless struggle, and was finally grounded near the shore; but the "Merrimac," selecting a position where her guns could rake her antagonist, after a bloody fight of more than an hour, with the commander killed and the ship on fire, the "Congress" struck her flag, and was soon blown up by the explosion of her magazine. Most fortunately for the Federal fleet, the "Merrimac" had not started out on its work of destruction until after midday. Its iron prow had been broken in breaching the "Cumberland," and after the fierce broadsides it had received from the "Congress" and the "Cumberland," with the other vessels firing repeatedly during the hand-to-hand conflict, the "Merrimac" was content to withdraw for the day, and anchored for the night under the Confederate shore batteries on Sewall's Point.

The night of March 8th was probably the gloomiest period of the war. It was well known at Fortress Monroe and at Washington that the "Merrimac" would resume its work on the following day, and it was equally well known that there were neither vessels nor batteries to offer any serious resistance to its work. With the fleet destroyed and the blockade raised, not only Washington, but even New York, might be at the mercy of this new and invincible engine of war. There did not seem to be even a silver lining to the dark cloud that hung over the Union cause; but

deliverance came most unexpectedly, as some time during the night the little "Monitor" was seen, by the light of the yet burning "Congress," towed into the waters of Hampton Roads. It was viewed with contempt by the naval officers and described as "a raft with a cheese box on top of it"; but Lieutenant Worden, who commanded the little iron-clad, after being advised of the situation, boldly took his position, after midnight, near the still helpless "Minnesota," thus challenging the whole fury of the "Merrimac" upon the "Monitor." On Sunday morning, the 9th of March, the "Merrimac" sailed out defiantly to complete its work of destruction and thus make itself master of the capital, of New York, and, presumably, end the Richmond campaign then contem

MOIST WEATHER AT THE FRONT.

O C

plated, and the little "Monitor" sailed out boldly to meet it. The history of that conflict need not be repeated. To the utter amazement of the commander of the "Merrimac," the "Monitor" was impervious to its terrible broadsides, while its lightness and shallow draft enabled it to out-manœuvre its antagonist at every turn; and while it did not fire one gun for ten of its adversary, its aim was precise and the "Merrimac" was materially worsted in the conflict. After three hours of desperate battle the defiant and invincible "Merrimac" of the day before was compelled to give up the contest and retreat back to Norfolk.

It was this single naval conflict, and the signal triumph of the little "Monitor," that revolutionized the whole naval warfare of the world in a single day, and from that time until the present the study of all nations for aggressive or defensive warfare has been the perfection of the iron-clad. To the people of the present time the iron-clad is so familiar, and its discussion so common, that few recall the fact that only thirty years ago it was unknown, and little dreamed of as an important implement of war. It is notable that neither of those vessels which inaugurated iron-clad warfare, and made it at once the accepted method of naval combat for the world, ever afterward engaged in battle during the three years of war which continued. The "Merrimac" was constantly feared as likely to make a new incursion against our fleet, but her commander never again ventured to lock horns with the "Monitor" and the additional iron-clads which were soon added to the navy. Early in May the capture of Norfolk by General Wool placed the "Merrimac" in a position of such peril that on the 11th of May, 1862, she was fired by her commander and crew and abandoned, and soon after was made a hopeless wreck by the explosion of her magazine. The fate of the "Monitor" was even more tragic. The following December, when being towed off Cape Hatteras, she foundered in a gale and went to the bottom with a portion of her officers and men; but she had taught the practicability of iron-clads in naval warfare, and when she went down a whole fleet was under construction after her own model, and some vessels already in active service.

One of the forgotten lessons of the war is given in the singular fatality that attended the formidable iron-clad vessels constructed by the Confederacy. The South not only furnished the first iron-clad of the war, but it constructed others which were confidently and reasonably relied upon to raise the blockade in both Savannah and New Orleans. The Confederates had converted the English iron clad steamer Fingal, one of the successful blockade runners, into one of the most powerful iron-clad war vessels constructed by either side during the war. It was regarded by all as the most dangerous engine of war that had yet been produced; and when Admiral Dupont ordered two of his best monitors, the "Weehawken" and the "Nahant," to accept the "Atlanta's" challenge of battle, the gravest fears were cherished by the Admiral as to the issue of the conflict.

So confident were the officers of the "Atlanta" and the people of Savannah of the speedy and complete victory of the new Confederate iron-clad, that when the "Atlanta," on the 17th of June, 1863, steamed out to give battle, it was accompanied by steamers brilliantly decorated with flags and crowded with men and women, the elite of the city, to witness the destruction of the Union fleet.

DEATH OF MAXIMILIAN.

demolished the pilot house; and the fourth and final shot crashed through a port shutter. So stunning was the first shot received by the "Atlanta" from the "Weehawken" that the "Atlanta" never again fired a gun, as it became unmanageable and entirely at the mercy of its adversary. Thus in a very few minutes after the battle opened the Confederate iron-clad displaced its colors with the white flag, and it was regarded as one of the grandest naval prizes of the war. The captured iron-clad was towed away by the victors and reconstructed for service in the Federal navy, but on the 6th of December, 1863, when with the fleet within Charleston Harbor, a rough sea caught it, heavily laden with shells, and before relief could come it sunk to the bottom with some twenty-five officers and men.

Such was the fate of the two great iron-clads of the Confederacy that were completed and put into action. Each fought one battle and both perished soon thereafter; but the most formidable of all the iron-clads constructed by the South during the war, was within a few weeks of completion when Admiral Farragut captured New Orleans. The Admiral was advised of the construction of this vessel, and the fear of its completion certainly hastened his aggressive action in attacking the Confederate forts and fleet on the Mississippi, to enter New Orleans. Neither was his information in any degree at fault as to the invulnerable character of the new iron-clad. After the capture of New Orleans, Admiral Farragut and General Butler informed themselves minutely of this new engine of war, and both confessed that had it been completed before the capture of the city, it would have been capable of destroying Farragut's entire fleet, raising the blockade and defending New Orleans from capture. Most fortunately for the Union cause, with all the haste that could be practiced in the construction of this vessel, it could not be made serviceable until after Farragut's heroic and successful assault, and it shared the fate of the first of the Confederate iron-clads by being blown up by those who had staked the highest hopes upon its achievements. Thus while the Confederates were eminently successful with their free-lance vessels assailing our commerce on the seas of the world, and while they conceived and accomplished much in the construction of great iron-clads, their vessels were all singularly fated to be valueless in promoting the Confederate cause. When it is remembered that had the Federal blockade been raised in any of our leading ports and an open port maintained, as was possible by each of these Confederate iron-clads, the recognition of the Confederacy by England and France would have speedily followed, we may justly appreciate the magnitude of the succession of disasters that attended these Confederate engines of war.

The civilized world dates the emancipation of slaves in the United States with President Lincoln's proclamation of January 1st, 1863, and all historians of the future will date the overthrow of bondage in our land with that immortal instrument. But the Emancipation Proclamation was not the end of slavery; it was simply the means that crystallized the forces that led to universal freedom within the limits of the Republic. In point of fact, President Lincoln's Emancipation Proclamation did not liberate a single slave, and it did not even assume to overthrow slavery in all the States of the Union. Tennessee, Maryland, and Delaware, three slave States then in partial accord with the Government, and nearly one-half the territory of Virginia and

BIRD'S-EYE VIEW OF THE NORTH END OF ANDERSONVILLE PRISON.
(From a photograph.)

In the middle-ground midway of the swamp is the "Island" which was covered with shelters after the higher ground had all been occupied.

considerable portion of the territory of Louisiana, were expressly excluded from the operations of the proclamation. It was an exercise of the extreme authority of the Executive under the war powers of the Constitution, and had it been thus carried into effect, it would have left slavery existing in five of the States. Congress had advanced toward emancipation to the extent of giving freedom to every slave that reached the Federal lines whose master was in rebellion against the Government, and the Emancipation

Proclamation practically accomplished nothing more. While it proclaimed freedom to all the slaves within the States and territory named, their actual freedom was not attained until our victorious armies brought them within our lines, and possessed the territory of the slave States.

President Lincoln well appreciated the fact that his proclamation was simply the final step toward the utter overthrow of slavery, and that other and most important agencies were essential to the completion of the great work with which his name must ever be associated. A prompt movement was made in Congress to give completeness to the emancipation policy by a constitutional amendment forbidding slavery in every State and Territory of the Union, and one of the most desperate Congressional struggles of the war was precipitated by that effort. It was defeated in 1864, wanting

LIBBY PRISON IN 1865.

several votes of the necessary two-thirds in the House, but the same House, during the second session, finally adopted it, and thus slavery was abolished throughout the length and breadth of the land, and thus the complete triumph of Lincoln's Emancipation Policy was attained. But none the less will future generations turn back to Lincoln's Emancipation Proclamation, as we do now, to date the deliverance of the great Republic of the world from the blistering stain of human bondage, and throughout all the peoples of the earth where the altar of liberty shall be known, there will the name of Abraham Lincoln be honored, because it gave freedom to 4,000,000 of bondmen.

There are very many forgotten lessons taught on the bloody battle fields of our Civil War which will never be recorded in history. The battle of Gettysburg, the Waterloo of the Confederacy, furnishes some most conspicuous instances of the apparent accidents which control the destiny of great armies, and possibly the destiny of nations. That great battle-field had not been chosen by the leaders of either army. It was accident or fate, or the omnipotent power that rules over all, that doomed the Confederate army to be defeated when it was most confident of victory and best equipped in numbers, munitions, and confidence for a triumphant campaign. The first day was an appalling disaster to the Federal army. Two army corps, embracing probably one-fourth of Meade's entire force, were not only defeated but routed in that engagement, the commanding officer killed, and the demoralized Federal forces driven through Gettysburg to Cemetery Hill. Had they been pursued by the Con-

LIBBY PRISON IN 1884, BEFORE ITS REMOVAL TO CHICAGO.

federate force that had defeated them, they could have been captured or scattered so as to be ineffective in the future battle; and even after the pursuit had been abandoned and Confederate headquarters established on Seminary Hill, Round Top, that commanded the left of the Federal position, and Culp's Hill, that commanded its right, could have been taken without firing a gun. Had that been done, the most impregnable position between Williamsport and Washington could not have been held an hour the following morning, the great decisive battle of the war, fought between the opposing lines on Cemetery and Seminary Hills, would have been unknown to history, and on no other field chosen by the Federal commander could Lee have been compelled to fight at such a disadvantage. Had Meade been defeated at Gettysburg who could measure the consequences? Baltimore, Philadelphia, all the teeming wealth of the Lancaster and Cumberland valleys, and possibly even the Capital itself, would have been at the mercy of the Southern victors.

Three days' delay in the arrival of pontoon trains at Fredericksburg not only lost Burnside that battle, but ended in one of the most bloody assaults of the war, and one that was equaled only by Pickett's assault at Gettysburg in the wanton sacrifice of life. Burnside's delay, caused by the failure of his pontoon trains, gave Lee ample time to concentrate his army and entrench himself on the heights of Fredericksburg, and the defeat of the Federal army, with 16,000 killed and wounded, was the sequel of the blunder. The mistake of a single officer in choosing a road when executing the orders of General Meade in marching upon Mine Run, in all human probability, saved Lee from a most disastrous defeat, and compelled Meade to retire and close the campaign. Had his plans been executed he would have suddenly thrown his entire army between Lee's divided forces, fought them in detail and defeated them ; but the mistaken march of part of his army separated his own forces and enabled Lee to concentrate at Mine Run, where he was so strongly entrenched that his position was absolutely impregnable. Many such instances might be cited, and results no less momentous frequently depended upon the condition of the roads and bridges, or of the weather, for " moist weather at the front " meant indefinite delay in the movement of trains and utter uncertainty as to the time in which necessary movements could be executed. The most heroic strategy of the war was exhibited by General Grant, when he swung his army away from the Mississippi River around to Jackson, defeated General Johnson in several pitched battles, separated him finally from General Pemberton, and shut Pemberton up in Vicksburg for his memorable siege that ended in the surrender of Pemberton's army six weeks thereafter. Grant is the only General of the army who would have made that campaign, and he did it against the advice of his subordinate officers and even against the written protest of General Sherman. It was a most perilous venture, but it meant the surrender and early capture of Vicksburg if successful, and Grant made it a success by his indomitable courage and celerity of movement. How he moved may be understood when it is stated that he was himself entirely without personal baggage, and he was so swift in his marches and in his attacks upon the enemy that when Johnson was defeated in the first battle, he was never given time to concentrate for another. But for that heroic movement it is doubtful whether Vicksburg could have been captured at all, and it is reasonably certain that, if captured, it would have been months later and after fearful sacrifice of life.

It was the deep-seated personal prejudice of Jefferson Davis that made Sherman's romantic march to the sea possible, in 1864. General Joseph E. Johnson was not in favor with the Confederate President. A short time before he capture of Atlanta, Davis appeared there in person, removed Johnson from command and substituted General Hood, who was a brave but unskillful General; and in a public speech Davis gave notice that the Confederate army vas to assume the aggressive. Hood speedily justified the prediction of Davis

THE CAPTURE OF BOOTH, THE SLAYER OF LINCOLN.

y making a desperate assault upon Sherman's lines to raise the siege of Atlanta. : was one of the bloodiest conflicts of the war, and for an hour or more after IcPherson fell victory seemed to tremble in the balance, but Hood's army was nally defeated after terrible slaughter, and so impaired in strength that herman was soon able to manœuvre him out of Atlanta without another great battle. Had General Johnson remained in command at Atlanta, it is entirely safe to say that General Sherman never would have attempted his march to the sea.

Stonewall Jackson made the most heroic and perilous movement at Chancellorsville ever made by the Confederate army. He divided Lee's forces in the face of an enemy overwhelmingly superior in numbers, made a long march to strike General Hooker's right, surprised it, routed it and compelled Hooker's retreat back across the Rapidan without the two great armies meeting face to face in a general engagement. That movement cost Jackson his life and the Confederate army, confessedly, its ablest Lieutenant. Had Jackson opened the battle of Gettysburg there would have been no battle fought on Cemetery Hill. He would have possessed the strong positions on both flanks of that line, and the battle on the second day would not have been delayed until after mid-day. That delay enabled Meade largely to increase his army by the arrival of fresh corps and to make his position impregnable by fortification. It was the absence of the special qualities possessed by Jackson that lost Lee more than an even chance for winning that desperate and decisive conflict. There was but one General in the Union army who could have captured Lee at Appomattox. It was General Sheridan, and Sheridan alone, who made Lee's escape impossible. He was the very fiend of battle, capable of greater endurance than any other officer in the field, and inspired as he was by the hope of making Lee captive, he neither slept nor rested after the battle of Five Forks until the end came at Appomattox. Lee would have been defeated and routed without Sheridan, but he is the only General who would have forced Lee to surrender in an open country.

The general public has almost forgotten the latest attempt of a European government to gain a foothold in North America. The brief reign of Maximilian as Emperor of Mexico; his base desertion by the Emperor of the French when it became evident that the United States was to survive the rebellion as a united and powerful nation, and that the continued presence of a European army on American soil was regarded by the great Republic as a demonstration of hostility, and resented as such; the immediate collapse of the empire when foreign support was withdrawn and the tragic death of Maximilian, form one of the saddest, but one of the most instructive, chapters in American history.

Such are some of the forgotten lessons of the war, and if all of them were carefully studied and faithfully presented, they would fill a large volume of most interesting history; but the actors in that crimson drama are rapidly passing away. Not one of the great chieftains of either the blue or the gray now survives, and each year sadly thins the already narrow circle of those who can recall the many forgotten lessons which are so romantically or so tragically interwoven with the history of the most heroic conflict ever made in man's

16   WILLIAM T. SHERMAN.

struggle for man. It is well to believe that some of its lessons will never be forgotten. The horror of war which so hindered the prompt suppression of the Rebellion grew deeper and took firmer hold upon the minds of our people. To those communities, North and South, which sent out their best and bravest to unknown graves on distant battle-fields ; to those families who waited with fear and trembling to know at what cost to them was purchased the last great victory ; to those who saw their loved ones painfully hobbling upon crutches, or carrying an empty sleeve, or returning, the shadow of their former selves, from the horror of Andersonville or Libby Prison ; to these, and they were our whole people, war was, and is, utterly horrible.

It is well to remember how the great man whose election to the presidency precipitated the conflict in those four years of supreme trial, of sadness and of victory, bound to him the hearts of the people ; and it is well to remember how, even in that terrible time when Lincoln was assassinated, and when his slayer was being pursued and captured, in the hour which might seem to invite anarchy, our national administration was equal to every emergency, and the government was undisturbed. That a government of the people can live through such catastrophes is a lesson not soon to be forgotten. The great lesson of the war is the permanency, the adaptability and the adequacy of republican institutions.

A. K. McCLURE.

The Story of Our Navy and Great Naval Battles.

FIGHT BETWEEN HON HOMME RICHARD AND SERAPIS.

PRIOR to the breaking out of the Revolutionary War, America had no navy. The colonists had before this time looked to the mother country for protection on the seas. But in the fall of 1775, when war seemed imminent, the building of thirteen war-cruisers was begun. Only one of these ships-of-the-line was built—the "America"—and she was given to France before she was launched. During the whole war, a total of twenty small frigates and twenty-one sloops flew the American flag; and fifteen of the former and ten of the latter were either captured or destroyed. What cockle-shells they were, and how slight in armament, compared with the floating fortresses of to-day, may be reckoned from the fact that twelve-pounders were their heaviest guns. Beside these, of course, there were many privateers, sent out to prey upon the enemy's commerce. These swift fishing craft ventured even to cruise along the very coast of England, and down to the time of the French alliance captured more than six hundred English vessels.

In the annals of the regular navy, there are but three great captains' names: Wickes, Conyngham, and Jones. It was Lambert Wickes who, on his little steen-gun "Reprisal," first bore the American war-flag to the shores of Europe, and made it a terror to the great power that claimed to "rule the waves." After a brilliant cruise the "Reprisal" went down, with all hands, in the summer of 1777, on the treacherous banks of Newfoundland. Then Gustavus Conyngham took up the work, with his "Surprise" and "Revenge," and that very summer so scourged the might of England in the North Sea and in the British Channel itself, that the ports were crowded with ships that dared not venture out, and the rates of marine insurance rose to fabulous figures.

But the one splendid name of that era was that of a canny young Scotch-man, John Paul Jones. Eighteenth he stood on the list of captains commissioned by the Congress, but on the scroll of fame, for those times, first—and there is no second. Coming to Virginia in boyhood, he entered the mercantile marine. When the war broke out he offered his services to the Congress, and was made a captain. And in 1778 he was sent with the "Ranger," of eighteen guns, to follow where Wickes and Conyngham had led. He swept with his tiny craft up and down the Irish Channel, entered Whitehaven and burned the shipping at the docks; captured off Carrickfergus the British war-sloop "Drake," larger than his own ship, and then made his way to Brest with all his prizes in tow.

Next year he set out on his immortal cruise, with a squadron of five ships. His flagship was an old merchantman, the "Duras," fitted up for fighting and renamed the "Bon Homme Richard," in honor of Franklin and his "Poor Richard's Almanac." She was a clumsy affair, armed with thirty-two twelve-pounders and six old eighteen-pounders not fit for use, and manned by 380 men of every race, from New Englanders to Malays. The "Pallas" was also a merchantman transformed into a thirty-two gun frigate. The "Vengeance" and the "Cerf" were much smaller; quite insignificant. The "Alliance" was a new ship, built in Massachusetts for the navy, but unhappily commanded by a Frenchman named Landais, half fool, half knave. Indeed, all the vessels save the flagship were commanded by Frenchmen, who were openly insubordinate, refusing half the time to recognize the commodore's authority, and often leaving him to cruise and fight alone. Yet the motley squadron did much execution along the shores of Britain. It all but captured the city of Leith, and entered Humber and destroyed much shipping.

But the crowning glory came on September 23, 1779. On that immortal date Jones espied, off Flamborough Head, a fleet of forty British merchantmen, guarded by two frigates, bound for the Baltic. At once he gave chase. He had, besides his own ship, only the "Pallas" and the "Alliance," but they would be sufficient to capture the whole fleet. But the miserable Landais refused to obey the signal, and kept out of the action. So the fight began, two and two. Jones, with the "Bon Homme Richard," attacked the "Serapis," Captain Pearson, and the "Pallas" engaged the "Countess of Scarborough." The "Sera-pis" had fifty guns and was much faster and stronger than Jones's ship. **The**

"Countess of Scarborough," on the other hand, was much inferior to the "Pallas" and proved an early victim.

It was growing dark, on a cloudy evening, and the sea was smooth as a mill-pond, when the "Bon Homme Richard" and the "Serapis" began their awful duel. Both fired full broadsides at the same instant. Two of Jones's old eighteen-pounders burst, killing twelve men, and the others were at once abandoned. So all through the fight, after that first volley, he had only his thirty-two twelve-pounders against the fifty guns—twenty of them eighteen-pounders, twenty nine-pounders, and ten six-pounders—of the "Serapis." For an hour they fought and manœuvred, then came together with a crash. An instant, the firing ceased. "Have you struck your colors?" demanded Pearson. "I have not yet begun to fight!" replied Jones. Then with his own hands Jones lashed the two ships together, and inseparably joined, their sides actually touching, they battled on. Solid shot and canister swept through both ships like hail, while musket-men on the decks and in the rigging exchanged storms of bullets. For an hour and a half the conflict raged. Then Landais came up with the "Alliance" and began firing

PAUL JONES.

equally on both. Jones ordered him to go to the other side of the "Serapis" and board, and his answer was to turn helm and go out of the fight altogether. Now the fighting ships were both afire, and both leaking and sinking. Most of the guns were disabled, and three-fourths of the men were killed or wounded. The gallant Pearson stood almost alone on the deck of the doomed "Serapis," not one of his men able to fight longer. Jones was as solitary on the "Bon Homme Richard," all his men still able-bodied being at the pumps, striving to keep the ship afloat. With his own hands he trained a gun upon the mainmast of the "Serapis," and cut it down; and then Pearson surrendered. The "Pallas" and "Alliance" came up and took off the men, and in a few hours the two ships sank, still bound together in the clasp of death.

This was not only one of the most desperate and deadly naval battles in history. Its moral effect was epoch-making. John Paul Jones was the hero of the day, and Europe showered honors upon him. The American flag was hailed as a rival to that of England on the seas, and all Europe was encouraged to unite against England and force her to abate her arrogant pretensions, and to accede to a more just and liberal code of international maritime law than had before prevailed. In view of this latter fact, this battle must be ranked among the three or four most important in the naval history of the world. It was this battle that inspired Catharine of Russia to enunciate the doctrine of the rights of neutrals in maritime affairs; and the tardy acquiescence of England, eighty years later, in that now universal principle, was brought about by the blow struck by John Paul Jones off Flamborough Head.

There were no other naval operations of importance during the Revolution, save those of the French fleet at Yorktown. But soon after the declaration of peace, new complications arose, threatening a war at sea. England and France were fighting each other, and commerce was therefore diverted to the shipping of other nations. A very large share of Europe's carrying trade was done by American vessels. But these were between two fires. England insisted that she had a right to stop and search American ships and take from them all sailors of English birth; actually taking whom she pleased; and France made free to seize any American ships she pleased, under the pretext that there were English goods aboard; and when she captured an English ship and found on board an American seaman who had been impressed, instead of treating him as a prisoner of war, like the others, she hanged him as a pirate.

Naturally indignation rose high, and preparations were made for war with France. In July, 1798, the three famous frigates, the "Constellation," the "United States," and the "Constitution," best known as "Old Ironsides," were sent to sea, and Congress authorized the navy to be increased to include six frigates, twelve sloops, and six smaller craft. Among the officers commissioned, were the illustrious Bainbridge, Hull, Decatur, Rodgers, and Stewart. Actual hostilities soon began. French piratical cruisers were captured, and an American squadron sailed for the West Indies to deal with the French privateers that abounded there, in which work it was generally successful. In January, 1799, Congress voted a million dollars, for building six ships of the line and six sloops. Soon after, on February 9, occurred the first engagement between vessels of the American and French navies. The "Constellation," Captain Truxton, overhauled "L'Insurgente," at St. Kitts, in the West Indies, and after a fight of an hour and a quarter forced her to surrender. The "Constellation" had three men killed and one wounded ; "L'Insurgente" twenty killed and forty-six wounded.

Again, on February 1, 1800, Truxton with the "Constellation" came up, at Guadeloupe, with the French Frigate "La Vengeance." After chasing her two days he brought on an action. The two ships fought all night. In the morning, "La Vengeance," completely silenced and shattered, drew away and escaped to Curacoa, where she was condemned as unfit for further service. The "Constellation" was little injured save in her rigging. For his gallantry, Truxton received a gold medal from Congress. Later in that year there were some minor engagements, in which Americans were successful.

By the spring of 1801, friendly relations with France were restored. The President was accordingly authorized to dispose of all the navy, save thirteen ships, six of which were to be kept constantly in commission, and to dismiss from the service all officers save nine captains, thirty-six lieutenants, and one hundred and fifty midshipmen. At about this time ground was purchased and navy-yards established at Portsmouth, Boston, New York, Philadelphia, Washington and Norfolk, and half a million dollars was appropriated for the completion of six seventy-four gun ships.

Now came on real war. For many years the pirate ships of the Barbary States, Algeria and Tripoli, had been the scourge of the Mediterranean. The commerce of every land had suffered. European powers did not venture to suppress the evil, but some of them basely purchased immunity by paying tribute to the pirates. America, too, at first followed this humiliating course, actually thus paying millions of dollars. In September, 1800, Captain Bainbridge went with the frigate "George Washington" to bear to the Dey of Algeria the annual tribute. The Dey took the money, and then impressed Bainbridge and his ship into his own service for a time, to go on an errand to Constantinople. Bainbridge reported this to Congress, adding, "I hope I shall never again be sent with tribute, unless to deliver it from the mouth of our cannon." However, Bainbridge was received courteously at Constantinople, and his ship was the first to display the American flag there.

Captain Dale was sent with a squadron to the Mediterranean in 1801, to repress the pirates of Tripoli. One of his ships, the schooner "Experiment," captured a Tripolitan cruiser, and this checked for a time the ardor of the pirates. But open war was soon declared between the two countries, and Congress authorized the sending of a larger fleet to the Mediterranean. The gallant Truxton was offered the command of it, but declined because the cheese-paring Administration was too parsimonious to allow him a proper staff of subordinates. Thereupon he was dismissed from the service, and Captain Morris sent in his place. But false economy had so enfeebled the navy that the fleet was able to do little. One Tripolitan ship was captured, however, and another destroyed.

Then the Government woke up, and began building new ships, and sent another squadron over, led by Preble with the "Constitution." He went first to Morocco, whose Sultan at once sued for peace; and then proceeded to Tripoli. Here he found that the frigate "Philadelphia," with Bainbridge and three hundred men aboard, had been captured and was being refitted by the Tripolitans for their own use. Decatur, commanding the "Enterprise," under Preble, determined upon a bold counter-stroke. Taking a small vessel, the "Intrepid," which he had captured from Tripoli, he sailed boldly into the harbor, flying the Tripolitan flag and pretending to be a merchant of that country. Running alongside the "Philadelphia," he boarded her, set her afire, and sailed away in safety, though amid a storm of shot and shell. The "Philadelphia" was burned to the water's edge.

Nothing more was done at the time, however, save to keep up a blockade, and Bainbridge and his men remained in captivity. In August, 1804, Preble and Decatur made a vigorous attack upon the harbor, and destroyed two and captured three vessels. A few days later other attacks were made. Then a new squadron under Commodore Barron came to the scene, and Preble was superseded. No other naval operations of importance occurred, and peace was finally concluded in 1805.

Troubles with England now grew more serious. That country persisted in searching American ships and taking from them all whom she chose to call deserters from the British service. And so the two powers drifted into the war of 1812. In that struggle, the Americans were badly worsted on land, but won victories of the first magnitude on the lakes and ocean. America had only nine frigates and a score of smaller craft, while England had a hundred ships of the line. Yet the honors of the war on the sea rested with the former. Her triumphs startled the world. The destruction of the "Guerriere" by the "Constitution," Captain Hull, marked an epoch in naval history. Then the "United States," Captain Decatur, vanquished the "Macedonian;" the "Wasp," Captain Jones, the "Frolic;" the "Constitution," Captain Bainbridge, the "Java;" and the "Hornet" the "Peacock." On Lake Erie, Commodore Perry won a great victory, which he announced in the famous message, "We have met the enemy, and they are ours." Equally brilliant was the victory of MacDonough on Lake Champlain. The most deplorable reverse was the destruction of the "Chesapeake" by the British ship "Shannon," the "Chesapeake's" commander, Lawrence, losing his life, but winning fame through his dying words, "Don't give up the ship!"

The conflicts of this war are more fully detailed elsewhere in this volume. It is needful here only to mention them briefly, as we have done. The cause of the surprising successes of the Americans may well be explained, however. It was due to that very inventive ingenuity that has made the history of the

world's industrial progress so largely a mere chronicle of "Yankee notions." The Americans had invented and were using sights on their cannon. That was all. But the result was that their aim was far more accurate and their fire far more effective than that of their opponents. This advantage, added to courage and skill in seamanship equal to any the world had known, gave them their victory.

This war was ended in February, 1815, and a month later another was begun. This was against the Dey of Algeria, who had broken the peace and seized an American ship, despite the fact that America had continued down to this time to pay tribute to him. It was now determined to make an end of the business; so Bainbridge was sent, as he had requested, to deliver the final tribute from his cannons' mouths. Before he got there, however, Decatur did the work. He captured an Algerine vessel; sailed into port and dictated an honorable peace; and then imposed like terms on Tripoli and Tunis, thus ending the tyranny of the Barbary States over the commerce of the world.

Thereafter for many years the navy had not much to do. Some vessels were used for purposes of exploration and research, and much was thereby added to the scientific knowledge of the world. During the Mexican war, naval operations were unimportant. But in 1846 complications with Japan were begun. In that year two ships were sent to the Island empire, on an errand of peaceful negotiation, which proved fruitless. Three years later another went, on a sterner errand, and rescued at the cannon's mouth a number of shipwrecked American sailors who had been thrown into captivity.

Finally the task of "opening Japan" to intercourse with the rest of the world, a task no other power had ventured to assume, was undertaken by America. On November 24, 1852, Commodore Perry set sail thither, with a powerful fleet. His commission was to "open Japan"; by peaceful diplomacy if he could, by force of arms if he must. The simple show of force was sufficient, and in 1854, he returned in triumph, bearing a treaty with Japan.

The most extended and important services of the United States navy were performed during the War of the Rebellion. At the outbreak of that conflict, in 1861, the whole navy comprised only forty-two vessels in commission. Nearly all of these were scattered in distant parts of the world, where they had been purposely sent by the conspirators at Washington. Most of those that remained were destroyed in port, so that there was actually for a time only one serviceable war-ship on the North Atlantic coast. But building and purchase soon increased the navy, so that before the end of the year it numbered two hundred and sixty-four, and was able to blockade all the ports of the Southern Confederacy. They were a motley set, vessels of every imaginable type, ferry-boats and freight steamers, even, being pressed into use; but they served.

The first important naval action was that at Hatteras Inlet, in August, 1861,

There Commodore Stringham, with a fleet of steam and sailing craft, bombarded a series of powerful forts and forced them to surrender, without the loss of a single man aboard the ships. Next came the storming of Port Royal. At the end of October Commodore Dupont and Commander Rodgers went thither with a strong squadron. They entered the harbor, and formed with their ships an ellipse, which kept constantly revolving, opposite the forts, and constantly pouring in a murderous fire. It was earthworks on land against old-fashioned wooden ships on the water; but the ships won, and the forts surrendered. A small flotilla of rebel gunboats came to the assistance of the forts, but were quickly repulsed by the heavy fire from the ships.

The next year saw much naval activity in many quarters. The blockade of all Southern ports was rigorously maintained, and there were some exciting engagements between the national ships and blockade runners. On the Cumberland, Ohio, Tennessee and Mississippi Rivers the gunboats of Foote and Porter greatly aided the land forces, in the campaigns against Fort Henry and Fort Donelson, at Island No. 10, and Vicksburg. Roanoke Island and New Berne, on the Carolina coast, were taken by a combined naval and military expedition.

One of the most striking events of the war was the entrance of the Mississippi and capture of New Orleans by Admiral Farragut. He had a fleet of forty vessels, all told. Opposed to him were two great and strong land forts, Jackson and St. Philip, one on each side of the river, mounting two hundred and twenty-five guns. From one to the other stretched a ponderous iron chain, completely barring the passage, and beyond this was a fleet of iron-clad gun-boats, fire-ships, etc. Military and naval authorities scouted the idea that Farragut's wooden ships could ever fight their way through. But Farragut quietly scouted the authorities. Making his way up to within range of the forts he began a bombardment. On the first day his guns threw 2000 shells at the enemy. A huge fire-raft was sent against him, but his ships avoided it and it passed harmlessly by. Another was sent down that night, a floating mountain of flame. But one of Farragut's captains deliberately ran his ship into it, turned a hose upon it, and towed it out of the way!

For a week the tremendous bombardment was kept up, 16,800 shells being thrown at the forts. Then Farragut cut the chain, and started to run the fiery gauntlet of the forts with his fleet. Before daylight one morning the mortar-boats opened a furious fire, under cover of which the ships steamed straight up the river. The forts opened on them with every gun, a perfect storm of shot and shell, and the ships replied with full broadsides. Five hundred cannon were thundering. One ship was disabled and dropped back. The rest swept on in a cloud of flame. Before they were past the forts, fire-ships came down upon them, and iron-clad gunboats attacked them. The "Varuna," Captain

Boggs, was surrounded by five rebel gunboats, and sank them all.　As the last of them sank, a sixth, a huge iron-clad ram, came rushing upon the "Varuna." Boggs saw he could not escape it, so he turned the "Varuna" so as to receive the blow squarely amidships.　The ram crushed her like an egg-shell, and in a few minutes she sank.　But her fearful broadsides, at such close range, riddled the ram, and the two went down together.　In an hour and a half, eleven rebel gunboats were sent to the bottom, and the fleet was past the forts.　Next

SINKING OF THE ALABAMA.

morning Farragut raised the national flag above the captured city of New Orleans.

　　This tremendous conflict was not, however, the most significant of that year.　There was another which, in a single hour, revolutionized the art of naval warfare.　When, at the outbreak of the war, the Norfolk Navy-yard had been destroyed to keep it from falling into rebel hands, one ship partially escaped the flames.　This was the great frigate "Merrimac," probably the finest ship in the whole navy. The Confederates took her hull, which remained uninjured, and covered it completely with a sloping roof of iron plates four inches thick, backed with heavy timbers, put a great iron ram at her bow, and fitted her with large guns and powerful engines. Then, to protect her further, she was coated thickly with tallow and plumbago. She was regarded as entirely invulnerable to cannon-shot, and her builders believed she would easily destroy all ships sent against her and place New York and all Northern seaports at the mercy of her guns. At the same time a curious little craft was built, hurriedly enough, in New York. It was designed by John Ericsson, and was called the "Monitor." It consisted of a hull nearly all submerged, its flat iron deck only a few inches above the water, and upon this a circular iron tower, which was turned round and round by machinery and which carried two large guns. Naval experts laughed at the "cheese-box on a plank," as they called it, and thought it unworthy of serious consideration.

A REVOLUTION IN NAVAL WARFARE.

At noon of Saturday, March 8, the mighty "Merrimac," a floating fortress of iron, came down the Elizabeth River to where the National fleet lay in Hampton Roads. The frigate "Congress" fired upon her, but she paid no attention to it, but moved on to the sloop-of-war "Cumberland," crushed her side in with a blow of her ram, riddled her with cannon-balls, and sent her to the bottom. The solid shot from the "Cumberland's" ten-inch guns glanced from the "Merrimac's" armor, harmless as so many peas. Then the monster turned back to the "Congress" and destroyed her. Next she attacked the frigate "Minnesota" and drove her aground, and then retired for the night, intending the next day to return, destroy the entire fleet, and proceed northward to bombard New York.

That night the "Monitor" arrived. She had been hurriedly completed. She had come down from New York in a storm, and was leaking and her machinery was out of order. She was not in condition for service. But she was all that lay between the "Merrimac" and the boundless destruction at which she aimed. So she anchored at the side of the "Minnesota" and waited for daylight. It came, a beautiful Sunday morning; and down came the huge "Merrimac" to continue her deadly work. Out steamed the tiny "Monitor" to meet her. The "Merrimac" sought to ignore her, and attacked the "Minnesota." But the "Monitor" would not be ignored. Captain Worden ran her alongside the "Merrimac," so that they almost touched, and hurled his 160-lb shot at the iron monster as rapidly as the two guns could be worked. Those shots, at that range, told, as all the broadsides of the frigates had not. The "Merrimac's" armor began to yield, while her own firing had no effect upon the "Monitor." It was seldom she could hit the little craft at all, and when she did the shots glanced off without harm. Five times she tried to ram the "Monitor," but the latter eluded her. A sixth time she tried it, and the "Monitor" stood still and let her come on The great iron beak that had crushed in the side of the "Cumberland" merely glanced on the "Monitor's" armor and glided upon her deck. The "Merrimac" was so lifted and tilted as to expose the unarmored part of her hull to the "Monitor's" deadly fire, while the "Monitor" quickly slid out from under her, uninjured. Then the "Merrimac" retreated up the river, and her career was ended. She was a mere wreck. But the "Monitor," though struck by twenty-two heavy shots, was practically uninjured. The only man hurt on the "Monitor" was the gallant Captain Worden. He was looking through the peep-hole when one of the "Merrimac's" last shots struck squarely just outside. He was stunned by the shock and half-blinded by splinters; but his first words on regaining consciousness were, "Have we saved the 'Minnesota'?"

The "Monitor" had saved the "Minnesota," and all the rest of the fleet, and probably many Northern cities. But, more than that, she had, in that grim duel, revolutionized naval warfare. In that hour England saw her great ships of the line condemned. The splendid frigates, with their tiers of guns, were thenceforth out of date and worthless. The "cheese-box on a plank" in a single day had vanquished all the navies of the world.

The success of Farragut in passing the Mississippi forts led Dupont, in April, 1863, to attempt in like manner to enter Charleston harbor; but in vain. The fire from the forts was too fierce, and his fleet was forced to fall back with heavy losses. But in August, 1864, Farragut repeated his former exploit at Mobile. Forming his ships in line of battle, he stood in the rigging of the "Hartford," glass in hand, and directed their movements. As Dupont had done at Port Royal, he swept round and round in a fiery ellipse. At a critical point in the battle the lookout reported, "Torpedoes ahead!" A cry arose to stop the ship. "Go ahead! Damn the torpedoes!" roared the great Admiral, and the ship went on. Then the huge iron ram "Tennessee" came forward, to crush them as the "Merrimac" had crushed the "Cumberland." But Farragut, with sublime audacity, turned the bow of his wooden ship upon her and ran her down. Thus the Mobile forts were silenced and the harbor cleared. Nor must the storming of Fort Fisher be forgotten. The first attack was made in December, 1864. Admiral Porter bombarded the place furiously, and then General Butler attempted to take it with land forces. He failed, and returned to Fortress Monroe, saying the place could not be taken. But Porter thought otherwise, and remained at his post with his fleet. General Terry then went down with an army. Porter renewed the bombardment, the fort was captured, and the last port of the Confederacy was closed.

While the National navy was thus carrying all before it along the coast, the Confederates were active elsewhere. Their swift, armed cruisers, fitted out

in English ports, scoured the seas and preyed upon American commerce everywhere, until the American merchant flag was almost banished from the ocean. The most famous of all these cruisers was the "Alabama," commanded by Raphael Semmes. During her career she destroyed more than ten million dollars' worth of American shipping. For a long time her speed and the skill and daring of her commander kept her out of the hands of the American navy. But at last, in June, 1864, Captain Winslow, with the ship "Kearsarge," came up with her in the neutral harbor of Cherbourg, France. Determined to make an end of her, he waited, just outside the harbor, for her to come out. Semmes soon accepted the challenge, and the duel occurred on Sunday, June 19. The shore was crowded with spectators, and many yachts and other craft came out, bearing hundreds anxious to see the battle. The vessels were not far from equal in strength. But the "Kearsarge" had two huge eleven-inch pivot guns, that made awful havoc on the "Alabama." The "Alabama," on the other hand, had more guns than the "Kearsarge." But the famous cruiser's time had come. As the two ships slowly circled round and round, keeping up a constant fire, every shot from the "Kearsarge" seemed to find its mark, while those of the "Alabama" went wide. And soon the "Alabama" sank, leaving the "Kearsarge" scarcely injured.

A volume might be filled with accounts of notable exploits of the navy which there is not room even to mention here. But one more must be named, so daring and so novel was it. In April, 1864, the great iron-clad ram, "Albemarle," was completed by the Confederates and sent forth to drive the National vessels from the sounds and harbors of the North Carolina coast. She came down the Roanoke River and boldly attacked the fleet, destroying one ship at the first onset and damaging others, while showing herself almost invulnerable. It was feared that she would actually succeed in raising the blockade, and extraordinary efforts were made to destroy her, but without avail.

At last the job was undertaken by a young officer, Lieutenant Cushing, who had already distinguished himself by his daring. He took a small steam launch, manned by himself and fifteen others, armed with a howitzer, and carrying a large torpedo. The "Albemarle" was at her dock at Plymouth, some miles up the river, and both banks of the narrow stream were closely lined with pickets and batteries. On a dark, stormy night the launch steamed boldly up the river and got within a short distance of the "Albemarle" before it was seen by the pickets. Instantly the alarm was given, and a hail of bullets fell upon the launch, doing, however, little harm. Cushing headed straight for the huge iron-clad, shouting at the top of his voice, in bravado, "Get off the ram! We're going to blow you up!" Running the launch up till its bow touched the side of the "Albemarle," he thrust the torpedo, at the end of a pole, under the latter and fired it. The explosion wrecked the "Albemarle" and sank her. The launch was also wrecked, and the sixteen men took to the water and sought to escape by swimming. All were, however, captured by the Confederates, save four. Of these, two were drowned, and the other two—one of them being Cushing himself—reached the other shore and got safely back to the fleet.

We have said that in the spring of 1861 there were only 42 vessels in commission in the navy. There were also 27 serviceable ships not in commission and 21 unserviceable, or 90 in all. During the four years of the war there were built and added to the navy 125 unarmored and 68 armored vessels, most of the latter being of the " Monitor " type. A few figures regarding some of the engagements will give a vivid idea of the manner in which the ships fought. In the futile attack of the iron-clads on the forts in Charleston harbor, April 7, 1863, nine vessels took part, using 23 guns and firing 139 times, at from 500 to 2100 yards range. They hit Fort Wagner twice, Fort Moultrie 12 times, and Fort Sumter 55 times, doing little damage. Against them the forts used 77 guns, firing 2229 times, and hitting the vessels 520 times, but doing little damage except to one monitor, which was sunk. In the second bombardment of Fort Fisher 21,716 projectiles, solid shot and shell, were thrown by the fleet.

But the most important thing achieved was the entire transformation effected in naval science. Hitherto the war-ship had been simply an armed merchant-ship, propelled by sails or, latterly, by steam, carrying a large number of small guns. American inventiveness made it, after the duel of the " Monitor " and " Merrimac," a floating fortress of iron or steel, carrying a few enormously heavy guns. The glory of the old line-of-battle ship, with three or four tiers of guns on each side and a big cloud of canvas overhead, firing rattling broadsides, and manœuvring to get and hold the weather-gauge of the enemy—all that was relegated to the past forever. In its place came the engine of war, with little pomp and circumstance, but with all the resources of science shut within its ugly, black iron hull.

John Paul Jones, with his " Bon Homme Richard," struck the blow that made universal the law of neutrals' rights. Hull, with the " Constitution," sending a British frigate to the bottom, showed what Yankee ingenuity in sighting guns could do. Ericsson and Worden, with the " Monitor," sent wooden navies to the hulk-yard and ushered in the era of iron and steel fighting-engines. These are the three great naval events of a century.

One of the most thrilling events in naval history occurred in a time of peace. It was in the harbor of Apia, Samoa, in March, 1889. A great storm struck the shipping and destroyed nearly every vessel there. Three German war-ships were wrecked. One English war-ship, by herculean efforts, was saved. Two American war-ships were wrecked, and one was saved after being run on the beach. This was the " Nipsic." The wrecked vessels were the

17

"Trenton" and the "Vandalia." The combined strength of their engines and anchors was not enough to keep them from being driven upon the fateful reefs. The "Vandalia" was already stranded and pounding to pieces, and the "Trenton" was drifting down upon her. "Suddenly," says a witness of the scene, "the Stars and Stripes were seen flying from the gaff of the 'Trenton.' Previous to this no vessel in the harbor had raised a flag, as the storm was raging so furiously at sunrise that that ceremony was neglected. It seemed now as if the gallant ship knew she was doomed, and had determined to go down with the flag of her country floating above the storm. Presently the last faint ray of daylight faded away, and night came down upon the awful scene. The storm was still raging with as much fury as at any time during the day. The poor creatures who had been clinging for hours to the rigging of the 'Vandalia' were bruised and bleeding, but they held on with the desperation of men who hang by a thread between life and death. The ropes had cut the flesh of their arms and legs, and their eyes were blinded by the salt spray which swept over them. Weak and exhausted as they were, they would be unable to stand the terrible strain much longer. They looked down upon the angry water below them, and knew that they had no strength left to battle with the waves. Their final hour seemed to be upon them. The great black hull of the 'Trenton' could be seen through the darkness, almost ready to crush into the stranded 'Vandalia' and grind her to atoms. Suddenly a shout was borne across the waters. The 'Trenton' was cheering the 'Vandalia.' The sound of 450 voices broke upon the air and was heard above the roar of the tempest. 'Three cheers for the "Vandalia!"' was the cry that warmed the hearts of the dying men in the rigging. The shout died away upon the storm, and there arose from the quivering masts of the sunken ship a response so feeble that it was scarcely heard on shore. The men who felt that they were looking death in the face aroused themselves to the effort and united in a faint cheer to the flagship. Those who were standing on shore listened in silence, for that feeble cry was the saddest they had ever heard. Every heart was melted to pity. 'God help them!' was passed from one man to another. The sound of music next came across the water. The 'Trenton's' band was playing 'The Star Spangled Banner.' The thousand men on sea and shore had never before heard strains of music at such a time as this." And so the good ships went to wreck, and many a life was lost; but a standard of endurance and of valor was there set up that shall command the reverence and wonder of the world as long as time shall endure.

During fifteen years of peace, following the War of the Rebellion, the navy was much neglected. No new ships were built, and the old ones fell into decay. In 1881, however, William H. Hunt, Secretary of the Navy appointed an Advisory Board to plan the building of a new navy adequate to the needs of the

nation.   From the deliberations of this Board and its
by Secretary Chandler, sprang the splendid new fleet.
mended the construction of four steel vessels: the "Cl
displacement; the "Boston" and "Atlanta," of 3189 to
and the "Dolphin," of 1485 tons displacement.   The dat
izing these vessels were August 5, 1882, and March 3, 1?
were taken for all four vessels by John Roach & Sons in

The pioneer of the new steel navy was the "Dolphin
as a "dispatch boat" in the Navy Register, she has we
first-class cruiser, and would be so classed if she had the
since she made a most successful cruise around the wo
miles of sea without a single mishap.   The "Dolphin" v
and she was finished in November, 1884, and although
were made in her she was kept in continuous service
After her trip around Cape Horn, and after ten months
thoroughly surveyed, and there was not a plate displaced
nor a timber strained, nor a spar out of gear.   At the enc
the world she was pronounced "the stanchest dispatch-bc
world."

The "Dolphin" is a single-screw vessel of the f
Length over all, 265½ feet; breadth of beam, 32 feet;
feet; displacement, 1485 tons.   Her armament consists c
firing guns; two six-pounder rapid-firing guns; four
Hotchkiss revolving cannon, and two Gatling guns.   S
torpedo tubes.   Her cost, exclusive of her guns, was $3
ment of crew consists of 10 officers and 98 enlisted men.

The first four vessels were called the "A, B, C, and
because of the first letters of their names—the "Atlanta,"
and "Dolphin."   The "Atlanta" and "Boston" are sist
were built from the same designs and their plates, etc., w
same patterns and they carry the same armament—hen
is a description of the other.   They followed the "Do
"Atlanta" being launched on October 9, 1884, and the "
4, 1884.   The "Atlanta" cost $619,000 and the "Bo:
official description of these vessels is that they "are c
single-deck, steel cruisers."   Their dimensions are: Len;
breadth of beam, 42 feet; mean draught, 17 feet; dis}
sail area, 10,400 square feet.   The armament of each coi
and six six-inch breech-loading rifles; two six-pounder, two
one-pounder rapid-firing guns; two 47-millimeter and tw
kiss revolving cannon, two Gatling guns, and a set of toi

Larger and finer still is the "Chicago," the flagship of the fleet, which was launched on December 5, 1885. She was the first vessel of the navy to have heavy guns mounted in half turrets, her four eight-inch cannon being carried on the spar-deck in half turrets built out from the ship's side, the guns being twenty-four and a-half feet above the water and together commanding the entire horizon. There are six six-inch guns in the broadside ports of the gun-deck and a six-inch gun on each bow. There are also two five-inch guns aft in the after portion of the cabin. Her secondary battery is two Gatlings, two six-pounders, two one-pounders, two 47-millimeter revolving cannon, and two 37-millimeter revolving cannon.

This auspicious start being made, the work of building the new navy went steadily on. Next came the protected cruisers "Baltimore," "Charleston," "Newark," "San Francisco," and "Philadelphia," big steel ships, costing from a million to nearly a million and a half dollars each. Much smaller cruisers, or gunboats, were the "Yorktown," "Concord," and "Bennington," and, smallest of all, the "Petrel." All these ships, though varying in size, are of the same general type. They are not heavily armored, and are not regarded as regular battle-ships, yet could doubtless give a good account of themselves in any conflict. They are chiefly intended, however, as auxiliaries to the real fighters, and as cruisers, commerce destroyers, etc.

The "Vesuvius," launched in April, 1888, is a "dynamite cruiser," a small, swift vessel, carrying three huge guns, each of fifteen inches bore, pointing directly forward and upward. From these, charges of dynamite are to be fired by compressed air. The "Cushing" is a swift torpedo boat, with three tubes for discharging the deadly missiles. It was launched in 1890, and named after the intrepid destroyer of the "Albemarle," whose feat has already been described. The "Stiletto" is a very small, wooden torpedo boat, of very great speed.

The new navy also contains a number of vessels intended for coast-defense, heavily armored for hard fighting. The "Monterey" is a vessel of the "Monitor" type invented by Ericsson. It has two turrets, or barbettes, each carrying two twelve-inch guns, and protected by from eleven to thirteen inches of armor. The bow is provided with a ram. The "Puritan" is a vessel of similar design, with fourteen inches of armor. Besides the four big guns there is a secondary battery of twelve rapid-firing guns, four Hotchkiss revolving cannon, and four Gatling guns. The "Miantonomah" is another double-turreted monitor. Her four ten-inch rifles have an effective range of thirteen miles, and she has a powerful secondary battery. Her big guns can send a five hundred-pound bolt of metal through twenty inches of armor, and she is herself heavily armored. This is a singularly powerful battle-ship, and would probably prove a match for any war ship in the world. In 1897 the Navy Department officials decided to paint these and every cruiser and battle-ship olive green in case of war.

The illfated "Maine," lost in Havana harbor February, 1898, was a heavily-armored cruiser, and, while intended for seagoing, was really a battle-ship. She had eleven inches of armor and carried four ten-inch rifles, besides numerous smaller guns. The "Texas" is a similar ship. The "Detroit," "Montgomery," and "Marblehead" are small, partially armored cruisers. The "New York" is a mighty armored cruiser, of 8,150 tons displacement, and is built on the most

"CHICAGO," U. S. N., ONE OF THE "WHITE SQUADRON" WAR SHIPS.

approved pattern for offensive and defensive power, endurance and speed. She is 380 feet 6½ inches long; steams 20 knots per hour; can go 13,000 miles without coaling; has from six to eight inches of armor, and carries six eight-inch and twelve four-inch rifles, and numerous smaller guns. The "Brooklyn," like the "New York," has 16,500 indicated horse power, is armored and designed on the same lines, with 1,000 tons more displacement.

The "Raleigh" and "Cincinnati" are protected cruisers of 3,183 tons displacement, and 10,000 horse power; while the "Olympia," of similar construction, has 5,500 tons displacement and 13,500 horse power.

The "Iowa" is an armored battle-ship of 11,296 tons displacement and 11,000 indicated horse-power, and of the same class are the "Oregon," "Massachusetts" and "Indiana," each of 10,200 tons displacement and 9,000 horse-power.

RECENT GROWTH OF OUR NAVY.

To our fleet of nineteen torpedo boats and destroying crafts were added, in 1897, three torpedo boats with a speed of thirty knots an hour, and six of lesser speed. Among the coast-defense vessels the ram "Katahdin," with a particularly ugly beak at the bow, deserves to be noted. Beyond a small secondary battery, she depends for offensive force upon her ability to ram a foe; to accomplish this purpose she can be submerged until only her turtle-back, funnel and ventilating shafts, all of which are armored, remain above water.

In 1898 the growth of our navy was greatly enhanced by the war with Spain. Early in April at Newport News the "Kearsarge" and the "Kentucky," the largest battle-ships in our navy, each of 11,525 tons displacement, were launched, and in May the "Alabama," a sister ship of the two just mentioned, was launched at Cramps' ship-yard. Two other battle-ships of the same size and pattern—namely, the "Illinois" and "Wisconsin"—are in course of construction at Newport News and San Francisco respectively. Our Government purchased in April from Brazil the two excellent cruisers, the "Amazonas" and "Abrouill," which names were changed to "New Orleans" and "Albany."

The "Amazonas" was delivered to the United States Battle-ship "San Francisco" on March 18, 1898, but the "Abrouill," which is a duplicate of the "Amazonas," was not completed until several months later. These foreign sisters are armed with guns in all respects of the best modern type. Their length is 330 feet; 43 feet 9 inches beam; draft 16 feet 10 inches, with a displacement of 3,450 tons; and a speed of about nineteen knots per hour. They are both built of steel, sheathed with teak and coppered, and enjoy the distinction of being the first sheathed ships in our navy. The cost to our Government for the two ships was $2,500,000. Numerous other ships of lesser importance were added, including the armored mercantile cruisers into which the magnificent ocean greyhounds "St. Paul," "St. Louis," "Paris" and others were transformed. Many private yachts were tendered by wealthy citizens and accepted. Congress also made appropriations for the building of several new battle-ships, torpedo boats and torpedo-boat destroyers, on which work was promptly begun.

All the great nations of the earth are increasing their navies as never before, and it is safe to say the United States is rapidly awakening to the importance of placing itself among the great naval powers of the earth.

The Story of Gold and Silver Mining.

Where the Precious Metals are Found and How Obtained.

READY FOR THE TRAIL.

THE explorations of Lieutenant Fremont made the possession of California a point most worth fighting for in the war with Mexico. The methods by which we obtained it were not entirely consistent with our boasted character as the most just and peace-loving nation of the world; but the part played in it by the American pioneers who settled in California exhibits our strongest national traits, both good and bad, in a scene half-heroic, half-comic, which will never be forgotten. In the words of Dr. Semple, one of their leaders, they "borrowed" supplies on the faith of the Bear-flag Government, assured that "their children in generations yet to come will look back with pleasure upon the commencement of a revolution carried on by their fathers upon principles high and holy as the laws of eternal justice." Another of the leaders of the revolutionists crowded the citizens of the captured town of Sonora between the four walls of their "calaboose," and there read to them a proclamation explaining that though he had for the moment deprived them of the liberty which is the right and privilege of all good and just men, it was only that they might become acquainted with his unalterable purpose to establish a government based upon the common rights of all men." All their proceedings, however, were brimful of the American spirit, and showed how the pioneers, though far outnumbered by the Spaniards, were inspired by a purpose which made them more than a match for the organized forces in guard of the Mexican province. The conquest of

277

California in this war simply prevented the peaceful annexation of the territory to our nation a year or so later. The American pioneers who poured in and developed the country had the might and the right to govern it, and the nation gained nothing which its children prize by violating its best instincts in acting the part of a bully toward our weaker Southern neighbor.

CLEARING UP UNDER-CURRENTS.

With the discovery of gold, however, California suddenly became a theatre toward which the eyes of the whole world were turned. The discovery was made by James Wilson Marshal, in January, 1848. Marshal had been employed to construct a mill on the estate of a hundred square miles which General John A. Sutter had received as a grant from the Spanish Government. Sutter's demesne had been the centre of the American colonies in California. General Sutter himself, a Swiss by birth, was a generous-minded visionary, who had shown himself so hospitable to all American immigrants, that he had attained to a certain pre-eminence in the affairs of the Territory, and was looked upon by many as a great and heroic figure. Up to the time of the discovery of gold upon his land, his fortunes had steadily mounted upward; from that time they went down, down. Marshal was an American by birth, born in a country town in New Jersey. He, too, was a courageous and kindly visionary, though sometimes he was aroused from his accustomed dreaminess into fierce action. His fortunes also became worse after his great discovery, and during his later life he was somewhat embittered by what he believed to be the injustice and neglect of his countrymen. "The enterprising energy of which the orators and editors of California's early golden days boasted so much, as belonging to Yankeedom," he wrote in 1857, "was not national but individual. Of the profits derived from the enterprise, it stands thus: Yankeedom, $600,000,000 ; myself, individually, $000,000,000. Ask the records of the country for the reason why. They will answer; I need not. Were I an Englishman, and had made my discovery on English soil, the case would have been different." For this last statement Marshal had some reason, for the discoverer of gold in Australia, whom Marshal claimed to have directed thither, received from the British Government, $25,000, and from the Australian Government, $50,000, while Marshal received nothing.

So much for the discoverer. Now for the discovery. It took place on the afternoon of the 24th of January, just after Sutter's mill had been completed, and Marshal and his men had made a perilous fight for two weeks to keep the dam from being destroyed by the heavy rains which had set in. In this contest with the water Marshal had exhibited a courage which made him half deserve the accidental fame that came through the finding of the gold. When his men were exhibiting to some amazed Indians the workings of their new saw-mill, Marshal was inspecting the lower end of the mill-race. He came back with the quiet remark, "Boys, I believe I have found a gold mine." He moved off to his cabin, went back to the race, and then again returned to his men, directing them early in the morning to shut down the head-gate and see what would come of it. The next morning the men did as they were told, and presently Marshal came back looking wonderfully pleased, carrying in his arms his old white hat, in the top of whose crown, sure enough, lay flakes and grains of the precious metal. Comparing these pieces with a gold coin one of the men happened to have in his pocket, they saw that the coin was a little lighter in color, and rightly attributed this to the presence of the alloy. Then all the men hurried down the race, and were soon engrossed in picking gold from the seams and crevices laid bare by the shutting down of the head-gate. In the midst of their excitement doubt would sometimes arise, and some of the metal was thrown into vinegar and some boiled in the soap-kettle, to see if it stood these tests. Then Marshal went off to General Sutter, and feverish with excitement, told him of what had come to light. When he returned to the men he said, "O boys, it's the pure stuff! I and the old Cap went into a room and locked ourselves up, and we were half a day trying it, and the regulars there wondered what the devil was up. They thought perhaps I had found quicksilver, as the woman did down toward Monterey. Well, we compared it with the encyclopedia, and it

agreed with it ; we tried aqua fortis, but it would have nothing to do with it.
Then we weighed it in water ; we took scales with silver coins in one side,
balanced with the dust in the other, and gently let them down into a basin of
water ; and the gold went down, and the silver came up. That told the story,
what it was."

That did tell the story, and though Sutter tried to keep the story a secret
until all the work in connection with the mills had been finished, the story
would not keep. A Swiss teamster learned it from a woman who did some of
the cooking about the mill, received a little of the gold, spent it for liquor at
the nearest store, and then the fame of the discovery swiftly flew to the ends

THE SLUICE.

of the earth. Gen-
eral Sutter had
been right in his
endeavor to keep
the discovery se-
cret as long as was
within his power,
for no sooner did
the gold hunters'
invasion set in than
it became impossi-
ble for him to get
men to work the
mill which he had
constructed. The
invaders carried
things with a high
hand, and ended by
setting aside his
title to his land and

establishing the claims which they had made upon it. Never was money made
with anything like such rapidity. Nearly every ravine contained gold in some
quantity or other. Nobody waited to get machinery to begin work. Knives,
picks, shovels, sticks, tin pans, wooden bowls, wicker baskets, were the only
implements needed for scraping the rocky beds, sifting the sand, or washing the
dirt for the gold. A letter in the New York *Journal of Commerce*, toward
the end of August, says of the hunt for gold : " At present the people are
running over the country and picking it out of the earth here and there, just
as dogs and hogs let loose in the forest would root up ground-nuts. Some get
even ten ounces a day, and the least active one or two. They make most who
employ the wild Indians to hunt it for them. There is one man who has sixty

Indians under his employ. His profits are a dollar a minute. The wild Indians know nothing of its value, and wonder what the pale-faces want to do with it, and they will give an ounce of it for the same weight of coin silver or a thimbleful of glass beads or a glass of grog, and white men, themselves, often give an ounce of it, which is worth in our mint $18 or more, for a bottle of brandy, a bottle of soda powders, or a plug of tobacco."

This newspaper writer had indeed some of the Munchausen qualities that his fellow craftsmen have nowadays, and his opportunities for exaggeration were increased by the remoteness of the scene and the inaccessibility of accurate information. California in those days was another part of the world. The journey to it overland took weeks, and even months, and was full of perils of starvation in case of storm and drought, and perils of slaughter if camps of hostile Indians were encountered. When things went well the life was pleasant enough, and is still most picturesque to look back upon. The buffalo hunts, the meetings with Indians, the kindling of the camp-fires at the centre of the great circle of wagons drawn up so as to form a bulwark against attack and a corral for the cattle, the story-telling in the light of these camp-fires—all present a picture which men will love to dwell upon so long as the memory of the Argonauts survives. But there were many times when the scenes were those of heart-sickening desolation. The attacks of the Indians were less horrible than attacks of hunger and disease which set in when the emigrant train reached a territory where the grass had been consumed, or lost their cattle in the terrible snow storms of the Sierras.

The journey by sea was hardly safer and was far less glorious. Every ship for California was loaded down with emigrants packed together as closely as so much baggage. Ships with a capacity for five hundred would crowd in fifteen hundred. The passage money was from $300 to $600. Often the ships were unseaworthy, often packed with coal in such a way that fires broke out. Against these dangers the passengers could not provide themselves and could not fight. The companies that were able to get their ships back again simply coined money, but it was no easy matter in those days to get a ship out of San Francisco harbor. The crews would instantly desert for the mines, and the wharves were lined with rotting vessels. The vessels which did make the return voyage were compelled to pay the California rate of wages. One ship in which the commander, engaged at New York, received $250 a month, had to pay on return $500 a month to the negro cook.

San Francisco in these days was the strangest place in the world. In February, 1848, it had hardly more than fifty houses; in August it contained five hundred, and had a large population that was not housed. A pamphlet written in the fall of that year says: "From eight to ten thousand inhabitants may be afloat in the streets of San Francisco; many live in shanties, many in tents, and many the best way they can." The best building in the town was the Parker House, an ordinary frame structure, a part of which was rented to gamblers for $60,000 a year. Even a higher sum than this was said, by Bayard Taylor, to have been paid. The accommodation was fearful. The worst that can be said of bad hotels may here be imagined. The pasteboard houses, hastily put up, were rented at far more than the cost of their construction, for every one figured that the land was as valuable as if it had been solid gold A correspondent of the New York *Evening Post*, in November, 1849, pictures in this way the land owners in San Francisco : "The people of San Francisco are

THE CRADLE.

mad, stark mad. A dozen times, in my work of the last four weeks, have I been taken by the arm by some of the millionaires—so they call themselves, I call them madmen—of San Francisco, looking wondrously dirty and out-at-elbows for men of such magnificent pretensions. They have dragged me about through the mud and filth almost up to my middle, from one pine-box to another, called mansions, hotels, banks and stores, as it may please the imagination, and have told me, with a sincerity that would have done credit to a Bedlamite, that these splendid structures were theirs, and they, the fortunate proprietors, were worth from three to four hundred thousand dollars a year each. . . . There must be nearly two thousand houses besides the tents, which are

still spread in numbers. . . . And what do you suppose to be the value, the yearly rental, of this card-house city? Not less, it is said, than twelve millions of dollars, and this with a population of about twelve thousand. New York, with its five hundred thousand inhabitants, does not give a rental of much more than this, if as much."

The greater part of this city was five times destroyed by fire in the first three years of its existence, but the people, with a hopefulness and energy which nothing could put down or burn up, would set to work and rebuild it, almost as quickly as the flames had swept it away. Everybody worked. The poorest man received unheard-of wages, and the richest man was obliged to do most things for himself.

When business of every sort was speculative to a degree so close akin to gambling, it is not strange that gambling itself took possession of the people and half frenzied them with its excitements. Physical insanity was a frequent result of the moral insanity of the community. There were few women in California, and most of these were of the worst sort. As a consequence, the men with no homes to go to in the evenings went into the gambling saloons, where they stayed till late at night. According to some descriptions, everybody gambled, but, as Royce points out in his admirable "History of California," the same men who talk half-boastfully of the recklessness and universality of the gambling, within the next breath speak with great fervor of the strength and genuineness of the religious life which soon showed itself in the community. There is no doubt that the forces for good as well as for evil were strong from the outset, and as the community grew older the forces for good kept growing stronger. More and more wives from the East had joined their husbands, and the young women who came from the East among the emigrants were married almost immediately on their arrival. Many a hotel keeper who engaged a servant girl at $200 a month, was disgusted to find that she married and left him before the month was over. With the introduction of family life came a return to saner moral conditions, and by 1853 the old distempered social order began to be spoken of as a thing of the past.

The great discovery of silver took place about ten years after the discovery of gold. In 1857 Allen and Hosea Grosch, two educated and serious-minded young men, from Reading, Pennsylvania, came upon the rich vein of silver afterward famous as "The Great Bonanza." These discoverers were even less fortunate than those who found gold in California. Before they could get together the capital necessary for the development of this mine, one of them struck a pick into his foot and died from blood-poisoning, while the other was caught in a terrible snow storm, and died as the result of the freezing of his legs, which he would not have amputated. These young men left papers describing their discovery in their cabin, which was placed in the charge of Henre C. T. Comstock. The descriptions were not explicit enough to determine the exact location, but Comstock remained in the cañon keeping watch upon the prospectors. During this time, by his constant watchfulness for a great discovery, he obtained the title of "Old Pancake" among the miners, because, as Wright narrates in his "Great Bonanza," "even as he stirred his pancake batter it is said he kept one eye on the head of some distant peak, and was lost in speculation in regard to the wealth of gold and silver that might rest somewhere beneath its rocky crest." At last on the 10th of June, 1859, **two prospectors named McLaughlin and O'Riley came upon a stratum of** strange-looking earth, the nature of which they did not understand. Comstock, who was immediately on the spot, exclaimed, "You've struck it, boys!" An arrangement was at once made to buy off the owners of the claims on which the vein was located. Three of the four owners were bought off for fifty dollars

GOLD-WASHING IN CALIFORNIA.

apiece ; the fourth sold at some higher figure to another miner named Winters, who obtained some inkling of the value of the claim.

A firm was formed, consisting of Comstock, McLaughlin, O'Riley, Winters, and a man named Penrod, who had been one of Comstock's two partners in the ownership of a spring necessary to the working of a mine. A third owner of this spring, called "Old Virginia," for whom Virginia City was named, was persuaded to sell his interest for an old blind horse. The new firm began the mining of silver on what came to be called the "Comstock lode." Very soon, however, they sold out to men of larger capital, who in turn sold to Mackay and Fair, famous the world over among America's millionaires. The subsequent fortunes of the firm which Comstock formed are interesting to follow, as they again illustrate the fate which came upon most of the men who brought to light the hidden mineral treasures of the Western territory. Comstock sold his interest for $11,000, became a merchant in Carson City, married the deserting wife of a Mormon, was soon in his turn deserted by her, failed in his business adventure, and ended his life by suicide. McLaughlin sold his interest at $3500, soon spent what he received, and afterward became a cook in a mine in California. Penrod and Winters were also soon poor men, while O'Riley, the last to sell, engaged in stock gambling with the $40,000 he received, was soon forced to resort to pick and pan for a living, and ended his life in a private asylum. The great fortunes, as has been said, were made by the later comers. Those who bought the mine from the original firm lost most that they made in litigation. Senator Stewart used to receive annually as much as $200,000 in fees as the principal attorney of some of the Comstock companies. He estimated the cost of litigation up to January, 1866, at $10,000,000. When the Comstock mines finally came into the hands of Fair, Mackay, and O'Brien, scientific methods were introduced, and the stock of the "Consolidated Virginia" rapidly rose from $85 a share in January, 1874, to $700 a share in January, 1875. The shares in another mine in the same lode rose to a like figure, and the two together had a market value of $160,000,000. During five years these mines produced over $100,000,000 worth of silver. After 1878 their product fell gradually, and the price of the stock went down. Bancroft, in his "History of Nevada," says that down to January 1, 1881, $306,000,000 worth of silver bullion was extracted from the Comstock lode. Yet he doubts whether that mountain of silver has proven a permanent advantage to Nevada. The wealth which came from her mines, he says, was to a large degree squandered by gamblers in New York and Paris, and used for purposes of political bribery and social corruption in Virginia City and San Francisco. The wealth that exists in Nevada to-day has come from improvements made by the people who came and developed the farms, made the roads, established the systems of irrigation, and built the stores, the factories, and the homes.

With the introduction of scientific mining, requiring mills and machinery costing vast sums of money, the wage system took the place of the free and independent mining of the earlier days. It is true that the mine laborers still remained their own masters, by organizing as workmen were never organized before, and compelling mine owners, for years, to pay four dollars a day as the minimum day's wages. But the mining life which came in with the wage system is the orderly life of to-day, not essentially different from that of Eastern communities. The life in the mining camps, to which all romances go back, was the life that prevailed when every laborer was his own capitalist, and every capitalist his own laborer. Never were so many men from so many places suddenly

AT WORK IN THE SILVER MINES OF NEVADA.

thrown together, as in California in '48 and '49. What came afterward in Nevada, and later still in Colorado, was like it in kind but not in degree. The Californians of the early days were without law, and thousands of miles away from established tribunals. Every man was a law unto himself, except when the community, as a whole, became aroused, and constituted itself a tribunal. The Territory was indeed nominally organized, but to wait for the regular process of law was to grant immunity to crime. The character of " miners' justice" may be illustrated by some of the scenes at Sonora, where gold was first discovered. Here there had been law and order previous to the miners' invasion, but with the invasion demoralization set in. In the fall of '48 the newcomers, following the Mexican fashion, elected two Alcaldes, but when one of the storekeepers at the settlement killed a man in a fight, both the officers promptly resigned rather than run the risk of arresting the homicide. Another storekeeper, however, called the people together to take action. This storekeeper was promptly elected Alcalde, and it was decided that one Alcalde was enough. A Prosecuting Attorney was likewise required, but no one was ready to take the office, and each person nominated promptly declined and nominated some one else. Finally the energetic storekeeper was obliged to accept this office also. The meeting succeeded in finding a second man to take the office of Sheriff. The offender was arrested, a jury impaneled, and the trial begun. The prisoner, on being brought in court, was requested to lay his arms on the table, and did so. On this table stood a plentiful supply of brandy and water, to which everybody in the court room helped himself at pleasure. The trial, however, proceeded with much attempt at legal form, and presently the Judge arose and began a plea for the prosecution. "Hold on, Brannan," said the prisoner, "you are the Judge." "I know it," replied that official, "and I am Prosecuting Attorney, too." He went on with his speech, and ended it by an appeal to himself as Judge in connection with the jury. When he had finished, the prisoner, after helping himself to a glass of brandy, made an able speech in his own defense. Night came on and the jury scattered without bringing in a verdict. The prisoner was admitted to bail, because there was no prison to put him in. The next day the jury met, but disagreed about the verdict. A new trial was held and the prisoner acquitted.

In most of the mining camps the administration of justice fell into the hands of the Vigilance Committees. A great many wild stories have been written about the trials they held, and story writers have been fond of depicting scenes where a higher form of justice was carried out than the conventional trials in older communities permit. There were, indeed, occasions when sudden and powerful appeals to the emotions of the Committee produced sudden and good effects, but as a rule the hearts of the Committee were no more open than their reasons. That they had assembled at all usually meant that there had been an accumulation of wrongs unpunished, and the gathered indignation of the community vented itself upon the single individual who happened to be brought to trial. Miners' justice was indeed far better than lynch law. As Shinn has pointed out in his book on "Mining Camps": "Lynch law is carried out at night by a transient mob, which keeps no records, conceals the names of its ministers, and is in its essence disorderly. Miners' justice, on the other hand, was executed in broad daylight, by men well known, who gave the prisoner a hearing, and kept a careful record of their doings." Yet, in spite of this, the assembling of the Committee was so irregular, its constituency so doubtful, its verdicts either so ferocious or so inadequate, or both—as when the favorite penalty of flogging and banishment was imposed—that the establishment of regular tribunals was in every respect an important gain to the mining communities. This change took place about the time that scientific mining was introduced, with regular pay for regular work. Before that time California, both as regards the rewards of labor and the punishment of crime, had seemed a world ruled by chance.

WASHINGTON'S GRAVE

The Story of the Farmer and His Farm, from Primitive Colonial Days to the Present.

A PLANTATION GATEWAY.
(Entrance to the Estate of William Byrd, at Westover, Va.)

FROM the time when the first free home was builded on Plymouth Rock, and no king, no tax, no petty tyrant, nor grasping landlord met the venturesome home-seeker, America has offered, from the length and breadth and fullness of her possessions, the land upon which all wanderers on this shifting desert of circumstance may erect their altars and worship their God according to the dictates of their own consciences. No other country in the world offers such inducements as America. Its great home privileges extend from the ocean of storms to the ocean of peace, from the land of snows to the land of the orange.

There are two instincts which impel the foreigner to cast his lot with that of a new country. The love of home, the desire to have his own fireside where he may set up his own household gods, will always be the strongest feeling among civilized people. But there is another feeling that is stronger often than patriotism—the desire of possession, which may take the form of greed for land. Those vast territories of unoccupied land which the country continues to offer to the resident of the New World will probably all be dealt out in less than half a century, so mighty has become the tide of immigration. The qualifications for ownership are that the applicant must be twenty-one years of age, or at the head of a family, and a citizen, or one who has signified his intention of becoming such. Land to the amount of 160 acres, a quarter-section, may be had by the payment of $1.20 per acre, or if 80 acres or less, at $2.50 per acre. After five years' cultivation, conditioned by a residency during six months of the year, the holder or his family is entitled to a patent conferring full ownership upon the holder. If the homesteader has served as a soldier or sailor during the war, for a period of ninety days or longer, the time of actual service is deducted from the full time required for preëmption, and is equivalent to settlement. He is further allowed six months' time after filing his declaration and locating his homestead before beginning settlement. The soldier's family are entitled to the benefits given soldiers. Every advantage is given to the homesteader. If one-sixteenth of the land is under good timber cultivation, and certain requirements in the way of planting have been met, the holder is entitled to receive patent for his land upon application after three years' occupancy. The homesteader is further protected by the law which forbids the seizures of homestead lands for prior debt. The objects of the Government in thus allotting public lands are to make her citizens contented by giving them the opportunity of establishing homes and to encourage agriculture, which must be every nation's chief resource. No one can complain that he does not find in America abundant opportunity to collect the living which the world owes him.

Less than two-fifths of the land in the United States is under cultivation, the improved land being about 365,300,000 acres, and the vacant public lands amounting to 579,664,683 acres. Aside from other natural resources, the wealth of timber and mineral lands extending over thousands of square miles, there are fully fifteen hundred thousand square miles of arable land in the United States, and her agricultural resources, if fully developed, would support a billion people. Japan, with her 48,000,000 acres, supports a population of 41,000,000 on a soil whose limit of cultivation was reached 2000 years ago. In that country of fully developed resources there is an average of one acre to four persons, while in the United States there is an average of eight acres to one person. With a land rich in resource, with the advantages of modern machinery, and the benefits of increasing knowledge in the science of farming, our agricultural possibilities are almost limitless. There are 2,115,135 square miles west of the Mississippi and 854,865 east. The greater portion of the former belonged to the American desert, which is receding rapidly before the advance of civilization and will soon become mythical. Even that extensive territory in Nebraska and Dakota known as the Bad Lands, in distinction from the adjoining fertile regions, and the Staked Plain of Texas, form a grazing country abounding in valleys and fertile districts. Cultivation of the soil increases rainfall, and artesian wells that overflow help to make the lands arable. But without irrigation and artificial moisture there are vast tracts that would produce from 40 to 50 bushels of wheat and 70 to 80 bushels of corn per acre.

It may not be true that a nation's history can be read in her agricultural machines, but they show in a great measure the development made in agriculture, both as an industry and as a science. The modern farmer, particularly if he is progressive and has a commercial instinct, is ready to make use of all the scientific methods that are offered if he sees a possible chance of improving his land, his crops, and his income. He is not slow to learn that irrigation warms and lightens cold and heavy soils, and that the utilization of the sub-soil hastens the harvest by several weeks. The increase in crops every year is due to intelligent farming as well as to an increasing number of improved acres for farm lands.

The most important of our American crops are corn and wheat. The great bulk of corn is used at home, and the shipments vary according to the home demand. The foreign demand for the past twenty years has not exceeded 3.9 per cent. of the production. The largest rate of production is in the Ohio and Missouri River valleys, but it is grown successfully in every part of the country except at high elevations. The highest value per acre is in New Hampshire and the lowest in South Carolina, where the yield is

BAGGING WOOL FOR TRANSPORTATION.

low, although prices are high. No product has a greater local variation than corn, for while it is one of the simplest crops as regards cultivation, much depends upon the season.

The price of wheat is regulated largely by the foreign market, the home demand affecting it only slightly. During ten years the average yield per acre has not varied one-third of a bushel. The banner wheat-growing States are Minnesota and the Dakotas, while Kansas and California come next in rank.

While there has been a gradual decrease in the yield of oats since 1889, there has been a steady increase in demand, affected somewhat by a growing consumption of the grain for human food. The interchangeable use of oats and corn regulates the values of each in a degree. The average yield for a series of years has been twenty-seven bushels to the acre. The range of value per acre is from $18 or $19 in Colorado, to $4.50 or $5 in North Carolina, depending upon the yield and the cost for transportation. A crop that is not grown much in this country is rye. It is a crop for poor soils, and its value per acre is from $11 to $13. In the South it is grown for winter pasturage rather than for seed. The average yield per acre, for ten years, has been 26.6 bushels.

The potato crop, a never-failing one in this country, will always be an important staple industry. In Idaho, where the soil is particularly favorable to the culture of this plant, 500 bushels have been the average per acre. Nearly every soil is suited to its growth.

Tobacco has always been one of the chief crops from the time it was exchanged by the early immigrants for wives, and from the first it has been a regular export. The chief tobacco regions are in Kentucky, Virginia, Tennessee, North Carolina, and Maryland, while it is grown also in Connecticut and in certain portions of New York, Pennsylvania, Wisconsin, and other States. The yield in Kentucky is steadily increasing, and this State now has 39.62 per cent. of the total acreage, besides producing over 45 per cent. of the entire crop The seed-leaf varieties are produced more in the Northern States, while farther south the manufacturing and export varieties predominate.

It is often profitable for the farmer to cultivate fodder in the seasons unfavorable to the regular crops. The representative constituent of hay is timothy, mixed more or less with other varieties of grass. In Texas, the land of the enormous hay farms, the famous mesquite and the native prairie grass, growing ten or twelve inches high, very juicy and fine-speared, make the best hay in the world. If carefully protected from cattle and allowed to grow, it is sufficiently hardy to choke out the weeds. In Arizona and parts of California, wheat, barley, and winter rye are cultivated for forage. The hardier varieties of sorghum and the early spring or winter grains may always be relied upon for fodder.

The successful cultivation of cotton depends upon certain meteorological conditions which the Northern climate lacks. During the first period in the growth of the plant, tropical conditions—moisture in the soil from frequent rains, an invariable high temperature, hot sun, with little wind—will reduce evaporation and contribute to the hardy growth of the plant. During the second period, which is the period of fruition, the opposite conditions are necessary, both in relation to soil and climate, to arrest the growth of the stalk and develop the boll. So much depends upon these external conditions to produce a fine grade of cotton. The best quality is produced on the coast and low-lands. The fibre grown in the pine belt is coarser and has a lower value for manufacturing purposes.

Statistics of the great harvests of 1891 show that 2,075,000,000 bushels of corn were produced, 588,000,000 bushels of wheat, 758,000,000 bushels of oats, 80,000,000 bushels of barley, 34,000,000 bushels of rye,

14,000,000 bushels of buckwheat, 225,000,000 bushels of potatoes, with a total of 3,774,000,000 bushels. Also 523,000,000 pounds of tobacco were raised, 44,430,000 tons of hay, and 8,000,000 bales of cotton. The cotton receipts were the largest since the year 1860.

While market gardening may be carried on near local markets, where the producer often disposes of his goods to the consumer, truck-farming is usually carried on at a greater distance from the local points, on a greater scale. The total number of acres under cultivation for truck-farming is 534,400, with a total value of $76,517,155. In the district of New York and Philadelphia, nearly 109,000 acres are cultivated. Not far from

ENTRANCE TO A COTTON-YARD, NEW ORLEANS.

one hundred million dollars are invested in the industry, and much employment is afforded to women and children. The advantages to be derived from the industry are that nearly all vegetables may be had during the year, since the railroad facilities have made it possible to convey perishable products to remote markets in a short time. Florida and the regions of the Lower Mississippi Valley supply the Eastern and Central cities in the early spring and late fall, and California supplies the Western cities. During midsummer the immediate neighborhoods supply the cities.

A partial failure of any of the crops does not signify that the cities shall not be supplied from other sources. About the only products received from California in Chicago, St. Louis, and Kansas City are new potatoes, cauliflower, cabbage, garlic, and tomatoes. The more perishable vegetables cannot be sent such a distance. New England supplies the Eastern markets even in the early and late season with such products as are profitable even when raised in hot-houses. California has the advantage over other States, for in addition to a soil that grows every vegetable, she has a climate that does not endanger her winter vegetables by frost. Michigan supplies the Chicago and middle Western markets with a great proportion of their produce, while Charleston, Savannah, and Jacksonville ship enormous quantities of truck to New York several times a week. During the census year of 1890 an estimate shows that the value of the vegetable crop was $5,773,476.25.

The Colonial records show that early in the seventeenth century the production of plants brought from the mother country was from seeds and by budding, grafting, and layering. In the records of the Massachusetts Company a memorandum of March 16, 1629, shows that slips for vine planters were provided, and stores of all kinds of fruits, and a letter from George Fenwick, of Saybrook, Conn., to Governor Winthrop acknowledged the receipt of trees for which he had evidently sent. Nurseries and botanic gardens were established, later, about the middle of the last century, at Flushing, L. I., which for more than a hundred years were continued by the descendants of William Prince, the original owner; and another is on record as existing near Charleston, S. C., about 1760. A premium of £10 was awarded to Thomas Young, of Oyster Bay, in 1768, by the Society for Promotion of Arts.

The matter of census inquiry in regard to nurseries was taken up in 1891, and but little recorded data were found to aid in the work. The approximated figures show that about 4510 nurseries are now flourishing in the United States, occupying 172,806 acres of land and valued at $41,078,835.80. There are employed 45,657 men and 2279 women for propagating and cultivating trees and plants, with a total capital invested of $52,425,669.51. The estimates show that 95,025.42 acres are comprised in these nurseries, and that a total number of plants and trees of 3,386,825,778 are reported, of which less than one-sixth are fruit trees; about one-fourth of the number are grape-vines and small fruits, and the remainder are evergreen and deciduous trees, hardy shrubs, and roses. The increased taste in horticultural matters and the steadily increasing demand will cause the rapid growth of horticultural production.

Within recent years the division of labor in every industry has made it possible to develop every branch in a measure independently of the others, save only so far as there must exist a mutual interdependence between all industries. In the day of small beginnings the farmer saved his own seeds for successive plantings, and if he wished to vary his crops or add to his varieties, he made an exchange with his neighbors. Since the demand for seeds of all agricultural products, fruits, vegetables, and flowers, has made it profitable to raise seeds for commercial purposes, it has been found worth while to devote 169,831 acres of land exclusively to seed production. Nearly one-half of the 569 seed farmers are in the North Atlantic States, covering 47,813 acres, or an average of 185 acres per farm. In the North Central division there are 157 farms, with a total acreage of 787,096, or 555 acres per farm. The largest farms are reported in Nebraska and Iowa, with an average of 695 acres. Several of these farms average 3000 acres each. The industry is not a new one, for two seed farms were reported before 1800.

Commercial floriculture has made the greater part of its development within the past ten years, and there are in this country to-day 965 state and local floral societies and clubs, besides the Society of American Florists. It is probably due to the influence of these societies that there is a rapidly growing taste for the culture of flowers. More than in any other American industry are opportunities offered for women. Of the 4650 floral establishments reported in the census year, 312 were owned and conducted by women. These establishments are valued at $38,355,722.43, and the combined wages of the 16,847 men and 1958 women employed, amount to $8,500,000. The rose is the universally favorite flower, as shown by the report of products. Nearly fifty million roses were produced in the year, thirty-nine million hardy plants and shrubs, and 153,000,000 of all other plants. It may be of interest to note that the greatest area of glass in any one floral establishment was 150,000 square feet, and the smallest 60 square feet, an attachment to a New England farm-house where the woman of the house sells from $35 to $50 worth of plants and cut flowers each year. Every state and territory except Idaho, Nevada, Indian Territory, and Oklahoma, reported floral establishments.

No industry is more fascinating and compensating to the man who has an instinctive fondness for nature, than fruit culture. Aside from the pleasure of watching the growth in his orchards and on his plantations, from shoot to bud and bloom, through the whole ripening process to full fruitage, he is rewarded even further by the literal fruits of conscientious toil. But perhaps no agricultural product is more subject to the uncertainty of varying seasons.

Although extensive fruit farming is of comparatively recent date in America, statistics show that $85,000,000 was expended in the home markets during the last census year for orchard products. In addition, fully $20,000,000 was spent for imported fruits and nuts. There is every reason to believe that in a few years, with the certain development of our country's resources, and with our rapidly increasing fruit industry, we shall be able to supply, not only the domestic markets, but a large part of the foreign as well.

Fruit raising as a vocation was hardly known in the South until after the Civil War. It would have been beneath the dignity of the "fine old Southern gentleman" to part with his orchard delicacies for money. The best his land could produce belonged always to his family, his friends, and the chance stranger within his gates. But when the civil strife was over, and his occupation gone, the gentleman turned to the products of the rich soil for his livelihood. To-day we find much of our best and most abundant fruit is grown in the South, much of which is raised for early Northern markets.

THE "PROVENT TIER.

Fruit growers remember the wave of fruit culture which, beginning in Delaware, swept southward through Maryland, Virginia, the Carolinas, and all the States warmed by the Gulf Stream. The territorial limit has not yet been reached. The west, aside from California, has not yet disclosed all its resources to the fruit grower.

The apple seems to be peculiarly an American fruit, for it can be grown successfully in a variety of soils, and in nearly every part of the country. It probably thrives best in the hard, rocky land of New England, and there seems to be justice in that, for there is so much in the way of fruit cultivation that is denied the New Englander. It is often believed that the apple was the first fruit discovered in America; but the fox-grape was found here by the earliest explorers, and the apple was probably first introduced by the French missionaries. The Dutch and English colonists followed with varieties from their own countries. One branch of apple growing is strangely neglected, that of rearing and sending to market the early summer varieties.

For the propagation of the peach, which is believed to have been brought here by Spanish explorers, we are indebted to the Indians. The variety known as "Indian" peach, sometimes also called Columbia, which was introduced into Jersey, has, by cross-cultivation, given numberless varieties, from the white free-stone to the peculiar dark purple type. The list of hardy varieties is not a long one, the latest being known as the "Excelsior." A slight difference in the quality of the fruit makes considerable difference in the price, and the shrewd grower aims to produce a superior quality rather than a great yield. The process of thinning is strongly recommended. As soon as the blossoms have set, fully two-thirds are plucked, and another thinning should follow as soon as the color of the fruit begins to turn. The result, other things being equal, is a yield of magnificent specimens, large, finely marked, and delicious to the taste. Peach cultivation is a remunerative industry in more ways than one. There is always a demand for skilled labor in the picking and handling of the fruit, this work being regarded as an art in its way.

The process of thinning is also profitable with early apples and choice pears, especially with those growing in clusters. While California produces more pears than any other State, and the California pear has no rival in the regard in which it is popularly held, the Southern States, particularly Texas, are experimenting with the fruit and have already produced fine varieties. The objection to planting pear-trees commonly made, that one must wait so long for any returns, is met by the fact that the demand for fine pears, as for all high-class native fruit, is constantly increasing. A large capital is not necessary to insure success in this branch of the fruit industry. The grower needs only to avail himself of the experiences of others in regard to the best soil, best methods of producing, and best varieties for cultivation.

The orange industry is a recent one. The fruit was first raised in this country for market by Dr. Clayton Cargill, of Dover, Del., in 1865. Soon after this Mrs. Harriet Beecher Stowe, visiting the region of the St. John's River, in Florida, wrote glowing letters on the possibilities for orange culture. Since then the trackless pine woods have been converted into orange bowers, beautiful to look upon, delightful to the senses, and profitable to the owner. There are $10,000,000 invested in orange groves in Florida, with a yearly return of $2,000,000. Fifty varieties are yielded by the tall, graceful, shining-leaved trees in that State alone, and fully 10,000 square miles are adapted to the production of the bridal blossom. **The finest oranges in the world come from Florida, and are raised on the banks of the Indian River.** No apologies are needed for that fruit, and there are no vain regrets that such and such a quality is missing. The Gulf Stream weathers are favorable to a variety that is almost as large as a croquet ball, of a deep color, brown cheeked, thin skinned, plentifully juiced, and flavored to a nicety. It is difficult to believe that the orange is not a native product of American soil, so splendidly does it nurture this fruit. It is only a few hundred years that the orange has been known on this continent, and we are indebted to Spanish cavaliers for its introduction. Its home is supposed to be in Southeastern Asia.

California produces a superior quality of oranges, some perhaps equal to the " Indian Rivers." Charles Dudley Warner writes that as late as April, 1877, he could not find an excellent quality of oranges in California, but now quantities of delicious native fruits are easily obtainable. The question is often asked if it is feasible for one to attempt orange culture in California with small capital? In all probability twenty times the number of men who are interested in the business now could become wealthy if engaged in intelligent culture of the fruit.

A BEE RANCH
IN LOWER
CALIFORNIA.

Energy. pluck. patience, and faith in his Maker, are pronounced good qualities in a man who starts out to make his fortune in any branch of fruit raising.

Grape fruit is produced in Florida and the other Southern States, as is also the shaddock, a coarse, pumpkin-shaped fruit of the same variety, weighing from three to five pounds. The persimmon, lime, fig, prune, guava, pineapple, banana, etc., are cultivated in the same region. In the cultivation of the banana the utmost care must be taken in selecting the best soil for the tree. The average time required to bring it to fruition is about one year, but if planted in one locality it may mature in nine months, while in another, where there is, apparently, only a slight difference in the soil, from fifteen to sixteen months may be required. The shoots are set fifteen feet apart, thus giving the growing tree plenty of room to spread its broad, translucent leaves, under whose shelter is partially hidden the single bunch of fruit which it is its mission to bear. Having performed its duty, the tree proper dies, while fresh shoots come forth to produce in time more food for the sustenance of its master, man. People remote from the home of the banana are not grateful enough for this palatable, nourishing fruit. They nibble it simply as the relish or finishing touch of a meal, unconscious of the fact that it forms almost the whole subsistence of millions of natives of the Tropics. It is claimed that a banana contains as much nourishment as a pound of beef-steak, but the Northerner clings to the beef at twenty-five cents a pound in preference to the humble banana at "two for five." The banana harvest does not depend upon the time of year, but upon the time of planting. We have a continual banana season, although the best market is between the first of March and the last of June. The large bunches, often weighing sixty pounds, are cut while green by machinery, and are caught by the laborer, as they fall, without breaking or bruising a single fruit. The bunches for transportation are wrapped in the dead leaves of the plant, which are used wet to insure pliability. The growth of the banana industry in this country is almost marvelous. Each of the large cities, Boston, New York, and Philadelphia, receives from seventeen to thirty thousand bunches a day. As in other branches of fruit-raising, the supply does not equal the demand. We pay Jamaica alone $1,000,000 a year for bananas, and the possibilities in the way of cultivation of this fruit should be a stimulus to encourage the industry. There are many "banana walks" along the irrigation canals in our Southern States, and there is room for many more. The enterprising young man with a few hundred dollars will find rich returns for intelligent investment in banana fields.

Pineapple culture in this country is still in its infancy. The largest plantation in Florida is owned by Thomas E. Richards, the pioneer in the industry, who began to plant in 1879. It is not yet known how much of our land is adapted to the pineapple, nor are the best methods of culture yet determined.

Much can be learned from the pioneer growers, who have already achieved encouraging results, but the pineapple planter is still an experimenter. The number of crops that a plant can profitably yield is a disputed question. Reports show that three crops are the limit under certain conditions of culture, four crops can be grown under other conditions, while one grower maintains that five crops can be easily yielded before the plants need to be replaced. A larger capital for investment—not less than $3000 or $4000—will be required

VALLEY IRRIGATION IN SOUTHERN CALIFORNIA.

to yield satisfactory returns in this branch of fruit culture, than in any other. While the experiment may be regarded as more or less hazardous, the returns are often gratifying. In some cases $700 an acre, with a net of $300, was reported, and the results are quick. The orange requires seven or eight years to reach fruition, and the pineapple plant bears a full crop in a year and a half from the time of setting. This delicious fruit, whether canned or fresh, will always be the *piece de resistance* of every thrifty housewife, and until its culture becomes a flourishing American industry she must continue to pay from twenty-five to seventy-five cents apiece for these luxurious necessities.

Of the progress made in the cultivation of the smaller garden fruits comparatively little has been written. They have been overshadowed by the larger enterprises devoted to the culture of larger fruits, and it has been said of them that except to the enthusiast they are, like Heaven, "objects of special interest and general neglect."

Our greatest fruit industry is grape culture. It is strange that no foreign grapes have yet been raised east of the Rocky Mountains. The experimenter has tried again and again to propagate European varieties, but all his efforts have been unsuccessful except in California. A few years ago E. W. Bull began experimenting with the wild fox-grape, and his efforts have met with gratifying success. The Ives Seedling, Lady Woodruff, and the luscious Concord are direct descendants of the humble "Fox." The Delaware, Isabella, and Catawba are accidental varieties.

The American wild grape and its cultivated varieties are peculiarly adapted for wine making, and it is encouraging to learn that France, which produces finer table grapes than any other country, is experimenting with our grapes for wine purposes. It is probable that the United States will eventually supply the world with the best vineyard varieties. Less than half a century ago a venturesome grower of grapes in the Lake Keuka district, N. Y., sent to New York city his full crop, consisting of fifty pounds. To his surprise, the entire shipment was sold. Growing reckless with his success, he sent during the following year about 250 pounds, and broke the market! In 1891 about 20,000 tons were consumed through the markets of New York, Boston, and Philadelphia. During the same year California alone manufactured 16,500,000 gallons of wine, besides producing 235,526 pounds of table grapes, and preparing 2,107,463 boxes of raisins, with prospects of increasing the yield of raisins within the next five years to 10,000,000 boxes. In the vineyards alone 100,422 men were employed, and the importance of the industry can scarcely be estimated.

Raisin making is a comparatively simple process. On the fruit ranches in California the grapes are simply cut from the stem and left on the ground for the sun to dry.

Statistics show that New York State produced 60,687 pounds of grapes for table use during the year and made 2,528,250 gallons of wine, employing 25,500 men for the work. However, the figures do not indicate that the consumption of wine has increased alarmingly, but that the wine consumer has transferred his patronage to home-made goods. It may be of interest here to note that the largest wine cask in the world is in the Lake Erie district. It is made of Ohio oak and holds 36,000 gallons. California can boast of the largest as well as of the smallest vineyard in the world. The former is at Tehama and

19

contains 3800 acres, to which 1000 acres are to be added within a year.   The smallest vineyard is in Santa Barbara county, and consists of a single vine which was planted by a Mexican woman about sixty-nine years ago.   Its trunk has a diameter of twelve inches, its branches extend over an area of 12,000 feet, and it produces annually from 10,000 to 12,000 pounds of grapes, of the famous Mission variety, the bunches frequently weighing six or seven pounds each.   The old lady to whose thrift the present owners are indebted died in 1865, at the age of 107.

The total number of acres included in the vineyards of the various States and Territories is 307,575, giving employment to 200,780 laborers.   The average number employed in the outdoor work, in the cultivating of the fruit, is one person to three acres.   As growers become more familiar with the use of spraying apparatus and fungicides, the harvests will be more certain.   It may be a long time before we shall achieve a parallel to the grapes of Eshcol, though our own product guarantees great possibilities in viticulture.

Aside from the small fruit farms, and hot-houses for the cultivation of blackberries, raspberries, and strawberries, much of the small fruit for market comes from the woods and marshes, where they grow in a semi-wild state.   Their yield as regards quantity and market price, is almost marvelous.

In many New England localities, the small farms that once were the source of livelihood of the Yankee and his family have weather-stained boards across their front gates bearing the sign, "For Sale," or "To Let."   The pear and apple orchards, clover meadows, and small fields, well enough for the sedate fathers, are too small to bound the aspirations and energies of the younger generation.   The soil which has borne harvests and fruitage for ten generations is not so responsive as the soil of the New West.   The young men who do not turn their attention to the more lucrative trades and professions of the cities, venture into farming on a large scale in the West, where the indolent tiller reaps almost as rich harvests as the energetic one.   The yielding capacity of the wheat farms of the New West is almost incredible.   If the native grass is burned off or turned under, and seed is scattered on top of a light plowing, the tender grain springs up and yields good returns with but little effort on the part of the tiller.   On the other hand, when great capital is invested, improved methods and machinery used, and efficient labor employed, wheat farming in these regions yields returns that would seem incredible to the old-fashioned farmer.   The supply of grain is limited only by the acreage under cultivation.   From 12,000 to 40,000 acres are comprised in single farms, and the number of buildings, granaries, elevators and windmills on each give the appearance at a short distance of little villages.   Farming on such a scale is simply a business venture, controlled by monopolies or wealthy capitalists, who leave the entire charge of the business with superintendents.   About 150 men are employed during the harvest season, with daily wages averaging $1.50 per capita, and thousands of dollars are invested in machinery and horses. The small farmer in the West has no chance in his competition with monopolies, and while companies are becoming wealthy, the communities receive little of the benefit. There is no home-life on these large Western farms, and the only society is that of the laborers, often uneducated foreigners.

The great fertile district extending from the Gulf of Mexico to the Panhandle of Texas, from the curving boundary lines of the Carolinas, Georgia, Alabama, Mississippi, and Louisiana to the Rio Grande River, has been called the Land of Cotton. The most beautiful, as well as the most typical plantations are those in the valleys of the Red and the Mississippi Rivers, where the soil is a rich red loam, easily cultivated as well as productive and responsive. The climate is mild and salubrious, and all natural conditions are favorable to the cultivation of the cotton. In all its different stages of growth it is the most interesting of those plants that fall under the class commonly designated as "useful." Its very seed is a mystery of the life principle, for that small, woolly, rusty little cocoon conceals the warp and woof of the great proportion of humanity's covering. After lying all winter in the neglected heaps about the old gins and barns, the seed are tossed into the moist earth, and soon the three-leaved plants appear, running in long straight rows for miles across the fields of bottom-land. The blossom, appearing as a pink bud, becomes white-

WIND-BREAK OF EUCALYPTUS TREES, TO PROTECT ORCHARDS.

petaled, filling the land with a rare fragrance. All the while the process of cultivation goes on, the dark-faced laborers plowing, thinning, hoeing, and weeding. It is a leisurely work which suits the indolent nature of the negro, the ordained cultivator of cotton.

During the summer drouth, the green stalks turn brown, and the leaves fall away, giving place to the cooped boll with its contents of snow. Soon these bolls burst, and out comes the fine dry fabric. "Cotton-pickin' time" begins, the merriest, jolliest, "flushest" season the darkies ever know. With good-natured hardihood they desert their town homes, for it doesn't pay to tend horses, run errands, nurse and cook, while the vast fields of cotton stretching beyond invite their nimble fingers, and promise pay for actual number of pounds picked.

Some of these plantations are small colonies in themselves. Their boundaries include many miles square of prairie and timber lands. Upon each is the store for general merchandise, a post-office, church, and school house, besides the mill, gin, press, compress, and warehouses. There are the renters' houses, the "hands'" cabins, each with its truck patch and pig pen, the owner's house, with its long, rose-bowered verandas, its beautiful lawns and flower gardens, the stables, barns, and carriage houses. There are an ice-house, a dairy, an apple-house and smoke house, and buildings innumerable. Fruit orchards and vineyards, hammocks and rustic seats, all contribute to make the life of the Southerners as enviable as possible. About these old plantations lingers the atmosphere of ante-bellum grandee life. Things are done on a large scale. Supplies are laid in by the barrel and hogshead, and produce is planted and garnered accordingly. Yet everything is subservient to King Cotton, who fills the measure of the hearts and expectations of his subjects. Year after year, and crop after crop, bring no great profits to the owner. He does not seem to take into consideration the difference between the former times, when he owned both labor and product, and the present conditions, with its divided interest, daily wages, inequality of labor, and decreasing capabilities, which have warped the conditions of the industry since the war. Paid labor is not equal in many ways to slave labor, for the slaves worked for the interest of their masters. As many as five hundred slaves often grew up together on one plantation. They knew but one home and one occupation. Their first toddling steps were between the rows of young cotton, and they learned to sing the cotton field songs as soon as they could talk. Their wants were few; their knowledge of life and its possibilities was bounded by the blue rim of the horizon which set on their master's plantation. Now they are a set of shiftless nomads, wearying of the new broom of their spasmodic energies at one plantation, and moving on to a fitful spell of work at another. This in a great measure accounts for the uncertainties. Employer and employee have no longer a mutual interest. As for white cotton-hands, they do not pay. The hot seasons are too intense for them and the returns too precarious. Yet the Southener clings to his cotton fields. He cannot believe that Egyptian and other foreign cottons are competing successfully with his. He cannot understand why it is that he makes as many bales to the acre as he did in the old time yet clears no money. He only knows that if raised at all it must be raised in large quantities. The cost of labor is nearly equal to the returns of the crop. He hauls his bales into town to be sampled and bid upon by merchants and buyers, and is satisfied if the net profits are sufficient to pay off last year's store-bills. The system of

SURRENDER OF GENERAL LEE TO GENERAL GRANT AT APPOMATTOX COURTHOUSE, APRIL 9, 1365

The two generals met at the house of Major McLean, in the hamlet of Appomattox Courthouse, where Lee surrendered. All that remained of the Confederate army, which for nearly four years had beaten back every attempt to capture Richmond. Grant's terms, as usual, were generous. He did not ask for Confederate troops, who, demanded only that Lee and his men should agree not again to bear arms against the Government of the United States.

THE ATTACK ON FORT DONELSON

This memorable battle of February, 1862, was the first serious blow to the Confederate cause. It was also Grant's first victory of importance, and marks the beginning of his rise to fame. Fifteen thousand prisoners were taken. Grant generously allowed the Confederates to retain their personal baggage, and the officers to keep their side arms. General Buckner expressed his thanks for this chivalrous act, and later on his became Grant's personal friend.

monthly and yearly credit is, of itself, the ruin of the Southern farmer. He is even handicapped by his tenants. He must advance them provisions while they are working in his employ. If his crop runs short he is in debt to his merchants and his tenants are in debt to him. He has not a diversity of crops to fall back upon in an unfavorable year. So all depends upon the season, upon the drouth, or overflow, or boll-worm.

Yet the business possesses a peculiar fascination. There are the green fields in the spring-time ; the blossom fields in the summer ; the brown fields of early autumn ; and the snow fields of harvest-time. There are the pickers in wagon-loads and tramping crowds, weary and care-free. They sing all day as they fill their baskets, joking and depreciating each other's skill as they wait about the weigher's stand at night for their weights and pay, and singing again to the merry tinkle of the banjo, as they lounge about their cabin doors before bedtime. There are the gins with their creaking machinery and snow-drifting lint room ; presses with the ties and bagging, rolling out great bales, which are crowded into a sixth of their original size by the mighty elbows of the com-presses. Then there are the wagons, loaded bale upon bale, jogging along the road, the happy tenant driving, wife and children perched upon the bales, "goin' to trade." There are visions of cotton exchanges, where gambling in futures runs high, and millions change hands every day ; of huge vessels at the seaport and long freight cars in the inland, laden and groaning with the precious freight.

One of the devices of greatest interest to the visitor in many parts of the West is the device which makes man a special providence in sections which were formerly arid wastes because of lack of rain. In an admirable discussion of the subject of irrigation, General Irwin quotes the phrase "irrigation makes homes for millions, better than the rain makes homes." In former times irriga-tion would undoubtedly have been regarded as a device of Satan, since it attempts to supplement the work of Providence in making the earth fruitful. The change in twenty years by the introduction of water into sections where no water was has been marvelous, but it is only prophetic of the still greater changes to come. It is not many years since the maps of the Western country were interspersed with forbidding dots, marked deserts, which were universally regarded as waste places forever. In the map of the near future there will be no American desert. Irrigation will have made almost every acre of land available, and those sections which seem to-day almost beyond redemption by artificial fertilization, will undoubtedly yield to the increasing inventiveness and ingenuity of man.

The arid area in this country, according to Major Powell, is fifteen hundred miles in its widest part, from east to west, and a thousand miles from north to south, containing over a million of square miles, over six hundred millions of

statements make the importance of irrigation evident at the first glance. Within the limits of this natural desert lie Arizona, Colorado, Nevada, Wyoming, New Mexico, Idaho, and parts of Montana, of the Dakotas, of Texas, of Kansas, of Nebraska, of Washington, of Oregon, and of California. The Secretary of the Interior, in his report for 1891, declared "that 120,000,000 acres that are now desert may be redeemed by irrigation so as to produce the cereals, fruits, and garden products possible in the climate where the lands are located." It is to the Mormons that we owe the first practical and successful use of irrigation on a large scale; a scale so large and so impressive that it became a great object-lesson in the whole West. There are now under the influence of irrigation nearly four million acres of land, penetrated by more than fifteen thousand miles of artificial water-ways in the form of canals and ditches. The condition of the cultivator of irrigated lands is, in one important respect, more assured than that of the cultivator of lands within the rain belt, for while rains fail, and droughts are of frequent occurrence, to the disaster and discouragement of the cultivator, irrigation is unfailing.

In California, the price of water is regulated by law, and it is likely that the other States and territories in which irrigation is used will, sooner or later, regulate the matter just as other States regulate and control the freight charges of the railroads. The greatest need in irrigated countries is the building of large reservoirs for water storage, for the purpose of securing an equalization of distribution. The dry regions contain hills and valleys, and the soil which is furnished by the valley is supplied with water by the mountains, and all that is needed is the utilization and equalization of the supply which nature furnishes. The main question now is how shall this be done. The Secretary of the Interior, in the report already quoted from, says that private corporations and associations are now substantially given the field of water supply for that domain which may be redeemed by irrigation, and that this field is being rapidly seized upon. The United States does not retain control, but establishes States or Territories, by which the control is handed over to corporations. In the Secretary's opinion the General Government should not release altogether its hold upon water supplies. No one can compute the future populousness and value of the arid Territory, and no one can compute, therefore, the future value of privileges which are now being given away. It will not be long before the matter of water supply will be one of the highest national importance, both as regards the value of the control to the Government and its importance to settlers who are dependent upon it. In a recent message to Congress, the President said "the Government should not part with its ownership of the water sources, except on the condition of insuring water to settlers at reasonable rates." The appliances of irrigation add not a little to the picturesqueness of the country, and the wind-mills often may be made as effective as the mills of Holland, if proportion and color are taken into account.

The Marvelous Story of Our Great Industries.

MARBLE is, of all stones used for building or sculpture, the best known and the most anciently used. The earliest records of human architecture tell of its employment. The Egyptians used it before they built the Pyramids. The temples and palaces of Greece were built of it; and it was the boast of an Emperor that he had found Rome brick and had left it marble. From Mount Pentelicus and from the Isle of Paros came the snowy stone of which the Parthenon and its fellow-gems of architecture were built, and in which were wrought the masterpieces of Phidias and Praxiteles, while the artists of Rome sought their supplies at Carrara, on the Gulf of Spezzia.

It is a far cry from Mount Pentelicus to Otter Creek. Yet the fame of the former for this beautiful stone is rapidly being transferred to the latter. The hills that border that humble stream in Central Vermont are green without, as their name implies. But within they have been found to have hearts of snowy marble, rivaling that of Italy and Greece in purity and texture. A considerable quantity of it is perfectly suited to the finest statuary work, while the amount available for architectural purposes is practically inexhaustible.

This Rutland County marble, for which Vermont is famous, is of the age of the Trenton limestone of New York, and forms a huge layer, 2000 feet thick, underlying hundreds of square miles of country. Not all portions of the layer, however, are valuable. Where it crops out at the surface of the ground, or nearly reaches it, the upper part, for a depth of from ten to fifty feet, is worthless, because of the action of the weather. At West Rutland the vein of perfectly pure statuary marble, rivaling that of Paros and Carrara, is only four feet thick. But there are fifty feet more of superb clouded and colored marble for architectural use. At Sutherland Falls the vein of building marble is seventy-five feet thick, and at Pittsford it is more than six hundred feet thick, with scarcely a seam or a flaw. Other less valuable deposits of marble, white, clouded, or colored, are found at Lee, Mass., Tuckahoe and Sing Sing, N. Y., Louisa County, Va., and other places in the Appalachian Mountain belt. At Shoreham, Vt., and Glen's Falls, N. Y., black marble is found. Burlington, Vt., furnishes the beautiful variegated "Winooski" marble. But the mountains of Tennessee are the chief source of this last-named kind, yielding seemingly endless quantities of fine-textured stone, colored in every imaginable hue and tint, and veined and streaked and mottled in the most bewilderingly beautiful manner.

IN THE QUARRY.
(A Marble Quarry in Vermont.)

So it came to pass that when the hardy Green Mountain farmer found his fields becoming sterile and unprofitable, he looked below the surface, and there found a richer and surer harvest than ever had appeared above. And while on the Gulf of Spezzia the quarrymen clung to the primitive methods of work, slow, laborious, and wasteful, the New Englanders utilized in quarrying the latest devices of Yankee ingenuity.

The first thing to do is to clear away the surface rock, which heat and cold and other conditions have partially decomposed and rendered worthless. This is largely done by blasting, great care being exercised to use light charges, acting upward, so as not to injure the sound marble below. After this "cap-rock" is thus removed and a "sound" floor secured there is no more blasting. The stone is too valuable to be shattered into useless fragments.

Instead of gunpowder, steam-power is used. There are two kinds of "channeling machines" in use. One drives a set of chisels, the other a series of drills. Both effect the same purpose, the cutting of straight, narrow,

SLUICE-GATE.

parallel channels in the marble floor, five or six feet deep and perhaps the same distance apart. Other channels are then cut at right angles to the first, dividing the floor into squares. One of these huge blocks is next broken loose, by means of wedges, and lifted out. Into the cavity thus formed a workman gets down, and directs a drill or set of chisels horizontally against the bases of the other blocks, which are thus one by one cut off—"gadding," the work is called—and lifted out. When all are removed, a fresh "floor" is presented and the "channeling machines" are set at work again, cutting their deep, narrow trenches and dividing the "floor" into another series of blocks. The cost of thus cutting marble and raising it from the quarry is from seventy-five cents to a dollar the cubic foot.

These huge cubes of marble are taken from the quarry to the mill, to be cut into smaller blocks or slabs for building purposes. The cutting is done by means of gangs of horizontal saws, made of soft iron and having no teeth, but being fed with sand and water. They are operated by steam or water power. The polishing of the blocks and slabs is also done by power. The pieces of marble are placed in a "rubbing-bed" and ground and polished with sand and emery by a rubber, which works on them with either a rotary or a to-and-fro motion.

Pieces of marble of extraordinary size, for monolithic columns, obelisks, etc., are cut and fashioned in the same way. Much of the fluting and other carving on ornamental stonework is done by machinery in the mills. Sometimes hand-carving is done there also, and sometimes it is left until the stones are actually in place in the structure of which they are to form a part.

The American marble industry is a comparatively young one. It began about 1836, with the burning of some of the

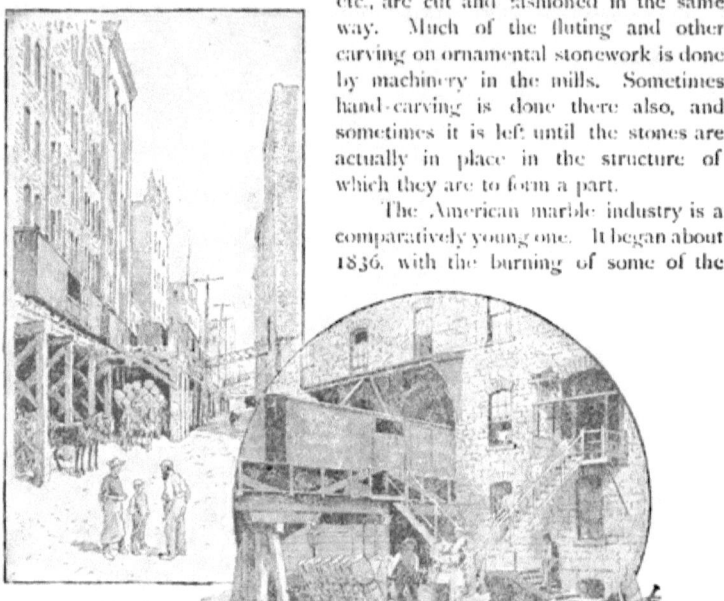

BETWEEN THE MILLS.

BARREL-HOIST AND TUNNEL THROUGH THE WASHBURN MILL.

surface marble, at West Rutland, for lime. Then a few tombstones were cut. After a dozen years systematic quarrying was begun; but it was difficult to persuade the public that Vermont marble was as good as that imported from Europe. That it is as good, if not better, is, however, now amply established, and the quarrying of it has become a mammoth industry. Where once were barren sheep-pastures, worth a few dollars an acre, are now vast and increasing caverns, with snowy walls, from which busy toilers armed with steel and steam have taken millions of dollars worth of stone, enough of it, and good enough, to have built all Athens in the age of Pericles.

"The old order changeth, giving place to new." But only the means are new, and not the ends. Before history began, bread was the staff of life, and in the Stone Age the grain of the field was ground into meal for food.

Among the earliest implements of human ingenuity were the two stones between which the corns of wheat or barley were crushed, and those very implements are in use to-day in savage lands. Civilization still clings to bread as the staff of life, and still grinds the grain between two stones. They are large stones, now, and they are operated by steam or water power. But the result is the same in kind as it was uncounted ages ago.

The well-nigh universal method of grinding grain is that of the common village mill. Two huge disc-shaped stones are placed one above the other, the faces which come together being grooved in a peculiar fashion.

SHOOTING A WELL.

Through the upper stone there is a hole, through which the grain trickles from a hopper and enters the narrow space between the stones. Then, as the upper stone whirls swiftly round and round upon its axis, the grain is finely ground, thereafter to be screened, so as to separate the fine flour from the coarser bran. To this day, with few exceptions, that is the process used in flour mills, great and small.

About 1870, however, some millers in Hungary began experimenting with a view of improving the milling process, and the result was the Walz Muhl, or cylinder-mill, called also the gradual reduction mill, and, in this country, the "new process." In this system no millstones are used, but, in their stead, many pairs of small, horizontal steel rollers, their surfaces traversed by small, sharp grooves, sometimes spiral, sometimes parallel

OPENING A WILD CAT WELL.

with the axes. These pairs of rollers are arranged in sets of at least three, one above the other, with a space between. The grain passes between the uppermost pair and is crushed. Falling through the intervening space it is cooled, and then goes between the second pair and is crushed more finely. Again it is cooled by falling to the third set, and again is crushed more finely still. The finest grades of flour are thus passed through eighteen or twenty sets of rollers.

This is the "new process" used in the great mills of Minnesota, perhaps the most important seat of the flour-making industry in the world. Here the famous and picturesque Falls of St. Anthony, on the Mississippi River, furnish practically unlimited water-power, through systems of turbine wheels. Anthony Trollope—not the Anthony for whom the falls were named—once said that he never could believe, until he actually saw it, that there was a place, inhabited by rational men, called Minneapolis. The name is a queer mixture of Indian and Greek. But never mind. Philology may stand aghast, but all the same a very great share of the world must get its bread from this same Minneapolis. Here huge mills form a city in themselves. For their supply cartage would be absurd; the railroads run directly into them. Daily long trains bear in the harvest of the wheat fields and bear out the finished flour, the finest in the world. There is no tumult or clatter; the thousands of cylinders are

THE SINKING OF THE "ALABAMA," THE MOST FAMOUS OF ALL CONFEDERATE CRUISERS

The battle between the *Kearsarge* and the *Alabama* took place off Cherbourg, France, June, 1864. "The Lancaster ranged up alongside, down, and the broadside of the *Kearsarge* were fired as fast as the guns could be worked, the fire focused upon the *Alabama*; the monster ship pumped out of sight, and the crew were hurried in to help the drowning men. The crew were rescued; the boats of the *Alabama* were too shattered . . . . . ."

FIRST BATTLE OF BULL RUN 1861

whirling with only a low, continuous hum. There is no dust in the air, with its death-dealing power. Once mills were pervaded with a fine, impalpable dust. This one day exploded, with the force of gunpowder, wrecking one of the largest mills and destroying many lives. Since then elaborate systems of air-currents have been devised, keeping the atmosphere of the mills always free from dust, and cool.

Thousands of barrels of flour daily are turned out of one of these mammoth mills, and thousands of empty barrels must be daily received to contain the snowy product. With a task of such magnitude on hand, the old-fashioned cooper's shop is use-less. Great factories have taken its place, where saws and knives, driven by steam power, in whole-sale fashion transform forests into flour barrels. These go in towering loads to the mills, and are hurried in the grasp of an end-less chain to where the perfected flour is pour-ing from the whirring rollers and through the quivering silken screens.

Starting from bins in the upper story, the wheat travels through the vast building, from floor to floor, from side

GAS WELLS.

to side, untouched by human hands; now being cleansed from impurities, now being crushed finer and finer, now being sifted again and again; until at last, encased in barrels of one hundred and ninety-six pounds each, it issues forth by the carload to feed the millions of the world. Half a billion bushels, or thirty billion pounds, are the inconceivable figures that represent the annual wheat crop of America; and the mills of Minneapolis and Rochester and other cities are worthy, in magnitude and perfection of equipment, to deal with the large share of it that forms their grist. True, they are doing, in kind, only what the squalid wild woman of the cave-dwelling race did with stone

bowl and grinder. But in degree, how different! And though the end be th
same, in means how has the old order changed and given place to the new!

The use of petroleum in various forms is of unremembered origir
Nineveh and Babylon knew it well, the "slime" of the Old Testament bein;
merely crude petroleum, partially evaporated. To this day the oil wells o
Is, on the Euphrates, which supplied "slime" or mortar for the building o
Babylon, are still flowing. Other ancient wells are in the Ionian Islands; a
Amiano, Italy; on the Persian Shore of the Caspian Sea, and in Burmal
Pliny tells of the use of this oil in lamps in his day, and the city of Geno
was largely lighted with it centuries ago. But it did not play a great part i
the world's economy until an American "struck oil" in the latter half of th
present century.

As early as 1819 petroleum was collected from wells in Ohio and pu
to various uses. In 1850 the manufacture of the oil from coal was begui
and rapidly increased until it became an important industry. But not ye
was the true vein struck. The honor of at last doing this was reserved fo
Colonel G. L. Drake, who, in 1858, began to bore, on Oil Creek, Venang
County, Pa., an artesian well. "What for?" his neighbors asked. "Fo
oil," was his reply; and they laughed him to scorn. But on August 28, 185
at a depth of 71 feet, he "struck oil." It flowed at the rate of 400 gallon
a day, and he sold it for 55 cents a gallon; and his neighbors stopped laughing

Seldom has the world seen such a rush for wealth as the oil country the
beheld. Wells were sunk everywhere. A forest of derricks arose. Farms tha
had been worth five dollars were largely purchased at a thousand dollars a
acre. One farmer sold out for a round million. Another would not sell, bu
got $3000 a day in royalties on wells sunk on his farm. Fabulous fortune
were amassed. One well, the Noble, in a little more than a year, yielde
500,000 barrels without pumping. The principal oil field was in Pennsyl
vania, but many wells were sunk in adjacent counties of New York and i
Ohio and West Virginia.

In time the freely flowing wells began to fail and pumping had to be re
sorted to, under which process the yield was maintained, though the profits were
slightly lessened. Another system of renewing the flow of exhausted wells wa
invented some years ago and is widely and successfully practiced. This i
called "shooting," or "torpedoing." A gallon or so of nitro-glycerine, enclose
in a long and slender tin can, is lowered to the bottom of the well and exploded
The shock shatters the oil-bearing slate and sandstone for a considerable dis
tance around the bore, and jars it much further, and the result is an immediat
rush of oil, often spurting high in air, like a geyser. This process is patented
and the work is done by a single company, whose agents drive about the oi
country, over rough roads, in a most reckless fashion, with cans of nitro-gly

cerine under the wagon-seat. Now and then a jolt of the wagon causes an
explosion. There is a tremendous noise and a hole in the ground; that is all.
Man, horse, and wagon are literally blown to atoms. "Moonlighting" is the
name applied to the surreptitious "shooting" of wells by unauthorized persons
—owners of wells who thus evade paying royalty to the company holding the
patent.

"Wild-cat" wells, so called, are shafts sunk secretly, or so guarded that
none but the owners can approach them to ascertain their value. Such wells
are surrounded by armed sentries, who promptly repel curious visitors at
the rifle's muzzle. If the well proves profitable, the owners are able thus

to secure other territory around it
before the price is enhanced by the
knowledge that they have "struck
oil."

The crude oil is stored in huge
tanks, and then shipped to the refi-
neries, at New York and elsewhere.
Once it was all conveyed in casks.
Then huge iron tanks, resembling a

TRANSPORTING OIL FROM THE PIPE-LINES TO THE
CARS.

locomotive boiler in size and shape, were made, each being mounted on a flat
railroad car and holding about 25,000 gallons. This method of transportation
is still much used. In 1865, however, another plan was devised, which is now
the characteristic method. This is the pumping of the oil through pipes, laid
on or under the ground. These pipes are from four to six inches in diameter,
and on the long lines have pumping stations at intervals of about twenty-five
miles. Twenty thousand barrels of oil may be sent daily through a six-inch
pipe. The oil country is fairly gridironed with these pipe-lines; and there are
two lines reaching from Olean to New York Bay, 300 miles, and many others
from fifty to 175 miles long.

In late years natural gas has become an important product of the oil fields. Exhausted oil wells often furnish it, and so do wells driven for the purpose. The gas rushes from the well in a powerful current, and when ignited forms a perpetual torch perhaps a hundred feet high, a very "pillar of fire." This gas is conveyed through pipes to towns and cities, where it is used in place of the manufactured gas for illuminating purposes. It is also much used for fuel in private houses and in manufacturing establishments. It is found to be cheaper than coal, its fires more easily regulated, and the unpleasant features of smoke, cinders, and ashes are entirely avoided.

Although the day of phenomenal "gushers" among oil wells seems well-nigh past, the industry maintains mammoth proportions. Thus in the month of May, 1892, in the Pennsylvania field alone 183 new wells were sunk, 43 of them being dry. The product of the new wells was 7795 barrels. In 1889 the oil fields of Pennsylvania and New York produced 21,486,403 barrels (of 42 gallons each,) those of Ohio, 12,471,665, and those of West Virginia, Colorado, California, Indiana, Kentucky, Illinois, Kansas and Texas enough to bring the total for the United States up to 34,820,306 barrels. That produced in Ohio, Indiana, and California was used chiefly for fuel, and the rest for illuminating purposes, excepting 109,891 barrels used for lubricating. The total value of the year's yield in its crude state was $26,554,652. The total product of the United States from 1859 to 1889, inclusive, was 407,985,503 barrels, or 17,135,391,126 gallons of crude oil.

The Thrilling Story of Life on the Frontier.

ILLUSTRATED BY FREDERIC REMINGTON.

A CHEYENNE.

MONG the unique and interesting figures that have entered into the history of the West is the squatter. His species has become almost extinct. He will soon be driven out, ground down, and reduced by the leveling arm of civilization to an ordinary American citizen, with every trace of picturesqueness lost. He may still be seen in the more thickly settled regions of the West. His people are a mongrel set. They generally came from one of the Middle States, a family at a time, in an old ox-wagon, whose cover was drawn in at the ends like the back of an old-fashioned sunbonnet, and from under whose tattered edges a row of pink-faced, white-haired children peeped out upon the new Canaan of their rightful possessions. Inside, wielding his long whip, sat the solemn pioneer. Outside, walking behind a retinue consisting of a cow, a calf, a sad-looking horse, and several yellow dogs, came the wind-tanned mother and the eldest, bare-legged boy. Over the wheels of the wagon dangled a few rush-bottomed chairs, an old pine bedstead, and the simplest household utensils. The father chewed his tobacco and cracked his whip, the children chattered, the big boy shied clods of earth at the quail and meadow lark, and the mother trudged on in silence.

When they came to a place that suited them, where there was timber, light, sandy soil, and water, they constructed a rude cabin and settled down for a season. It did not occur to them to ask whose land it was. They did not want to sign deeds, pay taxes, and build fences; they simply wanted a home where the father could return after his fishing and hunting and the mother could piece her rag-quilts and dip her snuff in peace. They cut a few poles and built a rude log cabin, roofed it with brush and sod, and smoothed the earthen floor. The old chairs and three-legged bedstead that had been nailed to the wall soon gave it a home-like air. A bee-gum spring was sunk, a brushwood fence was built for the calf, and a clearing made for the little garden. When they had found out the nearest mill their wants were supplied. They had no need for a school, a church, a physician, or a preacher. The mother knew of herbs and liniments, and as for education, the children needed to learn only to swim and climb, to ride and shoot, and, later in life, to shift for themselves.

But often the squatter does not even have a rude cabin to boast of. If he has the roving spirit that cannot settle down long enough in any one place to make it worth his while to construct a cabin, he will pitch a tent, and he and his family will live there in the most aboriginal fashion for a season or two, perhaps, before moving on. He may be a trapper, and in that case he gets a fair livelihood if his luck is good. When the owner decides to claim his land the squatter and his family move on. Perhaps the mother will fret a little over her ash-hopper, her setting hens, and her turnip patch; but the children like the travel, and the oldest boy is wild to ride the first mustang pony he has broken. They have prospered in the West, and this time the cart, followed by the inevitable yellow dogs, is loaded. There are plenty of other spring branches and tempting locations. The whole West is before them from which to make a more fortunate selection for a home.

In sharp contradistinction to the squatter is the settler, who knows the homestead law, takes up his one hundred and sixty acres, publishes his claim, and settles down to live unbrokenly upon it for the required six months each year. When his deeds read right and field notices have been properly witnessed and recorded, he is ready to begin life as a citizen and landholder. He hews and splits the tough post-oaks and black-jacks, builds strong "worm" fences around his possessions, and is ready when the season opens to begin his work. He plants his crop, digs his well, sets out the little fruit orchard, drains and irrigates, plows and grubs. The scent of the new earth is on his clothing and the sweetness and wholesomeness of it are in his heart. If he is progressive, public-spirited, and thoroughly imbued with the spirit of the West, he will immediately show some indication of his enterprise. He will meet his fellow-citizens, boom the lands, work for a new railroad, subscribe for schools and churches, and work for better laws. He is bound to succeed. His children will be sent away to be educated, and they will have a better inheritance than was left to their parents. Probably this independent, self-reliant, and public-spirited settler will aspire to political honors. Politics are contagious in the West, and nearly every young man looks forward to a seat in the Legislature, if not in Congress. But whether he represents a county or a district, the thoroughly and typically Western man will always carry with him the opinions that have been ground into him by his rough contact with a hard world.

There is another class of settlers in the West who remain hopelessly poor in spite of sobriety, hard work, and good intentions. They are the people whom luck seems to turn against. Whatever he undertakes, this settler seems to be unfortunate. He sells his land to a speculator, and the unearned increment goes into the hands of a shrewder person. He sees men all around him getting suddenly rich, and in time he gets used to seeing others profit by his toil. His wife must always be an overworked creature, for it takes the united toil of both to get a living. It is a wonder that these pioneer women of the West do not more frequently lose courage. But in times of grasshoppers or severe

A TUMBLE FROM THE TRAIL.

drought, of destruction of crops by wind or hail, she never gives up. She has the temperament that can endure. The woman who has always known hardship and toil, who marched in behind wagons, her face burned and hardened by exposure to wind and sun in varying seasons, is not the person to become faint-hearted. Hard-featured but tender-hearted, brown-skinned but white-souled, she holds her own with her sturdy husband and plodding sons. She takes upon her shoulders the helpmeet's half of a pioneer life. She is up with the dawn, milks her dozen cows, carries her water for cooking and washing purposes from the nearest branch, a quarter of a mile away, cuts her own wood, and makes her own fires. Uncomplaining and unresentful, she sings at her work, and is always ready to cheer and comfort. Side by side with the men, she plows and hoes the new fields, or, mounted on her own broncho, participates in the round-up or "stands herd" while the boys take their noontide nap in the chapparal bush. She teaches her children to ride, swim, and to look out for themselves at a tender age.

Childhood as it is known in cities and in older States, with its prattling ignorance and pretty dependencies, is almost extinguished in the far West. The boys assume responsibilities beyond their years, and the girls soon learn to share the mother's household cares. The substantial facts and practical experiences with which the life of their elders is guided has an early influence upon their own. They learn the time of day by the sun, and predict changes of weather by the hazes and rings about the moon. They learn the ages and distinctive qualities in the herds. The hills are their schools, pebbles and wild flowers their books, and the horses their playmates. They become sophisticated with a rare impersonal knowledge of nature and things created.

The cattle business, as the practical ranchman calls his vocation, has undergone a decided change during the past twenty years. The wholesale and loosely managed business of the '60's has given way to the statistical and close-margined system of the present. It has grown, with the tendency of modern practical and domestic economy, toward a basis of real valuations. It is the scope and territory of the business that have been so reduced, while the results remain practically the same. The last census bulletin, reporting on live stock on ranges, gives a summary of 517,128 head of horses, 5,433 mules, 14,100 asses or burros, 6,828,182 head of cattle, 6,676,902 sheep, and 17,276 swine. The sales of horses amounted to $1,418,205; cattle, $17,913,712; sheep, $2,669,663, and swine, $27,132. The total number of men in charge of the ranches was 15,390. As to territory for stock-raising, nature has made a generous provision. The immense Panhandle of Texas, which, with its fertility of soil and abundance of rainfall, must not be confounded with the arid Pecos regions or the Llano Estacado, or Staked Plains, embraces hundreds of square miles of juicy grass-range. Even the Staked Plains, considered useless for years, are gradually being converted into good pasture regions by means of irrigation and artificial forestry. The prairies of Kansas and the rolling stretches of the Indian Territory are used for no other purpose than as the feeding-ground for thousands of herds.

Until the passage of the Oklahoma Bill the Indian country was an Eldorado for Kansas and Texas cattlemen. The withdrawal of the country was a great backset to the cattle business in the Southwest. The Texas mesquite grass is superb winter forage, keeping its nutritive and sustaining qualities long after it appears dried up and juiceless, but it is not as fattening as the Territory grass. Every winter the Oklahoma district was overrun with herds driven from the surrounding country, and while in the Territory among the helpless Indians the cattleman resorted to his primitive system of commission. He knew he had no right to the Indian's land, and the Indian knew it too, but, so long as he was not inconvenienced for the time being, he made no resistance to the usurpation of his land. The stockmen pacified the Indians for the use of their pasturing grounds by supplying some of their more immediate wants, giving them fresh beef and cows and a generous amount of tobacco, whisky, and worthless trinkets for the squaws.

The pleasant little game of reciprocity was broken up by the President's fiat forbidding foreign stockmen to drive their herds into the Territory. There was no penalty attached, and there was, naturally, considerable manœuvring on the part of the stockmen to evade the law and its inconvenient requirements. The United States troops stationed at Forts Sill and Reno were commissioned to enforce the law and to order all foreign stockmen then in the Territory to vacate immediately. One stubborn old-timer from Texas, who was peacefully teaching his herd to eat forbidden grass, came under the official eye and gave no small amount of trouble. After numerous attempts at resistance, he finally rounded up his herd and marched to the border; but, as there was no fiat to forbid his return, deliberately marched back. Several official orders were sent him; each time he obeyed, and each time he returned. Finally two companies of cavalry were sent out to insist upon the enforcement of the law. The mounted cavalry, in their brave uniforms, riding their stall-fed and stiff-kneed horses, did not find the matter as simple as they perhaps had anticipated. They set out, solemnly marching in fours, before, behind, or in the midst, wherever they could keep their places in the disorganized herd of long-horns. The drive occurred in April, when most of the cows were calving, and the young calves, unable to keep up in the line of march, fell behind. The infuriated mothers continually broke ranks to rush back after their wailing offspring. The captain's roaring command, "Charge the brute!" would be countermanded by the order, "Retreat! Retreat!" when a maddened animal bore down upon the solemn fours. This weary war between the staid soldiers and the resisting herd of cattle went on for two days and nights. A combination of forces more incongruous can scarcely be imagined. The calm, rimless stretch of prairie was the scene of battle between man and beast. The dignified soldiers, in their unwonted service, contrasted with the infuriated mob of cattle; the flashing of arms and the prancing of terrified army horses; the confusion of orders; the lowing of the cows, bellowing of steers, and cries of deserted calves; the little knot of cowboys and their leader riding submissively apart, watching the pro-

A PUCKING BRONCHO.

ceedings with amused interest, wondering what the result would be.

The troops were called upon a number of times during the season to preserve the majesty of the law before the country was finally deserted by the stock-men. The Territories and new States of the Northwest still supply unlimited range and pasturage. The plains extending from the Black Hills and the mountain ranges of Wyoming, from Fort Collins to the Montana border, and between Pike's Peak and Denver, as well as the greater part of the mild-wintered New Mexi-co Territory, are rich in grasses and well watered lands yet open to the stock raiser.

The Colorado plains are particularly adapted to sheep raising, which is one of the leading industries of that State. The range is cut up by mountains and cañons into small ranches, where sheep can be raised to better advantage than cattle. The business is more hazardous than cattle raising, but it has competed successfully with it. There has long been a feudal rivalry between the two classes of ranchmen.

Until 1876 the Texas cattlemen had a monopoly of the business. They dealt entirely in common stock cattle, or stock-horns, that required no provision further than that afforded by a mild climate, sufficient grass, and water. The business was carried on with primitive simplicity. The herders, who were hired for twelve or fifteen dollars a month, furnished their own outfits, and a few pack-mules were sufficient to carry all necessary camp supplies. Even prices were established by the ranchmen to suit themselves, for competition was not strong enough to regulate them. When the Texas range became insufficient, and the stockmen drove their herds to the northwest, to Nebraska, Wyoming, and Colorado, a rivalry sprang up and a new impetus was given to the industry. In the year 1891 the Swan Land and Cattle Company pastured no less than 80,000 head of cattle in eastern Wyoming, and smaller companies owned from 14,000 to 50,000 stock and horses. A depression in the stock business was aggravated by the mixing of native and foreign breeds, and the spreading of various contagious and infectious diseases. Beef that had sold for $25 per head depreciated to $10 and $12. Stock cattle remained more nearly stationary in price, but there was a rapid falling off in numbers, due to both the rage of epidemic, and the general neglect of the business. When things were at their worst for both stock and stockmen, syndicates from the North and from foreign countries gave the trade a new boom. Capital was plentiful for a while; ranches and ranges were bought or leased in great numbers, and prices were pushed up by conventions and unions to something near their original fictitious bases. This state of affairs did not last long, and there was a gradual falling in prices to actual values. "Corn-fed" and refrigerated beef held its own, and people soon learned that 1000 head of cattle sheltered, fed, watered, and judicially disposed of paid better in the long run than 100,000 running wild on insufficient ranges, starving, famishing, and dying of "pink-eye" and epizoöty. Ranches were cut up into farms and orchards; the herds were reduced in numbers and made to supply the same demand as existed in the time of such unwieldy conditions.

The introduction of fine-blooded short-horned breeds into the Northwestern and Southwestern ranges has not proven profitable. The summers are too long, the winters too severe, and the country itself unsuited to the successful raising of cattle that require the best forage and shelter, as well as careful handling. The cattle and sheep that thrive in the West must be able to obtain their own subsistence all the year round, and to live without shelter, except that provided by nature in the ravines and wind-breaks. During the summer and winter they roam at will over the plains, frequently wandering long distances from the home range. At the fall and spring round-ups, when the stragglers are hunted up, an enumeration made, calves branded and beeves selected for market, the cattle are brought together from points a hundred miles or more apart. The different ranchmen pick out their own cattle, recognizable by the brand, which is recorded like the deed of property. It is interesting to study the effect of climatic and physical conditions of the country upon the cattle running wild. Even the proportion of the young is regulated by the characteristics of the country. Each member of a herd seems to know its place, and always prefers its own to any other herd. These dumb creatures have more intelligence than is usually credited to them.

The so-called wild cattle of Texas bear a close resemblance in many ways to the deer. The large development of horn, the pointed nose, the lustrous eye, and above all, the thinness of flank and length of leg, together with the fleetness, are the main characteristics. The spring "round up," which is held in May and early June, is the busiest time of the year. A captain is chosen from each district, and the stockmen and cattle boys belonging to fifteen or twenty ranges in each work under him. The work is apportioned, and the helpers are under semi-military organization. Each cowboy has eight or ten horses, and the whole district, sometimes covering hundreds of square miles, is laid out in daily rides. A month or more time is generally required to cover the country. It is said that the cowboys track cattle as the Indian tracks his game. The watercourses must be followed, and the country carefully searched for stragglers, some of which sometimes turn up after several years' absence. The boys are up at four or five o'clock in the morning, and frequently are in the saddle sixteen or seventeen hours a day. While the work is hard, the boys look forward to it for months. It is preferable to the monotonous life at the ranch, with no diversion but euchre or poker, or an occasional novel. The cowboy must have a constitution of iron to endure the hardships of prairie life. He is obliged to work, when after cattle, in all weathers. He must stand severe heat and drenching rains, with no prospect of relief from duty until after the work of the "round up" is finished. He must know the business of a ranchman thoroughly, and understand every detail of the work, whether that of day-watcher, herder, or night-watchman, or that of captain of a district. He must be a good horseman, know how to break a wild pony, and to ride it when broken, must be keen-witted, and never lose presence of mind, or he may lose his life in a stampede. Furthermore he must be a skillful lariat thrower. He cannot hope to handle his hempen rifle with any degree of skill until he has had at least two years of practice, and it will be much longer than that before he can throw it with anything like a sure aim.

The lariat is generally made of native grass, braided and twisted. It is forty-five feet long, and from three-eighths to one and a half inches in thickness. The end is wound with waxed shoemakers' thread and the whole boiled in oil to give it strength and pliability. The loop is often made of leather which has been soaked, stretched and scraped, and "seasoned." The success in handling the lariat depends entirely upon the strength and movement of the wrist.

The cowboy has been called the King of the Cattle Country. It may be only to a limited extent that he is monarch of all he surveys, but in his happy careless way he dominates even the master of the ranch. In former times he was only the son and grandson of a cowboy, and was relegated to a distinct class in the social scale. He inherited even the bow-legs of his pony straddling ancestors, and all the physical characteristics which the occupation stamped

A DISPUTE OVER A BRAND.

upon them. It was almost literally true of him that "he was born in the saddle." To-day the cowboy is sometimes the son of a well-to-do family in an eastern or middle State, and is led by a spirit of adventure to experience something of life in the West. The dash of the winds, the roar and swell and freedom of the prairies, delight him. Colleges seem small and limited, books and papers tame and unvarying. The prairies exhilarate and depress him by turns. He becomes contemplative and introspective, taciturn and uncommunicative, by reason of his surroundings. He is to be seen standing about the station at train time, in some western town, or more likely sitting sideways on his highpommeled Mexican saddle, watching the people that crowd off or on the cars with much the same expression that shows in his pony's eyes—an expression that can be best described by lack of alertness.

In dress he has escaped from every restraint of conventionality. He hates a coat, wears a coarse shirt of blue, gray, or red twilled flannel, as loose as a blouse, confined at the waist by a leather belt. His sombrero may be decorated with a gold or silver band, and tassels dangling at the side. His trousers fit his muscular legs with unfashionable snugness, and his hair is several seasons too long. His swearing is only a provincial sin, and his dram drinking a companionable custom. He is quick to join a lynching party, a band of serenaders *en route* to a ranch where an Eastern girl is visiting, a posse after a horse-thief, or an old folks' band to a camp-meeting, entering upon each with impartial enthusiasm. He sits his horse like an Arab, and handles his lariat as a professional trickster his cards. That unwieldy-looking coil of grass rope tied to his saddle-skirts is as dangerous a weapon as one could wish for. It has taken long practice to wield it dexterously, and the cowboy takes a natural pride in his accomplishment. If a steer or buffalo straying from its herd crosses his path, out springs his lasso in rhythmical sweeps over the rider's head, then off to one side, falling in a sure slip-knot over the animal's head, or around the fore legs, and by a twirl of the rope and a sudden movement of the wrist the victim is thrown upon the soft turf. In all feats of esquestrianism the cowboy excels the Indian; apparently as reckless, but more judicious and unerring in his movements. Even the cow-pony, the faithful friend of the cowboy, has a divination that is almost human. He enjoys the chase as a dog the hunt, the cowboy's "Halloo-oo-oo!" being to him what the hunter's horn is to the hound. He understands every movement of his rider. When the master coils the lasso about his head, the pony slows up; when the rope coils into nooses ahead of him, he advances; as the noose slips over the animal's head or leg, he halts, jerking back his head, stiffening his neck, and planting his forefeet into the ground, aiding the lariat thrower in landing the victim. It is peculiar that the pony never becomes tame. He submits to the girth and bit unwillingly, and each time he is turned loose upon the range imagines his apprenticeship to control is over. When he is captured again he shies and balks, flashes his eyes, chews the bit, and resents the whip. It is only an illustration of nature's refutation of man's superiority.

The pony, too, comes from the range; his progenitors were the wild horses of the West; his education is practical and experimental. His endurance is something marvelous. He can outrun two ordinary horses, and endure hunger and thirst with an indifference almost equal to that of the horned frog. He comes near his abstemious cousin, the burro, as regards provender. His intelligence is phenomenal, and the understanding between him and his master is fraternal. When the rider wishes to start on a gallop, he raises his elbows, giving them a slight shake, and he is borne away. A touch of the hand on the neck will bring the horse to a sudden standstill, without the use of the rein. It is no wonder that the two have become inseparably associated, and the horse is named "Friend" or "Little Brother." In his lonely ride the cowboy sings his strange ballads with all the devotion and fervor of an Oriental lover.

There are some branches of industry that are retarded, if not destroyed, by civilization. One of these is ranching, as it was followed in the wide scope pasturage and free grass of a quarter of a century ago. Then no man thought of claiming more land than he needed or cared to fence for his own homestead purposes. As free as the air he breathed, or the blue sky over him, was the land that lay before him. In a primitive and fraternal fashion the early stock-men availed themselves of the privileges of commission. In a land where range and booty alike were free, the first man out in the spring caught the first calf, and the tiny bit of communistic property belonged to the man who branded it. There was a premium on the early bird, and the prosperous stockman who believed that all was fair in love and war and cattle raising might at times hear the epithet: "That man? Why, he'd steal yearlings!" applied to himself. He reasoned that a crime confessed is not a crime, and a bad deed done in the light of day is not bad. Even the round-ups were a sort of barbarous Derby-day or hurdle-race, where stakes were open and entry was free, and where no hard feeling existed.

AN INDIAN WARRIOR.

The big-hearted and free-handed pioneer might forgive this wholesale thievery, but the law did not, which came with the homesteader and syndicates and barbed wire fences. Signs appeared on the pasture gates warning trespassers against appropriation of private land, wagon roads were forced to turn out of their way, railroads came into the Territories, and the free citizen was restrained by monopolies. With improved methods of cross feeding and ensilage, with winter sheds and artificial lakes, drouth and famine were circumvented, and stock raising settled down into a safer and smaller business.

In old times a ranchman was content with his dozen "hands," each one furnishing his own two ponies, and riding away the season at fifteen dollars a month. The ranchman was content, also, to live in his log cabin, or even "dug-out," while he could count his herds by the thousands. His manner of business was primitive and economical. His pack-mules carried all necessary camping and cooking utensils. Nowadays he must have fifty, instead of a dozen "hands." He must mount each one, allowing several good horses to each, besides furnishing a big round up wagon with its stove and gasoline and coal-oil, and supplies of canned fruits, meats, and delicacies of all kinds. He builds fine houses, wind-mills, patent gates, and commodious barns, and lives not only in comfort, but in luxury. The old-fashioned "round up" on the southern ranch was a merry time for all, from the children on the ranches to the horses, who enjoyed the race immensely. Ponies were driven from the range and "broke" to the dominion of girth and bridle; gray blankets were sunned, rolled up with a suit of flannel underwear, and strapped on to the back of the patient pack-horse; saddle-bags and grip-sacks were brought forth and filled, one side with cold biscuits, corn dodgers, sugar, and coffee, and the other side with streaked bacon, salt, pepper, and raw onions. Over the gray bundles on the pack-horse's back dangled frying pans, tin cups, an iron pot, and a home-made cedar bucket. The cowboys, booted, spurred, and sombreroed, wearing buckskin gauntlets and leather belt holding pistol, bowie knife, shot and powder horns, and a canteen of whisky, are off to the round up. The old ranch is left almost deserted for a few weeks until the herds are brought back. The roaring and lowing of the approaching cattle can be heard for miles. The tramping of thousands of restless hoofs and the bleating of thousands of thirsty tongues announce the approach of the cattle, and all work or play is stopped until after the herds come in. The cowboys chant a weird halloo-oo-oo! as they canter on their ponies amid the bellowing, hooting animals. Such a little thing may cause a stampede; the sudden whirl of an obstreperous pony, the dropping of a red handkerchief, the low flight of a hawk or turkey buzzard, and off go the cattle and pandemonium reigns. In vain the boys surround the herd, chanting their persuasive "Halloo-oo-oo!" which is unheeded by the frightened animals. They break ranks and scatter, pawing up the hot sand or loose grass, and flinging it, hoof-load after hoof-load, over their backs. Bellowing, lowing, and bleating, they rush back to their wild haunts on the range. Thus the entire work of a round-up may be lost in a few hours. But if the herd is once within the stockpens, all is safe. The cattle are separated, yearlings numbered, calves branded, and the old cattle turned loose upon the range.

One of the most remarkable yet common scenes about a ranch is a cattle funeral. Let a beef be killed, no matter how far away from the general range, nor how deeply the spilled blood be covered up, its kindred seem instinctively to know of the slaughter, and resent it with all the force of their dumb natures. They will come running for miles, tongue out, eyes red, back bristling, to find and keep watch over the murdered mate. They keep up the most mournful lowing, and as the crowds become thicker, the weird, resounding echoes of the

AN INDIAN TRAPPER—A STUDY OF A HORSE AND RIDER

plain are terrifying to one unused to such scenes. Those who come first seem to agree upon a kind of solemn courtesy to the new comers. They move back and the new relay rushes in in an orderly circle. They lower their horns and paw up the earth, bawling dismally, till a new committee arrives, and they in turn move back to allow the new comers to continue the tragic ceremonies. And woe to any human being who arrives upon the scene! With instinctive resentment, the brutes recognize their bloody-handed master, and plunge at him to rend him to pieces in their frenzy. Sometimes this awful death watch is kept up for twenty-four hours. It makes one nervous and apprehensive. It is as if Nature rose in her might, declaring, "Thou shalt not kill!" Ranchmen, of course, get accustomed to this weird spectacle, but when they cannot endure the maddened mob of upbraiding dumb creatures about their door, the yearlings for beef are driven several miles away to be killed, and hauled back to the ranch proper.

No sketch of the West is complete without some allusion to the far-famed woman of the ranch.

The cattle queen, who has held a conspicuous place in the narrator's tale of the West for a quarter of a century, belongs to the old days of typical ranch life, the merry round-ups, barbecues, log-raisings, and sheep shearings. At her best she was a much gilded and idealized creature. In fiction, she was daring and fearless, wore buckskin leggings, a black-plumed sombrero, high-heeled boots, and gold-spiked spurs. She swore lightly, with a pretty flirt of her skirt, carried her brace of Colt's revolvers, counted her thousand cattle on her thousand hills, rode into town and shipped them, depositing her good paper in the Stockmen's Bank. In life, the ranch woman was a hard-faced, hard-worked female cattleman, who trusted to others and was swindled out of her rights, who drove into town four times a year in her piano-box buggy and paid her lawyer half she made. She did not often, however, manage the business for herself. If she was the widow of a cattle king, she lived in her large town house, made occasional visits to the ranch, and reaped the profits left by her swindling superintendents.

The Interesting Story of Our Difficulties with Foreign Powers.

JAMES MONROE, AUTHOR OF "THE MONROE DOCTRINE."

On a bright spring morning, the date, April 30, 1789, amid the booming of cannon, the plaudits of the multitude, and the general rejoicing of the people of the whole country, Washington had been inaugurated President of the United States. That day saw one of the most significant events accomplished in the history of the world; for there in the city of New York, where the inauguration took place, a nation was born in a day. The old Confederacy was gone; the new nation stood forth "like a giant ready to run a race." And what a race it has run since that time history has told.

The United States was destined to prove no exception to the course marked out by all other nations and enjoy perpetual peace. The fact is, the seeds of conflict were already sown and were destined to bear fruit, both in civil and foreign war.

THE DIFFICULTY WITH THE BARBARY STATES.

If the reader will look at any map of Africa he will see on the northern coast, defining the southern limits of the Mediterranean, four States, Morocco, Algeria, Tunis, and Tripoli, running east and west a distance of 1800 miles. These powers had for centuries maintained a state of semi-independency by paying tribute to Turkey. But this did not suit Algeria, the strongest and most warlike of the North African States; and in the year 1710 the natives overthrew the rule of the Turkish Pasha, expelled him from the country, and united his office to that of the Dey. The Dey thus governed the country by means of a Divan or Council of State chosen from the principal civic functionaries. The Algerians, with the other "Barbary States," as the piratical States were called, defied the Powers of Europe. France alone successfully resisted

331

these depredations, but only partially, for after she had repeatedly chastised the Algerians, the strongest of the northern piratical States, and had induced the Dey to sign a treaty of peace, they would bide their time, and after a time return to their bloody work. It was Algiers which was destined to force the United States to resort to arms in the defense of its persecuted countrymen ; the result is a matter of history.

The truth is, this conflict was no less irrepressible than that greater conflict which a century later deluged the land in blood. For, before the Constitution had been adopted, two American vessels flying the flag of thirteen stripes and only thirteen stars, instead of the forty-four which now form our national constellation, while sailing the Mediterranean had fallen a prey to the swift, heavily armed Algerian cruisers. The vessels were confiscated and the crews, to the number of twenty-one persons, had been held for ransom, for which an enormous sum was demanded.

This sum our Government had been unwilling to pay, as to do so would be to establish a precedent not only with Algeria, but with Tunis, Tripoli, and Morocco as well, for each of these African piratical States was in league with the others, and all had to be separately conciliated.

But, after all, what else could the Government do ? The country had no navy. It could not undertake in improvised ships to go forth and fight the swift, heavily armed cruisers of the African pirates—States so strong that the commercial nations were glad to win exemption from their depredations by annual payments. Why not, then, ransom these American captives by the payment of money and construct a navy sufficiently strong to resist their encroachments in the future ? This feeling on the part of the Government was shared by the people of the country, and so it was, Congress finally authorized the building of six frigates, and by another act empowered President Washington to borrow a million of dollars for purchasing peace. Eventually the money was paid to all the four Powers, and it was hoped all difficulty was at an end. The work of constructing the new war-ships was pushed with expedition, and as will be seen, it was well that it was so.

We are now brought to the year 1800. Tripoli, angry at not receiving as much money as was paid to Algiers, declared war against the United States ; but now circumstances had changed for the better. For our new navy, a small but most efficient one, was completed, and a squadron consisting of the frigates "Essex," Captain Bainbridge, the "Philadelphia," the "President," and the schooner "Experiment," was in Mediterranean waters. Two Tripolitan cruisers lying at Gibraltar on the watch for American vessels, were blockaded by the "Philadelphia." Cruising off Tripoli the "Experiment" fell in with a Tripolitan cruiser of fourteen guns, and after three hours' hard fighting captured her. The Tripolitans lost twenty killed and thirty wounded ; this brilliant result had a marked effect in quieting the turbulent pirates.

But peace was not yet assured. In 1815, while this country was at war with England, the Dey of Algiers unceremoniously dismissed the American Consul and declared war against the United States; and all because he had not received the articles demanded under the tribute treaty. This time the Government was well prepared for the issue. The population of the country had increased to over eight millions. The military spirit of the nation had been aroused by the war with Great Britain, ending in the splendid victory at New Orleans under General Jackson. Besides this, the navy had been increased and made far more effective. The Administration,

A RAILROAD BATTERY.

with Madison at its head, decided to submit to no further extortions from the Mediterranean pirates, and the President sent in a forcible message to Congress on the subject, taking high American ground. The result was a prompt acceptance of the Algerian declaration of war. Events succeeded each other in rapid succession. Ships new and old were at once fitted out. On May 15, 1815, Decatur sailed from New York to the Mediterranean. His squadron comprised the frigates "Guerriere," "Macedonian," and "Constellation," the new sloop of war "Ontario," and four brigs and two schooners in addition.

On June 17, the second day after entering the Mediterranean, Decatur

23

captured the largest frigate in the Algerian navy, having forty-four guns. **The** next day an Algerian brig was taken, and in less than two weeks after his first capture Decatur, with his entire squadron, appeared off Algiers. The end had come! The Dey's courage, like that of Bob Acres, oozed out at his fingers' ends. The terrified Dey sued for peace, which Decatur compelled him to sign on the quarter-deck of the "Guerriere." In this treaty it was agreed by the Dey to surrender all prisoners, pay a heavy indemnity, and renounce all tribute from America in the future. Decatur also secured indemnity from Tunis and Tripoli for American vessels captured under the guns of their forts by British cruisers during the late war.

This ended at once and forever the payment of tribute to the piratical States of North Africa. All Europe, as well as our own country, rang with the splendid achievements of our navy; and surely the stars and stripes had never before floated more proudly from the mast-head of an American vessel, and they are flying as proudly to-day.

KING BOMBA BROUGHT TO TERMS.

It was seventeen years later, in 1832, under the administration of General Jackson, that one of the most interesting cases of difficulty with a foreign power arose. As with Algeria and Tripoli, so now, our navy was resorted to for the purpose of exacting reparation. This time the trouble was with Italy, or rather that part of Italy known at that time as the Kingdom of Naples, which had been wrested from Spain by Napoleon, who placed successively his brother Joseph and Murat, Prince, Marshal of France, and brother-in-law of Napoleon, on the throne of Naples and the two Sicilies. During the years 1809–12 the Neapolitan Government under Joseph and Murat successively had confiscated numerous American ships with their cargoes. The total amount of the American claims against Naples, as filed in the State Department, when Jackson's Administration assumed control, was $1,734,994. They were held by various insurance companies and by citizens, principally of Baltimore. Demands for the payment of these claims had from time to time been made by our Government, but Naples had always refused to settle them.

Jackson and his Cabinet took a decided stand, and determined that the Neapolitan Government, then in the hands of Ferdinand II—subsequently nicknamed Bomba because of his cruelties—should make due reparation for the losses sustained by American citizens. The Hon. John Nelson of Frederick, Maryland, was appointed Minister to Naples and ordered to insist upon a settlement. Commodore Daniel Patterson,* who aided in the defense of New

---

* Daniel T. Patterson was born on Long Island, New York, March 6, 1786; was appointed midshipman in the navy, 1800; was attached to the frigate "Philadelphia" when he ran upon a reef near Tripoli; was captured and a prisoner until 1805; was made lieutenant in 1807 **and**

Orleans in 1815, was put in command of the Mediterranean squadron and ordered to coöperate with Minister Nelson in enforcing his demands. But Naples persisted in her refusal to render satisfaction, and a warlike demonstration was decided upon, the whole matter being placed, under instructions, in the hands of Commodore Patterson.

The entire force at his command consisted of three fifty-gun frigates and three twenty-gun corvettes. So as not to precipitate matters too hastily, the plan was for three vessels to appear in the Neapolitan waters, one at a time, and

UNITED STATES MILITARY TELEGRAPH WAGON.

instructions were given accordingly. The "Brandywine," with Minister Nelson on board, went first. Mr. Nelson repeated the demands for a settlement, and they were refused ; there was nothing in the appearance of a Yankee envoy and a single ship to trouble King Bomba and his little kingdom. The "Brandy-

master-commandant in 1813. In 1814 he won great credit as commander of naval forces at New Orleans, and received the thanks of Congress. He commanded the flotilla which destroyed the fort and defenses of Lafitte, the pirate. He was made captain in 1815 ; Navy Commissioner, 1828 to 1832, and commanded the Mediterranean Squadron, 1832–1835. He died on August 15, 1839, being then in command of the Washington Navy Yard.

wine " cast anchor in the harbor and the humbled Envoy waited patiently for a few days. Then another American flag appeared on the horizon, and the frigate " United States " floated into the harbor and came to anchor. Mr. Nelson repeated his demands, and they were again refused. Four days slipped away, and the stars and stripes again appeared off the harbor. King Bomba, looking out from his palace windows, saw the fifty-gun frigate " Concord " sail into the harbor and drop her anchor. Then unmistakable signs of uneasiness began to show themselves. Forts were repaired, troops drilled, and more cannon mounted on the coast. The demands were reiterated, but the Neapolitan Government still refused. Two days later another war-ship made her way into the harbor. It was the " John Adams." When the fifth ship sailed gallantly in, the Bourbon Government seemed almost on the point of yielding ; but three days later Mr. Nelson sent word home that he was still unable to collect the bill. But the end was not yet. Three days later, and the sixth sail showed itself on the blue waters of the peerless bay. It was the handwriting on the wall for King Bomba, and his Government announced that they would accede to the American demands. The negotiations were promptly resumed and speedily closed, the payment of the principal in installments with interest being guaranteed. Pending negotiations, from August 28 to September 15 the entire squadron remained in the Bay of Naples, and then the ships sailed away and separated. So, happily and bloodlessly, ended a difficulty which at one time threatened most serious results.

AUSTRIA AND THE KOSZTA CASE.

Another demonstration, less imposing in numbers but quite as spirited, and, indeed, more intensely dramatic, occurred at Smyrna in 1853, when Captain Duncan N. Ingraham, with a single sloop-of-war, trained his broadsides on a fleet of Austrian war-ships in the harbor. The episode was a most thrilling one, and " The Story of America " would indeed be incomplete were so dramatic an affair left unrecorded on its pages. And this is the record :—

When the revolution of Hungary against Austria was put down, Kossuth, Koszta, and other leading revolutionists fled to Smyrna, and the Turkish Government, after long negotiations, refused to give them up. Koszta soon after came to the United States, and in July, 1852, declared under oath his intention of becoming an American citizen. He resided in New York city a year and eleven months.

The next year Koszta went to Smyrna on business, where he remained for a time undisturbed. He had so inflamed the Austrian Government against him, however, that a plot was formed to capture him. On June 21, 1853, while he was seated on the Marina, a public resort in Smyrna, a band of Greek mercenaries, hired by the Austrian Consul, seized him and carried him off to an Austrian ship-of-war, the Huzzar, then lying in the harbor. On board the vessel

Archduke John, brother of the
Emperor, was said to be in
command. Koszta was put
in irons and treated as a
criminal. The next day an
American sloop-of-war, the
"St. Louis," commanded by
Capt. Duncan N. Ingraham, *
sailed into the harbor. Learning what had happened, Capt.
Ingraham immediately sent
on board the "Huzzar" and
courteously asked permission
to see Koszta. His request
was granted, and Captain
Ingraham assured himself
that Koszta was entitled to
the protection of the American flag. He demanded
Koszta's release of the Austrian commander. When it
was refused he communi-
cated with the nearest United
States official, Consul Brown,
at Constantinople. While he
was waiting for an answer
six Austrian war-ships sailed
—

* Duncan Nathaniel Ingraham
was born December 6, 1802, at
Charleston, South Carolina. He
entered the United States Navy in
1812 as midshipman, and became a
captain September 14, 1855. In
March, 1856, he was appointed Chief
of the Bureau of Ordnance and Hy-
drography of the Navy Department,
a position which he held until South
Carolina passed her ordinance of
secession in 1860. He then resigned
his commission in the navy and took
service under the Confederate States,
in which he rose to the rank of
Commodore. He died in 1891.

THE PORT OF COLON—TERMINUS OF PANAMA RAILROAD.

into the harbor and came to anchor in positions near the "Huzzar." **On June 29th,** before Captain Ingraham had received any answer from the American Consul, he noticed unusual signs of activity on board the "Huzzar," and before long she began to get under way. The American Captain made up his mind immediately. He put the "St. Louis" straight in the "Huzzar's" course and cleared his guns for action. The "Huzzar" hove to, and Captain Ingraham went on board and demanded the meaning of the "Huzzar's" action.

"We propose to sail for home," replied the Austrian. "The Consul has ordered us to take our prisoner to Austria."

"You will pardon me," said Captain Ingraham, "but if you attempt to leave this port with that American on board I shall be compelled to resort to extreme measures."

The Austrian glanced around at the fleet of Austrian war-ships and the single American sloop-of-war. Then he smiled pleasantly, and intimated that the "Huzzar" would do as she pleased.

Captain Ingraham bowed and returned to the "St. Louis." He had no sooner reached her deck than he called out: "Clear the guns for action!"

The Archduke of Austria saw the batteries of the "St. Louis" turned on him, and he realized that he was in the wrong. The "Huzzar" was put about and sailed back to her old anchorage. Word was sent to Captain Ingraham that the Austrian would await the arrival of the note from Mr. Brown.

The Consul's note, which came on July 1st, commended Captain Ingraham's course and advised him to take whatever action he thought the situation demanded.

At eight o'clock on the morning of July 2d, Captain Ingraham sent a note to the commander of the "Huzzar," formally demanding the release of Mr. Koszta. Unless the prisoner was delivered on board the "St. Louis" before four o'clock the next afternoon, Captain Ingraham would take him from the Austrians by force. The Archduke sent back a formal refusal. At eight o'clock the next morning Captain Ingraham once more ordered the decks cleared for action and trained his batteries on the "Huzzar." The seven Austrian war vessels cleared their decks and put their men at the guns.

At ten o'clock an Austrian officer came to Captain Ingraham and began to temporize. Captain Ingraham refused to listen to him.

"To avoid the worst," he said, "I will agree to let the man be delivered to the French Consul at Smyrna until you have opportunity to communicate with your Government. But he must be delivered there, or I will take him. I have stated the time."

At twelve o'clock a boat left the "Huzzar" with Koszta in it, and an hour later the French Consul sent word that Koszta was in his keeping. Then several of the Austrian war-vessels sailed out of the harbor. Long negotiations between the two Governments followed, and in the end Austria admitted that the United States was in the right, and apologized.

Scarcely had the plaudits which greeted Captain Ingraham's intrepid course died away, when, the next year, another occasion arose where our Government was obliged to resort to the force of arms. This time Nicaragua was the country involved. Early in June, 1854, after repeated but unsuccessful attempts at a settlement had been made by the United States, our Government—Franklin Pierce was then President—determined to secure a settlement by appeal to arms. Various outrages, it was the contention of our Government, had been committed on the persons and property of American citizens dwelling in Nicaragua. The repeated demands for redress were not complied with. Peaceful negotiations having failed, in June, 1854, Commander Hollins, with the sloop-of-war "Cyane," was ordered to proceed to the town of San Juan, or Greytown, which lies on the Mosquito coast of Nicaragua, and to insist on favorable action from the Nicaraguan Government. Captain Hollins came to anchor off the coast and placed his demands before the authorities. He waited patiently for a response, but no satisfactory one was offered him. After waiting in vain for a number of days he made a final appeal and then proceeded

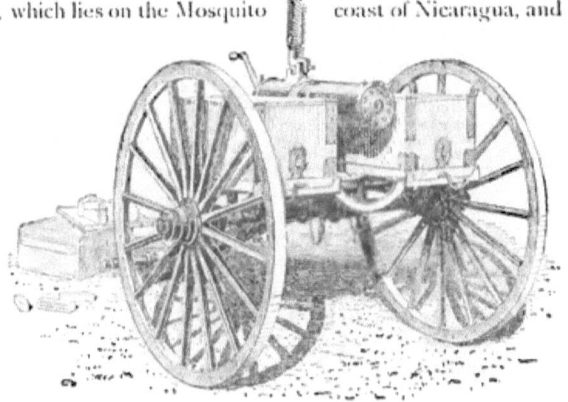

LATEST MODEL OF GATLING FIELD GUN.

to carry out instructions. On the morning of July 13th he directed his batteries on the town of San Juan and opened fire. Until four o'clock in the afternoon the cannon poured out broadsides as fast as they could be loaded. By that time the greater part of the town had been destroyed. Then a party of marines was put on shore, and they completed the destruction of the place by burning the houses.

A lieutenant of the British navy commanding a small vessel of war was in the harbor at the time. England claimed a species of protectorate over the settlement, and the British officer raised violent protest against the action taken by America's representative. Captain Hollins, however, paid no attention to the interference and carried out his instructions. The United States Government later sustained Captain Hollins in everything that he did, and England thereupon thought best to let the matter drop. In this they were unquestionably wise.

At this time the United States seems to have entered upon a period of international conflict. For no sooner had the difficulties with Austria and Nicaragua been adjusted, than another war-cloud appeared on the horizon. Here again but a year from the last conflict had elapsed, for in 1855 an offense was committed against the United States by Paraguay. We now have to go back three years. In 1852 Captain Thomas J. Page,* commanding a small light-draught steamer, the "Water Witch," by direction of his Government started for South America to explore the river La Plata and its large tributaries, with a view to opening up commercial intercourse between the United States and the interior States of South America. We have said the expedition was ordered by our Government; it also remains to be noted that the expedition was undertaken with the full consent and approbation of the countries having jurisdiction over those waters. Slowly, but surely, the little steamer pushed her way up the river, making soundings and charting the river as she proceeded. All went well until February 1, 1855, when the first sign of trouble appeared.

It was a lovely day in early summer—the summer begins in February in that latitude—and nothing appeared to indicate the slightest disturbance. The little "Water Witch" was quietly steaming up the River Paraná, which forms the northern boundary of the State of Corrientes, separating it from Paraguay, when suddenly, without a moment's warning, a battery from Fort Itaparu, on the Paraguayan shore, opened fire upon the little steamer, immediately killing one of her crew who at that time was at the wheel. The "Water Witch" was not fitted for hostilities; least of all could it assume the risk of attempting to run the batteries of the fort. Accordingly, Captain Page put the steamer about, and was soon out of range. It should here be explained that at that time President Carlos A. Lopez was the autocratic ruler of Paraguay, and that he had previously received Captain Page with every assurance of friendship. A few months previous, however, Lopez had been antagonized by the United States Consul at Ascencion, who, in addition to his official position, acted as agent for an American mercantile company, of which Lopez disapproved and went so far as to break up the business of the company. He also issued a decree forbidding foreign vessels of war from navigating the Paraná or any of the waters bounding Paraguay, which he clearly had no right to do, as half the stream belonged to the State bordering on the other side.

* Thomas Jefferson Page was born in Virginia in 1815. He entered the navy as midshipman in October, 1827, and was promoted to a lieutenancy in June, 1833. In September, 1855, he became a commander. In 1861, his State having passed the ordinance of secession, he resigned from the United States Navy, joining that of the Confederate States, where he attained the rank of Commodore.

Captain Page, finding it impracticable to prosecute his exploration any further, at once returned to the United States, giving the Washington authorities a detailed account of the occurrence. It was claimed by our Government that the "Water Witch" was not subject to the jurisdiction of Paraguay, as the channel was the equal property of the Argentine Republic. It was further claimed that even if she were within the jurisdiction of Paraguay she was not properly a vessel of war, but a Government boat employed for scientific purposes. And even were the vessel supposed to be a war vessel, it was contended that it was a gross violation of international right and courtesy to fire shot at the vessel of a friendly power without first resorting to more peaceful means. At that time William L. Marcy, one of the foremost statesmen of his day, was Secretary of State. Mr. Marcy at once wrote a strong letter to the Paraguayan Government, stating the facts of the case, declaring that the action of Paraguay in

EIGHT-INCH GUN AND CARRIAGE OF THE "BALTIMORE."
(Built at the Washington Navy-Yard, of American Steel.)

firing upon the "Water Witch" would not be submitted to, and demanding ample apology and compensation. All efforts in this direction, however, proved fruitless. Lopez refused to give any reparation; and not only so, but declared no American vessel would be allowed to ascend the Paraná for the purpose indicated.

The event, as it became known, aroused not a little excitement; and while there were some who "deprecated a resort to extreme measures"—a euphemistic phrase frequently resorted to by those who would neither resent an insult nor take umbrage at an intended offense—the general sentiment of the country was decidedly manifested in favor of an assertion of our rights in the premises. Accordingly, President Pierce sent a message to Congress stating that a peaceful adjustment of the difficulty was impossible, and asking that he be authorized to send such a naval force to Paraguay as would compel her arbitrary ruler to give the full satisfaction demanded.

To this request Congress promptly and almost unanimously gave assent, and one of the strongest naval expeditions ever fitted out by the United States up to that time was ordered to assemble at the mouth of La Plata River. The fleet was a most imposing one and comprised nineteen vessels, seven of which were steamers specially chartered for the purpose, as our largest war vessels were of too deep draught to ascend La Plata and Paraná. The entire squadron carried 200 guns and 2500 men, and was commanded by Flag Officer, afterward Rear Admiral, Shubrick,* one of the oldest officers of our navy, and one of the most gallant men that ever trod a quarter deck. Flag Officer Shubrick was accompanied by United States Commissioner Bowlin, to whom was intrusted negotiations for the settlement of the difficulty. Three years and eleven months had now passed since the "Water Witch" was fired upon, and President Buchanan had succeeded Franklin Pierce. The winter of 1859 was just closing in at the North; the streams were closed by ice, and the lakes were ice-bound, but the palm trees at the South were displaying their fresh green leaves, like so many fringed banners, in the warm tropical air when the United States squadron assembled at Montevideo [Montevidéo]. As has been said, the force was an imposing one. There were two United States frigates, the "Sabine" and the "St. Lawrence;" two sloops-of-war, the "Falmouth" and the "Preble;" three brigs, the "Bainbridge," the "Dolphin," and the "Perry;" six steamers especially armed for the occasion, the "Memphis," the "Caledonia," the "Atlanta," the "Southern Star," the "Westernport," the "M. W. Chapin," and the "Metacomet;" two armed storeships, the "Supply" and the "Release;" the revenue steamer, "Harriet Lane;" and, lastly, the little "Water Witch" herself, no longer defenseless, but all in fighting trim for hostilities.

On the 25th of January, 1859, within just one week of four years from the firing upon the "Water Witch," the squadron got under way and came to anchor off Ascencion, the capital of Paraguay. Meanwhile President Urquiza, of the Argentine Republic, who had offered his services to mediate the difficulty, had arrived at Ascencion in advance of the squadron. The negotiations were reopened, and Commissioner Bowlin made his demand for instant reparation. All this time Flag Officer Shubrick was not idle. With such of our vessels as were capable of ascending the river, taking them through the difficulties created by the currents, shoals, and sand bars of the river, he brought

---

* William Branford Shubrick was one of the most illustrious men whose name has appeared on the roll of United States naval officers. He was born in 1790; appointed midshipman United States Navy June 20, 1806; joined the sloop-of-war "Wasp" 1812; a year later was transferred to the frigate "Constellation;" aided in the capture of the British vessels "Cyane" and "Levant;" and in 1815 was awarded a sword by his native State. In 1820 was made commander; in 1820 commanded the "Lexington;" in 1846 commanded the Pacific squadron, and filled various prominent positions extending over a period of sixty-one years, till May 12, 1876, when he died.

them to a chosen position, where they made ready in case of necessity to open fire. The force within striking distance of Paraguay consisted of 1740 men, besides the officers, and 78 guns, including 23 nine-inch shell guns and one shell gun of eleven inches.

Ships and guns proved to be very strong arguments with Lopez. It did not take the Dictator-President long to see that the United States meant business, and that the time for trifling had passed and the time for serious work had indeed begun. President Lopez's cerebral processes worked with remarkable and encouraging celerity. By February 5th, within less than two weeks of the starting of the squadron from Montevideo, Commissioner Bowlin's demands were all acceded to. Ample apologies were made for firing on the " Water

ONE OF THE "MIANTONOMAH'S" FOUR TEN-INCH BREECH-LOADING RIFLES.

Witch" and pecuniary compensation was given to the family of the sailor who had been killed. In addition to this, a new commercial treaty was made between the two countries, and cordial relations were fully restored between the two governments. When the squadron returned the Secretary of the Navy expressed the satisfaction of the government and the country in the following terms :—

"To the zeal, energy, discretion, and courteous and gallant bearing of Flag-officer Shubrick and the officers under his command, in conducting an expedition far into the interior of a remote country, encountering not only great physical difficulties, but the fears, apprehensions and prejudices of numerous States; and to the good conduct of the brave men under his command, is the country largely indebted, not only for the success of the enterprise, but for the friendly feeling towards the United States which now prevails in all that part of South America."

To such a happy and peaceful conclusion were our difficulties with Paraguay finally brought.

A period of thirty years elapsed before any serious difficulty occurred with any foreign powers. It was in 1891 that a serious difficulty threatened to disrupt our relations with Chili and possibly involve the United States in war with that power. Happily the matter reached a peaceful settlement. In January, 1891, civil war broke out in Chili, the cause of which was a contest between the legislative branch of the government and the executive, for the control of affairs. The President of Chili, General Balmaceda, began to assert authority which the legislature, or "the Congressionalists," as the opposing party was called, resisted as unconstitutional and oppressive, and they accordingly proceeded to interfere with Balmaceda's Cabinet in its efforts to carry out the despotic will of the executive.

Finally matters came to a point where appeal to arms was necessary. On the 9th of January the Congressional party took possession of the greater part of the Chilian fleet, the navy being in hearty sympathy with the Congressionalists, and the guns of the war-ships were turned against Balmaceda, Valparaiso, the capital, and other ports being blockaded by the ships. For a time Balmaceda maintained control of the capital and the southern part of the country. The key to the position was Valparaiso, which was strongly fortified, Balmaceda's army being massed there and placed at available points.

At last the Congressionalists determined to attack Balmaceda at his capital, and on August 21st landed every available fighting man at their disposal at Concon, about ten miles north of Valparaiso. They were attacked by the Dictator on the 22d, there being twenty thousand men on each side. The Dictator had the worst of it. Then he rallied his shattered forces, and made his last stand at Placillo, close to Valparaiso, on the 28th. The battle was hot, the carnage fearful, neither side asked or received quarter. The magazine rifles, with which the revolutionists were armed, did wonders. The odds were against Balmaceda; both his generals quarreled in face of the enemy; the army marched against the foe divided and demoralized. In the last battle both Balmaceda's generals were killed. The valor and the superior tactics of General Canto, leader of the Congressional army won the day. Balmaceda fled and eventually committed suicide, and the Congressionalists entered the capital in triumph.

Several incidents meantime had conspired, during the progress of this war, to rouse the animosity of the stronger party in Chili against the United States. Before the Congressionalists' triumph the steamship Itata, loaded with American arms and ammunition for Chili, sailed from San Francisco, and as this was a violation of the neutrality laws, a United States war vessel pursued her to the harbor of Iquique, where she surrendered. Then other troubles arose. Our minister at Valparaiso, Mr. Egan, was charged by the Congressionalists, now

In power, with disregarding international law in allowing the American Legation to become an asylum for the adherents of Balmaceda. Subsequently these refugees were permitted to go aboard American vessels and sail away. Then Admiral Brown, of the United States squadron, was, in Chili's opinion, guilty of having acted as a spy upon the movements of the Congressionalists' fleet at Quinteros, and of bringing intelligence of its movements to Balmaceda at Valparaiso. This, however, the Admiral stoutly denied.

AN ATTACK UPON AMERICAN SEAMEN.

The strong popular feeling of dislike which was engendered by this news culminated on the 16th of October, in an attack upon American seamen by a mob in the streets of the Chilian capital. Captain Schley, commander of the United States cruiser, Baltimore, had given shore-leave to a hundred and

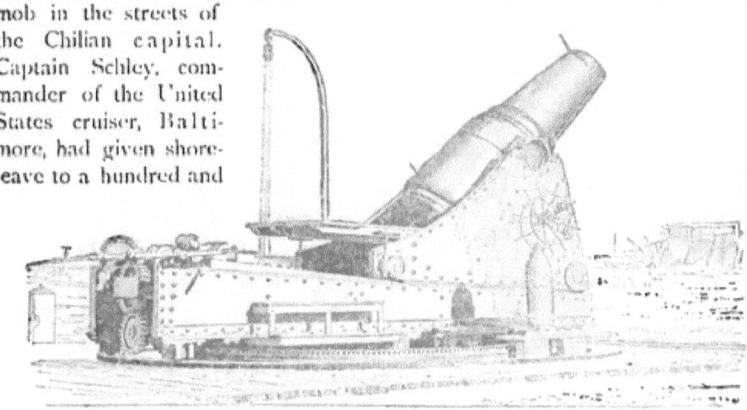

UNITED STATES 12-INCH BREECH-LOADING MORTAR, OR HOWITZER.

seventeen petty officers and seamen, some of whom, when they had been on shore for several hours, were set upon by Chilians. They took refuge in a street car, from which, however, they were soon driven and mercilessly beaten, and a subordinate officer named Riggen fell, apparently lifeless. The American sailors, according to Captain Schley's testimony, were sober and conducting themselves with propriety when the attack was made. They were not armed, even their knives having been taken from them before they left the vessel.

The assault upon those in the street car seemed to be only a signal for a general uprising; and a mob which is variously estimated at from one thousand to two thousand people attacked our sailors with such fury that in a little while these men, whom no investigation could find guilty of any breach of the peace, were fleeing for their lives before an overwhelming crowd, among which were a number of the police of Valparaiso. In this affray eighteen sailors were stabbed, several dying from their wounds.

Of course, the United States Government at once communicated with the Chilian authorities on the subject, expressing an intention to investigate the occurrence fully. The first reply made to the American Government by Signor Matta, the Chilian Minister of Foreign Affairs, was to the effect that Chili would not allow anything to interfere with her own official investigation.

An examination of all the facts was made on our part. It was careful and thorough, and showed that our flag had been insulted in the persons of American seamen. Yet, while the Chilian Court of Inquiry could present no extenuating facts, that country refused at first to offer apology or reparation for the affront.

In the course of the correspondence Minister Matta sent a note of instruction to Mr. Montt, Chilian representative at Washington, in which he used most offensive terms in relation to the United States, and directed that the letter be given to the press for publication.

After waiting for a long time for the result of the investigation at Valparaiso, and finding that, although no excuse or palliation had been found for the outrage, yet the Chilian authorities seemed reluctant to offer apology, the President of the United States, in a message to Congress, made an extended statement of the various incidents of the case and its legal aspect, and stated that on the 21st of January he had caused a peremptory communication to be presented to the Chilian Government, by the American Minister at Santiago, in which severance of diplomatic relations was threatened if our demands for satisfaction, which included the withdrawal of Mr. Matta's insulting note, were not complied with. At the time that this message was delivered no reply had been sent to this note.

Mr. Harrison's statement of the legal aspect of the case, upon which the final settlement of the difficulty was based was, that the presence of a war ship of any nation in a port belonging to a friendly power is by virtue of a general invitation which nations are held to extend to each other; that Commander Schley was invited, with his officers and crew, to enjoy the hospitality of Valparaiso; that while no claim that an attack which an individual sailor may be subjected to raises an international question, yet where the resident population assault sailors of another country's war vessels, as at Valparaiso, animated by an animosity against the government to which they belong, that government must show the same enquiry and jealousy as though the representatives or flag of the nation had been attacked; because the sailors are there by the order of their government.

Finally an ultimatum was sent from the State Department at Washington, on the 25th, to Minister Egan, and was by him transmitted to the proper Chilian authorities. It demanded the retraction of Mr. Matta's note and suit ble apology and reparation for the insult and injury sustained by the United States. On the 28th of January, 1892, a dispatch from Chili was received, in which the demands of our Government were fully acceded to, the offensive letter was withdrawn and regret was expressed for the trouble. In his relation to this particular case Minister Egan's conduct received the entire approval of his Government.

While the United States looked for a peaceful solution of this annoying international episode, the proper preparations were made for a less desirable

MONROE DOCTRINE.

When the great Napoleon was overthrown, France, Russia, Prussia and Austria formed an alliance for preserving the "balance of power" and for suppressing revolutions within one another's dominions. This was at the time the Spanish South American colonies were in revolt, and there was a strong suspicion that the alliance intended to unite in their reduction. George Canning, the English Secretary of State, proposed to our country that we should unite with England in preventing such an outrage against civilization. It was a momentous question, and President Monroe consulted with Jefferson, Madison, Calhoun, and John Quincy Adams, the Secretary of State, before making answer. The decision being reached, President Monroe embodied in his annual message to Congress in December, 1823, a clause which formulated what has ever since been known as the "Monroe Doctrine." It was written by John Quincy Adams, and, referring to the intervention of the allied Powers, said that we "should consider any attempt on their part to extend their system to any portion of this hemisphere as dangerous to our peace and safety;" and further, "that the American continents, by the free and independent condition which they have assumed and maintain, are henceforth not to be considered as subjects for future colonization by any European Powers."

BEHRING SEA TROUBLE.

Since the purchase of Alaska it has been difficult to come to an agreement with England upon the water territory over which the United States has jurisdiction, to prevent the hunters from slaughtering the animals out of season (from May 1st to July 1st), and to exclude Canadian fishermen from American waters. We maintained that the islands we acquired with Alaska pushed our borders far out into the ocean, and gave us authority to claim Behring Sea as inland, but this was ruled against us by a "Fisheries Commission" appointed by the governments of the United States and Great Britain to decide that question, and to settle claims against fishermen sealing in the waters of the neighboring nation

ALASKA DISPUTE.

It is the Southerly branch of Alaska which presents serious difficulties between the United States and Great Britain. When the United States bought Alaska from Russia it was stipulated that the Southerly boundry be thirty miles from the coast until the line reaches the 141st meridian. So far as the line can be definitely fixed, it begins at the southernmost point of Prince of Wales Island. The treaty signed on January 30th, 1897, applies only to that of the 141st meridian in the northerly part of Alaska. Until a treaty determining where the coast is from which the thirty mile strip is measured, it is felt that the most difficult questions are still unsettled. The main point involved is whether the boundry is to be measured from the mainland or from the outer fringe of islands along the coast. It is a repetition of the old contest over a closed sea, or mare clausum, which brought on the dispute referred to the Fisheries Commission.

THE SPANISH-AMERICAN WAR.

On the 25th day of April, 1898, war was declared by the United States
Government against the Kingdom of Spain. The causes which led to the declaration of hostilities were, first, the inhuman treatment of the Cubans by the
Spanish Government; and, second, the destruction of the United States Battle-
ship "Maine" in the harbor of Havana.

In 1895 a revolution began in Cuba, led by the brave Generals Maximo
Gomez and Antonio Maceo. Within three years Spain had sent an army of
nearly quarter of a million soldiers to the island but had failed to quell the rebellion. The country was laid waste by fire and sword, and the Spanish, under
the guise of protection, gathered the non-combatant Cubans into towns. The
news soon flashed over the wires that these *reconcentrados*, as those in the
garrisoned towns were called, were dying by thousands from starvation.

United States Consul-General Fitz-Hugh Lee reported also that American
citizens of the island had suffered greatly. Accordingly on January 25th the
Battle-ship "Maine" was dispatched to Havana, with the consent of the Spanish
Government, on a friendly visit, it being arranged that the Spanish Battle-ship
"Vizcaya" should visit New York in return.

On the evening of February 15th, 1898, between nine and ten o'clock, the
"Maine," while lying at anchor in Havana harbor, was blown to pieces and 266 of
her crew were killed. The belief prevailed throughout the country that Spanish
officials knew of or participated in the plans for destroying our battle-ship,
and the official inquiry seemed to justify this belief.

In the meantime Senators Proctor, Thurston and others visited Cuba, and,
returning, delivered speeches in the United States Senate which revealed a most
shocking condition of affairs. They deemed it impossible for Spain to subdue the
island except by practically exterminating its population, by starving the women
and children which seemed to be their policy. These reports were confirmed by
Consul-General Lee, and he also shared the belief that the "Maine" had been
destroyed through Spanish treachery. The whole nation was intensely aroused.

On March 8th, $50,000,000 had been voted to strengthen our coast defenses.
Heated debates in Congress followed. On April 19th a joint resolution was
passed by both Houses and signed by the President, declaring "that the people
of the island of Cuba are, and of a right ought to be, free and independent."
The Government of Spain was ordered to release its authority and withdraw its
land and naval forces from the island. The Spanish Minister, Polo, requested
and was given his passport and departed for Canada, and United States Minister
Woodford, at Madrid, was promptly dismissed by that Government before he
could present the President's ultimatum to Spain.

Friday night, April 22d, the United States fleet blockaded Havana and a call
was promptly made by the United States for 125,000 volunteers.

22

REVIEW OF UNION ARMIES AT WASHINGTON, AT THE CLOSE OF THE WAR.

EIGHT-INCH GUN AND CARRIAGE OF THE "BALTIMORE."
(Built at the Washington Navy Yard, of American Steel.)

THE STORY OF OUR WAR WITH SPAIN FOR CUBA'S FREEDOM.

PERHAPS no conflict within the past thirty years has so aroused and interested the world as the war begun in the spring of 1898 between the Kingdom of Spain and the United States of America. This conflict in some respects might be called a holy war, for it was inaugurated with the distinct object of relieving suffering humanity from oppression, tyranny, and abuses worse than slavery in the island of Cuba. It was undertaken by the United States, not for revenge on account of the lost battleship *Maine;* nor was it for conquest or hope of reward. We were the nearest neighbors to this suffering and oppressed land, and as such this country felt it incumbent upon it to take at least the initiatory steps towards the relief of those who suffered such tyrannical injustice at our doors. The causes leading to declaration of hostilities have been previously recited in the chapter entitled "Difficulties with Foreign Powers," to which the reader is respectfully referred. Diplomatic relations were broken off between the two countries April 21st. Thus the barriers were all removed and the two nations were ready for the conflict. On April 22d the United States fleet was ordered to blockade Havana. On the 24th Spain declared war, and the United States Congress followed with a similar declaration on the 25th. The call for 75,000 volunteer troops was increased to 125,000 and subsequently to 200,000. The massing of men and stores was rapidly begun throughout the country. Within a month expeditions were organized for various points of attack, war vessels were bought, and ocean passenger steamers were converted into auxiliary cruisers and transports. By the first of July about 40,000 soldiers had been sent to Cuba and the Philippine Islands. The rapidity with which preparations were made and the victories gained and the progress shown by the

Americans at once astonished and challenged the admiration of foreign nations, who had regarded America as a country unprepared for war by land or sea.

On April 27th, following the declaration of war on the 25th, Admiral Sampson, having previously blockaded the harbor of Havana, was reconnoitering with three vessels in the vicinity of Matanzas, Cuba, when he discovered the Spanish forces building earthworks, and ventured so close in his efforts to investigate the same that a challenge shot was fired from the fortification, Rubal Cava. Admiral Sampson quickly formed the *New York*, *Cincinnati*, and *Puritan* into a triangle and opened fire with their eight-inch guns. The action was very spirited on both sides for the space of eighteen minutes, at the expiration of which time the Spanish batteries were silenced and the earthworks destroyed, without casualty on the American side, though two shells burst dangerously near the *New York*. The last shot fired by the Americans was from one of the *Puritan's* thirteen-inch guns, which landed with deadly accuracy in the very centre of Rubal Cava and, exploding, completely destroyed the earthworks. This was the first action of the war, though it could hardly be dignified by the name of a battle.

GEORGE DEWEY

THE BATTLE OF MANILA.

It was expected that the next engagement would be the bombardment of Morro Castle, at Havana. But it is the unexpected that often happens in war. In the Philippine Islands, on the other side of the world, the first real battle—one of the most remarkable in history—was to occur.

On April 25th the following dispatch of eight potent words was cabled to Commodore Dewey on the coast of China: "Capture or destroy the Spanish squadron at Manila." "Never," says James Gordon Bennett, "were instructions more effectively carried out. Within seven hours after arriving on the scene of action nothing remained to be done." It was on the 27th that Dewey sailed from Mirs Bay, China, and on the night of the 30th he lay before the entrance of the harbor of Manila, seven hundred miles distant. Under the cover of darkness, with all lights extinguished on his ships, he daringly steamed into this

THE MOUTH OF THE PASIG RIVER

The city of old Manila is surrounded by water. On the west is the sea, to the north is the Pasig River, while moats, connected with the river by sluices, flank the other two sides. All the principal warehouses are on the Pasig, and ships deliver and receive their cargoes direct, without the necessity of cartage.

PRESIDENT McKINLEY'S LOVE FOR CHILDREN

Giving his buttonhole carnation to a little girl at one of his receptions

dangerous harbor, which he believed to be strewn with mines, and at daybreak engaged the Spanish fleet. Commodore Dewey knew it meant everything for him and his fleet to win or lose this battle. He was in the enemy's country, 7000 miles from home. The issue of this battle must mean victory, Spanish dungeons, or the bottom of the ocean. *"Keep cool and obey orders"* was the signal he gave to his fleet, and then came the order to fire. The Americans had seven ships, the *Olympia, Baltimore, Raleigh, Petrel, Concord, Boston,* and the dispatch-boat *McCullough.* The Spaniards had eleven, the *Reina Christina, Castilla, Don Antonio de Ulloa, Isla de Luzon, Isla de Cuba, General Lezo, Marquis de Duero, Cano, Velasco, Isla de Mindanao,* and a transport.

From the beginning Commodore Dewey fought on the offensive, and, after the manner of Nelson and Farragut, concentrated his fire upon the strongest ships one after another with terrible execution. The Spanish ships were inferior to his, but there were more of them, and they were under the protection of the land batteries. The fire of the Americans was especially noted for its terrific rapidity and the accuracy of its aim. The battle lasted for about five hours, and resulted in the destruction of all the Spanish ships and the silencing of the land batteries. The Spanish loss in killed and wounded was estimated to be fully one thousand men, while on the American side not a ship was even seriously damaged and not a single man was killed outright, and only six were wounded. More than a month after the battle, Captain Charles B. Gridley, Commander of the *Olympia,* died, though his death was the result of an accident received in the discharge of his duty during the battle, and not from a wound. On May 2d Commodore Dewey cut the cable connecting Manila with Hong Kong, and destroyed the fortifications at the entrance of Manila Bay, and took possession of the naval station at Cavite. This was to prevent communication between the Philippine Islands and the Government at Madrid, and necessitated the sending of Commodore Dewey's official account of the battle by the dispatch-boat *McCullough* to Hong Kong, whence it was cabled to the United States. After its receipt, May 9th, both Houses adopted resolutions of congratulation to Commodore Dewey and his officers and men for their gallantry at Manila, voted an appropriation for medals for the crew and a fine sword for the gallant Commander, and also passed a bill authorizing the President to appoint another Rear-Admiral, which honor was promptly conferred upon Commodore Dewey, accompanied by the thanks of the President and of the nation for the admirable and heroic services rendered his country.

The Battle of Manila must ever remain a monument to the daring and courage of Admiral Dewey. However unevenly matched the two fleets may have been, the world agrees with the eminent foreign naval critic who declared: " This complete victory was the product of forethought, cool, well-balanced judgment, discipline, and bravery. It was a magnificent achievement, and Dewey will go down in history ranking with John Paul Jones and Lord Nelson as a naval hero."

Admiral Dewey might have taken possession of the city of Manila immediately. He cabled the United States that he could do so, but the fact remained that he had not sufficient men to care for his ships and at the same time effect a successful landing in the town of Manila. Therefore he chose to remain on his ships, and though the city was at his mercy, he refrained from a bombardment because he believed it would lead to a massacre of the Spaniards on the part of the insurgents surrounding the city, which it would be beyond his power to stop. This humane disposition toward the conquered foe adds to the lustre of the hero's crown, and at the same time places the seal of greatness upon the brow of the victor. He not only refrained from bombarding the city, but received and cared for the wounded Spaniards upon his own vessels. Thus, while he did all that was required of him without depriving his country of the life of a single citizen, he manifested a spirit of humanity and generosity toward the vanquished foe fully in keeping with the sympathetic spirit which involved this nation in the war for humanity's sake.

The Battle of Manila further demonstrated that a fleet with heavier guns is virtually invulnerable in a campaign with a squadron bearing lighter metal, however gallantly the crew of the latter may fight.

After the Battle of Manila it was recognized that the Government had serious work on its hands. On May 4th President McKinley nominated ten new Major-Generals, including Thomas H. Wilson, Fitzhugh Lee, Wm. J. Sewell, and Joseph Wheeler, from private life, and promoted Brigadier-Generals Breckenridge, Otis, Coppinger, Shafter, Graham, Wade, and Merriam, from the regular army. The organization and mobilization of troops was promptly begun and rapidly pushed. Meantime our naval vessels were actively cruising around the Island of Cuba, expecting the appearance of the Spanish fleet.

THE FIRST AMERICAN LOSS OF LIFE.

On May 11th the gunboat *Wilmington*, revenue-cutter *Hudson*, and the torpedo-boat *Winslow* entered Cardenas Bay, Cuba, to attack the defenses and three small Spanish gunboats that had taken refuge in the harbor. The *Winslow* being of light draft took the lead, and when within eight hundred yards of the fort was fired upon with disastrous effect, being struck eighteen times and rendered helpless. For more than an hour the frail little craft was at the mercy of the enemy's batteries. The revenue-cutter *Hudson* quickly answered her signal of distress by coming to the rescue, and as she was in the act of drawing the disabled boat away a shell from the enemy burst on the *Winslow's* deck, killing three of her crew outright and wounding many more. Ensign Worth Bagley, of the *Winslow*, who had recently entered active service, was one of the killed.

He was the first officer who lost his life in the war. The same shell badly wounded Lieutenant Bernadou, Commander of the boat. The *Hudson*, amidst a rain of fire from the Spanish gunboats and fortifications, succeeded in towing the *Winslow* to Key West, where the bodies of the dead were prepared for burial and the vessel was placed in repair. On May 12th the First Infantry landed near Port Cabanas, Cuba, with supplies for the insurgents, which they succeeded in delivering after a skirmish with the Spanish troops. This was the first land engagement of the war.

THE BOMBARDMENT OF SAN JUAN, PORTO RICO.

On the same date Admiral Sampson's squadron arrived at San Juan, Porto Rico, whither it had gone in the expectation of meeting with Admiral Cervera's fleet, which had sailed westward from the Cape Verde Islands on April 29th, after Portugal's declaration of neutrality. The Spanish fleet, however, did not materialize, and Admiral Sampson, while on the ground, concluded it would be well to draw the fire of the forts that he might at least judge of their strength and efficiency, if indeed he should not render them incapable of assisting the Spanish fleet in the event of its resorting to this port at a later period. Accordingly, Sampson bombarded the batteries defending San Juan, inflicting much damage and sustaining a loss of two men killed and six wounded. The loss of the enemy is not known. The American warships sustained only trivial injuries, but after the engagement it could be plainly seen that one end of Morro Castle was in ruins. The Cabras Island fort was silenced and the San Carlos battery was damaged. No shots were aimed at the city by the American fleet.

Deeming it unnecessary to wait for the Spanish warships in the vicinity of San Juan, Sampson withdrew his squadron and sailed westward in the hope of finding Cervera's fleet, which was dodging about the Caribbean Sea. It was first heard of at the French island, Martinique, whence after a short stay it sailed westward. Two days later it halted at the Dutch island, Curaçoa, for coal and supplies. After leaving this point it was again lost sight of. Then began the chase of Commodore Schley and Admiral Sampson to catch the fugitive. Schley, with his flying squadron, sailed from Key West around the western end of Cuba, and Sampson kept guard over the Windward and other passages to the east of the island. It was expected that one or the other of these fleets would encounter the Spaniard on the open sea, but in this they were mistaken. Cervera was not making his way to the Mexican shore on the west, as some said, nor was he seeking to slip through one of the passages into the Atlantic and sail home to Spain, nor attack Commodore Watson's blockading vessels before Havana, according to other expert opinions expressed and widely published. For many days the hunt of the warships went on like a fox-chase. On May 23d Commodore Schley blockaded Cienfuegos, supposing that Cervera was inside the harbor, but on the 24th he discovered his mistake and sailed to Santiago, where he lay before the entrance to the harbor for three days, not knowing whether or not the Spaniard was inside. On May 28th it was positively discovered that he had Cervera bottled up in the narrow harbor of Santiago. He had been there since the 19th, and had landed 800 men, 20,000 Mauser rifles, a great supply of ammunition, and four great guns for the defense of the city.

Operations Against Santiago.

On May 31st Commodore Schley opened fire on the fortifications at the mouth of the harbor, which lasted for about half an hour. This was for the purpose of discovering the location and strength of the batteries, some of which were concealed, and in this he was completely successful. Two of the batteries were silenced, and the flagship of the Spaniards, which took part in the engagement, was damaged. The Americans received no injury to vessels and no loss of men. On June 1st Admiral Sampson arrived before Santiago, and relieved Commodore Schley of the chief command of the forces, then consisting of sixteen war-ships.

WILLIAM R. SHAFTER.

Admiral Sampson, naturally a cautious commander, suffered great apprehension lest Cervera might slip out of the harbor and escape during the darkness of the night or the pro-gress of a storm, which would compel the blockading fleet to stand far off shore. There was a point in the channel wide enough for only one warship to pass at a time, and if this could be rendered impassable Cervera's doom would be sealed. How to reach and close this passage was the difficult problem to be solved. On either shore of the narrow channel stood frowning forts with cannon, and there were other fortifications to be passed before it could be reached. Young Lieutenant Hobson, a naval engineer, had attached himself to Admiral Sampson's flagship, *New York*, just before it sailed from Key West, and it was this young man of less than thirty years who solved the problem for Admiral Sampson by a plan all his own, which he executed with a heroic daring that finds

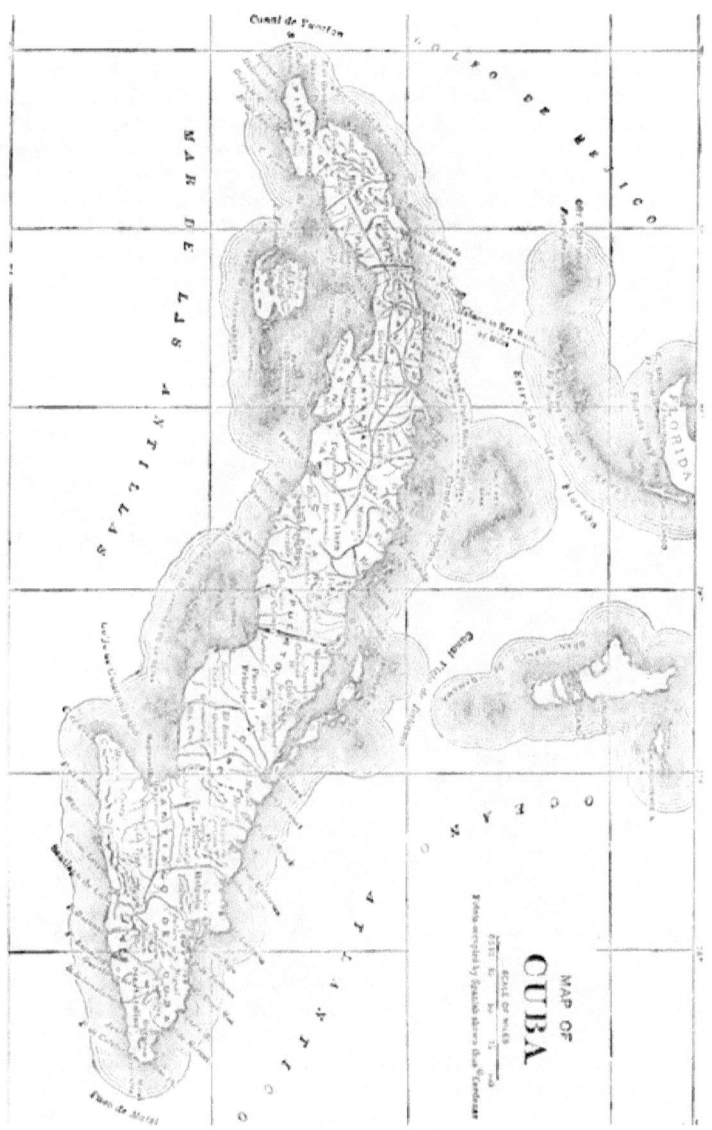

MAP OF
CUBA

SCALE OF MILES

Miles occupied by Spanish above 0 to Cárdenas

perhaps no parallel in all naval history. At three o'clock A. M., June 3d, in company with seven volunteers from the *New York* and other ships, he took the United States collier *Merrimac*, a large vessel with 600 tons of coal on board, and started with the purpose of sinking it in the channel. The chances were ten to one that the batteries from the forts would sink the vessel before it could reach the narrow neck, and the chances were hardly one in one hundred that any of the men on board the collier would come out of this daring attempt alive. The ship had hardly started when the forts opened fire, and amid the thunder of artillery and a rain of steel and bursting shells the boat with its eight brave heroes held on its way, as steadily as if they knew not their danger. The channel was reached, and the boat turned straight across the channel. The sea-doors were opened and torpedoes exploded by the intrepid crew, sinking the vessel almost instantly near the position desired. As the ship went down the men, with side-arms buckled on, took to a small boat, and, escape being impossible, they surrendered to the enemy. It seems scarcely less than a miracle that any of the eight men escaped, yet the fact remained that not one of them was seriously injured. The Spaniards were so impressed with this act of bravery and heroism that they treated the prisoners with the utmost courtesy, confined them in Morro Castle, and Admiral Cervera promptly sent a special officer, under a flag of truce, to inform Admiral Sampson of their safety. The prisoners were kept confined in Morro Castle for some days, when they were removed to a place of greater safety, where they were held until exchanged on July 7th.

THE SECOND BOMBARDMENT OF SANTIAGO AND THE COMING OF THE ARMY.

On the 6th of June the American fleet under Admiral Sampson bombarded the forts of Santiago for about three hours. The gunners were all instructed, however, to spare Morro Castle lest they should inflict injury upon Hobson and his heroic companions, who were then confined within its walls. Nearly all of the fortifications at the entrance of the harbor were silenced. An examination after the fleet had withdrawn revealed the fact that no lives were lost on the American side, and none of the vessels were seriously injured. The Spanish ship *Reina Mercedes* was sunk in the harbor, she being the only ship from the enemy's fleet which ventured within the range of the Americans' guns.

The danger of entering the narrow harbor in the face of Cervera's fleet rendered it necessary to take the city by land, and the Government began preparations to send General Shafter with a large force from Tampa to aid the fleet in reducing the city. Some 15,000 men, including the now famous Rough Riders of New York, were hurried upon transports, and under the greatest convoy of gunboats, cruisers, and battleships which ever escorted an army started for the western end of the island of Cuba.

But the honor of making the first landing on Cuban soil belongs to the marines. It was on June the 10th, a few days before the army of General Shafter sailed from Tampa, that a landing was effected by Colonel Huntington's six hundred marines at Caimanera, Guantanomo Bay, some distance east of Santiago. The object of this landing was twofold: first, to secure a place where our warships could safely take on coal from colliers, and, second, to unite if possible with the insurgents in harassing the Spaniards until General Shafter's army could arrive. Furthermore, Guantanomo Bay furnished the American ships a safe harbor in case of storm.

In the whole history of the war few more thrilling passages are to be found than the record of this brave band's achievements. The place of landing was a low, round, bush-covered hill on the eastern side of the bay. On the crest of the hill was a small clearing occupied by an advance post of the Spanish army. When the marines landed and began to climb the hill, the enemy with little resistance retreated to the woods, and the marines were soon occupying the cleared space abandoned by them. They had scarcely begun to compliment themselves on their easy victory when they discovered that the retreat had only been a snare to lure them into the open space, while unfortunately all around the clearing the woods grew thick, and their unprotected position was also overlooked by a range of higher hills covered with a dense undergrowth. Thus the Spanish were able under cover of the bushes to creep close up to our forces, and

MAJOR-GENERAL FITZHUGH LEE.

they soon began to fire upon them from the higher ground of the wooded range. The marines replied vigorously to the fire of their hidden foe, and thus continued their hit-and-miss engagement for a period of four days and nights, with only occasional intermissions. Perhaps the poor marksmanship of the Spaniards is to be thanked for the fact that they were not utterly annihilated. On the fourth day the Spanish gave up the contest and abandoned the field.

Major Henry C. Cochrane, second in command, states that he slept only an hour and a half in the four days, and that many of his men became so exhausted that they fell asleep standing on their feet with their rifles in their hands. It is remarkable that during the four days the Americans lost only six killed and about twenty wounded. The Spaniards suffered a loss several times as great, fifteen of them having been found by the Americans dead on the field. It is not known how many they carried away or how many were wounded.

THE LANDING OF SHAFTER'S ARMY.

On June 13th troops began to leave Tampa and Key West for operations against Santiago, and on June 20th the transports bearing them arrived off that city. Two days later General Shafter landed his army of 16,000 soldiers at Biaquiri, a short distance east of the entrance to the harbor, with the loss of only two men, and they by accident. Before the coming of the troops the Spanish had evacuated the village of Biaquiri, which is a little inland from the anchorage bearing the same name, and set fire to the town, blowing up two magazines and destroying the railroad round-house containing several locomotives. As the transports neared the landing-place Sampson's ships opened fire upon Juragua, engaging all the forts for about six miles to the west. This was done to distract the attention of the Spanish from the landing soldiers, and was entirely successful. After the forts were silenced the *New Orleans* and several gunboats shelled the woods in advance of the landing troops. The soldiers went ashore in full fighting trim, each man carrying thirty-six rations, two hundred rounds of ammunition for his rifle, and a shelter tent.

While the troops were landing at Biaquiri, the battleship *Texas*, hitherto considered as an unfortunate ship by the attachés of the navy, completely changed her reputation and distinguished herself by assailing and silencing, unaided, the Spanish battery La Socapa at Santiago, which had hitherto withstood the attacks against it, though all the ships of Commodore Schley's command had twice fiercely bombarded it without result. Captain Philip and his men were complimented in warm terms of praise by Admiral Sampson. The *Texas* was struck but once, and that by the last shot from the Spanish fort, killing one man and wounding eight others, seriously damaging the ship.

THE VICTORY OF THE ROUGH RIDERS.

On June 24th the force under General Shafter reached Jaragua, and the battle by land was now really to begin. It was about ten miles out from Santiago at a point known as Las Guasimas. The country was covered with high grass and chaparral, and in this and on the wooded hills a strong force of Spaniards was hidden. Lieutenant-Colonel Roosevelt's Rough Riders, technically known as the First Volunteer Cavalry, under command of Colonel Wood, were in the fight, and it is to their bravery and dash that the glory of the day chiefly belongs. Troops under command of General Young had been sent out in advance, with the Rough Riders on his flank. There were about 1200 of the

THE ELECTRIC TOWER, PAN-AMERICAN EXPOSITION

This magnificent architectural centrepiece of the Exposition is 400 feet in height. The main body of the tower is nearly 300 feet high and 50 feet square. The statue of the Goddess of Light which crowns the tower is 18 feet tall. The tower stands in the centre of the great basin, all about its base are many fountains playing, and from the southern face a cascade, 50 feet wide and 75 feet high, pours like a bridal veil. There are nearly 150 searchlights used in this tower, and it is illuminated by 30,000 incandescent lamps. It looks like a pillar of fire at night.

GREATER NEW YORK

On January 1, 1898, Greater New York was created by the union of New York, Brooklyn, Long Island City, and Staten Island, into one municipality. The city now covers nearly 326 square miles, contains over three and one-half million inhabitants, and, next to London, is the largest city in the world.

cavalry in all, including the Rough Riders and the First and Tenth Regulars. They encountered a body of two thousand Spaniards in a thicket, whom they fought dismounted. The volunteers were especially eager for the fight, and, perhaps due somewhat to their own imprudence, were led into an ambuscade, as perfect as was ever planned by an Indian. The main body of the Spaniards was posted on a hill approached by two heavily wooded slopes and fortified by two blockhouses flanked by intrenchments of stones and fallen trees. At the bottom of these hills run two roads, along one of which the Rough Riders marched, and along the other eight troops of the Eighth and Tenth Cavalry under General Young. These roads are little more than gullies, very narrow, and at places almost impassable. Nearly half a mile separated Roosevelt's men from the Regulars, and it was in these trails that the battle began.

For an hour they held their position in the midst of an unseen force, which poured a perfect hail of bullets upon them from in front and on both sides. At length, seeing that their only way of escape was by dashing boldly at the hidden foe, Colonel Wood took command on the right of his column of Rough Riders, placing Lieutenant-Colonel Roosevelt at the left, and thus, with a rousing yell, they led their soldiers in a rushing charge before which the Spaniards fled from the hills and the victorious assailants took the blockhouses. The Americans had sixteen killed and fifty-two wounded,

ADMIRAL WILLIAM T. SAMPSON.

forty-two of the casualties occurring to the Rough Riders and twenty-six among the Regulars. It is estimated that the Spanish killed were nearly or quite one hundred. Thirty-seven were found by the Americans dead on the ground. They had carried off their wounded, and doubtless thought they had taken most of the killed away also.

PREPARING FOR THE ASSAULT UPON SANTIAGO.

The victory of the Rough Riders and the Regulars at La Quasina, though so dearly bought, stimulated the soldiers of the whole army with the spirit of war and the desire for an opportunity to join in the conquest. They had not long to wait. The advance upon Santiago was vigorously prosecuted on the land side, while the ships stood guard over the entrapped Spanish Admiral Cervera in the harbor, and, anon, shelled every fort that manifested signs of activity. On June 25th, Sevilla, within sight of Santiago, was taken by General Chaffee, and an advance upon the city was planned to be made in three columns by way of Altares, Firmeza, and Juragua. General Garcia with 5000 Cuban insurgents had placed himself some time before at the command of the American leader. On the 28th of June another large expedition of troops was landed, so that the entire force under General Shafter, including the Cuban allies, numbered over 22,000 fighting men.

The enemy fell back at all points until the right of the American column was within three miles of Santiago, and by the end of June the two armies had well-defined positions. The Spanish intrenchments extended around the city, being kept at a distance of about three and one-half miles from the corporation limits. The trenches were occupied by about 12,000 Spanish soldiers, and there were some good fortifications along the line.

It was the policy of General Shafter to distribute his forces so as to face this entire line as nearly as possible. A week was consumed, after the landing was completed, in making these arrangements and in sending forward the artillery, during which time the battle of La Quasina, referred to, and other skirmishes and engagements occurred. Meantime the ships of Admiral Sampson had dragged up the cables and connected them by tap-wires with Shafter's headquarters, thus establishing communication directly with Washington from the scene of battle.

THE BATTLES OF SAN JUAN AND EL CANEY.

The attack began July 1st, involving the whole line, but the main struggle occurred opposite the left centre of the column on the heights of San Juan, and the next greatest engagement was on the right of the American line at the little town of El Caney. These two points are several miles apart, the city of Santiago occupying very nearly the apex of a triangle of which a line connecting these two positions would form the base. John R. Church thus described the battles of July 1st and 2d:

"El Caney was taken by General Lawton's men after a sharp contest and severe loss on both sides. Here as everywhere there were blockhouses and trenches to be carried in the face of a hot fire from Mauser rifles, and the rifles were well served. The jungle must disturb the aim seriously, for our men did not suffer severely while under its cover, but in crossing clearings the rapid fire of the repeating rifles told with deadly effect. The object of the attack on El Caney was to crush the Spanish lines at a point near the city and allow us to gain a high hill from which the place could be bombarded if necessary. In all of this we were entirely successful. The engagement began at 6.40 A. M., and by 4 o'clock the Spaniards were forced to abandon the place and retreat toward their lines nearer the city. The fight was opened by Capron's battery, at a range of 2400 yards, and the troops engaged were Chaffee's brigade, the Seventh, Twelfth, and Seventeenth Infantry, who moved on Caney from the east; Colonel Miles' brigade of the First, Fourth, and Twenty-fifth Infantry, operating from the south; while Ludlow's brigade, containing the Eighth and Twenty-second Infantry and Second Massachusetts, made a detour to attack from the southwest. The Spanish force is thought to have been 1500 to 2000 strong. It certainly fought our men for nine hours, but of course had the advantage of a fort and strong intrenchments.

"The operations of our centre were calculated to cut the communications of Santiago with El Morro and permit our forces to advance to the bay, and the principal effort of General Linares, the Spanish commander in the field, seems to have been to defeat this movement. He had fortified San Juan strongly, throwing up on it intrenchments that in the hands of a more determined force would have been impregnable.

COMMODORE JOHN CRITTENDEN WATSON,
Commander of the Blockading Fleet at Havana.

"The battle of San Juan was opened by Grimes' battery, to which the enemy replied with shrapnell. The cavalry, dismounted, supported by Hawkins' brigade, advanced up the valley from the hill of El Pozo, forded several streams, where they lost heavily, and deployed at the foot of the series of hills known as San Juan under a sharp fire from all sides, which was exceedingly annoying because the enemy could not be discerned, owing to the long range and smokeless powder. They were under fire for two hours before the charge could be made and a position reached under the brow of the hill. It was not until nearly 4 o'clock that the neighboring hills were occupied by our troops and the final successful effort to crown the ridge could be made. The obstacles interposed by the Spaniards made these charges anything but the 'rushes' which war histories mention so often. They were slow and painful advances through difficult obstacles and a withering fire. The last 'charge' lasted an hour, but at 4.45 the fire ceased, with San Juan in our possession.

"The Spaniards made liberal use of barbed-wire fencing, which proved to be so effective as a stop to our advance that it is likely to take its place among approved defensive materials in future wars. It was used in two ways: Wires were stretched near the ground to trip up our men when on the run. Beyond them were fences in parallel lines, some being too high to be vaulted over.

"The object of our attack was a blockhouse on the top of the hill of San Juan, guarded by trenches and the defenses spoken of, a mile and a half long. Our troops advanced steadily against a hot fire maintained by the enemy, who used their rifles with accuracy, but did not cling to their works stubbornly when we reached them. San Juan was carried in the afternoon. The attack on Aguadores was also successful, though it was not intended to be more than a feint to draw off men who might otherwise have increased our difficulties at San Juan. By nightfall General Shafter was able to telegraph that he had carried all the outworks and was within three-quarters of a mile of the city.

"Though the enemy's lines were broken in the principal places, they yielded no more than was forced from them, and the battle was resumed on the 2d. The last day saw our left flank resting on the bay and our lines drawn around the city within easy gun-fire. Fears were entertained that the enemy would evacuate the place, and the right flank was pushed around to the north and eventually to the northwest of the city."

In the fight at San Juan General Linares, commanding the Spanish forces in Santiago, was severely wounded and transferred the command to General José Toral, second in authority.

THE DESTRUCTION OF CERVERA'S FLEET.

During the previous two days' fight by land the fleet of Admiral Cervera in Santiago harbor had taken an active part in shelling our positions, with no inconsiderable effect; and General Shafter, largely on this account, had about despaired of taking the city, with the force at his command. In fact, he went so far on the morning of July 3d as to telegraph Washington that his losses had been greatly underestimated, that he met with stronger resistance than he had anticipated, and was seriously considering falling back to a position five miles to the rear to await reinforcements. He was also anxious for an interview with Admiral Sampson. The fleet had been shelling the enemy during the two days' fight, but it was necessary that the navy and army have a clearer understanding; and at 8.30 o'clock on Sunday morning Admiral Sampson with his flagship *New York* steamed eastward for the purpose of conferring with the General.

General Miles telegraphed General Shafter, in response to his request, to hold his position, that he would be with him in a week with strong reinforcements; and he promptly started two expeditions, aggregating over 6000 men, which reached Santiago on the 8th and 10th respectively, in time to witness the closing engagements and surrender of the city. But fortune again favored our cause and completely changed the situation, unexpectedly to the American commanders of the land and naval forces.

It was on Sunday morning, July 3d, just before Sampson landed to meet Shafter, that Admiral Cervera, in obedience to commands from his home government, endeavored to run his fleet past the blockading squadron of the Americans, with the result that all of his ships were destroyed, nearly 500 of his men killed and wounded, and himself and about 1300 others were made prisoners. This naval engagement was one of the most dramatic and terrible in all the history of conflict upon the seas; and, as it was really the beginning of the end of what promised to be a long and terrible struggle, it was undoubtedly the most important battle of the war.

REAR-ADMIRAL WINFIELD SCOTT SCHLEY.

It had been just one month, to a day, since Hobson sunk the *Merrimac* at the harbor's mouth to keep Cervera in, and for nearly one month and a half the fleets of Schley and Sampson had lain like watch-dogs before the gate without for one moment relaxing their vigilance. The quiet of Sunday morning brooded over the scene. Even the winds seemed resting from their labors and the sea lay smooth as glass. For two days before, July 1st and 2d, the fleets had bombarded the forts of Santiago for the fourth time, and all the ships except the *Oregon* had steam down so low as to allow them a speed of only five knots an hour. At half-past nine o'clock the bugler sounded the call to quarters, and the Jackies appeared on deck rigged in their cleanest clothes for their regular Sunday inspection. On board the *Texas* the devout Captain Philip had sounded the trumpet-call to religious services. In an instant a line of smoke was seen coming out of the harbor by the watch on the *Iowa*, and from that vessel's yard a signal was run up—"The enemy is escaping to the westward." Simultaneously, from her bridge a six-pounder boomed on the still air to draw the attention of the other ships to her fluttering signal. On every vessel white masses were seen scrambling forward. Jackies and firemen tumbled over one another rushing to their stations. Officers jumped into the turrets through manholes, dressed in their best uniforms, and captains rushed to their conning towers. There was no time to waste—scarcely enough to get the battle-hatches screwed on tight. Jingle, jingle, went the signal-bells in the engine-rooms and "Steam! Steam!" the captains cried through the tubes. Far below decks, in 125 to 150 degrees of heat, naked men shoveled in the black coal and forced drafts were put on.

One minute after the *Iowa* fired her signal-gun she was moving toward the harbor. From under the Castle of Morro came Admiral Cervera's flagship, the *Infanta Maria Teresa*, followed by her sister armored cruisers, *Almirante Oquendo* and *Vizcaya*—so much alike that they could not be distinguished at any distance. There was also the splendid *Cristobal Colon*, and after them all the two magnificent torpedo destroyers, *Pluton* and *Furor*. The *Teresa* opened fire as she sighted the American vessels, as did all of her companions, and the forts from the heights belched forth at the same time. Countless geysers around our slowly approaching battleships showed where the Spanish shells exploded in the water. The Americans replied. The battle was on, but at a long range of two or three miles, so that the secondary batteries could not be called into use; but thirteen-inch shells from the *Oregon* and *Indiana* and the twelve-inch shells from the *Texas* and *Iowa* were churning up the water around the enemy. At this juncture it seemed impossible for the Americans to head off the Spanish cruisers from passing the western point, for they had come out of the harbor at a speed of thirteen and one-half knots an hour, for which the blockading fleet was not prepared. But Admiral Sampson's instructions were simple and well understood—"Should the enemy come out, close in and head him off"—and every ship was now endeavoring to obey that standing command while they piled on coal and steamed up.

Meanwhile from the rapidly approaching *New York* the signal fluttered—"Close into the mouth of the harbor and engage the enemy;" but the Admiral was too far away, or the men were too busy to see this signal, which they were nevertheless obeying to the letter.

It was not until the leading Spanish cruiser had almost reached the western point of the bay, and when it was evident that Cervera was leading his entire fleet in one direction, that the battle commenced in its fury. The *Iowa* and the *Oregon* headed straight for the shore, intending to ram if possible one or more of the Spaniards. The *Indiana* and the *Texas* were following, and the *Brooklyn*, in the endeavor to cut off the advance ship, was headed straight for the western point. The little unprotected *Gloucester* steamed right across the harbor mouth and engaged the *Oquendo* at closer range than any of the other ships, at the same time firing on the *Furor* and *Pluton*, which were rapidly approaching.

It then became apparent that the *Oregon* and *Iowa* could not ram and that the

Brooklyn could not head them off as she had hoped, and, turning in a parallel course with them, a running fight ensued. Broadside after broadside came fast with terrific slaughter. The rapid-fire guns of the *Iowa* nearest the *Teresa* enveloped the former vessel in a mantle of smoke and flame. She was followed by the *Oregon, Indiana, Texas,* and *Brooklyn,* all pouring a rain of red-hot steel and exploding shell into the fleeing cruisers as they passed along in their desperate effort to escape. The *Furor* and *Pluton* dashed like mad colts for the *Brooklyn,* and Commodore Schley signaled—"Repel torpedo destroyers." All the heavy ships turned their guns upon the little monsters. It was short work. Clouds of black smoke rising from their thin sides showed how seriously they suffered as they floundered in the sea.

The *Brooklyn* and *Oregon* dashed on after the cruisers, followed by the other big ships, leaving the *Furor* and *Pluton* to the *Gloucester,* hoping the *New York,* which was coming in the distance, would arrive in time to help her out if she needed it. The firing from the main and second batteries of all the battle-ships, *Oregon, Iowa, Texas,* and also the *Brooklyn,* was turned upon the *Vizcaya, Teresa,* and *Oquendo* with such terrific broadsides and accuracy of aim that the Spaniards were driven from their guns repeatedly; but the officers gave the men liquor and drove them back, beating and sometimes shooting down those who weakened, without mercy; but under the terrific fire of the Americans the poor wretches were again driven away or fell mangled by their guns or stunned from the concussions of the missiles on the sides of their ships.

Presently flames and smoke burst out from the *Teresa* and the *Oquendo.* The fire leaped from the port-holes; and amid the din of battle and above it all rose the wild cheers of the Americans as both these splendid ships slowly reeled like drunken men and headed for the shore. "They are on fire! We've finished them," shouted the gunners. Down came the Spanish flags. The news went all over the ships—it being commanded by Commodore Schley to keep every-one informed, even those far below in the fire-rooms—and from engineers and firemen in the hot bowels of the great leviathans to the men in the fighting-tops the welkin rang until the old ships reverberated with exuberant cheers.

This was 10.20 A.M. Previously, the two torpedo boats had gone down, and only two dozen of their 140 men survived, these having been picked up by the *Gloucester,* which plucky little unprotected "dare-devil," not content with the destruction she had courted and escaped only as one of the unexplainable mysteries of Spanish gunnery, was coming up to join the chase after bigger game; and it was to Lieutenant Wainwright, her commander, that Admiral Cervera surrendered. The *Maine was* avenged. (Lieutenant Wainwright was executive officer on that ill-fated vessel when she was blown up, February 15th.) Cervera was wounded, hatless, and almost naked when he was taken on board the *Gloucester.* Lieutenant Wainwright cordially saluted him and grasped him by the hand, saying,

"I congratulate you, Admiral Cervera, upon as gallant a fight as was ever made upon the sea." He placed his cabin at the service of Cervera and his officers, while his surgeon dressed their wounds and his men did all they could for their comfort. Wainwright supplying the Admiral with clothing. Cervera was overcome with emotion and the face of the old gray-bearded warrior was suffused in tears. The *Iowa* and *Indiana* came up soon after the *Gloucester* and assisted in the rescue of the drowning Spaniards from the *Oquendo* and *Teresa*, after which they all hurried on after the vanishing *Brooklyn* and *Oregon*, which were pursuing the *Vizaya* and *Colon*, the only two remaining vessels of Cervera's splendid fleet. From pursuer and pursued the smoke rose in volumes and the booming guns over the waters sang the song of destruction.

In twenty-four minutes after the sinking of the *Teresa* and *Oquendo*, the *Vizaya*, riddled by the *Oregon's* great shells and burning fiercely, hauled down her flag and headed for the shore, where she hung upon the rocks. In a dying effort she had tried to ram the *Brooklyn*, but the fire of the big cruiser was too hot for her. The *Texas* and the little *Vixen* were seen to be about a mile to the rear, and the *Vizaya* was left to them and the *Iowa*, the latter staying by her finally, while the *Texas* and *Vixen* followed on.

It looked like a forlorn hope to catch the *Colon*. She was four and one-half miles away. But the *Brooklyn* and the *Oregon* were running like express trains, and the *Texas* sped after the fugitives with all her might. The chase lasted two hours. Firing ceased, and every power of the ship and the nerve of commodore, captains, and officers were devoted to increasing the speed. Men from the guns, naked to the waist and perspiring in streams, were called on deck for rest and an airing. It was a grimy and dirty but jolly set of Jackies, and jokes were merrily cracked as they sped on and waited. Only the men in the fire-rooms were working as never before. It was their battle now, a battle of speed. At 12.30 it was seen the Americans were gaining. Cheers went up and all was made ready. "We may wing that fellow yet," said Commodore Schley, as he commanded Captain Clark to try a big thirteen-inch shell. "Remember the Maine" was flung out on a pennant from the mast-head of the *Oregon*, and at 8,500 yards she began to send her 1,000-pound shots shrieking over the *Brooklyn* after the flying Spaniard. One threw tons of water on board the fugitive, and the *Brooklyn* a few minutes later with eight-inch guns began to pelt her sides. Everyone expected a game fight from the proud and splendid *Colon* with her smokeless powder and rapid-fire guns; but all were surprised when, after a feeble resistance, at 1.15 o'clock her captain struck his colors and ran his ship ashore sixty miles from Santiago, opening her sea-valves to sink her after she had surrendered.

Victory was at last complete. As the *Brooklyn* and *Oregon* moved upon the prey word of the surrender was sent below, and naked men poured out of the fire-rooms, black with smoke and dirt and glistening with perspiration, but

THE SURRENDER OF SANTIAGO, JULY 17, 1898

After a little ceremony, the two commanding generals faced each other as the trumpet-sounding in Spanish said: "Through five times four the city and through land of the city of Santiago." General Shafter in reply said "I now take the city in the name of the surrender of the American Army, the city and its through of the United States."

SAN JUAN, PORTO RICO

This city, the capital of Porto Rico, was founded by Ponce de Leon in 1511. It is a fine specimen of an old walled town, having portcullis, gates, walls and battlements which cost millions of dollars. It is built on a long, narrow island, connected with the mainland by a bridge. Its population in 1897, estimated at 23,000

wild with joy. Commodore Schley gazed down at the grimy, gruesome, joyous firemen with glistening eyes suspicious of tears, and said, in husky voice, eloquent with emotion. "*Those are the fellows who made this day.*" Then he signaled— "The enemy has surrendered." The *Texas*, five miles to the east, repeated the signal to Admiral Sampson some miles further away, coming at top speed of the *New York.* Next the Commodore signaled the Admiral—"*A glorious victory has been achieved. Details communicated later.*" And then, to all the ships, "*This is a great day for our country,*" all of which were repeated by the *Texas* to the ships further east. The cheering was wild. Such a scene was never, perhaps, witnessed upon the ocean. Admiral Sampson arrived before the *Colon* sank, and placing the great nose of the New York against that vessel pushed her into shallow water, where she sank, but was not entirely submerged. Thus perished from the earth the bulk of the sea power of Spain.

The Spanish losses were 1,800 men killed, wounded, and made prisoners, and six ships destroyed or sunk, the property loss being about $12,000,000. The American loss was one man killed and three wounded, all from the *Brooklyn*, a result little short of a miracle from the fact that the *Brooklyn* was hit thirty-six times and nearly all the ships were struck more than once.

The prisoners were treated with the utmost courtesy. Many of them were taken or rescued entirely naked, and scores of them were wounded. Their behavior was manly and their fortitude won the admiration of their captors. Whatever may be said of Spanish marksmanship, there is no discount on Spanish courage. After a short detention Cervera and his captured sailors were sent north to New Hampshire and thence to Annapolis, where they were held until released by order of President McKinley, August 31st.

THREATENED BOMBARDMENT OF SANTIAGO AND FLIGHT OF THE REFUGEES.

On July the 3d, while the great naval duel was in progress upon the sea, General Shafter demanded the surrender of Santiago upon pain of bombardment. The demand was refused by General Toral, who commanded the forces after the wounding of General Linares. General Shafter stated that he would postpone the bombardment until noon of July 5th to allow foreigners and non-combatants to get out of the city, and he urged General Toral in the name of humanity to use his influence and aid to facilitate the rapid departure of unarmed citizens and foreigners. Accordingly late in the afternoon of July 4th General Toral posted notices upon the walls of Santiago advising all women, children, and non-combatants that between five and nine o'clock on the morning of the 5th they might pass out by any gate of the city, all pilgrims going on foot, no carriages being allowed, and stating that stretchers would be provided for the crippled.

Promptly at five o'clock on the following morning a great line of pilgrims wound out of Santiago. It was no rabble, but well-behaved crowds of men and women, with great droves of children. About four hundred persons were carried out on litters. Many of the poorer women wore large crucifixes and some entered El Caney telling their beads. But there were many not so fortunate as to reach the city. Along the highroads in all directions thousands of families squatted entirely without food or shelter, and many deaths occurred among them. The Red Cross Society did much to relieve the suffering, but it lacked means of transporting supplies to the front.

While the flag of truce was still flying on the morning of July 6th a communication was received from General Toral requesting that the time of truce be further extended, as he wanted to communicate again with the Spanish Government at Madrid concerning the surrender of the city, and, further, that the cable operators, who were Englishmen and had fled to El Caney with the refugees, be returned to the city that he might do so. General Shafter extended the truce until four o'clock on Sunday, July 10th, and the operators returned from El Caney to work the wires for General Toral. During all this time the refugees continued to throng the roads to Siboney and El Caney, until 20,000 fugitives were congregated at the two points. It is a disgraceful fact, however, that while this truce was granted at the request of the Spanish General, it was taken advantage of by the troops under him to loot the city. Both Cuban and Spanish families suffered from their rapacity.

THE LAST BATTLE AND THE SURRENDER OF THE CITY.

On July 8th and 10th the two expeditions of General Miles arrived, reinforcing General Shafter's army with over 6,000 men. General Toral was acquainted with the fact of their presence, and General Miles urgently impressed upon him that further resistance could but result in a useless loss of life. The Spanish commander replied that he had not received permission to surrender, and if the Americans would not wait longer he could only obey orders of his government, and that he and his men would die fighting. Accordingly a joint bombardment by the army and navy was begun. The artillery reply of the Spaniards was feeble and spiritless, though our attack on the city was chiefly with artillery. They seemed to depend most upon their small arms, and returned the volleys fired from the trenches vigorously. Our lines were elaborately protected with over 22,000 sand bags, while the Spaniards were protected with bamboo poles filled with earth. In this engagement the dynamite gun of the Rough Riders did excellent service, striking the enemy's trenches and blowing field-pieces into the air. The bombardment continued until the afternoon of the second day, when a flag of truce was displayed over the city. It was thought that General Toral was about to surrender, but instead he only asked more time.

On the advice of General Miles, General Shafter consented to another truce, and, at last, on July 14th, after an interview with Generals Miles and Shafter, in which he agreed to give up the city on condition that the army would be returned to Spain at the expense of America, General Toral surrendered. On July 16th the agreement, with the formal approval of the Madrid and Washington Governments, was signed in duplicate by the commissioners, each side retaining a copy. This event was accepted throughout the world as marking the end of the Spanish-American War.

The conditions of the surrender involved the following points:

"(1) The 20,000 refugees at El Caney and Siboney to be sent back to the city. (2) An American infantry patrol to be posted on the roads surrounding the city and in the country between it and the American cavalry. (3) Our hospital corps to give attention, as far as possible, to the sick and wounded Spanish soldiers in Santiago. (4) All the Spanish troops in the province, except ten thousand men at Holguin, under command of General Luque, to come into the city and surrender. (5) The guns and defenses of the city to be turned over to the Americans in good condition. (6) The Americans to have full use of the Juragua Railroad, which belongs to the Spanish Government. (7) The Spaniards to surrender their arms. (8) All the Spaniards to be conveyed to Spain on board of American transports with the least possible delay, and be permitted to take portable church property with them."

MAJOR-GENERAL NELSON A. MILES.

TAKING POSSESSION OF SANTIAGO AND RAISING THE AMERICAN FLAG.

The formality of taking possession of the city yet remained to be done. To that end, immediately after the signing of the agreement by the commissioners, General Shafter notified General Toral that he would formally receive his surrender of the city the next day, Sunday, July 17th, at nine o'clock in the morning. Accordingly at about 8.30 A. M., Sunday, General Shafter, accompanied by the commander of the American army, General Nelson A. Miles, Generals Wheeler and Lawton, and several officers, walked slowly down the hill to the road leading to Santiago. Under the great mango tree which had witnessed all the negotiations, General Toral, in full uniform, accompanied by 200 Spanish officers, met the Americans. After a little ceremony in military manœuvring, the two commanding generals faced each other, and General Toral, speaking in Spanish, said:

"Through fate I am forced to surrender to General Shafter of the American army the city and the strongholds of the city of Santiago."

General Toral's voice trembled with emotion as he spoke the words giving up the town to his victorious enemy. As he finished speaking the Spanish officers presented arms.

General Shafter, in reply, said:

"I receive the city in the name of the Government of the United States."

The officers of the Spanish General then wheeled about, presenting arms, and General Shafter, with the American officers, cavalry, and infantry chosen for the occasion, passed into the city and on to the governor's palace, where a crowd numbering 3,000 persons had gathered. As the great bell in the tower of the cathedral nearby gave the first stroke of twelve o'clock the American flag was run up from the flagpole on the palace, and as it floated to the breeze all hats were removed by the spectators, while the soldiers presented arms. As the cathedral bell tolled the last stroke of the hour the military band began to play "The Star-Spangled Banner," which was followed by "Three Cheers for the Red, White, and Blue." The cheering of the soldiers was joined by more than half of the people, who seemed greatly pleased and yelled "Viva los Americanos." The soldiers along almost the whole of the American line could see and had watched with alternating silence and cheers the entire proceeding.

GENERAL SHAFTER'S ANNOUNCEMENT OF THE VICTORY.

Having assigned soldiers to patrol and preserve order within the city, General Shafter and his staff returned to their quarters at camp, and the victorious commander, who two weeks before was almost disheartened, sent a dispatch announcing the formal surrender of Santiago. It was the first dispatch of the kind received at Washington from a foreign country for more than fifty years. The following extract from General Shafter's telegram sums up the situation:

"I have the honor to announce that the American flag has been this instant, 12 noon, hoisted over the house of the civil government in the city of Santiago. An immense concourse of people was present, a squadron of cavalry and a regiment of infantry presenting arms, and a band playing national airs. A light battery fired a salute of twenty-one guns.

"Perfect order is being maintained by the municipal government. The distress is very great but there is little sickness in town and scarcely any yellow fever.

"A small gunboat and about 200 seamen left by Cervera have surrendered to me. Obstructions are being removed from the mouth of the harbor.

"Upon coming into the city I discovered a perfect entanglement of defenses. Fighting as the Spaniards did the first day, it would have cost five thousand lives to have taken it.

"Battalions of Spanish troops have been depositing arms since daylight in the armory, over which I have a guard. General Toral formally surrendered the plaza and all stores at 9 A. M. About ",000 rifles, 600,000 cartridges, and many fine modern guns were given up.

"This important victory, with its substantial fruits of conquest, was won by a loss of 1,593 men killed, wounded, and missing. Lawton, who had the severe fighting around El Caney, lost 410 men. Kent lost 859 men in the still more severe assault on San Juan and the other conflicts of the centre. The cavalry lost 285 men, many of whom fell at El Caney, and the feint at Aguadores cost thirty-seven men. One man of the Signal Corps was killed and one wounded. Trying as it is to bear the casualties of the first fight, there can be no doubt that in a military sense our success was not dearly won."

Thus within less than thirty days from the time Shafter's army landed upon Cuban soil he had received the surrender not only of the city of Santiago, but nearly the whole of the province of that name—or about one-tenth of the entire island.

MAJOR-GENERAL WESLEY MERRITT.

There were three expeditions sent. The first under General Miles sailed from Guantanamo Bay, Cuba, July 21st; the second under General Ernst on the same day sailed from Charleston, S. C.; the third under General Brooke embarked at Newport News on July 26th. All of these expeditions, aggregating about 11,000 men, were convoyed by warships, and successfully landed. The first under General Miles reached Guanica at daylight on July 25th, where a Spanish force attempted to resist their landing, but a few well-directed shells from the *Massachusetts*, *Gloucester*, and *Columbia* soon put the enemy to flight. A party then went ashore and pulled down the Spanish flag from the blockhouse—the first trophy of war from Porto Rican soil. As the troops began to land the Spaniards opened fire upon them. The Americans replied with their rifles and machine guns, and the ships also shelled the enemy from the harbor. Five dead Spaniards were found after the firing had ceased. Not an American was touched.

Before nightfall all the troops were landed. The next day General Miles marched toward Ponce. Four men were wounded in a skirmish at Yauco on the way, but at Ponce, where General Ernst's expedition from Charleston met them and disembarked on July 28th, the Spaniards fled on the approach of the Americans, whom the mayor of the city and the people welcomed with joy, making many demonstrations in their honor and offering their services to hunt and fight the Spaniards. General Miles issued a proclamation to the people declaring clearly the United States' purpose of annexing them. The mayor of Ponce published this proclamation, with an appeal from himself to the people to salute and hail the American flag as their own, and to welcome and aid the American soldiers as their deliverers and brothers.

On August 4th General Brooke arrived, and the fleet Commander, Captain Higginson, with little resistance opened the port of Arroyo, where they were successfully landed the next day, and General Haines' brigade captured the place with a few prisoners.

The Americans were then in possession of all the principal ports on the south coast, covering between fifty and sixty miles of that shore. A forward movement was inaugurated in three divisions—all of which we will consider together—the object of General Miles being to occupy the island and drive the Spanish forces before him into San Juan, and by the aid of the fleet capture them there in a body, though the Spanish forces numbered 8,000 regulars and 9,000 volunteers, against which were the 11,000 land forces of the Americans and also their fleet.

The town of Coamo was captured August 9th after half an hour of fighting by Generals Ernst and Wilson, the Americans driving the Spaniards from their trenches and sustaining a loss of six wounded. On the 10th General Schwan encountered 1,000 Spaniards at Rosario River. This was the most severe engagement in Porto Rico. The Spaniards were routed, with what loss is unknown. The Americans had two killed and sixteen wounded.

On the 11th General Wilson moved on to Abonito and found the enemy strongly intrenched in the mountain fastnesses along the road. He ventured an attack with artillery, sustaining a loss of one man killed and four wounded. On pain of another attack he sent a messenger demanding the surrender of the town of Abonito; but the soldierly answer was sent back: "Tell General Wilson to stay where he is if he wishes to avoid the shedding of much blood." General Wilson concluded to delay until General Brooke could come up before making the assault, and, while thus waiting, the news of peace arrived.

Meantime General Brooke had been operating around Guayama, where he had five men wounded. At three o'clock, August 12th, the battle was just opening in good order, and a great fight was anticipated. The gunners were sighting their first pieces when one of the signal corps galloped up with the telegram announcing *peace*. "You came just fifteen minutes too soon. The troops will be disappointed," said General Brooke, and they were.

So ended the well-planned campaign of Porto Rico, in which General Miles had arranged, by a masterly operation with 11,000 men, the occupation of an island 108 miles long by thirty-seven broad. As it was, he had already occupied about one-third of the island with a loss of only three killed and twenty-eight wounded, against a preponderating force of 17,000 Spaniards.

After the signing of the protocol of peace General Brooke was left in charge of about half the forces in Porto Rico, pending a final peace, while General Miles with the other half returned to the United States, where he arrived early in September and was received with fitting ovations in New York, Philadelphia, and Washington, at which latter city he again took up his quarters as the Commander of the American Army.

THE CONQUEST OF THE PHILIPPINES.

After Dewey's victory at Manila, already referred to, it became evident that he must have the co-operation of an army in capturing and controlling the city. The insurgents under General Aguinaldo appeared anxious to assist Admiral Dewey, but it was feared that he could not control them. Accordingly, the big monitor *Monterey* was started for Manila and orders were given for the immediate outfitting of expeditions from San Francisco under command of Major-General Wesley Merritt. The first expedition consisted of between 2,500 and 3,000 troops commanded by Brigadier-General Anderson, carried on three ships, the *Charleston*, the *City of Pekin*, and the *City of Sydney*. This was the longest expedition (about 6,000 miles) on which American troops were ever sent, and the men carried supplies to last a year. The *Charleston* got away on the 22d, and the other two vessels followed three days later. The expedition went

through safely, arriving at Manila July 1st. The *Charleston* had stopped e
June 21st at the Ladrone Islands and captured the island of Guam withou
resistance. The soldiers of the garrison were taken on as prisoners to Manila
and a garrison of American soldiers left in charge, with the stars and stripes
waving over the fortifications.

The second expedition of 3,500 men sailed June 15th under General Greene,
who used the steamer *China* as his flagship. This expedition landed July 16th
at Cavite in the midst of considera-
ble excitement on account of the
aggressive movements of the insurgents and the daily encounters and
skirmishes between them and the
Spanish forces.

On June 23d the monitor *Mo-
nadnoc* sailed to further reinforce
Admiral Dewey, and four days later
the third expedition of 4,000 troops
under General McArthur passed out
of the Golden Gate amid the cheers
of the multitude, as the others had
done; and on the 29th General Merritt followed on the *Newport*. Nearly
one month later, July 23d, General
H. G. Otis, with 900 men, sailed on
the *City of Rio de Janeiro* from San
Francisco, thus making a total of
nearly 12,000 men, all told, sent to
the Philippine Islands.

General Merritt arrived at Cavite July 25th, and on July 29th the
American forces advanced from Cavite toward Manila. On the 31st,

MAP OF PHILIPPINE ISLANDS.

while enroute, they were attacked at Malate by 3,000 Spaniards, whom they
repulsed, but sustained a loss of nine men killed and forty-seven wounded,
nine of them seriously. This was the first loss of life on the part of the
Americans in action in the Philippines. The Spanish casualties were much
heavier. On the same day General McArthur's reinforcements arrived at
Cavite, and several days were devoted to preparations for a combined land and
naval attack.

On August 7th Admiral Dewey and General Merritt demanded the surrender of the city within forty-eight hours, and foreign warships took their

IN THE WAR ROOM AT WASHINGTON

The plan adopted was by President McKinley, Secretary Long, Secretary Alger, and Major-General Miles, consulting the map during the progress of the Spanish-American War. It was in this room that the points of combination, the war by land and sea, were formulated, and the commands for action were issued for the fleet and the army.

AMERICANS STORMING SAN JUAN HILL

The most dramatic scene and the most destructive battle of the Spanish War

respective subjects on board for protection. On August 9th the Spaniards asked more time to hear from Madrid, but this was refused, and on the 13th a final demand was made for immediate surrender, which Governor-General Augusti refused and embarked with his family on board a German man-of-war, which sailed with him for Hong Kong.

At 9.30 o'clock the bombardment began with fury, all of the vessels sending hot shot at the doomed city.

In the midst of the bombardment by the fleet American soldiers under Generals McArthur and Greene were ordered to storm the Spanish trenches which extended ten miles around the city. The soldiers rose cheering and dashed for the Spanish earthworks. A deadly fire met them, but the men rushed on and swept the enemy from their outer defences, forcing them to their inner trenches. A second charge was made upon these, and the Spaniards retreated into the walled city, where they promptly sent up a white flag. The ships at once ceased firing, and the victorious Americans entered the city after six hours' fighting. General Merritt took command as military governor. The Spanish forces numbered 7,000 and the Americans 10,000 men. The loss to the Americans was about fifty killed, wounded, and missing, which was very small under the circumstances.

In the meantime the insurgents had formed a government with Aguinaldo as president. They declared themselves most friendly to American occupation of the islands, with a view to aiding them to establish an independent government, which they hoped would be granted to them. On September 15th they opened their republican congress at Malolos, and President Aguinaldo made the opening address, expressing warm appreciation of Americans and indulging the hope that they meant to establish the independence of the islands. On September 16th, however, in obedience to the command of General Otis, they withdrew their forces from the vicinity of Manila.

PEACE NEGOTIATIONS AND THE PROTOCOL.

Precisely how to open the negotiations for peace was a delicate and difficult question. Its solution, however, proved easy enough when the attempt was made. During the latter part of July the Spanish Government, through M. Jules Cambon, the French Ambassador at Washington, submitted a note, asking the United States Government for a statement of the ground on which it would be willing to cease hostilities and arrange for a peaceable settlement. Accordingly, on July 30th, a statement, embodying President McKinley's views, was transmitted to Spain, and on August 2d Spain virtually accepted the terms by cable. On August 9th Spain's formal reply was presented by M. Cambon, and on the next day he and Secretary Day agreed upon terms of a protocol, to be sent to Spain for her approval. Two days later, the 12th inst., the French

Ambassador was authorized to sign the protocol for Spain, and the signatures were affixed the same afternoon at the White House (M. Cambon signing for Spain and Secretary Day for the United States), in the presence of President McKinley and the chief assistants of the Department of State. The six main points covered by the protocol were as follows:

"1. That Spain will relinquish all claim of sovereignty over and title to Cuba.

"2. That Porto Rico and other Spanish islands in the West Indies, and an island in the Ladrones, to be selected by the United States, shall be ceded to the latter.

"3. That the United States will occupy and hold the city, bay, and harbor of Manila, pending the conclusion of a treaty of peace which shall determine the control, disposition, and government of the Philippines.

"4. That Cuba, Porto Rico, and other Spanish islands in the West Indies shall be immediately evacuated, and that commissioners, to be appointed within ten days, shall, within thirty days from the signing of the protocol, meet at Havana and San Juan, respectively, to arrange and execute the details of the evacuation.

"5. That the United States and Spain will each appoint not more than five commissioners to negotiate and conclude a treaty of peace. The commissioners are to meet at Paris not later than October 1st.

"6. On the signing of the protocol, hostilities will be suspended and notice to that effect will be given as soon as possible by each Government to the commanders of its military and naval forces."

On the very same afternoon President McKinley issued a proclamation announcing on the part of the United States a suspension of hostilities, and over the wires the word went ringing throughout the length and breadth of the land and under the ocean that peace was restored. The cable from Hong Kong to Manila, however, had not been repaired for use since Dewey had cut it in May; consequently it was several days before tidings could reach General Merritt and Admiral Dewey; and meantime the battle of Manila, which occurred on the 13th, was fought.

On August 17th President McKinley named commissioners to adjust the Spanish evacuation of Cuba and Porto Rico, in accordance with the terms of the protocol. Rear-Admiral Wm. T. Sampson, Senator Matthew C. Butler, and Major-General James F. Wade were appointed for Cuba, and Rear-Admiral W. S. Schley, Brigadier-General Wm. W. Gordon, and Major-General John R. Brooke for Porto Rico. In due time Spain announced her commissioners, and, as agreed, they met in September and the arrangements for evacuation were speedily completed and carried out.

President McKinley appointed as the National Peace Commission, Secretary of State Wm. R. Day, Senator Cushman K. Davis of Minnesota, Senator Wm. P. Frye of Maine, Senator George Gray of Maryland, and Mr. Whitelaw Reid of New York. Secretary Day resigned his State portfolio September 16th, in which he was succeeded by Colonel John Hay, former Ambassador to England. With ex-Secretary Day at their head the Americans sailed from New York, September 17th, met the Spanish Commissioners at Paris, France, as agreed, and arranged the details of the final peace between the two nations. Thus ended the Spanish-American War.

HOME-COMING OF OUR SOLDIERS.

After Spain's virtual acceptance of the terms of peace contained in President McKinley's note of July 30th, it was deemed unnecessary to keep all the forces unoccupied in the fever districts of Cuba and the unsanitary camps of our own country; consequently the next day after receipt of Spain's message of August 2d, on August 3d, the home-coming was inaugurated by ordering all cavalry under General Shafter at Santiago to be transported to Montauk Point, Long Island, and on the 6th inst. transports sailed bearing those who were to come north. These were followed rapidly by others from Santiago, and

EX-SECRETARY OF STATE WM. R. DAY,
Head of Peace Commission to Paris.

later by about half the forces from Porto Rico under General Miles, and others from the various camps, so that by the end of September, 1898, nearly half of the great army of 268,000 men had been mustered out of service or sent home on furlough.

regular force of less than 30,000 men, that an army of a quarter of a million could be built up out of volunteers who had to be collected, trained, clothed, equipped and provisioned, and a war waged and won on two sides of the globe, in a little over three months, without much suffering and many mistakes.

With the conquest of Cuba, Porto Rico and the Philippine Islands a new era has dawned in the history of our country. The United States must now take their place among the first nations of the world, and stand with England, if not as a colonizer, at least as a civilizer; and whatever else this war with Spain may do for us, it is bound to open up new avenues of trade in her colonies in the East and West Indies. The islands of Cuba and Porto Rico on the eastern coast, and the Philippines, Carolines and Ladrones, together with our newly acquired Hawaiian possessions on the west, furnish fields for marvelous developments and unique trade opportunities. All of these islands lie in the tropics where heretofore not an acre of our country has extended. Expert observers of commerce declare that "the natural avenues of trade are not with the sun along parallel lines of latitude, but north and south between zones of differing climates." Hence, these island groups are most favorably located. They can send us the fruits of the tropics, which our temperate climate produces too sparingly or not at all, and receive in return our grain and manufactures—an exchange mutually desirable and useful. Thus there is scarcely a product in the world that could not be raised within our enlarged borders.

The territory of which we have acquired control is equal to nine good States. Cuba, 800 miles long and from 30 to 125 miles wide, with an area about equal to that of the State of Ohio, and a population estimated before the war at 1,750,000, lies within a few hours of our Florida coast. Porto Rico, the gateway of the West Indies, and easily reached from the great harbors of the Atlantic, is equal in size to Long Island and has 800,000 inhabitants. In the Pacific, in line with our rapidly expanding trade with Japan, China, and Australia, lie the 2,000 Philippine and other Spanish islands. The island of Luzon alone, which we keep directly by our peace with Spain, has over 4,000,000 inhabitants, contains 57,505 square miles, equal in size to the States of New York and Massachusetts combined, and upon this island stands the city of Manila. With the other Spanish islands of the Philippine group we enjoy superior trade facilities, without the burden of directly administering their affairs. Here, then, are Cuba and Porto Rico in the Atlantic and the Hawaiian and Philippine groups in the Pacific, whose destiny has become closely intertwined with our own. Their combined area is 168,000 square miles, equaling New England, New York, Pennsylvania, and New Jersey. Their combined population is about 10,000,000, or perhaps one-half that of the nine home States mentioned, and among all this vast number of people there are very few manufactures of any kind to be found. Thus this war has opened an avenue for American products destined to give such an impetus to American manufacturing as our country has never enjoyed. Cuba which, in 1902, took so happily her place as a new free Republic, is and must be closely connected with our country in all industrial and commercial enterprises and become a market for our products.

THE TREATY OF PEACE.

December 10, 1898, was one of the most eventful days in the past decade, one fraught with great interest to the world, and involving the destiny of more than 10,000,000 of people. At nine o'clock on the evening of that day the commissioners of the United States and those of Spain met for the last time, after about eleven weeks of deliberation, in the magnificent apartments of the foreign ministry at the French capital, and signed the Treaty of Peace, which finally marked the end of the Spanish-American War.

This treaty transformed the political geography of the world by establishing the United States' authority in both hemispheres, and also in the tropics, where it had never before extended. It, furthermore, brought under our dominion and obligated us for the government of strange and widely isolated peoples, who have little or no knowledge of liberty and government as measured by the American standards. In this new assumption of responsibility America essayed a difficult problem, the solving of which involved results that could not fail to influence the destiny of our nation and the future history of the whole world.

On January 3, 1899, the Hon. John Hay, Secretary of State, delivered the Treaty of Peace to President McKinley, who, on January 4th, forwarded the same to the Senate of the United States with a view to its ratification. Below will be found the complete text of the treaty as submitted by the President.

The Queen Regent of Spain signed the ratification of the Treaty of Peace on March 17, 1899, and the final act took place on the afternoon of April 11th, when copies of the final protocol were exchanged at Washington by President McKinley and the French ambassador, M. Cambon, representing Spain. The President immediately issued a proclamation of peace, and thus the Spanish-American War came to an official end. A few weeks later the sum of $20,000,000 was paid to Spain, in accordance with the treaty, as partial compensation for the surrender of her rights in the Philippines, and diplomatic relations between the Latin kingdom and the United States were resumed.

The treaty with Spain was finally consummated on July 3, 1899, on which day it was ratified by the Spanish Cortes.

24

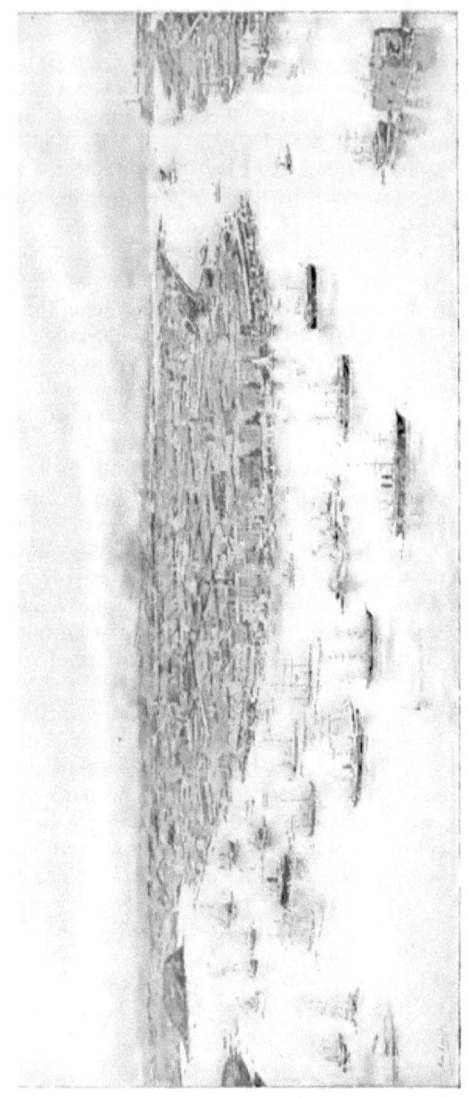

CITY OF HAVANA AND HARBOR, SHOWING WRECK OF THE BATTLESHIP "MAINE."

The United States Becomes a World Power.

The New Century Brings New Problems of
Colonization and Foreign Co-operation.

On the last day of 1898 the Spanish troops were withdrawn from Havana, and on the first day of 1899 the stars and stripes proudly floated over that queen city of the American tropics. But this was only for a time. The United States was pledged to give freedom to Cuba, and no man in authority thought of breaking this pledge, for the honor of the country was involved.

In the summer of 1900 the Cuban people were asked to hold a convention and form a Constitution, with the single proviso that it should contain no clauses favoring European aggression or inimical to American interests. This done, American troops and officials would be withdrawn and Cuba be given over to the Cubans.

The occupation of Porto Rico, on the contrary, was permanent. It had been fully ceded to the United States, and steps were taken to make it a constituent part of that country. But the period of transition from Spanish to American rule was not favorable to the interests of the people, who suffered severely, their business being wrecked by tariff discrimination. Action by Congress was demanded, and a bill was passed greatly reducing the tariff in Porto Rico, but not giving free trade with the United States, though many held that this was the Constitutional right of the islanders. Under this new tariff business was resumed, and the lost prosperity of the island was gradually restored.

The occupation of our new possessions in the Pacific presented serious difficulties. This was not the case with Hawaii, which fell peacefully under its new rule, and in 1900 was made a Territory of the United States. With the Philippine Islands the case was different. There hostility to American rule

383

soon showed itself, and eventually an insurrection began, leading to a war, which proved far more protracted and sanguinary than that with Spain.

DEWEY RETURNS HOME.

Shortly after these troubles began Admiral Dewey received a well-merited reward. On the 3d of March, 1899, he was promoted by President McKinley and the Senate from the rank of rear-admiral to that of full admiral, a grade of high honor which only two Americans, Farragut and Porter, had borne before him. Worn out with his labors, this distinguished officer soon after set out for home. His journey was a

leisurely one, and he was the recipient of the highest honors at every stopping-place on his route. On reaching his own country he found himself a great popular hero, and was everywhere greeted with enthusiastic applause. His reception at New York was one of the striking events of the century, and as a lasting testimonial of appreciation and esteem his grateful countrymen purchased him a beautiful residence in Washington. Here, taking to himself a wife, the Admiral settled down to peace and domestic comfort after his stormy career.

THE PHILIPPINE INSURRECTION.

Dewey left the Philippines in a state of convulsion. On the 30th of December, 1898, President McKinley had issued a proclamation offering the natives, under American supremacy,

MAJOR-GENERAL ELWELL S. OTIS.

acy, a considerable measure of home rule, including a voice in local government, the right to hold office, a fair judiciary, and freedom of speech and of the press. These concessions were not satisfactory to Emilio Aguinaldo, the leader in the late insurrection against Spain, who demanded independence for the islands. He claimed that Dewey had promised it to him in return for his aid in the capture of Manila—a claim which Dewey positively denied.

General Elwell S. Otis, who had succeeded General Merritt as military governor of the islands, found himself plunged into the midst of an active war. The difficulty with which General Otis had to contend was one in which the navy was not specially concerned, it being almost wholly a military affair. It had its origin in a variety of causes, beginning with the irritation of the Filipino forces in not being permitted to enter Manila after its capture—presumably with the purpose of loot and outrage. This irritation was added to by growing relations of hostility between the American and the Philippine forces. Little was done to adjust this trouble, and the hostile attitude of the Filipinos steadily increased. Not until after fighting had actually begun was an effort at an amicable settlement made, and in this Dewey took part.

Before his return he had served on a commission, organized with the hope of reaching a peaceful end of the difficulties. The other members of the commission were General Otis, Jacob G. Shurman, President of Cornell University, Professor Dean Worcester, and Charles Denby, late Minister to China. The commission began its work on April 4, 1899, by issuing a proclamation to the Philippine people, offering them, under the supremacy of the United States, an abundant measure of civil rights, honest administration, reform of abuses, and development of the resources of the country. This proclamation fell stillborn, so far as the insurgent forces were concerned, Aguinaldo issuing counter proclamations and calling on the people to fight for complete independence. It was evident that the settlement of the affair would depend on the rifle and the sword rather than on paper proclamations and promises.

THE INSURRECTION IN LUZON.

On the 30th of December, 1898, President McKinley had issued a proclamation to the Philippine people, in which he offered them a large measure of local self-government, the right to hold office, a fair judiciary and freedom of speech and of the press. These concessions were not satisfactory to their leaders, and in January, 1899, a conference was held with General Otis in which the Philippine spokesman demanded a greater degree of self-government than he had authority to grant. As the debate in the Senate upon the treaty of peace with Spain approached its termination, and promised to end in the ratification of the treaty and the cession of the islands to the United States, the restlessness and hostility of the natives increased, and on the night of February 4th the threatened outbreak came, in a fierce attack on the American outposts at Manila. A severe battle ensued, continuing for two days, and ending in the defeat of the natives, who had suffered severely and were driven back for miles beyond the city limits.

Meanwhile a republic had been proclaimed by the Philippine leaders,

Aguinaldo being chosen president and commander-in-chief of the native armies. He immediately issued a declaration of war, and both sides prepared for active hostilities. The first step taken by the Filipinos was a desperate one—an attempt at wholesale arson. On the night of February 22d the city of Manila was set on fire at several points, and the soldiers and firemen who sought to extinguish the flames were fired upon from many of the houses. The result was not serious except to the natives themselves, since the conflagration was in great part confined to their quarter of the city. General Otis took vigilant precautions to prevent the recurrence of such an attempt, and from that time forward Manila, though full of secret hostiles, was safe from the peril of incendiarism.

THE CAMPAIGN OF 1899.

The American forces, being strengthened with reinforcements, began their advance on March 25th. They met with sharp resistance, the Filipinos having thrown up earthworks at every defensible point, and being well armed with Mauser rifles. But they nowhere seemed able to sustain the vigorous onsets of the Americans, who did not hesitate to charge their works and swim wide rivers in face of their fire, and they were driven back from a long succession of fortified places. On March 31st Malolos, the capital of Aguinaldo, was occupied. Calumpit, another Philippine stronghold, was taken near the end of April. General Lawton, an old Indian fighter, who had recently reached the islands, led an expedition northward through the foothills and captured San Isidro, the second insurgent capital. Various other places were taken, and at the beginning of July, when the coming on of the rainy season put an end to active operations, a large and populous district to the north and west of Manila was in American hands.

By this time it had become evident that a larger army was needed to complete the task, and reinforcements were now hurried across the ocean. With them was sent a considerable body of cavalry, the lack of which had seriously handicapped the troops in the spring campaign. Fighting was resumed in mid-autumn, and Aguinaldo's new capital of Tarlac quickly fell. The insurgents seemed to have lost heart from their reverses in the spring, and defended themselves with less courage and persistence, the result being that by the 1st of December the Americans were masters of the whole line of the Manila-Dagupan Railway and the broad plain through which it ran, and the Filipinos were in full flight for the mountains, hotly pursued by Lawton and Young, with their cavalry and scouts.

From that time forward there was no Filipino army, properly so-called, Aguinaldo's forces being broken up into fugitive bands, capable only of guerilla warfare. The American troops traversed the island from end to end, having frequent collisions with small parties of the enemy, in one of which, unfortunately, the gallant Lawton was shot dead. Many of the insurgent leaders were captured or surrendered, but Aguinaldo continued at large, and the hope of a final end of the war came to depend largely upon the event of his capture.

In November the Philippine Commission made its report to the government, and a system which was thought to be well adapted to the situation was formulated at Washington. This declared that the people of the Philippines, while many of them were intelligent and capable, had no experience in self-government, and that it was necessary for the United States to retain a firm political control, while giving them such share in the government as they were fitted to exercise, increasing this as they gained political training. In accordance with this policy, local governments were established in those localities which had become pacified, and with very promising effect. By the summer of 1900 the resistance to American domination had so much decreased that President McKinley issued a proclamation of amnesty, with the hope that the natives still in arms would take advantage of the opportunity to cease their desultory resistance.

THE SITUATION IN CHINA.

While this was going on in the Philippines a disturbed condition of affairs suddenly developed in a new quarter, the ancient and populous empire of China. It is necessary to go a step backwards to trace the course of events leading to this unlooked-for situation. The whole intercourse of European nations with China had been of a character to create indignation and hatred of foreigners in the populace of that country. The Japano-Chinese war increased this feeling, while demonstrating the incapacity of the Chinese to cope in war with modern nations. In the years that followed, the best statesmen of China vividly realized the defects of their system, and recognized that a radical reform was necessary to save the nation from a total collapse. The nations of Europe were seizing the best ports of the empire and threatening to divide the whole country between them, a peril which it needed vigorous measures to avert.

The result was an effort to modernize the administration. Railroads had long been practically forbidden, but now concessions for the building of hundreds of miles of road were granted. Modern implements of war were purchased in great quantities, and the European drill and discipline were introduced into the imperial army. The young emperor became strongly imbued with the spirit of reform, and ordered radical changes in the administration of affairs. In short, a promising beginning was made in the modernization of the ancient empire.

A movement of this kind in a country so rigidly conservative as China could scarcely fail to produce a revulsion. The party of ancient prejudice and conservative sentiment—a party comprising the bulk of the nation—took the alarm. The empress-dowager, who had recently laid down the reins of government as regent, took them up again, under the support of the conservative leaders, seized and held in palace seclusion the emperor, put to death his advisers, and restored the old methods of administration.

THE BOXER OUTBREAK.

This revolution in the palace soon made itself felt in the hovel. A secret society of the common people, known as "The Boxers," rose in arms, made a murderous onslaught upon the missionaries, who were widely domiciled within the realm, and soon appeared in the capital. Here, aided by many of the soldiers, and led by men high in rank in the anti-foreign party, they made a virulent assault upon the legation buildings, and put the ministers of the nations in imminent peril of their lives. These exalted officials were cut off from all communication with their governments, stories of their massacre alone filtering through, and the powers, roused to desperation by the danger of their envoys, sent ships and troops in all haste to the nearest point to Pekin. In this movement the United States actively joined, its minister, Edwin H. Conger, and the members of the embassy sharing the common peril.

What followed must be briefly told. A small force, made up of soldiers and marines of various nations, under Admiral Seymour, of the British navy, set out on June 11th for Pekin. This movement failed. The railroad was found to be torn up, a strong force of Chinese blocked the way, and Seymour and his men were forced to turn back and barely escaped with their lives.

At the same time a naval attack was made on the forts at Taku; Admiral Remey, of the United States navy, refusing to take part in this ill-advised action. Its immediate result was an assault in force by Boxers and troops on the foreign quarter of the city of Tien Tsin, in which the Chinese fought with an unexpected skill and persistence. They were repulsed, but only after the hardest fight which foreigners had ever experienced on Chinese soil.

THE RESCUE OF THE MINISTERS.

As the month of July went on the mystery at Pekin deepened. It became known that the German minister had been murdered, and doubtful reports of the slaughter of all the foreigners in the capital were cabled. As it seemed impossible to obtain authentic news, the greatest possible haste was made to collect an army strong enough to march to Pekin, and early in August this force, consisting of some 16,000 Japanese, Russians, Americans and British, set out. A severe struggle was looked for, and their ability to reach Pekin seemed very doubtful. At Peitsang, some twelve miles on the route, the Chinese made a desperate resistance, which augured ill for the enterprise; but their defeat there seemed to rob them of spirit, and the gates of Pekin were reached with little more fighting. On the 14th the gates were assailed, the feeble opposition from within was overcome, and the troops marched in triumph to the British legation, the stout walls of which had offered a haven of refuge to the imperilled legationers.

Glad, indeed, were the souls of the beleaguered men and women within, so long in peril of death from torture or starvation, to see the stars and stripes and the union jack waving over the coming troops. Only then was the mystery surrounding their fate made clear and the safety of all the ministers, except the representative of Germany, assured. So far as the United States was concerned, the work was at an end. That country wanted no share in the partition of China. All it demanded was an "open door" to commerce, an equal share in the important Chinese trade. No sooner was its minister rescued than it was announced that the American troops would be withdrawn as soon as proper relations with the Chinese government had been consummated, and that in no case would the United States support any land-seizing projects of the nations of Europe.

THE POLITICAL CAMPAIGN OF 1900.

In the summer of 1900 the national conventions of the political parties were held to nominate candidates and formulate platforms for the presidential campaign of that year. The candidates for President proved to be the same as in 1896, William McKinley being chosen by the Republicans, William J. Bryan by the Democrats and Populists. For Vice-President, Adlai E. Stevenson, who had filled that office under Cleveland, was selected by the Democrat and Populist parties; Theodore Roosevelt, Governor of New York and the hero of the battle of San Juan, by the Republicans.

The platforms of the parties were significant in that the old party war cries sank into the background and new principles rose into prominence. The tariff, so long the leading issue, vanished from sight. The question of free silver coinage, so prominent in 1896, became a minor issue. The new points in debate were the trusts and the policy of so-called Imperialism. The trusts, however, could not be made a leading question. Both parties condemned them in their platforms, though the Democrats maintained that they were supported by the existing administration, and that the Republican party was the sustainer of monopoly. This left as the leading issue the question of Imperialism *versus*

Anti-Imperialism, a controversy based on the effort of the administration to subdue and control the people of the Philippines. The persons opposed to this policy had grown in numbers until Anti-Imperialism was taken up as the main principle of the Democratic platform. The country became divided upon this great question, and the campaign orators fulminated pro and con, with all their eloquence, upon the grand problem of the conquest or the independence of the Filipinos. The result of the election proved favorable to the Republican candidates, William McKinley being re-elected President by a considerably larger majority than in 1896. On March 4, 1901, he was duly re-inaugurated President of the United States, and Theodore Roosevelt, the new Vice-President, took his seat as presiding officer of the United States Senate.

THE CENSUS OF 1900.

Much interest was taken throughout the United States in the results of the twelfth census which was taken in July, 1900, under the direction of William R. Merriam. Elaborate preparations were made and numerous calculating and registering machines were employed to facilitate the work. The country was divided into 52,600 districts, and from these the returns showed a total population of over 76,000,000 against 62,600,000 by the census of 1890. For many years it had been predicted that the census of 1900 would show a population of 100,000,000. There being less public land to be distributed for homes has reduced immigration, and been one of the reasons that the percentage of increase in population has diminished. The census of 1900 shows that about thirty-three per cent. of the population is living in cities or towns of 8,000 inhabitants or over. In 1890 this percentage was 29. The centre of population for the United States in 1880 was near Columbus, Indiana, and in 1900 it had moved to a point seven miles southwest of this city.

The following table shows the aggregate population of twenty cities by the twelfth census, in their order, in comparison with that of the eleventh:

	12th Census 1900.	11th Census 1890.
Greater New York	3,437,202	2,507,591
Chicago	1,698,575	1,099,850
Philadelphia	1,293,697	1,046,964
Brooklyn	1,166,582	806,343
St. Louis	575,238	451,770
Boston	560,892	448,477
Baltimore	508,957	434,439
Cleveland	381,768	261,353
Buffalo	352,219	255,664
San Francisco	342,782	298,997
Cincinnati	325,902	296,908
Pittsburg	321,616	238,617
New Orleans	287,104	242,039
Detroit	285,704	205,876
Milwaukee	285,315	204,468
Washington	278,718	230,392
Newark	246,070	181,830
Jersey City	206,433	163,003
Louisville	204,731	161,129
Minneapolis	202,718	164,738

GENERAL ARTHUR MacARTHUR

GENERAL CHARLES KING

GENERAL HENRY W. LAWTON

GENERAL JOSEPH WHEELER

POPULAR COMMANDERS IN THE FILIPINO WAR

391

AMERICA'S LARGEST CITIES—CENSUS OF 1900

The following table shows the population of 32 of the largest cities of the United States. They are arranged and numbered according to population; and, in the same line with the name of the city, appear the date on which it was incorporated, the number of acres within the corporate limits, the population according to the census of June 1, 1900, the death rate per thousand population, the net debt per capita, the net debt of the city after deducting the sinking fund, the total property valuation and the tax rate per thousand on property. In a very few instances, where the information desired is not given, the space is left blank.

The average density of population in any city may be estimated by comparing the number of acres with the number of inhabitants. It will be noticed that St. Louis, Mo., with a population greater than Boston, occupies less than two-thirds as much territory as her Eastern rival. The comparison between Boston and Baltimore is still more striking, the Southern city crowding into a little over one-third the space of B-ston about seven-eighths as many people. The last decade has developed a remarkable disposition to spread the corporate limits of large cities. The trolley car and rapid transit justifies such extension of the boundary lines.

Marginal Number	CITIES	Incorporated	Area (acres)	Population at Twelfth Census, June 1, 1900	Death rate on basis of population at Twelfth Census (not including still-births)	Net Debt per capita	Net Debt after deducting Sinking Fund	Property total valuation	Tax rate per $1,000	Marginal Number
1	New York, N. Y.	1614	197,192.00	3,437,202	19.01	$73.21	$251,632,705	$3,478,352,029	$47.61	1
2	Chicago, Ill.	1837	122,249.00	1,698,575	15.01	17.17	29,163,723	345,196,419	18.50	2
3	Philadelphia, Pa.	1701	54,913.12	1,293,697	18.96	31.86	41,211,030	800,935,205	19.50	3
4	St. Louis, Mo.	1822	39,276.80	575,238	17.43	33.21	19,105,594	373,360,913	13.10	4
5	Boston, Mass.	1822	24,661.00	560,892	19.91	105.72	59,299,883	1,089,736,752	21.58	5
6	Baltimore, Md.	1797	21,190.00	508,957	19.95	64.70	32,928,106	388,112,020	29.40	6
7	Cleveland, Ohio	1836	25,343.57	381,768	14.55	32.04	12,233,020	145,971,985	23.29	7
8	Buffalo, N. Y.	1832	27,060.00	352,219	13.92	40.27	14,181,516	245,672,620	18.66	8
9	San Francisco, Cal.	1850	20,364.00	342,782	20.73	13.02	4,452,631	352,344,061	15.74	9
10	Cincinnati, Ohio	1819	19,418.17	325,902	18.41	83.65	27,265,313	260,820,520	17.69	10
11	Pittsburg, Pa.	1816	25,600.00	321,616	18.27	36.98	11,892,270	317,174,221	29.00	11
12	New Orleans, La.	1805	18,560.00	287,104	27.47	50.70	14,556,715	141,000,000	19.08	12
13	Detroit, Mich.	1824	13,624.32	285,704	15.89	16.13	4,609,732	216,971,000	22.07	13
14	Milwaukee, Wis.	1846	41,320.00	285,315	13.47	22.25	6,349,062	151,971,991		14
15	Washington, D. C.	1791	11,819.00	278,718	21.52	54.44	15,171,284	196,587,846	21.20	15
16	Newark, N. J.	1836	8,320.00	246,070	18.14	59.53	14,131,980	145,657,738	28.40	16
17	Jersey City, N. J.	1838	12,800.00	206,433	18.67	81.14	16,749,862	92,021,096	25.35	17
18	Louisville, Ky.	1828	34,105.00	204,731	17.19	43.96	9,003,888	119,695,947	23.15	18
19	Minneapolis, Minn.	1867	11,795.00	202,718	11.08	32.95	6,678,683	105,729,765	16.50	19
20	Providence, R. I.	1832	17,792.00	175,597	18.01	81.63	14,312,167	183,501,780	18.00	20
21	Indianapolis, Ind.	1847	16,640.00	169,164	15.22	18.29	3,094,073	123,395,849	28.80	21
22	Kansas City, Mo.	1853	35,453.39	163,752	16.45	28.00	4,585,426	71,052,135	22.20	22
23	St. Paul, Minn.	1854	11,635.00	163,612	10.79	45.88	7,506,107	91,891,590	21.79	23
24	Rochester, N. Y.	1834	31,485.00	162,435	14.12	61.58	10,002,762	120,430,972	37.70	24
25	Denver, Colo.	1861	18,284.20	133,859	15.05	19.66	2,631,253	62,202,495	33.20	25
26	Toledo, Ohio	1837	5,930.00	131,822	13.90	43.56	5,741,775	51,780,405	18.80	26
27	Allegheny, Pa.	1840	10,400.00	129,896	16.95	43.28	5,621,740	81,811,100	27.50	27
28	Columbus, Ohio	1834	21,272.80	125,560	10.83	48.26	6,059,146	64,344,999	16.00	28
29	Worcester, Mass.	1848	10,041.00	118,421	15.20	45.16	5,346,397	112,336,099	19.33	29
30	Syracuse, N. Y.	1857	10,240.00	108,374	13.49	68.09	7,379,339	80,759,231	21.00	30
31	New Haven, Conn.	1784	14,340.00	108,027	15.85	31.42	3,364,846	67,322,575	25.00	31
32	Paterson, N. J.	1851	3,357.00	105,171	19.34	32.67	3,435,820	47,575,561		32

33	Fall River, Mass.	1854	26,210.00	104,863	18.35	35.17	3,688,434	71,601,670	$17.80	33
34	St. Joseph, Mo.	1851	9,400.00	102,979	8.02	14.12	1,451,160	21,914,740	28.50	34
35	Omaha, Neb.	1857	15,680.00	102,555	11.57	55.26	5,607,631	34,907,399	50.16	35
36	Los Angeles, Cal.	1850	27,774.49	102,479	16.01	15.54	1,599,429	65,674,282	29.60	36
37	Memphis, Tenn.	1827	10,240.00	103,320	21.03	29.54	3,022,707	37,788,944	—	37
38	Scranton, Pa.	1866	12,160.40	102,026	16.88	8.37	853,915	21,749,891	37.30	38
39	Lowell, Mass.	1850	7,053.00	94,969	19.46	34.84	3,308,865	71,255,587	19.60	39
40	Albany, N. Y.	1605	9,207.00	94,151	20.90	35.45	3,337,821	66,841,295	22.60	40
41	Cambridge, Mass.	1846	4,182.48	91,886	16.75	65.58	6,026,182	91,542,795	17.10	41
42	Portland, Ore.	1851	25,600.10	90,426	9.51	61.81	5,589,325	38,685,411	32.00	42
43	Atlanta, Ga.	1837	7,030.00	89,872	23.01	31.25	2,808,910	52,249,058	21.60	43
44	Grand Rapids, Mich.	1850	11,200.00	87,565	13.16	22.28	1,980,822	27,271,186	30.32	44
45	Dayton, Ohio	1830	6,720.00	85,333	14.19	41.75	3,562,933	42,565,240	25.60	45
46	Richmond, Va.	1712	5,626.00	85,050	18.57	80.62	6,250,602	64,552,621	18.10	46
47	Nashville, Tenn.	1806	5,990.00	80,865	23.34	42.21	3,401,580	36,479,356	24.50	47
48	Seattle, Wash.	1869	30,750.00	80,671	7.43	56.65	3,570,765	32,193,262	22.50	48
49	Hartford, Conn.	1784	11,065.00	79,850	17.92	47.61	3,801,597	68,242,427	17.50	49
50	Reading, Pa.	1847	3,605.00	78,961	13.25	17.37	1,371,567	43,480,679	14.30	50
51	Wilmington, Del.	1732	6,519.00	76,508	16.91	26.48	2,025,701	26,597,162	20.60	51
52	Camden, N. J.	1828	5,640.00	75,935	16.53	32.31	2,453,772	30,833,581	22.60	52
53	Trenton, N. J.	1792	3,105.50	73,307	15.82	35.05	2,369,575	61,516,030	21.50	53
54	Bridgeport, Conn.	1836	8,570.00	70,996	15.09	18.31	1,299,976	51,091,948	12.92	54
55	Lynn, Mass.	1630	7,251.20	68,513	14.88	53.64	3,675,146	42,391,945	17.80	55
56	Oakland, Cal.	1854	20,480.00	66,960	13.49	7.24	454,600	30,914,722	24.10	56
57	Lawrence, Mass.	1853	4,577.00	62,559	19.73	23.79	1,488,162	56,107,413	15.60	57
58	New Bedford, Mass.	1847	12,373.00	62,442	18.59	49.35	3,081,820	14,324,950	19.29	58
59	Des Moines, Iowa	1857	34,560.00	62,139	10.75	12.42	771,953	69,970,747	13.60	59
60	Springfield, Mass.	1636	24,661.30	62,059	15.11	32.80	2,035,419	51,262,400	16.30	60
61	Somerville, Mass.	1842	2,720.80	61,643	12.99	29.24	1,502,500	47,626,797	17.66	61
62	Troy, N. Y.	1716	3,368.00	60,651	21.05	24.72	1,499,234	28,048,800	24.30	62
63	Hoboken, N. J.	1845	450.00	59,364	19.17	25.37	1,586,639	75,370,060	25.42	63
64	Evansville, Ind.	1847	3,589.00	59,007	18.27	36.35	2,144,492	34,491,784	19.30	64
65	Manchester, N. H.	1846	21,700.00	56,987	18.66	29.95	1,506,963	37,576,687	22.55	65
66	Utica, N. Y.	1832	6,400.00	56,383	17.55	6.10	344,041	8,013,556	84.50	66
67	Peoria, Ill.	1845	3,290.00	56,100	12.55	12.04	675,532	17,293,458	37.13	67
68	Charleston, S. C.	1755	2,278.80	55,807	34.94	68.06	3,297,200	36,562,759	26.15	68
69	Savannah, Ga.	1733	3,264.00	54,244	29.39	59.59	3,257,750	30,640,204	27.00	69
70	Salt Lake City, Utah	1760	32,840.00	53,531	11.99	63.80	3,115,354	31,602,458	27.00	70
71	San Antonio, Tex.	1842	23,040.00	53,321	27.02	41.55	2,215,705	26,459,935	24.50	71
72	Duluth, Minn.	1870	11,000.65	52,969	10.93	113.47	6,010,442	19,299,621	24.00	72
73	Erie, Pa.	1851	4,420.00	52,733	13.24	14.78	729,510	17,151,100	29.60	73
74	Elizabeth, N. J.	1855	5,760.00	52,130	18.44	62.03	3,233,721	17,975,180	12.88	74
75	Wilkesbarre, Pa.	1871	3,109.12	51,721	13.75	11.46	997,741	6,138,864	61.60	75
76	Kansas City, Kan.	1886	9,600.00	51,418		34.25	1,761,205	25,618,000	17.00	76
77	Harrisburg, Pa.	1860	3,734.46	50,167	14.07	25.17	1,262,688	44,639,950	21.00	77
78	Portland, Me.	1632	11,680.00	50,145	17.69	26.25	1,326,549	36,603,455	21.00	78
79	Yonkers, N. Y.	1871	13,470.00	47,931	16.42	62.03	3,271,369	26,120,750	21.00	79
80	Norfolk, Va.	1845	2,240.00	46,624	22.93	68.25	3,750,543	32,00		80
81	Waterbury, Conn.	1853	2,400.00	45,859	17.12	80.66	904,457	11,937,107		81

POPULATION AND POPULAR VOTE BY STATES FOR PRESIDENTIAL ELECTORS 1900.

	Population By Twelfth Census.	Electoral Votes. McKinley Rep.	Bryan.	McKinley (Rep.).	Bryan (Dem.).	Woolley (Proh.).	Barker (People's).	Debs (Soc. Dem.).	Malloney (Social Labor).
Alabama	1,828,697		11	55,669	96,368	1,407	3,797	. . .	. . .
Arkansas	1,311,564		8	44,800	81,142	584	972	. . .	. . .
California	1,485,053	9	. .	164,755	124,985	5,024	. . .	7,572	. . .
Colorado	539,700		4	93,072	122,733	3,790	389	684	714
Connecticut	908,355	6	. .	102,572	74,014	1,617	. . .	1,029	908
Delaware	184,735	3	. .	22,560	18,863	546	. . .	57	. . .
Florida	528,542		4	7,499	28,007	2,239	1,090	603	. . .
Georgia	2,216,329		13	35,036	81,700	1,396	4,584	. . .	. . .
Idaho	161,771		3	27,198	29,414	857	213	. . .	. . .
Illinois	4,821,550	24	. .	597,985	503,061	17,626	1,141	9,687	1,373
Indiana	2,516,463	15	. .	336,063	309,584	13,718	1,438	2,374	663
Iowa	2,251,829	13	. .	307,808	209,265	9,502	613	2,742	259
Kansas	1,469,496	10	. .	185,955	162,601	3,605	. . .	1,605	. . .
Kentucky	2,147,174		13	226,801	234,899	2,429	2,017	760	289
Louisiana	1,381,627		8	14,233	53,671	. . .	. . .	. . .	. . .
Maine	694,366	6	. .	65,415	36,823	2,585	. . .	878	. . .
Maryland	1,189,946	8	. .	136,212	122,271	4,582	. . .	908	391
Massachusetts	2,805,346	15	. .	239,147	157,016	6,208	. . .	9,716	2,610
Michigan	2,119,762	14	. .	316,269	211,685	11,859	837	2,826	903
Minnesota	1,751,395	9	. .	190,461	112,901	8,555	. . .	3,065	1,329
Mississippi	1,551,372		9	5,753	51,706	. . .	1,644	. . .	. . .
Missouri	3,107,117		17	314,093	351,913	5,963	4,244	6,128	1,249
Montana	243,289		3	25,373	37,146	298	. . .	708	116
Nebraska	1,068,901	8	. .	121,835	114,013	3,686	1,104	823	. . .
Nevada	42,334		3	3,849	6,347	. . .	. . .	. . .	. . .
New Hampshire	411,588	4	. .	54,798	35,489	1,261	. . .	790	. . .
New Jersey	1,883,669	10	. .	221,707	164,808	7,183	669	4,609	2,074
New York	7,268,009	36	. .	821,992	678,386	22,043	. . .	12,869	12,622
North Carolina	1,891,992		11	133,081	157,752	1,009	830	. . .	. . .
North Dakota	319,040	3	. .	35,891	20,519	731	110	518	. . .
Ohio	4,157,545	23	. .	543,918	474,882	10,203	251	4,847	1,688
Oregon	413,532	4	. .	46,526	33,385	2,536	275	1,494	. . .
Pennsylvania	6,301,365	32	. .	712,665	424,232	27,908	638	4,851	2,936
Rhode Island	428,566	4	. .	33,784	19,812	1,592	. . .	. . .	1,423
South Carolina	1,340,512		9	3,525	47,283	. . .	. . .	. . .	. . .
South Dakota	401,559	4	. .	54,530	39,544	1,542	339	169	. . .
Tennessee	2,022,728		12	123,608	145,250	3,900	1,368	410	. . .
Texas	3,048,828		15	130,641	267,132	2,644	20,981	1,846	192
Utah	276,565	3	. .	47,089	44,949	205	. . .	717	106
Vermont	343,641	4	. .	42,569	12,819	383	367	. . .	. . .
Virginia	1,854,184		12	115,895	146,080	2,150	. . .	. . .	. . .
Washington	517,672	4	. .	57,456	44,833	2,345	. . .	1,906	1,066
West Virginia	958,900	6	. .	119,851	98,791	1,586	279	286	. . .
Wisconsin	2,068,963	12	. .	265,866	159,285	10,124	. . .	7,095	524
Wyoming	92,531	3	. .	14,482	10,164	. . .	2	. . .	. . .
Total	74,627,907	292	153	7,217,677	6,357,853	207,368	50,192	94,551	33,450

TERRITORIES, ETC.

Alaska (estimate)	44,000	. .	. .	. .	. .	. .	. .	. .	. .
Arizona	122,212	. .	. .	. .	. .	. .	. .	. .	. .
District of Columbia	278,718	. .	. .	. .	. .	. .	. .	. .	. .
Hawaii	154,001	. .	. .	. .	. .	. .	. .	. .	. .
Indian Territory	391,960	. .	. .	. .	. .	. .	. .	. .	. .
New Mexico	193,777	. .	. .	. .	. .	. .	. .	. .	. .
Oklahoma	398,245	. .	. .	. .	. .	. .	. .	. .	. .
Total	76,210,820	. .	. .	. .	. .	. .	. .	. .	. .

In March, 1901, an event of leading importance took place in the Philippine Islands in the capture of Emile Aguinaldo, President of the Philippine government and commander-in-chief of its forces. On February 28th, General Funston had captured a messenger bearing letters from the insurgent leader, which revealed the fact that he was then at the town of Palanan, in northwest Luzon. Funston at once devised a plan and organized a force for his capture.

The expedition consisted of seventy-eight Macabebe scouts, dressed as insurgents and laborers, and four ex-insurgent officers. The only Americans were Funston and four other officers, who had disguised themselves as privates. Funston had prepared two decoy letters, apparently signed by the insurgent general Lacuna, whose seal and correspondence he had captured some time before. These stated that Lacuna was sending his superior the best company under his command.

Landing from the gunboat Vicksburg, the party made a toilsome march over a very rugged country. They reached Palanan on March 23d. Aguinaldo was completely deceived by the letters, and the story told him that the Americans were part of a surveying party which had been surprised on the march, part being killed and part taken. His household guards were drawn up to receive the visitors and their captives. Suddenly the mask was thrown off, firing began, and one of the ex-insurgent officers seized and held him firmly. His attendants and body-guard at once took to flight, and in a few minutes the affair was at an end, and the Filipino leader was a captive to the Americans. The expedition had proved a complete success. The important prisoner was brought to Manila, and confined there in the Malacanan Palace. Here he soon regained his calmness, talked freely, and was visited by a number of prominent Filipinos, who sought to convince him that the struggle was hopeless, and advised him to use his influence with the people to establish peace. Their arguments were effective, Aguinaldo expressed his satisfaction with the form of government, and on April 2d he took the oath of allegiance to the United States.

The effect of his capture proved highly favorable. Several prominent insurgent leaders at once surrendered themselves and their bands, and it seemed as if a new era of peace was about to dawn. Aguinaldo, who had apparently experienced a change of opinion, did his share towards hastening it by sending peace emissaries to the chiefs still in arms and signing a peace manifesto for distribution among the people. General Funston's brilliant exploit was not left unrewarded. Its value was heightened by the great risk he had run in his daring deed, and on March 30th President McKinley promoted him to the rank of Brigadier-General in the United States army. His comrades were also suitably rewarded for their participation in the exploit, which was looked upon as the most signal instance of courage and daring during the entire war.

A VIEW OF TEMPLE OF MUSIC, BUFFALO, PAN-AMERICAN EXPOSITION

After two years of more or less active warfare the struggle in the Philippines was practically at an end. There were still some bands of brigands in the mountains, as there had been for centuries, but the revolutionists ceased their opposition, and the Taft Commission, appointed by President McKinley to establish a liberal form of government in the islands, met with the greatest success in its work. At the same time a large number of teachers were sent out from the United States to establish schools in the islands, and thus confer upon their people the highest boon which this country was able to bestow—that of education on liberal principles.

PAN-AMERICAN EXPOSITION.

Among the events of the opening year of the twentieth century one of the most interesting was the Pan-American Exposition, held in the city of Buffalo, N. Y., from May 1 to November 1. This project was first planned in 1897, the exposition to be held on a small scale, in 1899, on Cayuga Island, near Niagara Falls. The Spanish-American War, however, checked this project, and when it was revived it was on a more ambitious scale. Buffalo was chosen as the site, and the original 50 acres were expanded into 350 acres, the ground chosen including the most beautiful portions of Delaware Park. A fund of $5,000,000 was provided by the city and citizens of Buffalo, appropriations were made by the State of New York and the Federal Government, and the work was begun on an estimate of $10,000,000 of expenditures.

The purpose of this Exposition is clearly indicated in its name. It concerned itself solely with the countries of the two Americas and the new possessions of the United States, of which it was proposed to show the progress during the nineteenth century, a leading object of the enterprise being to bring into closer relations, commercially and socially, the republics and colonies of the Western Hemisphere and promote intercourse between their peoples. The Department of State, in June, 1899, invited the various American governments to take part in the enterprise, and acceptances were very generally received.

The preparations made for the Exposition were of the most admirable character, and, when completed, the grounds and buildings presented a magnificent scene. While on a smaller scale than the Philadelphia and Chicago World's Fairs, the Buffalo Fair surpassed all previous ones in architectural beauty. Instead of presenting the pure white of the Columbian Exposition, there was a generous use of brilliant colors and rich tints, which gave a glowing rainbow effect to the artistically grouped buildings; the general style of architecture being a free treatment of the Spanish Renaissance, in compliment to the Latin-American countries taking part. The elaborate hydraulic and fountain

arrangements, the horticultural and floral settings, and the sculptural ornament-
ation, added greatly to the general effect.

Of the varied elements of the display, that of electricity stood first, the enormous electrical plant at Niagara and its connection by wire with Buffalo affording unequalled facilities in this direction.   The Electric Tower, 375 feet high, was
the centre-piece of the Exposition, the edifice itself being stately and beautiful
and its electric display on the grandest scale. The vari-colored electrical fountain
was strikingly beautiful.   There were winding canals, caverns and grottoes,
water cascades, towers, domes and pinnacles, and other objects of attraction, not
the least of them the Midway, with its diversified display, a feature which has
become indispensable to all recent enterprises of this character.

The exhibits were divided into fifteen classes, ranging from fine arts to
transportation, and including displays from the Hawaiian and Philippine
Islands.   During the summer and autumn the attendance was very large, the
near vicinity of Niagara Falls, with its supreme scenic grandeur, forming a
splendid addition to the commercial and industrial attractions of the Fair.

TRANS-CONTINENTAL TOUR OF THE PRESIDENT.

Another event of much public interest which marked the year 1901 was a
grand tour of the entire country projected by President McKinley, on a scale
far surpassing those undertaken by preceding Presidents, its limits being the
Atlantic and Pacific in the East and West, and the Gulf and Lake States in the
North and South.   Leaving Washington on May 7th in a special train, whose
cars were provided with every convenience and luxury which art could devise
and skill provide, and following roads where the utmost care and precaution
were taken to insure ease, safety and comfort of travel, the party proceeded
through the southern portion of its route, the President being received in all
the large cities and towns with a generous enthusiasm which spoke volumes for
the unity of sentiment throughout the country.   His appreciative remarks and
well-chosen responses to addresses of welcome added greatly to the kindly feeling with which he was everywhere received.   Unfortunately the severe illness
of Mrs. McKinley, after San Francisco had been reached, put an end to the
tour when half completed.   The life of the "Lady of the White House" was
despaired of, but she recovered sufficiently to be brought back by the shortest
route to Washington, attended at every point by her loving husband with the
most assiduous and anxious care.

The presence of the President in Washington was needed, for important
political questions had arisen demanding his immediate attention and extended
consultation with the members of his cabinet.   These arose in consequence of a
decision of the Supreme Court of the United States fixing the status of our

THE PRESIDENT'S TRAIN ON HIS CALIFORNIA TRIP

insular possessions. In a number of instances duties had been collected on goods imported from Porto Rico and Hawaii to this country, and in one instance fourteen diamonds brought by a soldier from the Philippine Islands had been seized for non-payment of duty. Several law-suits brought for the recovery of these duties, on the claim that they had been illegally exacted, were decided adversely to the claimants by the lower courts, and appeals were taken to the Supreme Court. A decision was rendered by this court on May 28, 1901, in the suit of DeLima & Co., merchants of New York, which covered all the cases involved except the Philippine one, which was left in doubt. This opinion, announced by Justice Brown, was concurred in by five members of the court, Chief Justice Fuller and Associate Justices Brown, Brewer, Harlan and Peckham, and dissented from by Justices Gray, Shiras, White and McKenna.

The decision was to the effect, that before the Treaty of Paris Porto Rico was a foreign country and its exports were subject to full duties. After that treaty it became a domestic territory, and as such subject to the jurisdiction of Congress while it continued a territorial possession, the decision being that Congress has the right to administer the government of a territory and to lay such duties upon its commerce as it deems suitable. The effect of this decision was that, from the signing of the Treaty of Paris till the passage of the Foraker act fixing the duties at 15 per cent., no duties could legally be collected on Porto Rican goods. After that act was passed the duties designated by it could be exacted.

This crucial decision fixes the status of all our insular possessions under civil control. But the court adjourned without rendering an opinion on the Philippine case, and as the Philippine Islands differed from Porto Rico in being under military control, the question as to the right of the government to collect duties upon Philippine goods remained unsettled. Many held that the President had no authority to exact duties, and that it would be necessary to call an extra session of Congress in order to pass a law governing the Philippine customs; but the President decided that this was not needed, and that existing acts of Congress governed this special case.

AFFAIRS IN CUBA AND CHINA.

This was one of the questions which confronted President McKinley on his return to Washington. Another had to do with Cuban affairs. The Cuban Constitutional Convention had accepted the Act of Congress fixing the relations between the United States and Cuba and establishing what might be called a mild form of protectorate over the island; but its acceptance was vitiated by conditions which the President declined to accept, and the question was returned to the convention with the decisive understanding that the Platt amendment must be accepted in its entirety, or the military occupation of Cuba would necessarily continue. On June 12, 1901, the Cuban Convention accepted this amendment in its original form, and the sole obstacle to Cuban independence was removed.

Meanwhile the Chinese situation had been modified by the withdrawal of the American troops, except a legation guard; other nations also ordering the withdrawal of their troops and restoring the government to the Chinese. The indemnity demanded from and accepted by China amounted to $237,000,000, with interest at not over 4 per cent. This large sum was objected to by the United States Government, but was adopted on the demand of the other nations concerned.

OTHER EVENTS OF NATIONAL IMPORTANCE.

Among other events of national importance was the settlement of the vexed question of the number of soldiers in the army. The provision to make it 100,000 men was modified on suggestion of General Miles, and the number fixed at 76,000, making one soldier for every 1000 of the population. The problem of a ship canal from the Atlantic to the Pacific was also given a new phase by a proposition from the French Panama Canal Company to sell their partly completed canal to the United States. This opened the question as to the comparative availability of the two routes, the Nicaragua and the Panama, and left the final choice open to future decision.

In the spring of 1901 a signal discovery of petroleum was made in the southwest, a well being opened at Beaumont, Texas, which threw a six-inch stream of oil a hundred feet into the air. Other rich wells were subsequently opened, some of them in Louisiana and Tennessee, and great excitement prevailed in the speculative world. The oil differed essentially from that of Pennsylvania, being ill adapted to refining and principally suitable for fuel.

One of the most striking events of the year was the formation of an industrial combination on an unprecedented scale, a gigantic union of the steel manufacturing interests of the country, with the immense capital of $1,100,000,000. A line of steamships was purchased in the interest of this concern, the railroad magnates of the country added to their holdings, and showed indications of an eventual general combination of transportation facilities, and the public stood aghast at these vast operations, in doubt as to where they would end, or how the interests of the great multitude would be affected. In the spring of 1902 this combination of interests was added to by a stupendous amalgamation of the trans-Atlantic steam-ship lines, embracing nearly all the great passenger and freight steam-ships plying between Europe and America; the whole controlled by the American capitalists, who were at the head of the new steel and railroad combinations. It was with such vast financial and industrial operations that the new century began its career.

On the afternoon of Friday, September 6, 1901, this country and the whole world were thrown into consternation as the news was flashed over the wires that President McKinley had fallen by the hand of an assassin. That day had been appointed as Presidents' Day at the Pan-American Exposition held at Buffalo, and elaborate preparations had been made to make this the event of the Exposition, all the high dignitaries of State, including the representatives of all the American governments, were in attendance. On September 5th the President delivered a speech, which was easily his greatest effort, advocating reciprocity in trade and greater encouragement to commerce. On the morning of the 6th, with his wife and party, he had visited Niagara Falls and inspected the Exposition. After luncheon he was to hold a public reception in the Temple of Music to meet his countrymen and take them by the hand. No trouble was anticipated, although precautions had been taken to avoid mishaps. President McKinley, assisted by President Milburn and others, received the people as they moved by in a long, continuous line, shaking hands and smiling upon each. The would-be assassin was a rather tall, boyish-looking fellow, apparently 25 years old; about his right hand was wrapped a handkerchief, giving the impression to the officers that his hand was injured, especially as he extended his left across the right to shake hands with the President.

Innocently facing the assassin, the President smiled as he extended his right hand to meet the left of the man before him. As the youth extended his left hand he suddenly raised his right, the one which held the pistol, and before any one knew what was transpiring two shots rang out, one following the other after the briefest portion of a second. For the first moment there was not a sound.

The President drew his right hand quickly to his chest, raised his head, and his eyes looked upward and rolled. He swerved a moment, reeled and was caught in the arms of Secretary Cortelyou to his right. Catching himself for the briefest second, President McKinley, whose face was now the whiteness of death, looked at the assassin as the officers and soldiers bore him to the floor, and said, feebly: "May God forgive him." The President was first helped to a chair but was quickly removed on a stretcher to the emergency hospital, and all the eminent surgeons within reach were summoned.

Two wounds were located, one in the breast, which was not serious, and the other in the abdomen, which proved fatal. There was every hope at first that he would recover, but after some days there came a relapse, and, although all that surgical and medical skill could do was done, President McKinley passed away early on the morning of September 14th. His last words were memorable: "It's God's way; His will, not ours, be done."

The world joined the American people in mourning the beloved President. He was given a state funeral at Washington, September 17th, and buried at Canton, his home city, September 19th, amid impressive ceremonies.

THE ASSASSIN.

The man who assassinated President McKinley was Leon Czolgosz, a Russian Pole and an anarchist. At the time of the assassination he was described as follows: "He is twenty-eight years of age, slim, of dark complexion, with an intelligent and rather pleasing face. His features are straight and regular. He dresses with considerable neatness. There is nothing in his appearance that would attract unusual attention. He is not a suspicious-looking person."

Czolgosz's parents were born in Russian Poland. They came to this country about 1865 as immigrants, and settled in the West. Czolgosz was born in Detroit, and hence was not an immigrant. He received some education in the common schools of that city, but left school and went to work when a boy as a blacksmith's apprentice. Later he read all the socialistic literature which he could obtain, and finally began to take part in socialistic meetings. In time he became fairly well known in Chicago, Cleveland and Detroit, not only as a socialist, but as an anarchist of the most bitter type.

Czolgosz was placed on trial in Buffalo, September 23d, and was given able counsel to protect his interests. After an unsensational and impartial trial he was found guilty, and, on September 26th, he was sentenced to die in the electric chair at Auburn Prison, in the State of New York. The execution took place in the early morning of October 29, 1901, in the presence of twenty-two witnesses and the prison officials.

PRESIDENT McKINLEY'S BODY IN THE EAST ROOM, THE WHITE HOUSE

The United States and the Twentieth Century Problems.

By the provision of the Constitution governing the succession, Theodore Roosevelt, the Vice-President, became President of the United States upon the death of William McKinley. He was at the time seeking recreation in the Adirondacks, but, on receiving the news, he sped with all haste to Buffalo, where, on September 14th, he took the oath of office, at the same time pledging himself to carry out the policy of his predecessor.

Theodore Roosevelt was born October 27, 1858, in the city of New York, and therefore attained to the Presidency in his forty-third year, being the youngest of all our Presidents. Graduating from Harvard University in 1880, he quickly grew active in New York politics, and in 1881 was elected a member of the Assembly. He served for three years in that body, in which he became influential and took a leading part in reform legislation for New York City.

In 1884 he was the Republican candidate for Mayor of New York, and, though defeated, received a large vote. He was appointed in 1889, by President Harrison, on the Civil Service Commission, and in 1895 became Police Commissioner of New York. His earnestness and energy for reform in both of these offices won him a national reputation, and led, in April, 1897, to his appointment as Assistant Secretary of the Navy. Here, too, he did excellent work, but as soon as war with Spain was assured he resigned, organized the regiment of cowboy cavalry familiarly known as " Roosevelt's Rough Riders," and made himself the most popular figure in the Santiago campaign in Cuba. Coming home as the real hero of the military part of the war, as Dewey was of the naval, he was, in the autumn of 1898, elected Governor of New York, and, in 1900, much against his own desire, was given the Republican nomination for Vice-President. Some of the party leaders hoped thus to " shelve " this energetic and unmanageable favorite of the people in a passive post of honor, but, as

405

events proved, the nomination led him to the highest office in the gift of the American people.

OPENING OF THE ADMINISTRATION.

The President's demeanor in the elevated position to which he had so suddenly and unexpectedly been raised was one that inspired public confidence and met with general approval. In addition to his pledge to conform to the policy of the McKinley administration, he requested all the members of the Cabinet to remain in office till the end of his term. These assurances dissipated the feeling of dread that the new President might inaugurate an untried and disastrous policy, as in some previous instances of the same kind.

The first official act of President Roosevelt was to issue a proclamation appointing Thursday, September 19th, as a day of mourning for the lamented late President. In the impressive funeral obsequies which followed he took part as chief mourner on the part of the nation, and comported himself with a grave dignity well suited to the situation, and winning him fresh public esteem.

THE NICARAGUA CANAL.

Several events of much importance took place in the early months of the new administration, chief among them being what is known as the Hay-Pauncefote Treaty—a convention between the United States and Great Britain to establish a new status of these powers in Nicaragua.

For years the desirability of constructing an inter-oceanic ship canal across Nicaragua or the Isthmus had been strongly felt. Much work in excavation had been done by private companies; but these having failed, Congress became inclined to make the enterprise a national one, the United States to construct and control the canal. Commissions of engineers were sent to investigate and report on the most available route, with the result of that across Nicaragua, via the San Juan River and Lake Nicaragua, being given the preference.

One thing stood in the way of this, the Clayton-Bulwer Treaty of 1850, which still held good in spite of various efforts for its repeal. This treaty established a joint control between the United States and Great Britain over any canal that might be made, an arrangement by no means satisfactory in case the United States should construct it alone. As this treaty had wrecked several efforts to carry a canal bill through Congress, a new treaty was negotiated in 1900, but failed of acceptance, as it did not remove the old difficulty. Finally, in 1901, a second treaty was prepared by Secretary Hay and Lord Pauncefote, the British Ambassador, in which the Clayton-Bulwer Treaty was formally set aside, and the United States given sole control of the canal; which, however, was to be free and open to the vessels of all nations. This treaty was ratified by the Senate on December 16, 1901.

Bills for the construction of a canal at the cost of the United States were now introduced into both Houses of Congress, the estimated cost being $189,-000,000. The House bill was passed early in January, 1902, with only two negative votes. But before the Senate could act the situation took on a new phase. The Panama Canal, partly excavated by the De Lesseps Company, and upon which a new company had been engaged, was offered to the United States at a cost of $40,000,000. As it was about two-fifths finished, it was estimated that at this price it could be completed more cheaply than the Nicaragua Canal. It presented other advantages also, and the commission now reported in its favor. The Senate, however, deferred action upon the subject.

PAN-AMERICAN CONGRESS.

On October 22, 1901, there met in the city of Mexico a congress of delegates from the United States and the various other American Republics, to consider questions of policy concerning the relations of the peoples of the Western Continent. The most important subject dealt with by this Pan-American Congress, as it was called, was that of international arbitration. An agreement was made to adopt the regulations made at the Hague Arbitration Conference, and a majority of the delegates went so far as to favor compulsory arbitration. This failed through the opposition of Chili, unanimous approval being necessary.

THE SCHLEY COURT OF INQUIRY.

A more immediate subject of interest was the action of the Naval Court of Inquiry convened at the request of Admiral Schley to investigate his conduct during the war with Spain. Since this war a controversy had existed between his friends and those of Admiral Sampson, one party claiming for Schley, the other for Sampson, the honor of commanding in the great fight with the Spanish squadron at Santiago. A scurrilous attack made upon Schley by the author of a history of the United States Navy, an extreme Sampson partisan, was the immediate cause of Admiral Schley's attempt to obtain vindication.

The court convened at Washington, September 12, 1901, with Admiral Dewey as presiding officer and Admirals Benham and Ramsay as the remaining members. Its decision was made public on December 13th. In this decision the majority of the court, while giving Schley credit for courage, found him blamable in several important particulars, including the famous "loop," or turn of the "Brooklyn" away from the Spanish vessels.

Admiral Dewey gave a minority report, in which he sustained Schley in most of these particulars, and said further: "He was in absolute command, and is entitled to the credit due to such commanding officer for the glorious victory which resulted in the total destruction of the Spanish ships."

Secretary of the Navy Long approved of the majority finding of the court, whereupon Admiral Schley made a personal appeal to the President for a revision of the case. After a full study of the evidence, Roosevelt dismissed the whole affair, with the implication that neither of the contestants had won any special honor, remarking that no action had been taken on any ship " in obedience to the orders of either Sampson or Schley, save on their own two vessels. It was a captain's fight." This decision was soon followed by the death of Admiral Sampson, which took place May 6, 1902.

EXPOSITIONS OF ART AND INDUSTRY.

The Pan-American Exposition at Buffalo closed at the beginning of November, and on December 1st there was inaugurated at Charleston, S. C., a South Carolina Inter-state and West Indian Exposition, to remain open for six months.

This exposition was opened by President Roosevelt, who touched an electric button in the White House, at Washington, and set the machinery in motion. It embraced a general exhibit of the results of industry in the South, while many Northern States and a number of the West India Islands contributed. While on a smaller scale than the Buffalo Exposition, the buildings were artistic and handsome, and the exhibits highly attractive, reflecting great credit on the enterprise and industry of the South. An exposition on a much larger scale, a World's Fair at St. Louis, commemorating the purchase of Louisiana Territory in 1803, is projected for 1904.

ROOSEVELT'S FIRST MESSAGE.

President Roosevelt's message to the Fifty-seventh Congress, at its opening session, was looked for with intense interest. During the brief period in which he had occupied the presidential chair he had won popular applause, while faith in his sturdy integrity and admiration for his stalwart independence of character gained him friends in all parties. But the exact stand he would take on the great public questions of the day was not known, and the people awaited his message with a degree of anxiety.

The document, when issued, was therefore read with avidity. It showed the hand of a practiced author and clear thinker, and its treatment of the varied topics reviewed was held to be able and promising. The hand of the earnest reformer, yet of the self-contained statesman, was evident throughout.

Several of the problems referred to in the President's message became subjects of Congressional action. Among these was the canal question, already mentioned, and the passage of a bill regulating tariff charges upon Philippine commerce. The tariff on exports from Porto Rico had been abolished by

President McKinley, in accordance with the terms of the act of Congress in the summer of 1901. On March 8, 1902, a Philippine tariff bill was enacted by which the duties on exports to the United States were reduced twenty-five per cent.

The war taxes imposed to provide funds for the war with Spain were found, after the expenses of this war had been met, to yield an excess of revenue. In consequence, a strong demand for their repeal was made. The principal stamp taxes had been taken off in 1901, and in 1902 the remainder of these taxes were repealed, the country returning to its ante-war revenue status. Another Congressional measure of importance had to do with the act for the exclusion of the Chinese. This expired in the spring of 1902, and a renewal of the " yellow-peril," in the form of a great influx of Chinese laborers, was threatened. This was prevented by a re-enactment of the law. It was made to apply also to the Philippine Islands, which had hitherto been freely open to Chinese immigration. Still another Congressional measure was the establishment of a permanent census bureau. The work in this field of labor had so increased that it was deemed necessary to keep it in continuous action.

CUBAN RECIPROCITY.

Among the measures considered during this session of Congress, one of the most important had to do with Cuban affairs. In accordance with the constitution adopted for the new Republic of Cuba, an election was held on the last day of 1901, Tomas Estrada Palma being chosen for President. The final act in giving full independence to the island republic was the withdrawal of United States troops, which was fixed to take place May 20, 1902.

But the Cubans found their new independence likely to prove a serious economic burden. Cuba being a foreign country, only temporarily under American supervision, the full tariff charges of the United States revenue law were enforced against its exports. Of these the most important was sugar, whose production was the leading industry of the island. This product was chiefly consumed in the United States. But it could not compete profitably with the beet-sugar of Europe, and unless some tariff concession was made the sugar planters would be in peril of ruin.

President Roosevelt, feeling that we owed some degree of protection to the country which we had launched on the high seas of independence, advocated in his message a measure of tariff reciprocity with Cuba, and a bill was introduced in Congress for a partial remission of the duty on sugar.

VISIT OF PRINCE HENRY.

A very interesting event of the spring of 1902 was the visit to this country of Prince Henry, brother of the Emperor William II. of Germany. A yacht, the *Meteor*, had been built for the Emperor at New York, and the ostensible purpose of the Prince's visit was to be present at the launching of this yacht. This took place immediately after his arrival, Miss Alice Roosevelt, eldest daughter of the President, being chosen to perform the christening ceremony.

Reaching New York on February 23d, the Prince was taken through a whirl of fêtes, receptions, dinners, and other excitements, enough to turn his head. He was rushed over the country at breakneck speed, the limits of his journey being Chattanooga in the South, and Chicago and Milwaukee in the North and West. He sailed again for Europe on March 11th, doubtless feeling a relief at his escape from the hands of his too ardent entertainers.

CABINET CHANGES.

Though when President Roosevelt took up the reins of office he did so under full relations of amity with the McKinley Cabinet and with a statement that he would make no changes in the personnel of this Cabinet, yet, from various causes, a number of changes took place before the expiration of his first year in office. In December the resignation of Charles Emory Smith, Postmaster-General, was handed in, the demands of business requiring him to withdraw from departmental duties. He was succeeded by Hon. Henry C. Payne, of Milwaukee.

A few months afterward Lyman D. Gage, Secretary of the Treasury, similarly resigned, also yielding to business necessities, and feeling that he had given to this high office all the time he could wisely devote to it. Hon. Leslie M. Shaw, the retiring governor of Iowa, was selected as his successor.

A third withdrawal was that of John D. Long, Secretary of the Navy, to take effect May 1, 1902. Hon. William H. Moody, of Massachusetts, was chosen to succeed him.

THE DANISH WEST INDIES AND THE PHILIPPINE QUESTION.

The year 1898 was the beginning of an epoch of island additions to United States territory, Porto Rico, the Philippines and Guam being obtained that year as a result of the war with Spain, and Hawaii by peaceful annexation. In 1899 Tutuila and some smaller islands of the Samoan group were acquired by treaty. The next island acquisition was the Danish West India possessions, including St. Thomas, St. Croix, and St. John, lying to the east of Porto Rico. These had been ceded to the United States in 1867 for $7,500,000, but the Senate had rejected the treaty. They were purchased in 1902 for $5,000,000. These islands are small, but contain the valuable harbor of St. Thomas, or Charlotte Amalia.

The question of what should be done with the Philippine Islands came prominently before Congress in the opening year of the Roosevelt administration. The capture of Aguinaldo had gone far toward bringing the guerrilla warfare in these islands to an end. It had been followed by numerous surrenders of leaders and soldiers, until the only active opposition was that maintained in two of the southern provinces of Luzon and the small island of Samar.

General Lukban, the Filipino leader in the latter, was captured in February, 1902, and in April his successor surrendered, with all his men. General Malvar, the leader in Batangas and Laguna, the insurgent provinces of Luzon, also surrendered, and all opposition, beyond that of the bands of brigands which had existed for centuries, was at an end.

There was a marked difference of policy in the platforms of the two great parties as to what should be done eventually with the Philippines. The Republicans proposed to give them a stable system of government and hold them as island possessions of the United States. The Democrats favored the establishment of a stable government, but demanded that they should then be set free, as Cuba had been, this country simply guaranteeing their independence.

Congress, after passing the Philippine tariff bill, took up the question of government of the islands, but soon found itself concerned with a related matter of less desirable character. Charges of cruelty by our soldiers in the islands had long been made, but the government had ignored them. They now became too direct to be set aside. Evidence of the frequent use of the " water cure "— a mode of torture in which the victim is filled with water, which is then forced out of him—was given by a number of witnesses.

Still more disturbing was the news from Samar, where General Smith had issued orders to kill, burn and destroy—boys of over ten years of age to be among the killed. These orders had been literally carried out by Major Waller. The President at once ordered a trial by court-martial of General Smith, and in this it appeared that Smith had some warrant for his act in orders issued by his superiors. It was evident that deeds disgraceful to American citizenship had been done in the islands, and that a state of affairs existed under which peace in the Philippines could never be assured.

President Roosevelt's determination to probe these outrages to the bottom, and to inaugurate a more humane system in these new possessions of our country, was the only method by which peaceful conditions could be assured and the Filipinos be made consenting wards of the United States. This reform of the conditions existing in the Philippines the President could be trusted to inaugurate, and it was felt that these barbarous relics of the passions of war would no longer be suffered to prevail in lands under American rule.

VIEW OF THE CAPITOL, WASHINGTON

How Our National Government Does its Work.

BY MISS ANNA L. DAWES.

Author of Life A Summer, etc

THE CAPITOL AT WASHINGTON.

The Government of the United States is unique in three respects: It is the largest and most successful democracy that has ever existed, it is a federal system, and it has a written Constitution. Perhaps it may be called unique in its methods also, for no other government is made up of three separate and yet equal branches, each in some sense the Government, but all necessary to any complete action of the nation; and still again those departments, the Legislative, the Executive, and the Judiciary, have each their own peculiar and distinctive features. Legislation is representative and not democratic. The Executive has not only the duty of executing the laws, but a power of veto over them, and the Supreme Court stands alone in all the world in its place and importance.

The Government of the United States, in the expressive phrase of Abraham Lincoln, is "A government by the people, of the people, and for the people." It is often claimed that England is more democratic in fact, Germany more attentive to the needs of the people; but Briton and German alike hold that power comes from the throne and its reserved rights remain with the throne. But every American believes that power comes from the people, the Executive is in some sense an agent, and the reserved rights remain with the people. The difference is not only fundamental, but there result from it doctrines and relations which run through all our system and our methods as well. No amount of superficial flexibility, as in England, or of temporary advantage, as in Germany, can at all compensate for this great and far-reaching distinction, this confidence in and dependence upon the people. Again, we have two kinds of law—that made by Congress as the needs of the time require, law which may be altered according to occasion, and the great permanent Constitution, which only the people and the States acting together can alter, and that after long and careful process, and to which all other law must conform. This Constitution is truly enough the bulwark of our liberties ; no sudden whims or changing passions can deprive us of the fundamental rights guaranteed by it ; the storm of battle has proved it strong enough to stand against all assaults, and the stress of unequaled growth has shown it broad enough for all demands. It seems, indeed, as if a superhuman wisdom was given to the forefathers. Molded by Hamilton, and Franklin, and the Adamses, and Madison, and Ellsworth, and many another great man, it drew its inspiration from French philosophers and Dutch methods, and the mingled love and hate for English practice. The government of a little Baptist church in Pennsylvania, and the Connecticut town-meeting, and the conflicting interests of different sections, and many other elements entered in to make this great instrument what it is. Under it we have lived for one hundred years, and have stretched our boundaries from one ocean to the other, from the frozen seas of the Arctic Circle to the tropical waters of the Gulf. We have endured three wars, and are grown so strong that the great governments of Europe hesitate to encounter us, and sit by our side in equal honor ; we have become sixty million people, and our riches are matched with imperial treasuries, but our doors are ever open to the laborer and we give him all opportunity, until he shall stand at the top if it pleases him. Side by side the rich and the poor, the learned and the unlearned, the chief among us and the least of all, hold the great gift of governing, and we count them each a man ; and the whole great and glorious structure rests on the firm and enduring rock of the Constitution.

The Government is carried on, according to the terms of this Constitution, and under its provisions, by three great branches ; Congress, which makes the laws ; the Judiciary, which interprets these laws and decides whether they agree with the Constitution ; and the Executive, which carries them out. And since this is a government of the people, Congress, which represents the people and expresses their will, is the centre around which the whole government turns.

Congress is composed of two houses, the House of Representatives and the Senate. The House of Representatives is elected every two years, and each member of it represents somewhat more than 150,000 people. Each State sends as many Congressmen as are necessary to represent its whole population, being divided into districts containing each a population of 150,000, from among which the members of Congress are chosen. The requirement that the representative shall live within the State is an important distinction between our system and that of England. An English district or borough may elect a member of Parliament from any part of the nation, and thus it is believed the House of Commons will be composed of the best men in the country ; but it is our purpose to have every part of the country represented, and, therefore, by an unwritten law, never disregarded, we require that each Congressman shal. reside in the district which chooses him. Thus, so far as possible, every man in the country is represented. It must always be remembered, however, that the government of the United States is not a pure democracy, but a republic. It is first and foremost a *representative* government. In every possible way endeavor is made that each man shall be represented, but he must act through a representative. The short term of service insures that these representatives shall reflect the changing will of the people, and furnishes a remedy for all unjust or foolish action. He shows an entire ignorance of our system who complains of the tyranny of government in the United States. The House of Representatives is its chief governing power, and, remade as it is by the people themselves once in two years, it is constantly controlled by the will of the people.

This very fact, the fact that the House of Representatives can be altered so readily, and always will reflect every passing change of public sentiment, made it necessary and highly desirable to add some more permanent element to Congress. For this, among other reasons, a Senate was created. Senators are elected once in six years, and represent the people of a whole State. Thus, because he is more permanent, and because he is chosen by a larger constituency, a senator represents the more stable elements of political thought, not so much the passing feeling of the moment, but the deep underlying opinions and wishes

JAMES G. BLAINE, EX-SECRETARY OF STATE.

of a large number of people. Moreover, as the Senate is so arranged that only one senator from a State is elected at a time, and only one-third of the senators go out of office on any given year, it becomes in some sense a stable body, and acts as a check upon the excitements and lack of wisdom natural to such a body as the House.

Still another reason, and that of great importance, marks the value of the Senate to the people. It is, in fact, more necessary to the preservation of our system than the House itself. The senators represent the States directly, and each State has two senators, no more and no less. This places each State on an equal footing with every other, a result obviously an important element in our political system, and of the greatest practical importance to our liberties. By reason of this provision in our Constitution, Delaware or Rhode Island are of equal power in the Senate with Texas or New York, furnishing a check upon the unregulated control of any one section. If the Senate, like the House, represented the population and not the States, shortly enough Congress would be controlled by the great cities, or, perhaps, by the great States. The tyranny of New York or Chicago would be replaced by the tyranny of California or Texas. The immense mass of their people would always control the country, and we should be at the mercy of a practical monarchy. The equal power of the small States in the Senate goes far to prevent this result and to preserve the rule of the whole people, an actual as well as a nominal democracy. The Senate is altogether necessary to the country, and he is a false friend who would persuade the country to undermine it or destroy its relations to the States by making it a popular body. So thoroughly was this understood by the men who made the Constitution that a unique provision was inserted forbidding any amendment which should deprive the States of their equal representation in the Senate without their own consent, practically a prohibition of such an amendment.

Congress has power to raise funds for our necessities by taxes, to borrow money, if necessary, to establish postal facilities, to coin or print our money, to regulate our foreign affairs, to make war, to control many other matters, and to make all the laws relative to these concerns.

It requires both houses of Congress to pass the laws that govern us. A bill originates in the House or the Senate, according to its nature, is debated and passed by that body, sent to the other, debated and passed by that, and then sent to the President, who signs it, and thereby it becomes a law. If any of these conditions fail it falls to the ground. Either branch can refuse to pass a measure, and the President may refuse to sign, or veto it. But in this latter case, since the will of the people is the supreme power, the vetoed bill may be passed again, over the head of the President, as the phrase goes, if two-thirds of each house of Congress can be thereafter induced to vote for it. All bills for furnishing money must originate in the House of Representatives, that the people, by controlling the purse strings, may still more thoroughly control the Government. The Senate, on the other hand, has the power to consider and pass upon our treaties, and has also the duty of confirming or refusing all appointments of any importance.

The officers of the House of Representatives are a Speaker, elected from among its members, who presides over its deliberations, a Clerk, a Sergeant-at-Arms, a Doorkeeper, and several smaller officers necessary to carry on its business. The Senate is presided over by the Vice-President of the United States, and in his absence by one of the senators, chosen by themselves for that duty, and known as the President *pro tempore*. This body has also a Clerk and Sergeant-at-Arms and minor officials. The business of Congress is largely done by its committees, which consider all important subjects before they are brought to the attention of either house. These committees are appointed by the Speaker in the House of Representatives, and in the Senate are selected by a committee of the senators. Each Congress lasts for two years, although not in session all of the time. Congress meets in the Capitol at Washington on the first Monday in December of every year. The first year the session lasts until both houses can agree to adjourn, thus giving time for free and ample discussion of every subject. These "long sessions" usually continue until July or August, and sometimes until October. On the alternate years Congress is directed by the Constitution to adjourn on the fourth day of March, thus pre-

SENATE CHAMBER.

venting the attempt to make any one Congress permanent. All Congressmen are paid a salary, in order that poor men may have an equal chance with the rich. This salary is $5000 for both senators and representatives, except in the case of the Speaker and President of the Senate, who each of them receive $8000. No religious tests are allowed, and any man may belong to either house who is a citizen of the United States, who resides in the State which elects him, and who is of suitable age, twenty-five years in the House and thirty years in the Senate.

When the laws are made they must be carried out; and this is the business of the Executive department of the Government, a co-equal branch with the Legislative department. The President is the chief executive officer of the nation, and as such is properly the chief personage and principal officer in the land. It is no mistake to style him the "chief ruler" of the United States, for although the people are our only rulers, they do this ruling through and by means of the President and Congress, and thus depute him to rule over them for the time being. The President is only in a limited sense the agent of the people, but he is their chosen, although temporary, ruler, who is to carry out their laws.

The President and Vice-President are chosen once in four years and elected

HOUSE OF REPRESENTATIVES.

by the people, who vote by States and not directly as a nation. The citizens of each State vote for a body of men called electors, equal in number to their Congressmen, who in turn choose the President a few weeks later. As a matter of fact, their choice is always known beforehand, as they are elected on the distinct understanding of their preference. Although the method is somewhat clumsy, the principle is most necessary. In all our affairs, so far as possible, we must continue to act by States. It is only thus that our federal system can be preserved, and in that lies our safety and success.

The qualifications for President are that he shall be a native-born American, who has resided in the country for fourteen years, and who is thirty-five years old. He is inaugurated with much pomp and ceremony on the fourth of March, every four years, and resides at the Executive Mansion, or White House, in Washington, during his term of office. He is paid a salary of $50,000, that he may keep up a suitable state and dignity as our chief ruler. If he is guilty of treason, or other "high crimes and misdemeanors," of such importance that his continuance in office is dangerous to our liberties, he may be impeached by the House of Representatives, tried by the Senate, and, if found guilty, deposed, in which case his office would fall to the Vice-President. An effort was made to impeach President Johnson in 1866, but there being no adequate ground for such action, he was acquitted.

THE WHITE HOUSE - MAIN ENTRANCE.

The duties of the Executive department are mostly connected with the administration of the laws. The President is Commander-in-Chief of the Army and Navy, and he also represents the nation in matters connected with foreign governments. To that end he sends out foreign ministers to other govern ments, and consuls, to conduct our business affairs in foreign ports. A large body of foreign ministers sent from other countries for a similar purpose reside at Washington, and throughout our cities are scattered foreign consuls for the transaction of commercial business.

The President is assisted in his duties by a body of advisers, known as the

Cabinet. This consists of eight officers of great importance, of his own selection and appointment, each of whom has control of affairs of the Government in his particular department. The Secretary of State conducts our foreign relations; the Secretary of the Treasury our financial affairs; the Secretary of War is over our armies; the Attorney General is the law officer of the Government; the Postmaster General superintends the postal service; the Secretary of the Navy commands our navy; the Secretary of the Interior is concerned with patents, the Indians, the public lands, and many other important matters; and the Secretary of Agriculture promotes the farming interests of the country. Each of these Secretaries has his office in Washington, where he attends to the enormous business of his department. Under him are an immense number of officers and clerks, all appointed either by the President or the head of the department, to carry on the business of Government. Each department is divided into bureaus, and much of the work is of the highest value and importance.

In case of the death or inability of the President, the duties of his office devolve upon the Vice-President, and after him would fall to the Cabinet successively, in the order already named. But should any member of the Cabinet be obliged to take this office, he would fill it only until a new election could be held.

We have had a long and remarkable list of Presidents, beginning with George Washington himself. There have been in all twenty-three different Presidents, by a curious coincidence covering twenty-four terms, and distributed among various political parties. Many of them were men of extraordinary ability. They have been strangely representative, some, like Washington and the Adamses being men of the aristocratic class, while others, like Jackson, and Lincoln, and Garfield, were proud of their origin from among the poorest of the people. Twice the descendant of a President has filled that high place—John Quincy Adams being the son of John Adams, and Benjamin Harrison the grandson of Wm. Henry Harrison. Two Presidents have brought beautiful and charming brides to the White House during their term of office—President Tyler, who married Miss Julia Gardner, and President Cleveland, who married Miss Frances Folsom. Many times the people have delighted to honor the heroes of our wars. As one epoch after another passed in our history the laurels of war were placed upon the heads of Washington, of Andrew Jackson, of Wm. Henry Harrison, of Taylor, of Grant, and Hayes, and Garfield, and the second Harrison. Many different States have claimed the honor of the Presidency, but we have never yet had an Executive from the great Western States. Several Presidents have been re-elected, but by an unwritten law no man ever serves but two terms. Four have died in office, two of them, Lincoln and Garfield, having been assassinated. There have been many great men and many wise men in this office, but among them all there are three who stand out beyond their fellows.

creators of history—George Washington, who founded the Republic ; Abraham Lincoln, the greatest of all our great men in any time, and Ulysses S. Grant, the chief among our generals.

An elaborate system of courts make up our national judiciary, and secure to the citizens protection and justice. In some respects the most extraordinary feature of our Government is the Supreme Court, which is unique in its power and importance. It is the business of this tribunal to construe the laws, to decide whether they agree with the Constitution, to settle any question as to

SMITHSONIAN INSTITUTE.

and void, and thus of no effect whatever. This court consists of nine judges, or justices as they are called, appointed for life or good behavior, by the President, and confirmed by the Senate. They are paid $10,000 a year, with a pension after they become too old for longer service. The head of the court, or the Chief Justice, administers the oath to the President on his inauguration, and many times stands next him in rank and position. Certainly no nobler illustration of the might and majesty of law can be given than this court, adjusting the affairs of the nation itself, to which President and people alike bow, in token that righteousness and justice are greater than power.

No account of our Government would be in any sense complete, nor indeed would it be intelligible, that did not take into account our Federal system. The whole country is divided into States, and each State is a separate and distinct government, having control of its local affairs, and responsible to its own people. In all those larger affairs which concern the whole country, it joins with its fellows in the general Government, but the power of this general Government comes from the States. The States are not given more or less power *by* the United States, but the States give more or less power *to* the United States and reserve the other rights to themselves. The United States, however, has supreme control over all matters relating to the nation, and will not allow any State to infringe upon the rights or jeopardize the safety of any other. For that reason it will not permit any State or States to secede, because the coöperation of them all is necessary to the safety of the Union. We are States united into a nation, but we are a nation, one and indissoluble.

The history of the country makes plain these relations. Thirteen colonies, settled by different peoples of different origins and for widely different reasons, joined each other for the sake of common safety and national prosperity. Practical necessity and political wisdom alike dictated that local affairs should continue under the control of each colony or State, while matters of general interest were decided by the whole acting together. To this end each colony gave up to the nation its general rights but reserved the power over its internal affairs. It is this federal system which makes it possible for a democratic government to rule such an immense country, and it is only this. Therefore while we are careful to retain the supreme control to the general Government we must more and more relegate sectional concerns, however large and important, to the States ; and we must guard against the centralizing of our affairs in the hands of the national Government, however much to our temporary advantage it may be. In the nature of the case we cannot govern territory of such enormous extent, with so various a population and such varying interest, by democratic methods unless we keep strictly to the federal idea. It is our only safety.

Each State has a Governor, Legislature, and Supreme Court of its own :

the Governor, Legislature, and, in some States, the Supreme Court, being elected by its own people. Different States require different qualifications in their voters; in some a man must be able to read and write; in some be possessed of certain property; in one there is no distinction between men and women; and various other requirements are found in the different States. Whatever makes a man a voter in his own State allows him to vote in that State in national elections also.

The term of office of State officers varies greatly, some States holding their Legislatures annually, and some biennially; some Governors being elected for one year and some for longer terms. In all these, its own affairs, the State is supreme. Each has its own courts, under its Supreme Court, for the furtherance of justice. Local affairs also are very variously administered, by townships, counties, parishes, and other subdivisions, many of them very ancient, and in like manner cities are governed in different ways. All this diversity in unity serves to make one homogeneous nation of this heterogeneous multitude of sixty million people.

The original thirteen States, little as they dreamed of the great territory over which the flag of the United States floats so proudly to-day, had no narrow idea of a nation, and provided for its expansion even better than they knew. The common land belonging to the nation, and as yet largely unsettled, is held by the common Government, in Territories. These are governed by officers appointed by the President, and are subject to United States laws only. Their own Legislatures arrange their local affairs, and each sends a delegate to Congress to look after its interests, but the law does not allow him to vote. As soon as any Territory contains a population large enough, Congress admits it to the Union as a State, with all the rights and privileges of its older sisters, the President proclaims that fact to the world, and a new commonwealth is added to the sisterhood, marked by the new star in the flag we honor. Thus one after another we have already seen thirty-one new States added to that little band of thirteen, some of them great and rich realms many times as large as the whole nation at its beginning.

The United States is indeed a land of the free, and its great written charter, the Constitution, itself protects the freedom of her citizens. The right to worship God as he will, the right to assemble when and where he will, freedom of speech and press, and of petition, the right to keep and bear arms—all these great gifts the United States gives to every person in all her broad borders. Nor is this enough; she preserves his house inviolate from search and seizure, and everywhere in all his relations throws the shield of the law over his person and possessions. If indeed he be accused of crime, she makes certain that he shall have justice, for by the right to a trial by jury and by many other careful provisions she protects both his person and property, and in the last and greatest articles of her great Magna Charta—articles for which she spent blood and treasure beyond the telling—she forbids all slavery within all her borders, and guarantees to every citizen his right to vote without regard to "race, color, or previous condition of servitude." For this is the duty which the United States asks of every man child within her borders, to help her govern herself. This is his proud privilege—to choose her officers, to control her policy, to sustain her laws, and through his representatives to make them; to develop the Nation and govern her. This is what it is to vote in the United States of America.

BAILEY'S DAM ON THE RED RIVER.

627

www.ingramcontent.com/pod-product-compliance
Lightning Source LLC
Chambersburg PA
CBHW030938110726
47900CB00004B/1044